The Elemental Odyssey

Tales of Zura

Book One

Derek J. Canyon

The Elemental Odyssey

Tales of Zura Book One

By

Derek J. Canyon

Copyright 2011 by Derek J. Canyon
www.derekjcanyon.com
Email: derek@derekjcanyon.com
If you operate a retail store and would like to order quantities of
this book for resale, please email derek@derekjcanyon.com.

ISBN-13: 978-1461111238
ISBN-10: 1461111234

Cover art by Igor Kieryluk
www.igorkieryluk.com

Editing by Joel David Palmer
joeldavidpalmer@gmail.com

For Shari

Without your love, support, and encouragement this book
would not have been possible.

CHAPTER 1

From time to time he appeared, between the dark shadows cast by the strange moon. The silvery light glinted along his wide grin as his sensitive nose savored the sweet vanilla aroma of the trees. His eager eyes sparkled under a wide-brimmed hat and behind a dark mask. Tonight, his part in shaping the future truly began.

He darted across a two-lane road that cut through the rugged forest and found a path on the far side. To his left, unwavering light illuminated a granite mountain with a massive sculpted face. As he moved through the trees, three more stone likenesses came into view, each towering high above. For a moment he paused to gaze up at the majestic visages, shining like beacons.

The path grew brighter as he descended into a slender valley and came upon a narrow but vast amphitheater, obviously designed to grant a spectacular view of the stone busts far above. He skulked in the shadows and observed hundreds of people listening to a woman as she spoke from the stage.

The prowler crept from tree to tree. He snuck around stone buildings and between distracted passersby. Behind the amphitheater, he hurried across a paved trail and up into a rocky stand of trees. Leaping over a black metal railing, he scurried between tall stone pillars decorated with dozens of distinctive banners quivering in the feeble night breeze.

Leaving the avenue of flags behind, he padded through the Ponderosa pines, caressing them with his hands. The crumbling bark felt rough and dry, leaving his palms and fingertips feeling fresh and clean. The vanilla and butterscotch scent of the trees teased his sensitive nose. It had been a long time since he had enjoyed the soothing sights, smells, sounds, and textures of such a rich forest.

"Hold it right there!" someone ordered, and a bright beam of light blinded him.

He raised his hands to ward off the dazzle.

"What are you?" someone asked hesitantly.

"I could ask you the same question," he responded, squinting into the glare.

The beam of light dropped away from his face. A man stepped out from behind a tree, clad in dark pants, a light-colored shirt, and a flat-brimmed hat. The beam of light shone from a thick rod in his left hand.

"I'm a park ranger," the man said, pointing at a golden brooch on his chest. "And you…don't look human."

"I am called Bozabrozy. And if I am not human, what would I be?" He bowed, but kept his hat on. He watched as the ranger neared, noting a black object attached to his hip, obviously a weapon of some sort.

"Are you saying that's a costume? It doesn't look like a costume."

Bozabrozy wore a dark, wide slouch hat. Beneath a short cloak he had wrapped several belts and bandoliers around his shoulders and waist. His shirt and pants were also dark, but he wore no shoes. Fur covered his feet and hands and head. His nose and mouth looked more like a snout and muzzle full of sharp teeth. He kept his ringed tail hidden behind him.

"In my home, it is customary to introduce yourself when you are gifted with the name of another."

"Park Ranger John Five Eagles," the man replied, stepping closer to Bozabrozy. "That's no costume. If I didn't know better, I'd say you were a spirit. Something my grandfather spins tales about."

"Five Eagles," Bozabrozy pondered. "That is a fine name. It speaks of the sky and, therefore, power and royalty. Your grandfather is proud of it, as is the rest of your family, no doubt. Mother, father, brother, and...sister?"

John Five Eagles ignored his question. "What are you doing sneaking through the park?"

"You have nothing to fear from me, John Five Eagles," Bozabrozy said, moving his hand to his chest and the pouch-laden bandoliers. "Just let me pass and all will be well."

"That's definitely no costume. You're some kind of...animal man!" The ranger stepped forward. "You're coming with me. Turn around and put your hands on your head."

"I don't have time for this. Great things are afoot. You must not interfere."

The ranger pulled the black weapon from his belt and pointed it at Bozabrozy.

"Turn around. Now!"

Bozabrozy sighed and obeyed.

"That's a tail!" Five Eagles gasped. "Hands on your head!"

Bozabrozy placed his hands on his head.

"This is not a very kind way to treat a guest."

Five Eagles stepped up behind Bozabrozy, returning his weapon to his belt. He grabbed Bozabrozy's wrist and pulled it down behind his back.

"No one is going to believe me if I don't take you in," he said. He noticed that Bozabrozy now had a small bottle in his left hand. "What's that?"

"You won't take me anywhere," Bozabrozy said, spinning around. With the reckless agility of a cornered rodent, he squirmed free of the ranger's grip and threw the bottle at his feet. Shimmering blue light erupted around them. The tree trunks gleamed like an undersea grotto.

Bozabrozy leapt away as the ranger stumbled amidst a shower of sparkling snowflakes.

"What?" John Five Eagles steadied himself and pulled out his weapon again. "What is this?"

The snowflakes swirled and eddied around the man, then swelled into a furious flurry. The air grew much colder. Snow gathered on the ranger's clothes and hair.

"This is what happens when you interfere in matters not your own," Bozabrozy said.

"Make it stop!" Five Eagles demanded, waving his arms to ward off the growing blizzard. His frantic efforts had no effect on the frigid little storm. Hoarfrost appeared on his face and hands.

"It would be best not to struggle," Bozabrozy warned.

Five Eagles raised his hand to point his weapon. "Stop it!" he said through chattering teeth.

Bozabrozy watched as the ranger froze in place, frost and rime covering his entire body, the ebbing blizzard coating him with a thick layer of snow and ice.

"It is stopped," Bozabrozy told the motionless figure of the park ranger as it glimmered brightly in the moonlight. A final few snowflakes drifted peacefully to the ground.

Without another glance, Bozabrozy sped away into the darkness, crossing a wide road, delving into deep woods, up this ridge and down that valley. He turned left at this landmark, or right at that one, as he had been told.

Ahead, through the thick tree trunks, a light shone. Sensing his destination, he stole to the edge of a clearing. A cabin stood at the far tree line, quiet and serene, its windows lit up against the night. On the porch stood a four-foot tall wooden statue of a rearing bear, sporting a red cap.

Nodding to himself, Bozabrozy's gaze rose to a second-story window.

4

CHAPTER 2

"And this is a trilobite, also, but from the Cambrian period," Jürgen explained, holding out another fossil to his friend.

Kyle took the rock, no bigger than a marble, and examined it. "It looks a lot like the other ones, just smaller."

"Of course, they're all trilobites. Same taxonomic class, just different orders."

"And your dad is here to find more of these?"

"Not only trilobites," Jürgen replied, squirming around on the floor to better position his bulky stomach. "The geologic formations around here have all sorts of fossils. Plants, fish, mammals, reptiles."

"You really like this stuff?" Kyle picked up another fossil. To him, it wasn't any different than the others, except for the size and color. It looked like a beetle made out of stone. "It's just a bunch of rocks."

"It's okay. But my parents spend a lot of time at fossil sites. Places like the Messel Pit and another near Mauer. They tell me all about the prehistory. Jurassic, Cambrian, Cretaceous."

"Sounds a lot like school to me. I'd rather spend my vacations having fun. Hiking, swimming, exploring. Stuff like that."

"Actually, paleontology is a lot like that. We hike and explore. We get to go into caves, also."

"That's fun! I can't wait to do some of that on this trip!" Kyle glanced over at his backpack full of hiking and caving equipment. "We're going to check out Wind and Jewel Caves. I've only been in Ape Cave by Mt. St. Helens. You're lucky you get to do that so often."

"I guess so, but only when they're not spending hours dusting and chipping at rocks. That's boring."

"Do you have to do that a lot?"

"Not usually. My parents let me wander around the sites. And they did get me an Xbox to play in the hotel rooms."

"Well, this time you don't have to spend all your vacation watching them dig up old bones." Kyle beamed. "We get to explore all the fun stuff around Mt. Rushmore."

"I can't wait," Jürgen said. "Thanks so much for inviting me!"

"No problem. When you said you were coming over with your dad on a working vacation I knew my dad would agree to come here. We've always wanted to visit. Lots of hiking and other stuff to do, like the Reptile Gardens."

"Too bad we didn't get much done on the first day," Jürgen lamented.

"Sorry about that," Kyle apologized. "We didn't have the money to fly over here so we had to drive. Seventeen hours on the road."

"*Unglaublich*," Jürgen said in German. "America is so big. Seventeen hours to drive halfway across. It only takes us six hours to drive all across Germany, from France to Poland."

"We can get started doing stuff tomorrow," Kyle said.

"You won't be too tired?"

"Nope, I slept most of the trip. My dad says it's one of the benefits of being twelve."

Jürgen laughed as he sat up. "I slept on the plane, also."

"Tomorrow morning, I say you make me some of the French toast you're always bragging about."

"Of course! I make the best French toast in Germany. My parents say so." He stood up and grabbed his ample

6

stomach. "How else do you think I get this fat?"

Kyle laughed. "Wiener schnitzel and bratwurst!"

"I see you were paying attention when I fragged you five to one in Halo."

"That wasn't a fair match! I was on a bad connection." Kyle objected.

"You won't have that excuse here."

"Is that a challenge?" Kyle asked, stepping over to the corner to grab an Xbox controller.

"Yes, it…" Jürgen paused. "What's that?"

Kyle held out a controller to his friend. "What's what?"

"That," Jürgen said, pointing. "In the window."

Even though the reflection of the room's lights made it difficult to see through the glass, there was definitely something out there. Peering closer, Kyle saw a black mask over a white face and dark eyes. "It's a raccoon!"

"A raccoon?" Jürgen squinted. "You mean a… *Waschbär*?"

"A raccoon. You know, masked face and a ringed tail."

"Yes, a *Waschbär*," Jürgen nodded. "We have them in Germany, also. They climb onto houses and knock over garbage cans."

"Same thing here." Kyle kept watching the raccoon through the window. It stared back in at them, its face only inches from the window pane. "I saw one run across the steps of a building at the University of Washington. It was night, but I could still tell that it was huge. It must have been as big as a dog. My dad said they get pretty big in the city where there's lots of food."

"This one is very big, also."

"Yeah, it is," Kyle agreed, moving closer to the window to try and see through the glare.

The raccoon placed both its paws on the window.

"It's trying to get in!" Jürgen exclaimed.

"Don't worry, Jürgen. The window's locked."

"Good. It could have *die Tollwut*."

"The Toll what?"

"*Tollwut*. The disease that makes the dogs foam at the mouth."

"Oh," Kyle said, "you mean rabies."

"*Jawohl*, that's it. Rabies. Raccoons can have rabies."

"Don't worry, it won't get in. Unless it crashes through the window."

As the boys watched, a hint of shimmering light played along the window and the glass melted away like thawing ice. In seconds the windowpane had dissolved completely. Kyle and Jürgen gaped in shock. The raccoon stared back as it leaned into the room.

CHAPTER 3

The raccoon dropped nimbly to the floor and bared its fangs at the boys. Rising on its hind legs it stood nearly five feet tall. It held a wide slouch hat and wore a cloak!

"A giant raccoon!" Jürgen exclaimed, jumping back against the bunk beds on the far side of the room. He clambered up onto the top bunk.

"And it's wearing clothes!" Kyle said, stumbling over game boxes and pressing against the far wall.

"I'm no raccoon!" it said.

"It talks!" the boys said in unison. "A giant raccoon that talks!"

The intruder raised its head. "I am not some mindless animal! I am a Zuran. More precisely, I am a rascan. And to be absolutely specific, I am Bozabrozy." He bowed, stood upright, and put on his hat with a practiced flourish.

Jürgen trembled under his blankets on the bunk bed, and Kyle stood frozen against the wall. They stared at Bozabrozy in fear.

Bozabrozy smiled, his sharp fangs bright. "Yes, yes. I am stunning, am I not? Dashing. Heroic, even?" He laughed.

Kyle relaxed a bit. The creature wasn't attacking. Its bared fangs weren't a snarl. It was…smiling. Maybe it wasn't dangerous.

Kyle finally got his mouth to work. "What are you?"

"I'm a rascan," Bozabrozy repeated. "From Zura."

Jürgen pulled the blanket from his face. "What is Zura?"

"Ah… Zura! It is a world of endless skies and wondrous

sights." The rascan waved his hands as he spoke, and began walking around the room. "Stone and sky and water and fire! All four providing protection, granting their magic to ensure law and order and prosperity! Zura is a world where magic reigns with a strict yet caring hand. At least that's what the Emperor says." He smirked as he stepped on a fossil.

Kyle shook his head in amazement. "What are you talking about?"

Bozabrozy picked up the trilobite, juggling it from hand to hand while he sniffed it. "Zura! Zura with its endless skies! The world where I was born. The realm I came from, to visit you here on Earth."

"You're not from Earth?" Jürgen asked in surprise and growing delight. He sat up on the bunk and tossed the blanket aside.

Bozabrozy snickered. "No, I am not. Have you ever seen a rascan before?" He deposited a few of the trilobites into one of the many pouches hanging from his belts.

"Hey! Those are mine!" Jürgen said, jumping off the bed, his fear dissipating as he witnessed the rascan steal his fossils.

"What? Oh, these?" Bozabrozy pulled the trilobites back out and handed them to Jürgen. "So sorry. I thought they were just stray rocks. Are they valuable?"

"Yes, of course they are!" Jürgen took the fossils and bent to collect the rest of his treasures still scattered across the floor.

"You can't go around taking other people's stuff," Kyle chastised Bozabrozy, stepping forward.

The furry creature rubbed his white muzzle. "Is that how it works here? That is very good to know." He picked up a flashlight from the bed. "But in my land, youngsters introduce themselves to their elders."

"I'm Kyle Morgan."

"My name is Jürgen Schmidt. I'm from Kaiserslautern.

It's in Germany."

"I'm from Seattle. It's here in America," Kyle quickly added.

"Nice to meet you both." He held out the flashlight. "What is this? A magic wand?"

"That's a flashlight," Kyle said. "Don't you have those on Zura?"

"No, nothing like this." He fiddled with the flashlight, finally pushing the switch. "Aha! I saw a park ranger use one of these. It will prove very useful on our quest." He flipped the light off and put it in his largest pouch.

"That's not yours, either," Kyle objected.

"I know that. But I'll just carry it for you in my pouch. Since you don't have a pouch. You don't have a pouch, do you?"

"We have these," Jürgen said as he stuffed fossils into a pocket of his backpack. "They're much better than your pouches."

Bozabrozy moved to stand beside Jürgen as he zipped up the pocket. "Another magical wonder!" He pawed at the backpack, feeling the material, the straps, and the zippers. "Pockets sealed with metal teeth! Ha! Will wonders never cease?"

"Hey," Jürgen said, "you have opposable thumbs!"

Bozabrozy's eyes widened and he stepped back. "What is an opposable thumb?"

"Your thumbs. You have thumbs."

The rascan held up his hands and wiggled his thumbs in the air. "Yes, so I do. Don't you?"

"Raccoons don't have opposable thumbs."

"Now, now," Bozabrozy said with a frown on his furry face, "I already told you I'm not a raccoon. There are many differences between the dumb animals and Zurans. One is 'opposable' thumbs."

"Sorry."

"Fret not, Jürgen. I'm sure you'll get used to me before

we've finished the quest." He swished his ringed tail.

"What's this quest you keep talking about?" Kyle asked.

The Zuran wandered over to the nightstand and opened the drawers, digging around in each. He pulled out t-shirts and pants and socks and underwear, tossing them on the floor. "The Zuran quest. That's why I'm here. To enlist your aid."

"Why do you need our help?" Jürgen asked.

"Your bear outside wears a hat like this." Bozabrozy picked up Kyle's Seattle Mariners baseball cap and donned it in place of his own. "I am new to your world. It is so vastly different from my own. Not enough sky, mostly. I feel pinched by all these mountains. So much stone. And I need to find some things."

"What things?" Kyle asked.

Bozabrozy leaned forward and crooked a forefinger at the boys. When they drew close he whispered, "Elemental quintessence."

"Come again?" said Kyle.

"The purest, most concentrated, and most valuable manifestation of the four elements of water, fire, stone, and sky."

"Why do you want the stuff?" Kyle grabbed his cap from Bozabrozy's head and put it on his own.

"Oh, it has many, many uses." The rascan fiddled with the Velcro dartboard hanging on the door. "Each kind can do so many things. Even I do not know them all. But Savakala does. She'll tell you, when you meet her."

"Savakala?"

"Yes, she leads this quest. She is a powerful magus."

"What's a magus?"

"One who can do wondrous magic with quintessence."

"You mean, like a wizard?" Jürgen wondered.

"No, not at all," Bozabrozy said. "Or, maybe. I guess so." He picked up paper and pens from a small table.

"Where is she?" Kyle asked.

"She awaits us in the wilderness. She is trying to use her powers of foresight to aid us in the quest." Bozabrozy scribbled on the note pad with a red pen. "Ah…a magic quill."

"It's not magic, it's just a pen."

"It matters not." The Zuran slid the pen and paper into a pouch. He put his hat on, and stood with his hands on his hips. "Well, Kyle Morgan from America and Jürgen Schmidt from Germany, are you ready to embark on the adventure of a lifetime?"

"Um…no," Kyle said. "Not before I get my dad. He'll never believe in a talking racc– I mean a talking rascan."

"Your sire is near?" Bozabrozy crouched and glanced about like a hunted animal.

"Both our dads are downstairs," Jürgen said. "Our mothers aren't here. This is a man's vacation." He smiled proudly, hands on his hips, posing like a daring explorer.

"Let's take Bozabrozy and introduce them. My dad will never believe it."

"Mine won't, also!"

Bozabrozy backed up toward the melted window. "I don't think that is wise."

"Why not?"

"No doubt your parents will beat you for speaking to me. And, sky knows, they would do far worse to me."

"My father doesn't beat me!" Jürgen objected.

"Mine neither!"

Bozabrozy shook his head. "Not even when you are bad, or don't do your chores? What about when they are angry at you for stealing the porridge? All the old tales start with the foster parents beating the orphaned children."

"We're not orphans."

"You're not?" Bozabrozy looked shocked. "That's most odd. Were your parents not eaten by beasts long ago?"

Kyle grimaced. "No, they weren't."

"They must mistreat you, then. Make you dig for tubers?

Sleep in caves? Starve you?" Bozabrozy looked at Jürgen. "Well, obviously they don't starve you. Maybe they force you to eat too much foul gruel?"

"Hey," Kyle said, "leave him alone."

The rascan frowned, his whiskers hanging down beside his white muzzle. "Even if you aren't mistreated by your parents, you'd still better come with me to escape your poverty."

"We aren't poor."

"Then perhaps you should leave before your disease leaves you all patchy and covered in sores."

"What are you talking about now?"

"That sickness you were lamenting before I came in," Bozabrozy said.

"You mean rabies?" Kyle asked. "We don't have rabies."

Bozabrozy looked at Jürgen. "You don't have it either?"

Jürgen shook his head.

"Thank sky!" Bozabrozy clapped and rubbed his hands. "I arrived just in time. Let us make haste so we can avoid any other illnesses."

"There aren't any diseases here," Kyle said.

"There aren't?" The rascan looked at the ceiling. "That doesn't seem right. Well, if your parents aren't beating you, and you aren't orphaned or poor or sick…" He pulled a stick out of a pouch, broke it, and threw it out the window. "The heroes in the old tales always have problems before the stories even start. Most of them are motherless and fatherless, of course, their parents eaten by fiends, furious or foul."

Jürgen stared at the Zuran in confusion and then looked at his friend.

Kyle sighed and walked to the door. "I'm going downstairs to tell my dad you're here."

Bozabrozy rushed over and held the door shut. "We don't have time for that. You are in great peril every moment you stay here."

"Are you always this much of a liar?" Kyle stared at him.

"I didn't want to tell you this," Bozabrozy bent down and whispered, "because you are so young and no doubt it will frighten you. But...other Zurans are here looking for the quintessence. They are not as kind as me, or even Savakala. They would use pain and torture to get you to aid them."

Jürgen eyes widened. "Why didn't you tell us this first? We should call the police!"

Kyle grabbed his friend's shoulder and tried to calm him. "Don't believe him, Jürgen. He's making all this stuff up to try and get us to go with him. Aren't you, Bozabrozy?"

"No, absolutely not! Okay, well, yes. I did make up the parts about mean parents and diseases. But I only did that to get you to come with me before the others find you. That part was true."

Kyle scowled. "Why should we believe you? You're a thief and a liar. I'm going to get my dad." He tried to pull the door open, but Bozabrozy leaned against it to hold it shut.

"I speak the truth," the rascan said. "You are in danger! At any moment the others could burst in and wreak havoc on you and your parents!"

Kyle opened his mouth to reply when a tremendous crash shook the cabin. At the same time, a bellowing roar thundered from beyond the door.

Chapter 4

"You don't want to go out there," Bozabrozy warned them, leaning against the door to prevent Kyle from opening it.

"Yes, I do!" Kyle replied as the roaring and crashing from downstairs continued. He pulled on the doorknob to no avail.

"Get away from the door!" Jürgen shouted. He grabbed the Zuran's arm and tried to pull him away. Between the two of them, Kyle and Jürgen were able to push Bozabrozy away and open the door. They ran into the hallway and down the stairs.

Below them, the front room of the cabin lay in shambled ruins. The front door was splintered and strewn across the room, along with a good portion of the wall. The sofa was ripped to shreds and the recliner suddenly flew through the air and hit the wall only a few feet from them.

They stopped halfway down the stairs and saw the source of the ferocious growling. A bear rampaged through the room, demolishing couches and end tables and wall hangings. The boys' fathers stood on the far side of the dining table, brandishing a floor lamp and a fire poker. The bear grabbed one of the dining chairs and flung it aside.

Kyle's dad noticed them standing on the stair. "Kyle! Jürgen! Get back upstairs into your room and lock the door!"

The boys stood shocked and motionless.

"NOW!"

"But the bear!"

"Do as he says!" Jürgen's father commanded loudly. *"Macht schnell!"*

"Jawohl!" Jürgen answered in German, yanking Kyle up the stairs.

The growling and roaring stopped. The bear turned from the half-eaten dining table and glared at the boys. It spat out wood splinters and snarled.

"Ah, there you are," it said in a deep, rumbling voice.

Paralyzed with shock, Kyle stared as the bear turned and lumbered from the dining room. It was at least eight feet tall, and held a dining chair in its left paw. No, not a paw. A huge furry hand, with talons and an opposable thumb! And the bear was wearing clothes!

Jürgen pulled on his friend's shirt. "Come on, Kyle!"

"The bear! It was another Zuran!" Kyle couldn't believe that he'd met two talking animal men in one night. He wished the bear was as friendly as the raccoon. He could hear it thumping up the stairs after them.

"It isn't a bear," Bozabrozy said as he stood at the bedroom door, motioning them back in, "it is an urgra. Very powerful. Very dangerous. Quick! Inside!" He followed the boys into the room and closed the door.

"That door isn't going to stop that thing!" Kyle said as heavy footsteps neared.

"No, it won't," Bozabrozy agreed. "I will delay him while you two escape into the woods. Take your fancy pouches and jump out the window!"

"Delay him? You're tiny and he's gigantic!"

"The elements are a great equalizer," Bozabrozy smiled, and pulled out a small key. It looked like it was made of ice. He touched the doorknob with it and the entire room shimmered in wavering blue lights. A burst of snowflakes swirled near the door and chill spread throughout the room. Ice formed on the door jamb.

"Unglaublich!" Jürgen gasped.

The heavy footsteps stopped just outside the door and it

shuddered with a heavy blow, but the thickening ice held.

"Go! Now! There will be more of them! Head toward the mountain of faces. Do not tarry here. I will catch up."

"But, our dads," Kyle objected.

"The urgra is after you, not them. They will be safe once you are away." The frosted door jolted again, and shards of ice flew off. "Go! I cannot keep it out much longer."

"Let's go, Kyle." Jürgen handed him his backpack and pulled him toward the window. The door quaked under another terrible blow and a huge paw splintered through it. Bozabrozy leapt back to avoid the flailing talons.

Jürgen climbed through the window onto the sloping roof. Kyle followed, but looked back into the room. The ice-reinforced door was giving way. Bozabrozy stood several feet from it, between the urgra and the window.

"I don't like heights," Jürgen complained as he crouched at the edge of the roof.

"It's only a one story drop," Kyle said without enthusiasm. He threw his pack to the ground and sat down on the edge. Taking a deep breath, he closed his eyes and pushed off. He landed unharmed. He opened his eyes and noticed the wooden bear statue toppled on the deck, its baseball cap nowhere to be seen. He looked back up. "Come on."

Jürgen threw him his pack and sat down heavily. He turned onto his ample stomach and dangled his legs over the edge.

Kyle heard a loud crash from above and knew the urgra had broken through the bedroom door. "Hurry! I'll catch you!"

Jürgen let himself slip over the edge, grabbing the gutter for support. It broke free in his grasp and he fell onto Kyle. They both collapsed in the dirt.

"Get off me!" Kyle moaned. Jürgen rolled away and with effort pushed himself to his feet. The boys grabbed their packs and backed away, looking up at the window.

Growling and roaring and smashing noises emanated from their bedroom. They could see a towering shaggy shape.

"We better get going," Jürgen said.

Kyle looked through the shattered front wall. He couldn't see his dad, but there were two more furry creatures in the room. They weren't as big as the urgra. They had long snouts and large ears and long furry tails. They stood on two legs, wore armor and brandished swords.

"They look like *Shäferhund*," Jürgen gasped.

"If that means German shepherd, you're right. And, they don't look friendly." They hurried away from the cabin into the trees, hiding behind a pile of wood stacked like a tepee. Crashing and roaring emanated from their room. One of the dog-men came outside and sniffed the wind.

"What do we do now?" Jürgen asked.

Kyle clamped a hand over his friend's mouth and whispered in his ear. "We go get help."

They snuck into the woods. There was very little undergrowth, but there were lots of sticks and pinecones. Jürgen's heavy trodding snapped too many twigs for Kyle's comfort.

"Try not to step on every branch you see," he whispered angrily.

"I can't see any branches, or anything else," Jürgen replied.

"Well, use your flashlight. Bozabrozy took mine."

Jürgen retrieved his light from his pack and turned it on. The forest around them burst into brightness. Kyle grabbed the flashlight and quickly turned it off again.

"Hey, turn it back on," Jürgen said. "We'll be able to go a lot quieter if we can see."

Kyle shook his head. "If we light up the forest we'll be seen a lot farther off."

"Oh. That's a good point."

"Let's find the driveway and run down to the road,"

Kyle suggested. "We'll be out of view of the cabin and we can make better time that way."

"Run?" Jürgen frowned.

They found the dirt road from the cabin and Kyle ran down the slope. Jürgen jogged heavily behind him. The driveway came out on U.S. Route 16A, also called Iron Mountain Road. Kyle waited for Jürgen to catch up. He noticed a swift fox skulking away into the trees.

The young German boy plodded up to the road, panting and wheezing.

"Not used to running?" Kyle asked, smiling.

Jürgen managed a weak grin between gasps. "Paleontologists don't usually have to escape from extraterrestrial bear-men."

"Let's keep moving." Kyle turned right and hurried down the road.

"Where are we going?" Jürgen said, struggling to keep up. "Are we going to Mt. Rushmore like Bozabrozy told us?"

"No. That would take too long. We can go to the next house. I don't think it's very far."

They hurried along, the moon lighting the way. No cars came by. After a while they crossed a bridge and the road curved sharply around and underneath the same bridge.

"Why curl a road over and under a bridge like this?" Jürgen asked as they walked under it. He stopped and flipped on his flashlight to look at the thick timbers that supported the bridge.

"I don't know."

"My dad didn't know why, also. He read that they're called the Pigtail Bridges. There are three of them."

"I've never seen anything like it before," Kyle admitted. "We better keep going."

"Do you think he's still alive?" Jürgen asked, wiping his sweaty forehead, but not moving.

"Your dad?"

"Yeah, him, also. But, I meant Bozabrozy."

"That bear was huge," Kyle said. "It could eat him in one bite."

"Bozabrozy had magic. Maybe he used magic to win. He made the door freeze and the window melt. I've never seen anything like that before."

"But he's never seen an ink pen or a flashlight," Kyle said. "He thought they were magical. Maybe his magic is technology, just different from ours."

"I guess so. But I'd rather think of it as magic."

"Let's just get help and figure this out later." Kyle walked down the road away from the bridge. The highway was dark and empty. "There should be cars. Why aren't there any cars?"

"Because America is a wilderness. So much empty land here."

"But Keystone is just a couple miles up the road. You'd think there would be more people out."

"It's late," Jürgen said.

"Not late for–" Kyle held his nose. A pungent odor, like a tanker truck full of cheap perfume had crashed, filled the air. "Eww…do you smell that?"

"Yuck! What is it?"

Jürgen pointed the flashlight into the trees. He saw nothing but the tree trunks and tepee-like piles of wood.

"Nothing in there," he said, then pointed the light down the road. A short distance away, a large ungainly figure trundled toward them up the center of Iron Mountain Road.

"Aaah!" Jürgen yelled. "It's the bear-man! It found us!"

Kyle peered into the night. "I don't think so…"

The figure moved into the beam of light. It was a woman. An incredibly fat woman, wearing a simple dress and moccasins. She huffed up to the boys and smiled at them. Her cheeks billowed like sails filled with wind.

"Why, hello there, dearies," she squealed in delight. "I'm so glad I found you!"

CHAPTER 5

"You were looking for us?" Jürgen asked as if she'd just told him the world wasn't round.

Kyle coughed, her perfume overwhelming him as the woman neared.

"Yes, I was," she replied. "Unless you aren't Bozabrozy's new friends?"

"You know Bozabrozy?" Kyle rubbed his eyes, which were beginning to water from the perfume.

"Yes, we're the dearest of friends." The woman patted them each on the shoulder. "And you must be the boys I'm looking for. He's very worried about you."

"We're worried about him," Jürgen said, waving a hand in front of his face to ward off the fumes. "He was fighting an ogre bear!"

"Urgra," Kyle corrected. He looked back at the obese woman. "But who are you?"

"My name is Barathrina and I'm here to take you back to Bozabrozy."

"He never mentioned you."

"He didn't?" Barathrina put her hands on her hips. "That naughty rascan! He was supposed to tell you all about me. It's so like him to play the lonely hero. Tsk, tsk. But it doesn't matter. I've found you now and we can go back and have him introduce us properly."

"We can't go back to the cabin," Jürgen warned. "There are bear and dog monsters there."

"Thunder and lightning, I know that. An urgra and

22

some canars. Bozabrozy told me all about them."

Kyle looked askance at her. "He did? Last time we saw him he was fighting the urgra."

"That doesn't sound like him at all. I bet he did what he does best: run away, and quickly. Well, second best. He's much better at sneaking. Or maybe third best, since he's quite good at stealing, too. We can ask him about it."

"You've seen him since he fought the urgra?" Kyle asked.

"Yes. He's searching for you in the forest and I'm searching for you on this road. Looks like I'm the lucky one who found you." She moved off the road and into the woods, motioning for the boys to follow.

"He sure got away from the urgra quickly," Kyle did not leave the road.

"Isn't that what I said? Bozabrozy is almost as fast getting out of trouble as he is getting into it." Barathrina made an odd snorting noise, which sounded a bit like laughter. "Now come along. Let's go find him."

Jürgen started to follow the large woman but Kyle pulled him back. "Why should we trust you?" he asked Barathrina.

"Why trust me?" She looked shocked. "Because I'm telling the truth. Come with me and ask him yourself."

"You could be lying. You could be with the urgra and not Bozabrozy."

"Oh, now that's just all kinds of cruel. Doubting my loyalties. I can assure you that I'm being truthful. In fact, I can prove it."

Kyle's eyes narrowed. "How?"

"Bozabrozy told me your names. Kyle and Jürgen. Tell me I'm wrong."

Jürgen nodded. "That's right. She's right, Kyle. Let's go, I don't want that bear to catch us alone on the road."

"Okay," Kyle said, but then whispered, "just keep your eyes open."

Barathrina led the way into the woods, plodding heavily. She made a great deal of noise, snapping branches and crushing old pinecones underfoot. She pushed her great bulk through the trees, grunting with the effort of climbing over logs, up hills, or around jumbles of boulders. She snorted or whined every time a creeper, twig, or bramble caught her dress or hair or cape. Kyle and Jürgen cringed with each sound she made, sure that she would lead the urgra to them.

"Do you think you can be less noisy?" Kyle pleaded in a whisper.

"What?" She stopped and rested against the thick bole of a towering Ponderosa pine. Jürgen thought he saw the tree lean from her weight. "I'm sorry, I can't hear you over the racket from this dratted forest."

"Can you try to be quieter?" Kyle asked. "You're making a lot of noise. That urgra will find us."

Barathrina wiped her brow. "Oh, we don't have to worry about making noise."

"Why not?" Jürgen asked.

"Because the canars can easily follow our scent. I'm sure they're already on our trail. Speed is more important than stealth at this point."

"What? They can track us by our scent?" Kyle exclaimed. "Then why in the world are you wearing so much perfume?"

"Because I like it, of course. The canars' big noses can find us whether or not I'm wearing perfume. They are master hunters."

Jürgen looked into the dark forest behind them, fearing a sudden rush of vicious dog-men. "Why didn't you tell us that before?"

"I don't see how that would have helped. It probably would have only scared you."

"Then why did you tell us now?" Jürgen asked, flabbergasted.

24

"Oh, right. Sorry."

"I'm afraid Barathrina isn't the best sneak," someone said from the shadows.

Barathrina, Kyle, and Jürgen jumped in alarm, but quickly calmed when Bozabrozy stepped into view.

"Don't do that!" Barathrina complained.

"Bozabrozy!" Jürgen smiled like he'd just found a German chocolate cake. "You escaped!"

"Of course." The rascan stepped forward and spread his hands at his sides. "That's what I do."

"What happened to my dad?" Kyle demanded.

"Your father is safe," Bozabrozy said, and then looked at Jürgen. "As is yours."

"Safe where?" Kyle asked.

"After you fled into the woods I managed to lead the urgra and the canars in another direction. Your fathers had fled, most likely to hide. I'm sure they've returned to the cabin by now to look for you."

"They'll call the police," Kyle said. "We should head back to the cabin and wait with them."

Bozabrozy shook his head. "That's not the thing to do, Kyle. The urgra will have left one of the canars to spy on the cabin. If they see you return it will only provoke another attack."

"Then what do we do?" Jürgen asked.

"Continue the quest!"

"With the canars hunting us down?"

"I took care of that," Bozabrozy said. "I threw them off the scent with a bit of elemental trickery."

"More magic?" Jürgen said, eager to learn more.

"Right you are, Jürgen. But it won't last forever. We should find shelter and take a nap before day returns."

Kyle was astounded at such a suggestion. "Nap? We don't have time to nap! There are aliens from another planet hunting us down. We need to find a park ranger. Or the police. Or the army!"

"They won't stop hunting you even if you gain the protection of your people," Barathrina said.

"She's right," Bozabrozy agreed. "The only way to stop them is to find the quintessence before they do. Once we have it and depart, they won't bother you again."

"My dad says that whenever I'm in trouble I should find a police officer," Kyle stood firm.

"Wise counsel, I am sure, for the events that usually transpire here," Bozabrozy said. "But I doubt your father was thinking of urgras and canars when he told you that."

"Kyle, listen to him," Jürgen said. "Bozabrozy is a Zuran. He knows how to deal with other Zurans."

Kyle turned on his friend. "Why are you on his side? He's done nothing but lie and trick us."

"Lie? Trick?" Bozabrozy frowned. "When have I done that?"

"Yeah," Jürgen objected. "He hasn't done that. He told us not to go downstairs because there was danger, and there was. He told us he would save us when we ran into the woods, and he did. You just don't like him."

"I..." Kyle stuttered, removed his cap, and rubbed his head, "I just...but...this is all too weird!"

Barathrina hugged Kyle's shoulder. "Now, now, dearie. From what I know of your world, we must seem awfully scary. You probably think we're all just big furry talking monsters, trying to eat you up!"

Kyle looked at her in confusion. "You're a Zuran?"

"Yes, this is just my disguise." She posed with hands on hips.

"But you look human," Jürgen said, and suddenly his eyes sparkled. "Is it magic?"

"How smart you are, Jürgen. Yes, it is magic." She pulled at her cape. "This very special cloak creates my illusion of humanity."

"Are you a rascan like Bozabrozy?"

"No, I'm a grunk."

"What's a grunk?"

"Let me show you." With pudgy hands, Barathrina fumbled with the clasp at her neck and finally pulled the cloak free. As she did so, her features blurred and wavered, like watching her through a distorted window. Her size and general shape didn't change much. She remained exceedingly obese and her perfume still reeked. But her features changed dramatically. Her ears widened and lengthened and poked out from her head. Her hair became short bristles that spread all over her face and body. Her nose and chin pushed out from her face and elongated into a pink muzzle with large flat snout. Her beady eyes remained beady, but moved farther apart.

"You're a pig!" Jürgen laughed.

"No, I'm a grunk."

"So there are four species of Zuran? Rascan, urgra, canar, and grunk," Jürgen counted on his fingers. "Wait. What kind of Zuran is Savakala?"

"An uburu."

"How many different Zuran species are there?" Jürgen asked, wanting to learn as much as he could about such a magical place.

"Many," Bozabrozy said. "But we'll have to wait to tell you about it until later. First, we must find a place for you to rest until morning while I go lead the canars farther away."

"I still think we should get help," Kyle said.

"We can get help in the morning," Jürgen disagreed. "Even though you didn't believe him, Bozabrozy has been right the whole time. And you didn't believe Barathrina either, but she's been telling the truth, also. Hasn't she?"

"Yeah, I guess you're right."

"Then it's settled." Bozabrozy rubbed his hands together and led the group off into the trees. Fifteen minutes later he found a small hollow in the side of a hill, hidden on one side by tall Ponderosa pines and brush. The other side, however, was open and exposed.

"This doesn't seem too safe," Kyle said. "Anyone can see us from that direction."

"Oh, not for long." Bozabrozy smiled, his fangs glinting in the moonlight. He pulled a bottle from one of his many pouches and sprinkled the liquid onto the ground. Almost immediately, sprouts burst up from the soil, pushing upward and growing swiftly. Weeds gave way to bushes, which gave way to saplings, and finally thick Black Hills spruce trees.

"*Unglaublich!*" Jürgen gaped.

"What does that mean?" Barathrina asked.

"It's German for 'incredible'," Jürgen said.

"He likes to say it. It is a pretty cool word, actually," Kyle said with a smile.

"What was that stuff you used?" Jürgen asked Bozabrozy.

"It's called a Verdurous Potion."

"Do you have more? That could save the rainforests."

"We'll see what we can do after the quest is over. Now, you two get some sleep."

"Was that like the key you used to freeze the door in the cabin?"

"No, that is the Everkey. It can both lock and unlock many things."

"I thought you said you weren't a wizard. You're doing all sorts of magic. You must be a magus. Like that Savakala person."

"No, she is an aeromagus. She deals in sky magic. I just use aquosian implements to my advantage," he said, whiskers twitching.

"What are aquosian implements?"

"Artifacts that let one do something magical with the element of water. Something specific. Like a potion that grows plants." Bozabrozy rolled his eyes. "Do you always ask so many questions?"

"Yes," Jürgen replied happily. "What other kinds of

magic can you do?"

"Enough questions. Get some sleep." He turned and walked to the other side of the hollow to talk to Barathrina.

"What other magic things do you think he has?" Jürgen asked Kyle. "He's like a magical vending machine."

"How should I know?" Kyle said, looking for a comfortable place to lie down.

"You were right, Bozabrozy," Barathrina said quietly, watching the children. "They're not branded. How will Savakala control them? They could be dangerous."

"Shhh!" Bozabrozy snarled. "Savakala knows what she's doing."

Chapter 6

Early the next morning Kyle was awakened by Bozabrozy pawing at him. "Hey! What do you think you're doing?"

"Waking you for the new day." Bozabrozy waved about him at the early morning light filtering through the tall pine forest. "I've led Rakanian's minions on a fruitless chase far from here. We are, for the time being, safe from his wickedness."

"Who's Rakanian?"

"He's the villain who sent the urgra after you."

Kyle yawned and rubbed his head with both hands, messing up his brown hair. He was still tired even though he had slept during much of the previous day's road trip across half the continent from Seattle to South Dakota. He scratched his back where a twig had poked him during the night. From where she slept nearby, Barathrina's reek overpowered the pleasant scent of the forest and her snores drowned out the chirps of the birds.

"What do we do now?"

Bozabrozy moved across the small glade and gently prodded Jürgen from his slumber. The boy woke slowly, stretching and yawning. "*Was ist los?*" he said. "Oh, I mean, what's happening? Where are we?"

"Same place you were when you fell asleep," Bozabrozy said. "Where else would you be?"

"That's right. I almost forgot what happened. It feels kind of like a dream, doesn't it, Kyle? But here we are, with two aliens."

"Yeah, and no breakfast."

Jürgen stood and his stomach growled. "I'm hungry, also."

"Guess we're not going to have that French toast," Kyle lamented.

"That's okay, I have some candy bars." Jürgen rummaged through his backpack and pulled out several chocolate bars. He handed a couple to Kyle.

Barathrina woke with a snort. "Rainbows and cool breezes! What's that delicious aroma?"

"Chocolate," Jürgen said. "Want one?"

Scratching her backside and yawning like a hippo, Barathrina hurried over to the boy. She took a candy bar he offered and munched off a large portion. "Mmmmm…. Yes, chocolate! They have chocolate ales in the taverns of Azuria. I miss all the sweet treats and tasty pastries… But I've never tasted anything like this before."

"What's Azuria?" Jürgen asked.

"Azuria is Zura's greatest empire," Bozabrozy said, speaking as if he was telling a well-worn story. "The benevolent Emperor Exeverius rules the endless skies, ensuring that the law is obeyed, order is maintained, and beasts are kept at bay. The Imperial Armada and Legion protect the citizenry from depredations of fiends both furious and foul, of which there are many."

"Don't forget the sky pirates," Barathrina mumbled with a giggle as she gobbled up the candy bar. "The Imperial Armada is always battling the sky pirates."

"Sky pirates?" Kyle asked. "Are they dangerous?"

"Oh, yes," Barathrina nodded. "You can be kidnapped by sky pirates and forced to help them smuggle quintessence. But there are even worse dangers. You could be sacrificed by the Dynasties of Kur. Or slaughtered in the Bosikor Expanse, or eaten by savage Zurans, or hunted in the Kingdoms of Yesterday and Tomorrow. Or even assassinated by the Murkbound! By the skies, I wouldn't want to forget them! Well, actually, I would. But I can't. Even though I almost did. You understand, of course. Of course you do. Who would want to ever even meet the Murkbound? Not me! Best to forget them. In fact, I never even mentioned them."

The two boys stared at her blankly. Bozabrozy rolled his eyes and his ringed tail twitched.

Finally, Kyle managed to say, "Zura sounds like a dangerous place."

"It is," Barathrina said. "Beyond the borders of Azuria is a wilderness of terrible peril."

"And untold riches," Bozabrozy added. "Don't forget the untold riches."

"Can we go to Zura with you?" Jürgen blurted, his eyes dancing with eagerness.

Kyle looked at his friend in disbelief. "What? Didn't you hear what she just said?"

The German boy nodded like a bobblehead. "Yeah! It sounds exciting! Can we go with you, Bozabrozy?"

"I don't see why not. But it is a long journey."

"How did you get here, then?" Kyle asked. "I've never heard of Zura. Is it in another solar system?"

Jürgen's eyes bulged like saucers. "Did you come here in a spaceship?"

"What is a spaceship? We did not come in a spaceship. We came in a skyship," Bozabrozy said. "It is called the Windrunner. It is the fastest ship in the Imperial Armada."

"You're a soldier?" Jürgen asked.

Barathrina grunted and laughed. "Bozabrozy a soldier? Hah! That would be a sight!"

"Barathrina is right. I could never be in the Legion or the Armada. Too strict, too confining. I prefer to keep all my options open, and I don't like following orders from stuffy officers."

"Like you've been doing for the whole journey,"

Barathrina scoffed.

"That's not my fault. Savakala tricked me…" The rascan looked sideways at the boys as his voice trailed off. "But that's beside the point. We have a quest to embark upon. I say we go and get it done!" He walked into the forest.

"Me, too!" Jürgen agreed, and hurried after the rascan like an eager puppy.

Kyle reluctantly followed the others. "As long as we can get to some police or rangers and tell them what's going on."

"That might not be the wisest thing to do, Kyle," Bozabrozy suggested as they walked.

"Why not?"

"No doubt your parents have already reported the urgra's attack of last night. So your rangers are already alerted. However, we are very different from any others here on Earth. New and different things are feared and often attacked. Don't you think your rangers would try to capture Barathrina and myself?"

"He's got a point," Jürgen agreed. "Just like in the movies. The government always grabs the aliens to hide and study them."

"We don't have time to be hidden and studied," Bozabrozy said. "Rakanian would beat us to the quintessence."

"Why is that stuff so important?" Kyle asked.

"Quintessence gives a magus wonderful powers," Barathrina said. "Zura has much of it, and it is the coin of the realm."

"Powers like melting glass, freezing doors, and growing plants," Jürgen said.

"You probably shouldn't ask a cook about magic," Bozabrozy warned. "They know how to make breakfast, not elixirs and artifacts."

"Stop belittling cooks!" Barathrina complained. "You'd better watch your tongue or it will be nothing but gruel and loaf heels for you on the way back."

Bozabrozy rolled his eyes. "Cooks are also very sensitive. At least, Barathrina is."

"All true artists are sensitive, Bozabrozy, and cooking is an art. How do you think I got to be this fat? By making bad food?"

"No, no, no," the rascan sighed. "By working beautiful magic with oven and skillet. But we'd best concentrate on thwarting Rakanian instead of eating chicken and dumplings."

They hiked along in the early morning, climbing up steep hills and then back down into narrow valleys. Bozabrozy led the way through the forest, often scraping the Ponderosa pines with his palms. Large boulders of sparkling stone loomed above or squatted beside their path, alone and in jumbles, surrounded by sparse grasses and infrequent bushes. They startled a small herd of mule deer, large ears twitching.

"Why is Rakanian so mean and dangerous?" Kyle asked.

"He's a villainous pirate king and magus," Barathrina said, panting like a tired dog as she trudged along through the wilderness.

"He came here on a skyship, too?"

"One can only assume so."

"How did the quest start? How did you know to come to Earth?" Jürgen asked.

"Savakala had a vision. With the help of elemental artifacts, we were sent on the Windrunner to undertake the quest."

Kyle shook his head. "I don't understand. How did you know how to get here? Travelling through space isn't easy. Did her vision give her galactic coordinates or something? Did she see us through a telescope? How far away is Zura? How many light years?"

"You are obviously schooled in arcane knowledge," Bozabrozy said, impressed. "You speak in strange words. I do not know what light years are, or many of the other things you mention. You should ask Savakala these questions. She will have the answers."

"That'd be good," Kyle said.

Bozabrozy held up a hand and stopped. "We're here."

Chapter 7

They descended a shallow slope, wending their way between trees and the piles of wood, and stopped at the top of a low rocky cliff. Below, a flat bare field separated them from Highway 244 and the entrance to the Mt. Rushmore National Memorial. The sprawling, three-level parking lot already boasted many cars, campers, and SUVs. Two large motor homes were parked directly across the highway from where they watched.

Beyond and to the left, the white stone faces of the presidents basked in the morning sun. From this angle, Thomas Jefferson and Teddy Roosevelt were partially obscured by George Washington, while Abraham Lincoln seemed to stare straight at them. Even at this distance, the images carved into the granite mountain were a sight to behold, and Kyle and Jürgen stared in awe.

"So, Kyle, what have you decided?" Bozabrozy asked, jolting them back to their current situation. "Will you join us in our quest until we locate the quintessence? After we find it, you can tell the world about us, if you wish. Or, will you now rush off to report the Zuran invaders to your rangers?"

Jürgen looked at his friend. "Come on, Kyle, let's help them. At least for today. When will you ever have another chance to go on a quest with aliens?"

Kyle looked at his new German friend. He'd been playing Xbox Live with Jürgen for months, but he'd only met him in person yesterday. He was obviously enthralled by the Zurans. And, Kyle had to admit that Bozabrozy was fantastic. A talking raccoon-man! But there was something strange about him and Barathrina. The whole situation seemed so unreal, like something out of an Xbox game.

"Well?" Jürgen prodded.

Kyle looked across the highway at the parking lot. A family of four emerged from an SUV. The mother checked to make sure everyone had enough water and trail bars, while the father fiddled with his camera. The kids jumped around excitedly, despite the early hour, looking forward to exploring the park.

That's exactly what Kyle and his dad had planned to do today: view the monument, hike the paths, visit the museum. Kyle thought about his dad. Was he all right? Did he escape from Rakanian's minions? According to Bozabrozy, their parents were okay, since Rakanian had no interest in them. But was the alien telling the truth?

If his dad was okay, he would have already called the police. They would be at the cabin, examining the damage. His dad would tell the cops that a bear had rampaged through the house and his son and friend were missing. Park rangers and police would be out searching for them. Actually, since the police would probably catch up to them pretty soon, it wouldn't hurt to go along with Bozabrozy. Jürgen was right; it was a strange and fantastic opportunity.

But, over to the right, Kyle saw the main entrance to the park, where rangers admitted the visitors. It would be so easy for him to dart across the road, waving and yelling, to warn the officers that alien creatures had destroyed his cabin last night. And the park rangers would laugh at him. Kyle realized that his story was completely unbelievable. The rangers would think he was lying to get attention.

"Okay, I'll help you," Kyle said. "Today. But tonight we go talk to the cops."

"Most assuredly we will, Kyle," Bozabrozy agreed. "I'm very happy that you're helping us."

Jürgen jumped up and down, his stomach jiggling.

"Awesome! This is going to be awesome! Imagine the stories we'll be able to tell!"

"What do we do now?" Kyle asked.

"Now you can help us with the riddle," Barathrina said.

"There's a riddle?" Jürgen asked. "I love riddles."

"Yes," Bozabrozy said. "It led us to the mountain with the faces. But we can't figure out the rest of it."

"Tell it to us!" Jürgen demanded.

Bozabrozy cleared his throat and then said:

> Four giant stone faces on a mountain high
> Nowhere is nearer the sky
> On a peak known by the daughter
> Look beneath the trapped water
> Near a place where fire is seen
> The path descends between

Jürgen and Kyle glanced at each other, completely clueless.

"What does that mean?" Jürgen shook his head.

"Is that even supposed to be helpful?" Kyle asked.

"The first line, of course, refers to your Mt. Rushmore," Bozabrozy said, pointing to the monument. "*Four giant stone faces on a mountain high.*"

"Yeah, that makes sense," Kyle agreed.

"Unless the riddle is talking about some other four stone faces," Jürgen suggested. "There are many giant statues in the world. Especially in Egypt."

"Savakala believes this mountain is the correct one. She glimpsed it in her vision."

"Why isn't she here?" Kyle asked. "If she's the one having visions and getting the riddles, wouldn't it be best if she were on this quest with us?"

"She's on the Windrunner," Barathrina said. "As the Minister of the Sky, she commands others to do her bidding."

"Shouldn't we go back to the ship, then?" Jürgen asked, eager to see the ship that carried the Zurans between worlds.

"No, not until we learn more," Bozabrozy said. "Savakala wants us to find out as much as possible before we return. She's trying to use her powers of foresight to decipher the riddle, but it is a daunting task."

"Well, if a powerful wizard like her can't do it, how can we?" Kyle asked.

"You are familiar with this world, we are not."

"I don't see how that can help much. That riddle is too hard."

"But," Jürgen interjected, "the riddle said "near" the mountain. We aren't very near the mountain here. Let's get closer."

"That's not a bad idea," Bozabrozy agreed. "Perhaps there are some other clues that we must find."

"How are we going to get closer?" Kyle asked. "As soon as we leave the woods and someone sees you there's going to be a riot."

"Use the magical cloak that turns you into a human," Jürgen suggested.

"An excellent course of action," Bozabrozy smiled at Jürgen. "Unfortunately, there is only one and Barathrina has it. Therefore, I shall use stealth to get near the mountain. The rest of you can walk straight there. Go to the large amphitheater at the end of the path."

Barathrina nodded. She put her magical cloak back on. Her form shimmered and altered, and the fat woman the boys met the previous night stood before them once again. Only her immense bulk and overpowering perfume remained the same.

While Bozabrozy snuck off into the woods, Barathrina led the way down a trail, across the field and highway, and through the parking lot. Kyle and Jürgen followed the disguised grunk, trying to stay out of her reeking wake. As they passed the granite pillars of the main entryway, Kyle saw a young girl with long black hair in a pony tail talking to a ranger.

"But my brother was supposed to meet me here so we could go hiking," the girl was saying.

"It's still early, Susie," the ranger replied. "I'm sure Johnny will be along sometime. He had the late shift last night. Maybe he just slept in on his day off."

"Okay," Susie sighed. "When you see him, tell him I'm just wandering around the park." Her nose wrinkled at an unfriendly smell and she turned from the ranger to see Barathrina lumbering along. Kyle held his nose and pointed at the disguised grunk. Susie giggled as the trio walked by.

Barathrina strode purposefully along the paved path, toward the stony presidents. They passed the Information Center, Audio Tour Building, Gift Shop, and Carvers Café. They crossed Borglum Court and hurried through the Avenue of Flags where flags from all the United States fluttered from thick stone pillars.

"Look," Kyle pointed at a green flag near the end. "That's the Washington State flag. It has a picture of George Washington on it."

"Just like on the mountain," Jürgen said.

"Let's not tarry," Barathrina admonished, hurrying onto the Grand View Terrace, a wide balcony overlooking the amphitheater and with a spectacular view of the mountain. They looked down over the railing.

"How do we get down there?" Barathrina asked. "I can't jump that far!"

Kyle pointed. "There are stairs over there."

They descended from the terrace and walked into the amphitheater. Many rows of wood and white stone benches extended from a broad stage behind which sat a blocky building with large steel doors. Behind the building a wooded slope led up to a massive pile of boulders and rocks below the enormous carved faces of George Washington, Thomas Jefferson, Theodore Roosevelt, and Abraham

Lincoln.

Barathrina trundled down a few steps between the rows of seats before plopping down and wiping her forehead.

"I really don't know why I was sent on this hiking foray," she said to no one in particular. "I'm not up to all this exertion, especially before breakfast."

Kyle sat down several feet away from her, hoping to avoid her smelly aura. He did not succeed. "Weren't those candy bars enough for you?"

"Sky, no! That was barely even half a snack. I'm accustomed to a well-stocked larder and full ovens with fruits and vegetables and meats and breads and spices and cakes and pies and ales and wines and much more." She stared dreamily off into the sky.

Jürgen pulled another candy bar from his backpack and handed it to Barathrina. "Here, have another. Maybe it will hold you over until we–" Jürgen froze in mid-sentence as the grunk snatched the bar from his hand, ripped off the wrapper and swallowed the entire bar in one gulp. "–can find more food."

"You don't seem like a quester to me, Barathrina," Kyle said. He looked around the outdoor theater but saw no sign of Bozabrozy. A few tourists wandered around, taking pictures, sipping coffee, or eating a sandwich from the cafe.

"I'm not a quester," Barathrina conceded. "I'm just the ship's cook. I shouldn't be wandering around, looking for elemental quintessence on a strange world full of skinny humans. I should be in the ship's galley eating. I mean cooking. I should be in the ship's galley cooking, of course."

Jürgen sat down across the aisle from her. "So what are you doing out here?"

"Following Savakala's orders. She is the emperor's delegate on this quest, you know. She was hand-picked to lead the expedition. Everyone must do what Savakala commands. Well, except Machadaro." She laughed. "He has fun disobeying Savakala's orders, I think. If someone as surly as him can have fun."

"Who's Machadaro?"

"He is the captain of the Windrunner. Strong, bold, and ferocious. You won't find a skyship captain with greater skill, daring, or fury."

"How come he can get away with disobeying orders when no one else can?"

"He's the ship's captain," Barathrina said. "A ship's captain has complete command of his vessel. Savakala can only tell him the course or destination. Machadaro decides how to fulfill those orders."

"And he's a quester, too?" Kyle asked.

"Will we meet him?" Jürgen asked.

"Yes, when we find the quintessence and deliver it to Savakala, I expect."

"I don't see how we can find that stuff," Kyle said. "That riddle doesn't help at all."

"Kyle is right," Jürgen agreed. "Can you give it to us again?"

Barathrina repeated the riddle.

"*Nowhere is nearer the sky,*" Kyle looked around. "That must mean Mt. Rushmore, too. I don't see anything taller."

"*On a peak known by the daughter.*" Jürgen frowned. "Who's daughter?"

"I have no idea," Barathrina shrugged.

"Maybe it means you," Kyle said. "You are someone's daughter, after all. Maybe the daughter in the riddle just means any woman. Not a specific person."

"Yes, I am someone's daughter, that's true. But I don't know any peaks on Earth. Other than that one." She pointed at Mt. Rushmore. "And I only know that one because you told me its name."

"So that means the first three lines all point to Mt. Rushmore," Jürgen said.

"What were the next lines?"

"*Look beneath the trapped water. Near a place where fire is seen. The path descends between."*

"Trapped water. That means water that can't escape. Maybe there's a swimming pool nearby?" Jürgen guessed.

"I wonder if there is? Or maybe there's a fountain. We'll need a map. They must have a map around here somewhere."

"Near a place where fire is seen," Jürgen said. "Where is a fire seen? A fireplace! We're looking for a swimming pool with a fireplace on top of Abraham Lincoln's head!"

Barathrina and Kyle remained silent and unconvinced.

"What?" Jürgen asked.

"That doesn't seem right," Kyle said. "Why would they have a swimming pool on top of his head?"

"Well, we need to come up with the answer to finish the quest," Jürgen said. "I think we should just start throwing out ideas. If we don't figure out the riddle, who will?"

"Me!" said someone with a high-pitched voice. They all turned to see a dark-haired girl sitting a few rows behind them, the girl Kyle had seen talking to the ranger. She had obviously been eavesdropping on their conversation.

"Who are you?" Barathrina snorted.

Chapter 8

"My name is Susie Five Eagles," the little girl replied proudly, her chin held high and her eyes dancing. "Who are you? Where are you from? I'm from the Sioux Nation."

Barathrina stood and glared at the girl. "Our names and origins are not your concern. You better go find your parents and leave us alone."

"But I have the answer to your riddle!"

"Hold on, Barathrina," Kyle motioned for the grunk to sit back down, which she did with a grunt. "Maybe she does know the answer."

"I do! I do!" Susie laughed. "I love riddles and that one is easy for anyone that knows the Black Hills like me."

"So, what's the answer?" Jürgen demanded.

"Harney Peak!"

"What's Harney Peak?" Kyle asked.

"And why is it the answer?" Jürgen added.

"Here's why," Susie began. "Harney Peak is the tallest mountain near Mt. Rushmore. I know about it, and I'm someone's daughter. There is an old fire watchtower on top of it. And behind the watch tower is a little dam with a pond." She crossed her arms and smiled.

"That's pretty good," Kyle said. Jürgen nodded in agreement.

"Where is this Harney Peak?" Barathrina asked.

Susie jerked a thumb to her left. "Over in that direction. I can take you to a spot where you can see it." They agreed to follow her and she led them from the amphitheater and along the Presidential Trail. After only a few minutes, she pointed through the trees and they could see a distant mountain swathed in Ponderosa pines. Thrusting up from the trees, tall cliffs looked like the walls of a castle. At the top, a tower squatted.

"That's the old fire watchtower."

Barathrina's shoulders sagged. "That's a long way off."

"By trail, it is," Susie admitted. "We could hike from here on the Blackberry Trail, but it's too late to do that. It'd take all day to get to the tower from here. But if we catch a ride with my brother we could go to Sylvan Lake. It's only three and a half miles from there to the mountaintop."

Kyle looked at the girl. "We?"

Susie grinned from ear to ear. "Sure! I love to hike. I've done all the trails in Rushmore and Custer State Park. I'm supposed to meet my brother Johnny here today for hiking anyway. I'll go see if he's here yet." She ran back toward the park buildings before they could say anything. "Meet you in a couple minutes at the Information Center!"

"Swooping sky!" Barathrina gasped, casting another fearful glance at the steep cliffs of Harney Peak. "That girl has too much energy. She actually expects me to trek across this wilderness all the way over to that mountain and then climb those cliffs?"

"It could be the answer to the riddle," Jürgen said.

"You solved the riddle?" Bozabrozy suddenly appeared from behind a tree, making all of them jump.

"Don't do that!" Barathrina held her chest. "I told you to stop that! You know I don't like it!"

"Can't be helped. I have to stay hidden so I'm not spotted by the other humans." The rascan turned to the boys. "Is it true, you've solved the riddle already? I couldn't hear what you were talking about with the girl."

The boys quickly explained Susie's riddle theory.

"It does sound promising." Bozabrozy looked at Harney Peak. "That's going to be a good hike."

"We don't have to hike from here," Jürgen said. "Susie is going to get us a ride to get closer."

"We don't have any food," Barathrina lamented.

"Wouldn't it be quicker to call the skyship and have it take us over there?" Kyle suggested.

"If only we could." Barathrina frowned. "The Windrunner was damaged on the way here. The captain and crew are repairing it."

"Our arrival was more like a crash than a landing," Bozabrozy admitted. "Besides, it would attract too much attention to have the Windrunner come flying over all these people."

"But the television news would love it," Kyle said, imagining the headlines. "UFO Visits Mt. Rushmore! Tourists Flee in Terror!" He and Jürgen laughed.

"I should return to the ship and inform Savakala of our progress," Barathrina volunteered.

Bozabrozy shook his head. "You need to go with the children. You have the Cloak of Humanity. I'll inform Savakala."

"I'll give you the cloak."

"Did Savakala give you permission to give away your artifacts?" Bozabrozy asked.

"No," Barathrina admitted reluctantly.

"You don't want to defy a magistrate, do you?"

"No. But you're just using that as an excuse. You've never obeyed the magistrates and their laws before. You always have contraband artifacts."

"Be that as it may," Bozabrozy said, "you can't go back to the ship without the cloak. She'll ask for it immediately. You'd have to face her wrath. Alone."

At that, Barathrina seemed to deflate. "But it's such a long way and I'm tired and hungry."

"I can buy you some food at the snack shop," Jürgen offered.

"Could you, dearie? That would be such a gift!"

"You three go with the little girl. I'll meet you there," said Bozabrozy, pointing at Harney Peak. The rascan disappeared into the woods.

Jürgen, with some extra money from Kyle, hurried off to get food for the trail.

"Why couldn't you give him the cloak?" Kyle asked the grunk as they walked back toward the park buildings.

"The Emperor owns all artifacts," Barathrina huffed. "The creation, possession, and use of artifacts are closely regulated by Imperial decree and enforced by the magistrates. Savakala is the only magistrate on this expedition, and she keeps all the artifacts in her cabin. She metes them out to those who need them."

Barathrina and Kyle arrived at the Information Center to find Susie talking to a ranger.

"Oh, here they are," Susie said. "Hi! This is Deborah. She's a ranger."

Kyle shook the ranger's hand. "Hi. I'm Kyle Morgan, and this is Barathrina... Schmidt."

"Nice to meet you folks," Deborah said with a smile, trying not to wince at the grunk's strong perfume. "You've got yourself a good little guide today. Susie knows more about these trails than anyone." The girl beamed.

"She's just a little dearie," Barathrina agreed.

"My brother's not here yet," Susie said, "and he's not answering his phone. But Deborah says she has to go on an errand to Custer City, and she can drop us off at Sylvan Lake. She's so nice!"

"I hope you've got enough food and water. It's a steep hike, and it looks like it's going to be a sunny day. You don't want to get dehydrated." The ranger seemed a bit dubious about Barathrina, who did not look like someone who could hike miles through mountainous terrain.

"I've got my water bottles," Susie said, referring to a backpack she had retrieved from somewhere. "Compass, matches, poncho, rope, first aid kit, plus all the fixings for

Susie Snacks."

"Excellent," Deborah said. "Johnny's got a good ranger-in-training here. What about your friends?"

"Jürgen is getting us some food," Kyle said. "And I've got some water."

"Who's Jürgen?"

"Jürgen Schmidt," Kyle said. "He's a friend of mine from Germany. There he is now." Jürgen jogged up, still stuffing items into the pockets of his backpack, which now bulged.

"I bought us some sandwiches, muffins, brownies, cookies, chips, and baked caramel pecan rolls. And energy drinks and Sioux City Sarsaparilla."

Susie squealed in delight. "I love Sioux City Sarsaparilla! It's the best soda ever!"

"It's even better than root beer,"Kyle agreed. "I wish we could get it in Seattle."

Deborah laughed. "All that sugar should give you enough energy for the hike. Everyone ready?"

Chapter 9

It was only a half hour drive from Mt. Rushmore to Sylvan Lake. Along the way, Barathrina sampled the snacks in Jürgen's backpack while the others enjoyed the mountainous scenery.

"What are all those weird piles of wood that look like tepees?" Jürgen asked, pointing at the side of the road.

"Those are slash piles," Deborah explained. "We stack the wood like that after cleaning up fallen branches and thinning the forest. It helps to prevent fires. It also helps keep the forest healthy, which slows down the Rocky Mountain pine beetle."

"What is that?"

"It's a tiny beetle that can kill the biggest Ponderosa pine tree." She pointed at a mountain and they saw that many of the trees on it were brown and dead.

"It's sad," Susie agreed. "But the pine beetles don't do as much damage if we keep the forests clean."

"Something like that," Deborah smiled, as they pulled in at Sylvan Lake. "Remember to sign-in on the trail, Susie. I'll tell Johnny where you are and maybe he'll catch up."

"I hope so." Susie waved as the ranger drove away.

Barathrina looked around. "So, where is this tower? I don't see it."

"You can't see it from here," Susie said. "We'll be able to see it after a couple hours of hiking."

"I thought we were going to get closer!"

"We're a lot closer. But we still have to hike more than

three miles."

Barathrina sighed, but followed Susie to the Sylvan Lake Trailhead: Trail #4, also called the Cathedral Spires Trail. The children cinched up their backpacks and they all set off. The ground sparkled with mica and other reflective minerals.

As they wound their way around giant grey boulders and through towering pines, Susie pointed out interesting trees and birds and rocks and mountain views. There were lots of wildflowers, tall yellow-blossomed common mullen and short purple bunches of silky aster and especially black-eyed Susans. A brown-feathered northern harrier soared overhead. Small bluebirds fluttered by. They saw the rocky formations of Little Devil's Tower and the majesitc Cathedral Spires.

They only saw a few other hikers, who smiled and wished them good luck. Two men, however, warned them that someone had seen bear tracks a few miles away. Kyle and Jürgen frowned at that.

Susie asked a lot of questions along the way. Where were they from? How did they meet? How long were they here for? When were they leaving? She did not get very satisfactory answers from Barathrina, who gasped and wheezed the whole time. They kept having to pause and wait for her to catch up.

"Why doesn't your mom like answering questions?" Susie asked Jürgen after a couple hours. They rested near a massive rock soaring dozens of feet into the sky. Barathrina lagged behind, plodding up the slope toward them.

"She's not my mom!" Jürgen objected between gulps of his energy drink.

"Oh, I thought she was. Kyle said her name was Schmidt." Susie turned to Kyle. "Is she your mom?"

"No. My mom's back in Seattle. She couldn't get off work for this trip."

"So who is she?"

"Jürgen's aunt," Kyle lied.

Susie watched the rotund woman stumble along the slope toward them. "She isn't in very good shape. And, she's hiding something."

"Hiding something?" Kyle said, suddenly worried that Susie might discover their secret. "Why do you say that?"

"Because you always answer whenever I ask her questions."

"Oh, she's just out of breath. She needs her energy for hiking, not talking."

"Right," Susie said doubtfully.

Barathrina finally caught up with them and leaned against a Ponderosa pine, wheezing. "I need another candy bar!" she demanded. Susie wondered if the tree would topple over from her weight.

"You've already eaten almost all the snacks I bought!" Jürgen complained, but handed her a Gutzon's Grab and Go sandwich.

"What's this?" Barathrina unwrapped the sandwich and smelled it. "Mmmm…. Ham!"

"You eat ham?" Jürgen asked. "Isn't that kind of like cannibalism?"

The grunk did not answer, but Susie said: "That's not very nice, Jürgen!"

"What? What did I say?"

"You just tried to be clever by calling her a pig, didn't you?"

"That's the last of our food," Kyle interjected, hoping to distract Susie.

Susie smiled and pulled a jar of peanut butter from her backpack. "Don't worry, I'll make you some Susie Snacks." She put soda crackers and chocolate chips next to the peanut butter.

"What are Susie Snacks?" Kyle asked.

"Trail snacks I invented! It's like a sandwich. But instead of bread you use two soda crackers, spread peanut butter on both, and then put five chocolate chips in between." She quickly demonstrated, using a pocket knife to spread the peanut butter.

Jürgen munched on the crumbly snack. "These are delicious!"

"No kidding," Kyle agreed. "I love peanut butter."

"It has sugar, protein, and salt. Great for hiking. You just have to carry a lot of water. They make you real thirsty."

"They sure do," said Jürgen, gulping down a bottle of sarsaparilla.

After dining on Susie Snacks, which Barathrina also found delicious, they started on their way again. After nearly four hours of hiking they neared the summit of Harney Peak. A huge boulder leaned over to create a short tunnel that led to a winding metal stairway. The fat grunk squeezed her way up the last leg of the journey while the children ran ahead.

"Wow! That is so cool," Kyle said as he stepped out on the walkway leading up to the fire tower. It squatted on the top of the granite peak, proud and intimidating, against blue skies colored with wisps of cloud. It reminded Kyle of a medieval castle from some movie about knights and dragons. It was made of irregular stones of gray, red, orange, and black, sparkling in the sun.

"It's so small," Jürgen said.

"Hey," Kyle frowned, "just because Germany has so many castles doesn't mean you have to complain about ours."

"That's not a castle," Jürgen said. "It's not even big enough to be a tower on a castle wall. Americans don't know how to build real castles, I guess."

"There's a great view," Susie said, hurrying ahead. "It's the highest spot from here to Europe. Race you to the top!"

Chapter 10

At the top of the stone steps was a tall doorway. A metal plaque explained the history of the tower.

HARNEY PEAK LOOKOUT
THE HARNEY PEAK FIRE LOOKOUT, DAM, AND PUMPHOUSE WERE BUILT BY THE CCC IN 1939 AND ARE LISTED IN THE NATIONAL REGISTER OF HISTORIC PLACES. HARNEY PEAK ELEVATION IS 2207 METERS (7242 FEET). THE PEAK IS THE HIGHEST POINT EAST OF THE ROCKY MOUNTAINS AND WEST OF THE PYRENEES MOUNTAINS OF EUROPE.

Inside, they climbed a steep metal stair, a ladder really, to the upper floor of the tower. Far away, they could see the back side of Mt. Rushmore and part of its parking lot, with the plains of South Dakota in the distance beyond. Grey mountains thrust up out of the forest in every direction.

"The views in Germany are better," Jürgen said. "We have the Alps, you know."

"I don't have to come up there, do I?" Barathrina called from where she leaned against a short wall that ran along the path below them.

"No. We're just enjoying the view," Susie replied. "But you can see five states from up here. Which ones do you think they are, Mrs. Schmidt?"

The fat woman collapsed on a boulder, sweating profusely, wheezing and unable to speak. Three chipmunks darted out onto the path, no doubt expecting her to feed them.

"South Dakota, North Dakota, and Montana," Jürgen guessed. He'd read up on the American heartland before leaving Germany.

"And two more," Susie looked over at Kyle.

"Um... Nebraska...and..."

Susie waited.

"Wyoming?" Kyle said hesitantly.

"Right!"

"Let's find the pool you were talking about," Jürgen said.

"It's right down there," Susie pointed. On the other side of the tower, a green pond was almost hidden in a small gorge. "Come on, Mrs. Schmidt. You need to go through the tower."

They met Barathrina at the doorway, and then descended another narrow ladder-stair. Barathrina almost got stuck, but Kyle and Jürgen pulled her down to the lower level. They passed some bare concrete rooms with small windows before exiting the tower and heading down another stone path. It turned and steepened into a ravine, the bottom of which was blocked by a small stone building with a gaping doorway.

"That's the old pumphouse," Susie said. "It was built in 1939."

"I know," Jürgen said. "I read the plaque up there."

Barathrina went into the one-room building and looked through the only window. She nearly filled the small room. "There's no way to get to the water."

"We have to go around out here," Susie said, squeezing between the ravine wall and the pumphouse.

"Thunder and clouds!" Barathrina shook her head. "I can't fit through that. Why is everything here so skinny?"

"We can help you through again," Kyle volunteered. With much effort and grunting, they tried to push and pull the grunk through the narrow gap. She squealed and protested and squirmed and finally got stuck.

"Oh, no!" she lamented. "I'm stuck! Help me! Pull me out!"

After even more effort, the kids managed to pull Barathrina back out onto the steps above the pumphouse.

"I am not trying that again." She went into the pumphouse and peered through the window. "You go down and I'll watch from here."

Kyle and Jürgen joined Susie beyond the pumphouse. Several chipmunks skittered along the granite rocks. The pond, which seemed to be only a couple feet deep, filled the small gorge. A dam held in the water.

"Here we are," Susie said. "Now, what was that riddle again?"

Through the window, Barathrina once again recited the riddle.

Four giant stone faces on a mountain high
Nowhere is nearer the sky
On a peak known by the daughter
Look beneath the trapped water
Near a place where fire is seen
The path descends between

"Okay," Susie said. "The first three lines are about Harney Peak. The fourth is about this pond and the fifth is about the fire tower. But I don't know what the last one means. What was this riddle for again? A school project?"

"Um...yeah," Kyle said.

"So where's the rest of your class? Isn't this a class project? Don't they get a chance to solve the riddle, too?"

"No, it's just for me. My...um...teacher has been here and when she heard I was coming she gave me the riddle for extra credit if I solve it before school starts."

Susie shrugged and said "whatever" but Kyle didn't think she believed him. She waded into the pond, but there was only silt and rocks. *"Look beneath the trapped water... I don't see anything. Just mud. What does that line mean?"*

"Bozabrozy knows what to do," Barathrina said from the pumphouse.

"Who's Bozabrozy?" Susie asked.

"I am!"

The rascan emerged from around the pumphouse.

Susie's eyes opened wide and her jaw dropped.

Bozabrozy tilted his head and looked at Kyle. "Have you not told her about me?"

Kyle shuffled. "No."

Susie pointed at Bozabrozy and splashed toward him. "You're an animal spirit! My grandpa talks about you all the time! Are you?"

"No, I'm a Zuran and a rascan."

"I don't know what those are. This is so cool! I wish my brother and grandfather were here. He used to tell us stories of animal spirits. I think raccoons were tricksters, like Coyote."

"I am Bozabrozy. So nice to meet you, Susie Five Eagles." He held out his hand and Susie gave it a good shake.

She turned to Kyle. "I knew you were hiding something!"

"He's from another planet," Jürgen said. "He's an alien. So is Barathrina."

Susie paused and looked at the fat woman in the pumphouse window. "From another planet? Wow! She doesn't look like an alien. She looks human."

"Wait until she takes off her magical cloak," Jürgen said.

"If you're from another planet, how do you know how to speak English?" Susie asked.

"Magic fish," Bozabrozy replied.

"Magic fish?" Kyle shook his head. "What do you mean, magic fish?"

"What do you mean, magic?" Susie asked.

"Bozabrozy is a wizard," Jürgen answered. "He can turn things into ice and make plants grow."

"You're alien wizards?" Susie exclaimed. "That's so…strange. Shouldn't you use ray guns and spaceships and stuff like that?"

"Not a spaceship. They call it a skyship," Jürgen replied. He then told Susie how Bozabrozy had arrived, about the urgra attack on their cabin, and their flight into the woods.

"I can hardly believe it," she said. "Except that he's standing right there and that's obviously no mask. And he has a cute tail!"

"We don't have time for this," Bozabrozy said. "More humans could be along at any moment. The problem, if my eavesdropping skills aren't failing me, is that we can't look beneath the water, as the riddle suggests?"

"Yes, we think the answer to the riddle is under the water, but we can't dig underwater even if we had shovels."

"Then I think what we need is less water." Bozabrozy reached into one of his pouches, pulled out a potion bottle and threw it over Susie's head. When the bottle hit the surface of the pond, the water exploded in a huge splash. The chipmunks scattered as it drenched everyone and splattered against the steep granite walls of the gorge. But, most of it flew so high that it washed over the dam and down the mountain.

"Storms and clouds!" Barathrina said, protected from the spray by the pumphouse. "I'm glad I'm not out there with you. I'd be all wet."

"It's only water," the rascan smiled, his fur dripping.

"That was amazing!" Kyle said. The pond was gone. Only small puddles of water remained in the gorge.

Susie, sopping wet, giggled uncontrollably as a fine spray drifted down over them. Jürgen took off his backpack and started wringing out his clothes as best he could.

"Now we can look under the trapped water," Bozabrozy said, feet squelching as he stepped into the mud.

"Yeah," Jürgen said, following him. He started kicking around. "You think the quintessence is buried under the mud?"

"The riddle says there is a path," Kyle disagreed. "There must be a secret tunnel somewhere."

"I've never heard of a secret tunnel under the pond," Susie frowned.

Jürgen stared at her. "Of course not. It's secret."

"Are you looking for a hidden door, Bozabrozy?" Kyle asked, watching the rascan splashing his hands around in a puddle.

"No. I am asking the water if there is a tunnel below."

"You can talk to water?" Susie said.

"Talk is perhaps too strong a word," the rascan nodded. "This is just normal water, not a water elemental, so I can only learn a few things from it. But I can find out where the water comes from and where it goes."

"How does that help?"

"By telling us that the water seeps out into a deep shaft right under here." Bozabrozy walked to the center of the gorge and pointed at the mud with a smile.

"I don't see a shaft," Jürgen said.

"I guess we get to dig," Susie said and dropped to her knees, pulling mud away. Kyle moved to help, as did Jürgen and Bozabrozy. As the work started, Barathrina disappeared from the pumphouse window.

"Wow!" Susie said as they dug. "This is like a story my grandpa would tell. Magic and talking animals and secret tunnels."

"It's a story we all get to tell when we've finished the quest," Jürgen said. "They'll probably make a movie out of us."

"Can I be in the movie, too?" Susie asked.

"You want to join the quest?" Jürgen said.

"Yes, it sounds like fun!" Susie's eyes twinkled and she grinned broadly. "Besides, we're at the last lines of the riddle. It won't take long, will it?"

After a short time, they had cleared away the mud from a wide area of bare rock with a few cracks.

"There's nothing here," Jürgen said. "There's no door or tunnel. The water lied to you."

"No." Bozabrozy stood. "There is a passage beneath the stone."

"How do we get to it?" Kyle asked.

"We must dig through the stone."

"That's impossible. We'd need a bunch of jackhammers."

"I don't know what jackhammers are," Bozabrozy said. "But we do have the Sundering Bardiche."

Jürgen puckered his brow. "The what what?"

"A weapon that Joromwor possesses."

"Who's Joromwor?"

"A warrior I brought along in case we encountered more of Rakanian's soldiers."

"Where is he?" Jürgen asked.

"Guarding the path to the gorge. I'll go get him." The rascan had started toward the pumphouse when suddenly everyone heard voices through the window.

"Who's talking to Barathrina?" Jürgen asked.

There was a loud roar and the back wall of the pumphouse burst outward in a shower of stone and mortar. A giant shaggy creature appeared in the gaping hole, glaring out into the gorge. Kyle stumbled backwards when he recognized the urgra that had attacked the cabin.

Chapter 11

"Look out!" Kyle yelled, and pulled Susie away from the pumphouse.

"What's the matter?" Bozabrozy said.

"It's the monster that attacked us!" Jürgen cringed against the wall of the gorge. There was no way to escape.

"No, it isn't," Bozabrozy said. "This is Joromwor, an Imperial Legionary."

"Imperial Legate," Joromwor corrected in a rumbling deep voice like boulders crashing down a mountainside. He jumped down from the shattered pumphouse and into the gorge. "I am no mere legionary. I command legions."

Unlike the furious urgra of the previous night, this one carried a huge weapon and wore ornate armor of overlapping metal plates. A chunk of stone dangled on a leather thong around his neck. Barathrina, unhurt, walked to the edge of the pumphouse but did not descend.

"He's a friend. No need to fret," Bozabrozy tried to calm the boys. "He came with us on the Windrunner and is here to protect Savakala. And the rest of us."

Joromwor grunted, striding through the mud.

"But he looks just like the other one," Jürgen said.

Bozabrozy nodded and snickered. "Urgras look alike to me, too."

Susie pulled free of Kyle's grasp and went up to the urgra. "I can't believe this! No one is ever going to believe me when I tell them."

Joromwor merely glared at the diminutive child from

his lofty height.

"But you shouldn't have smashed the pumphouse," Susie protested. "That's park property and very old. It's historical. You just did a very bad thing! Why didn't you go around?"

The urgra ignored her and spoke to the rascan. "I heard you needed help."

"To get through this stone," Bozabrozy pointed. "We think the path to the quintessence lies beneath."

Joromwor lumbered over to the bare patch of stone, hefting his weapon. It was a huge staff with a curved blade that ran along half its length.

"Move aside," he ordered.

"Do you do aquosian magic like Bozabrozy?" Jürgen asked.

Joromwor growled at the chubby boy. "Do I look like a wet rodent, whelp? No, you'll soon see that I am much better than a ring-tailed rascan!"

"What kind of weapon is that?" Jürgen asked.

"One that will hurt you lest you stand aside."

"That weapon," Bozabrozy explained, "is the Sundering Bardiche. It is crafted from geopsium and honed to a terribly sharp edge. It can cut through anything."

"Even rascans," Joromwor growled and pushed Bozabrozy away. "Everyone stand back."

The legate raised the bardiche and brought it down on the stone. The huge blade sliced through it like a knife through butter. Dust and rubble flew around him as he worked. Soon, his efforts revealed a dark hole in the ground.

Susie peered down the hole. "Where does that go?" she asked. It looked like a natural tunnel leading to darkness in the heart of Harney Peak.

Bozabrozy waved away the dust, looked into the fissure, and smiled. "To the quintessence. Who wants to go first?"

CHAPTER 12

"I don't have a flashlight," Susie said unhappily.

"Don't worry, I have one," Bozabrozy pulled Kyle's flashlight from his pouch and flipped it on. Kyle stepped forward and grabbed it from the Zuran.

"That's mine!"

"I have one, also," said Jürgen, pulling it from his backpack. "Before the aliens abducted us, we were planning to go spelunking in Jewel Cave."

"How deep is it?" Susie asked.

Jürgen pointed his light down the hole. They still could not see the bottom even though the beam shone down at least thirty feet.

"It could be hundreds of feet down there."

"We can find out for sure," Kyle said. He reached into his backpack, pulled out a glow stick and bent it with a snap. It immediately began glowing with a strong green light.

"That's a fine artifact!" Bozabrozy's whiskers twitched. "Can I have some?"

Kyle shook his head. "I don't have enough to hand out." He dropped the glow stick down the hole. It didn't fall for long before it landed on a rocky floor.

"That's probably only sixty feet," Susie guessed.

"That's a long way to climb," Kyle took a step back from the edge.

"It sure would be nice to have Savakala's cloak of flying right about now," Barathrina said.

"She'd never let anyone else use that," Bozabrozy said,

but produced a coil of slender rope from his pouches. "We'll use this instead. Joromwor will hold the rope. I'll go down first, then Barathrina. Then the children."

"Why do I have to go down there?" Barathrina asked from where she sat at the edge of the pumphouse. "You and Joromwor can take care of things now. I'll head back to the Windrunner."

"Alone? I don't think Rakanian will be too kind if he happens upon you."

"Is he still about?"

"His minions are. They are most assuredly looking for us."

Barathrina eyed the thin cord skeptically. "That won't hold me."

"It doesn't look very strong," Jürgen agreed.

"Yes, it will hold you. It's an elemental rope," Bozabrozy said. "Twisted from fibers of plants grown in soil enriched with pure geopsium to give it strength. The plants are watered with pure aquosia, to keep them supple and enduring."

"What is geopsium," Susie said. "And what is aquosia?"

"Geopsium is the elemental quintessence of stone," Joromwor replied. "Plants grown in earth salted with it are stronger and larger and tougher."

"And aquosia is the elemental quintessence of water," Bozabrozy said. "It is pure and cooling and life-giving. Aquosia can heal injuries and cure diseases and make things grow, among many other things."

"Which one are we looking for?" Susie asked.

The Zurans exchanged glances. "We're not sure," Bozabrozy said, "as the riddle is not explicit."

"It's geopsium," Jürgen guessed. "We're crawling down into the depths of the Earth, after all."

"You need quintessence to make all your magic stuff?" Kyle said. "Is that why you're here on Earth? Have you used up all the geopsium and aquosia on your planet and now you're here to take ours?"

Bozabrozy laughed. "No, Kyle, no. Zura is rich with quintessence of all kinds. Geopsium, aquosia, pyrophyra, aethrial. Emperor Exeverius has fleets of skyships scouring the endless skies for it. There are entire islands riddled with geopsium mines. Entire lakes of aquosia. The Empire has no lack of quintessence."

"Then why do you need the geopsium here?" Susie wondered.

"That is a question for Savakala," Bozabrozy said. "She is the commander of this quest. She sees the past and the future. When she feels it is right to tell us more, she will."

"Ooh. I'm looking forward to meeting her," Susie said. "It must be amazing to see visions of the future."

"But don't forget the past," Bozabrozy said. "It holds secrets, as well."

"Let's get going," Joromwor demanded, uncoiling the rope down the shaft. "We shouldn't waste time."

"Right you are," said Bozabrozy. He grabbed the rope and dropped down the hole with ease as the others watched.

"Get over here, grunk," Joromwor ordered as he pulled up the rope. Barathrina struggled down from the pumphouse and moped over to the hole. The urgra looped the rope around her and under her arms. She sat at the edge of the hole.

"I'm not too sure about this," she whined.

"Neither am I," Joromwor replied, and pushed her in. He held the other end and quickly lowered her down. Under his armor and fur, his muscles bulged with the effort of supporting the grunk's weight. The hole was narrow, and Barathrina could touch both sides, but she did little to help the urgra.

"You're really strong," Jürgen said.

"Lucky for that fat tub of lard," Joromwor growled.

"I'm next!" Susie jumped forward. She tied the rope around herself and descended into the mountain like it was an amusement park ride.

"Looks like she's done this before," Jürgen said admiringly.

Susie reached the bottom and got out of the rope. "I can't see much with just the glowstick. I should have brought one of their flashlights."

Bozabrozy handed her a small, clear bottle full of water.
"What's this?"

"It is a glimmerer," Bozabrozy told her. "Shake it."

She did. The bottle sparkled and the tunnel around them shimmered as if in sunlight reflecting off of a rippling pond. "That's neat!"

"Keep it with you," Bozabrozy said, handing another to Barathrina.

"Hey! Look out below!"

They glanced up to see Jürgen spinning at the end of the rope. They hopped aside as he plopped down next to them. "Sorry. I lost control."

Kyle also had a bit of trouble, but managed to keep his feet when he reached the bottom.

"How's he getting down?" Susie asked, pointing back up to the urgra.

"Stand back!" The legate bellowed down to them, and they moved away. A few seconds later, Joromwor's Sundering Bardiche plummeted down the hole and stuck solidly into the granite floor. The magic rope, coiled neatly, followed. Then came Joromwor, descending like a rock, letting gravity take hold. He scraped the walls with his massive claws, slowing his fall, and landed heavily and unperterbed amidst a shower of rocks. He retrieved his weapon and threw the rope back to Bozabrozy.

"Let's get going," he said gruffly.

The way continued downward, and descent was not easy. Joromwor's size was a problem, but he often used the Sundering Bardiche to enlarge passages and openings. There was one gap that was too narrow for even Jürgen to squeeze through until Joromwor chopped it larger. Barathrina's weight sometimes caused the rocks beneath her to break off and collapse, but someone was always near to save her from a fatal fall.

Fortunately, both Bozabrozy and Susie were accomplished climbers. The magic rope often came in handy to belay Barathrina or Joromwor when traversing the numerous cliffs they had to conquer.

Kyle felt sorry for Jürgen. He had a hard time with all the hiking and spelunking. Kyle enjoyed both, but even he was feeling tired. A restless night in the woods hadn't helped, especially after the long road trip from Seattle. After a lengthy hike in the mountains followed by hours of climbing rough rock in bottomless caverns, his muscles were aching. Kyle wondered how Jürgen was able to endure it. He wasn't used to such prolonged exertion. Slowly digging up fossils and dusting them with toothbrushes hadn't prepared him for this grueling trek. Neither had French toast, ice cream, and candy bars.

Kyle poked his friend as they all got up after a short break. "Jürgen, hey, wake up."

Jürgen stretched and yawned. "What? Already?"

"Yep."

"Are we there yet?"

Kyle pointed his flashlight down the chasm from their ledge. "No way to know, bud."

Jürgen's stomach rumbled loudly as he stood up. He'd run out of snacks, and drinks, long ago. "Okay, but whatever is at the end of this quest better be good!"

Kyle laughed. Despite Jürgen's weariness, hunger, thirst, scrapes, bruises, and blisters, he still wanted to press on. Kyle patted him on the back. "It'll be better than any Xbox game, I bet."

The questers continued downward, always downward. At the easiest times, they found themselves walking along sloping tunnels with sand and pebbles underfoot, the dry streambeds of some subterranean waterway. But these were rare, and usually they had to scramble across jumbles of sharp rocks, or squirm through gaps between boulders, or climb down sheer rock faces supported only by Bozabrozy's magical rope. Often, they felt a breeze blowing this way or that. Jürgen said it was caused by atmospheric pressure.

With each new bend of the tunnel, each new shaft they descended, and each new corner they turned, they found another demonstration of the beauty hidden beneath the Earth. They found strange stone honeycombs in the walls or ceilings, like thin blades intersecting at all angles. They waded across a cold shallow lake, on top of which floated thin wafers of stone, like rocky lily pads. Another cavern's floor was covered by small white protuberances like packing popcorn. The oddest thing they found was a forest of stone bushes that filled several caverns.

"These look like curly-fries," Susie said. "Look! This one is taller than me!"

"There's a whole clump of them over there that are twice as tall!" Kyle said. The shadows of the strange stone bushes groped along the cavern walls like skeletal fingers. "I think they look more like big clumps of worms."

"They're called helictite bushes," Jürgen said. "Don't touch them, they're very fragile."

Jürgen wasn't able to remember names for all of the geologic wonders they saw, but that didn't bother the kids in the least. They made up their own names for them.

After walking along a level, sand-strewn tunnel for half an hour, Kyle observed, "It's been a long time since we had to climb down."

"Maybe we're almost at the end," Susie said, still full of energy. She was used to physical exertion after all the hikes she'd been on.

"I hope so," Jürgen said as he stumbled along.

"I'd much rather not do any more climbing," Barathrina agreed. "Down, up, or sideways."

Bozabrozy stopped and pointed ahead. The tunnel seemed to end, except for a narrow opening lined with dark crystals, sharp and pointed. They looked like spearheads or the razor-sharp teeth of some terrible beast. There was a large opening beyond.

"That doesn't look very promising," Barathrina frowned.

Bozabrozy, not seeing any other options, said "And yet, that is where we are going." And with that, he leapt through the opening. Susie followed immediately after, holding her glimmerer in front of her.

"You go next, Jürgen," Kyle suggested. "That way we can help Barathrina through."

Jürgen stepped through the opening and waited on the other side. "Come on, Barathrina, it's not that hard."

"I'm four times bigger than you are," the grunk noted. "I don't think I'll fit."

"Come on, we'll help."

Barathrina moved into the opening. She tried to step gingerly over the jagged crystals, but she was about as sure-footed as a cross-eyed elephant on a lop-sided skateboard. A crystal sliced open her left boot. Her dress snagged on another and ripped, making her stumble into the opposite wall. She shrieked as dozens of crystals poked her. Jürgen pulled her as hard as she could, while Kyle pushed. All three toppled through the opening and into the cavernous chamber beyond.

Kyle rolled off of Barathrina, who then rolled off of Jürgen. The German gasped for breath. Kyle bent down and looked to make sure Barathrina wasn't bleeding all over, but she had only suffered a few pinpricks.

"Stand back," Joromwor ordered from the other side of the opening. When they obeyed, he ducked his head and crashed his way through. The razor-sharp crystals shattered against his armor, dark shards tinkling to the floor.

"Hey!" Susie complained. "Those were pretty! You

didn't have to break them all."

"Silence, whelp! I'll not take any sass from a furless child! If I had my way, we'd brand you and be done with it."

Susie cringed and hid behind Barathrina.

"We seem to be in a very large cavern," Bozabrozy said. Their glimmerers and flashlights didn't reveal any other walls besides the one they had just passed through. However, the room certainly felt large.

"We'll soon see how big it is," Bozabrozy said. He held yet another bottle. It sparkled, but brighter than a glimmerer.

"Where did you get that, rascan?" Joromwor's deep voice rumbled. "That's one of Savakala's Dawn Sparks. You aren't authorized to have that."

"Yes, I am," Bozabrozy said. "She gave me one in case we needed it." He threw it into the dark. It smashed against the floor and the sparks inside exploded outward, soaring into the air like a hundred Roman candles on the Fourth of July.

Kyle thought the Dawn Sparks were amazing, but not as much as what they illuminated.

CHAPTER 13

A vast cavern sprawled away from them, sloping gently downward for several dozen feet before leveling out into a wide field of fluorescent red helictite bushes. Large clumps of glinting crystals refracted the radiance from the Dawn Sparks in a kaleidoscopic explosion of light. The sudden illumination seemed to awaken an army of gleams and glimmers in the cavern. Splotches of phosphorescent fungi dotted the walls, and glowing shelf fungi clung to gigantic columns, stalactites, and stalagmites. The ceiling glistened as water seeped across it, down the stalactites, and dripped into innumerable puddles. Delicate white formations, like masses of snowflakes, spread across the rippled floor.

The far wall of the granite chamber, at least a hundred yards away, loomed a hundred feet high. Fractured and scored by countless tremors over hundreds of millennia, the ominous gray stone was shot through with pink striations, black splotches, and blue dots.

Jürgen gazed about in wonder. "I think if I were a bunch of geopsium, this is where I'd be."

"It's so bright in here now," Susie said.

"The crystals amplify our light, and those fungi emit even more," said Bozabrozy, pointing as he walked farther into the cavern.

As they moved toward the far wall, Kyle gawked at the display of geologic formations. There were rocks that looked like popcorn, frosty snowflakes, deflated balloons, drapes, icicles, flowers, melted plastic, waves, egg cartons, columns, stripes, and more. It was amazing that so many different shapes and patterns and colors could exist in one chamber.

"So," Susie said after a few minutes, "how do we find this geopsium stuff, anyway? Start digging?"

Before anyone could respond the cavern shuddered. A low, grating rumble grew from a whisper to a grumble to an intelligible voice!

"NO ONE DIGS HERE!"

The voice boomed like the collapse of a mountainside. They all covered their ears as the deafening words reverberated across the cavern. They peered past the columns and rocks, trying to find the source. The echoing softened and they realized that the voice emanated from the far granite wall. Even as they watched, a large horizontal fissure widened and opened to reveal massive chipped teeth. Above it, a bulge appeared in the stone, like a gigantic nose with deep caves for nostrils and a steep slope for a bridge. To the sides, the granite pulled back to reveal two enormous crystal eyes beneath a prominent brow.

"WHAT DO YOU WANT?" the vast stone face asked.

When the echoes died down, Susie said, "We're on the elemental quest! We want the geopsium!"

"No, no, wait!" said Bozabrozy, trying to stop her. "Let me speak. Care must be taken in dealing with such an elemental."

But it was too late. Her tiny voice carried to the far wall and the giant stone face frowned.

"WHAT DO I WANT?" it bellowed.

No one answered that question. Susie looked at Barathrina, who looked at Bozabrozy, who looked blankly at the stone wall. Joromwor merely glowered.

"What does that mean?" Jürgen asked. "It wants something?"

"I think it wants to trade," Kyle said.

"Of course, you fools," said Joromwor. He stepped forward until he was nearest the wall, and yelled out, "What do you want?"

The stone elemental's eyes narrowed, and its mouth opened to reveal more, sharper teeth. "WHAT DO I WANT?" it repeated angrily, and the entire cavern shook.

"Don't ask it that again!" Jürgen yelled as he held his ears.

When the booming echoes finally died out, the group gathered in the middle of the chamber. The elemental watched them in stony silence.

"For future reference," Bozabrozy said to Susie, "let me do the talking with elementals, right? Little girls and boys shouldn't speak out before their elders."

"That's an elemental?" Susie asked, unperturbed by the rascan's admonition. "What's an elemental?"

"An elemental is the living embodiment of an element," Bozabrozy explained. "In this case stone."

"It's alive?" Kyle looked up at the building-sized face in the wall.

"Not alive like you or me," Joromwor said. "But still alive. It sees, it hears, it senses. It thinks and reasons."

"But not like us," Bozabrozy said. "Elementals don't need to eat or drink or sleep. They even perceive time differently. They have goals and secrets unlike anything any of us could ever imagine."

"I imagine this one likes to be alone," Kyle said.

"Why do you say that?" Bozabrozy asked.

"Because it's here. Way down in the ground. Nobody ever comes down here. Well, except us. But I bet it hasn't had visitors in a long time, if ever. And it can probably move through the ground anytime it likes. So, since it's way down here, it must like it. Being alone, I mean."

"You think maybe it just wants us to leave?" Jürgen asked. It seemed far too simple and cheap a payment in exchange for magical geopsium.

"Unlikely," Bozabrozy said. "Elementals are rarely selfless. They realize their own worth and always demand

72

payment of some kind. Water elementals are the easiest to pay, because they aren't too demanding. Fire elementals just want to burn something. Sky elementals want freedom, but they almost always have that already."

"What do stone elementals want?"

"More stone, usually," Joromwor said.

Kyle waved his arms around, indicating their surroundings. "More stone? This one already has about as much stone as anyone could have. How could we give it something it doesn't already have?"

Bozabrozy frowned. "A very good question."

"Yeah, we should have brought a mountain with us," Susie said.

"Wait," Jürgen said. "Joromwor, you said it wants more stone. More of the kind it already has?"

"Not necessarily. Each elemental's desires are different."

Jürgen spun around, looking at the vast array of formations in the giant chamber. "Well, I think this is a private rock museum for this stone elemental. All sorts of cool things for it to look at and enjoy."

"Does that mean we have to go find it a new fancy rock?" Susie asked.

"We don't have to find it," Jürgen said, taking off his backpack and reaching into one of the pockets. "I have it right here. Fossils!"

"Fossils?" Joromwor didn't understand.

"Fossils are the preserved remains of ancient life that have turned into stone," Jürgen explained.

"You mean geothropes?" the bear-man asked.

"I don't know what those are. These fossils are trilobites, an extinct kind of crustacean. They're made out of stone now, but they used to be alive like us." He held out a handful of trilobites in his hand for the Zurans to see. The ground trembled and the floor under Jürgen's feet rose like a platform.

"Jürgen, look out!" Kyle yelled. He jumped up to grab

the edge of the stone column as it kept rising, but it crumbled under his hands and he fell back to the floor. Jürgen knelt on the rising rock as it rose higher and higher and moved closer to the face in the wall, like a long granite arm. The platform stopped near the elemental's face.

"WHAT DO I WANT?" it said, the voice like sand scraping along stone.

Jürgen held out the trilobites in his palm. The face peered down and one of the crystal eyes squinted at the tiny fossils. The giant eye sparkled like an emerald, and the mouth smiled. The platform moved away from the face and deposited Jürgen back on the ground. A huge hand-like stone erupted from the cavern floor in front of him. He put the trilobites into the cupped hand.

"MORE."

Jürgen nodded and took all the fossils from his backpack and gave them to the elemental. The hand submerged into the floor.

"Wow!" said Kyle. "That was so amazing!"

"I thought it was going to eat you!" Susie said. "I'm glad it didn't."

"Where's the geopsium?" Joromwor demanded, shoving Jürgen away and grabbing his backpack. He rummaged in it.

"No need to be so rough," Bozabrozy said. "I'm sure it will give us the quintessence."

"Don't command me, thief!" Joromwor snorted. "Savakala wants the geopsium, and she shall have it!"

"ACCEPT YOUR REWARD." Another rocky hand appeared.

"Yes! Yes!" Joromwor said eagerly, reaching out to the hand. "Bring it here!"

The hand moved toward Jürgen.

"No!" grunted the urgra. "I shall take it!" He rushed over and pushed Jürgen aside.

The cavern trembled again. "YOU DESERVE NO REWARD!" The hand balled into a fist and hit the urgra.

Despite his prodigious size and armor, the blow sent him catapulting across the chamber. He quickly stood up, and his armor was not even scratched. He glared at the elemental, but kept his distance.

The hand approached Jürgen and dropped a single pebble into Jürgen's outstretched hands. As the hand submerged again, the stone elemental spoke:

WHERE THIRST SCOURS THE LAND
AND UNDERFOOT GIANT BIRDS SOAR
UNEARTHED BY ANCIENT HANDS
FROM THE BEAK IT WILL POUR

Kyle hurried to Jürgen's side to look at the geopsium. It appeared to be a simple gray rock, rough-surfaced and a bit larger than a marble.

"That's it?" Susie asked. "That doesn't seem like much."

"Of all the elemental quintessences," Bozabrozy said, "geopsium comes in the most shapes and sizes. Just because it doesn't look fantastic, doesn't mean it is not valuable or powerful. That little pebble there is enough to–" The rascan's words died on his lips.

The geopsium pebble suddenly crumbled in Jürgen's palm, turning to a small pile of shards, which then burrowed into his flesh!

"Ow!" Jürgen screamed, holding his wrist and waving his hand around . "Ow! Ow! Ow! Make it stop! Make it stop!"

Kyle grabbed his friend's hand. Blood seeped from a dozen small punctures, but even as he watched, the wounds closed. Jürgen's palm turned from fleshy pink to light gray to dark grey. The skin of his hand took on the texture of hard granite, and it spread up his arm.

Jürgen pulled away from Kyle. "What's happening to me?" he cried in horror as his arm turned to solid stone. The transformation moved past his shoulder and spread to his face and body. Seconds later, a perfect stone statue of Jürgen stood before them, an eternal expression of terror etched on its petrified face.

Chapter 14

"No, no!" sobbed Barathrina.

Kyle ran over to Bozabrozy and shook him. "What happened?"

"Jürgen melded with the geopsium," the rascan replied.

"What does that mean?"

Joromwor said, "It means that Jürgen is a geomancer."

Bozabrozy looked down at Kyle. "Remain calm. Jürgen is unhurt. He melded with the geopsium, something not everyone can do. Those who can are called geomancers."

"He's not hurt?" Susie rapped on the silent and motionless statue. "But he turned into solid rock."

"That's probably temporary," Bozabrozy said.

"Probably?" she exclaimed.

"I'm not an expert on geomancers. Sometimes they absorb too much geopsium and are enslaved by it, becoming geothropes. But I believe that most survive the first merging."

"Some don't?" Kyle demanded.

"Alas, no."

Joromwor touched the Jürgen statue. "The geopsium is lost!" He paused, thinking. "Although, if we can get him back to the ship we might be able to pulverize the rock and find the geopsium dust."

"You're not going to pulverize Jürgen!" Kyle said angrily.

"Of course we're not," Bozabrozy said. "How dare you even suggest such a thing, Joromwor? Savakala will be quite pleased with our success at finding the geopsium."

"Success?" Joromwor scoffed. "It turned the boy to stone. That means we don't have it. How is that a success?"

"We will bring Jürgen to Savakala and she will know what to do," Bozabrozy said. "And we did get the riddle for the next quintessence from the stone elemental."

Joromwor growled, and tapped the statue. "That won't do us any good if we can't get the geopsium out of this."

"Stop fretting. One step of the quest is complete. It just completed a bit differently than we expected."

"Expected? What did we expect? Savakala doesn't tell us enough to know what is going on!"

"One step of the quest?" Kyle said. "What do you mean by that? I thought this was the whole quest? I thought we were done with the quest now."

"You are, Kyle," Bozabrozy said, smiling. "No need for you to continue with us. You've done your part. We'll take care of the rest."

"But what about Jürgen?"

"I'm sure Savakala will devise a plan to return him to normal before we've finished locating the other three quintessences."

"Other three? How long will that take?" Susie asked.

"I have no idea," Bozabrozy said with a shrug. "But the first step toward that goal is returning to the surface. With this statue of Jürgen, of course."

Kyle was taken aback. He stared at the rascan, then at the stony Jürgen. The descent to the cavern had been nearly impossible. There was absolutely no way they were going to get back up with the statue. Kyle doubted whether any of them could lift it, except maybe Joromwor.

"Getting back is going to be tough enough without the statue," Barathrina squealed.

"BEGONE!" the stone elemental bellowed like an avalanche.

"Easier said than done!" Barathrina yelled back.

The cavern shook. Stalagmites suddenly burst up around them, enclosing them in a stony fence. The floor beneath them rose quickly, heaving them up toward the ceiling. As they neared, their speed only increased.

"I don't think this is going to end well," Barathrina whimpered and dropped to the floor just as they slammed into the ceiling.

But the ceiling opened up and let them in unharmed. The stalagmite fence merged into the rock and Kyle gazed in wonder as stone and earth rumbled and groaned around them. It was like they were in a bubble. The platform on which they stood remained stable, but the ceiling, only a dozen or so feet above, cracked open continually as they rose up through solid Earth. He felt like he was in an elevator made of stone.

"What's going on?" Susie asked, covering her head as dust and pebbles fell around them.

"The stone elemental is taking us back to the surface!" Kyle smiled.

"Yay!"

While the descent into the depths of the Earth had been long and laborious, the ascent took only minutes. Before long, the rumbling intensified, the ceiling above suddenly parted, and they erupted onto the surface. The six of them (including the petrified Jürgen) found themselves standing on a large bare mountaintop. Beneath their feet was no evidence of their eruption. The Sun was low in the western sky, and bathed them in a rich golden glow.

"We're back at Mt. Rushmore!" Susie said.

Kyle spun around, looking for the familiar stone faces of Washington, Jefferson, Lincoln, and Roosevelt. "Where? I don't see it."

"Look between your feet, silly," said Susie.

"We're on top of it?" he asked.

"Yes." Susie pointed. "The presidents are below us, over there."

Kyle looked at Jürgen and wondered how they would get him down. Bozabrozy squeezed his shoulder. "Don't worry, Kyle. I'll go to the Windrunner and come back to get Jürgen. We'll find a way to depetrify him."

"How long will that take?"

"A long time, I'm sure," Joromwor said, glaring at Bozabrozy.

"Don't listen to him," Bozabrozy disagreed, "and don't fret. The clue that the stone elemental gave us will eventually lead us to the quintessence of elemental water. Aquosia has great healing and restorative powers. If Savakala isn't able to return Jürgen to normal, I'm sure the aquosia will."

"Is that what the elemental was talking about? Aquosia?"

"Yes, I believe so. The riddle mentioned thirst and pour. I believe those to be hints that the next part of the quest will be for pure elemental water."

"Where is it hidden?" Susie asked.

"I have no idea. Savakala will be able to divine more from the riddle than we, I'm sure."

"She wasn't able to figure out the first riddle," Susie reminded the rascan. "I think you're going to need our help again."

Bozabrozy shook his head. "No, I couldn't impose on Kyle any longer. He was loathe to start the quest in the first place, and he agreed only to aid us for the day. Kyle has done enough for Zura and I'll ask no more of him."

"That's not your decision, rascan," Joromwor rumbled quietly.

"But, Kyle," Susie said, "how are we going to get Jürgen back? Who knows how long they'll take? They don't know about Earth. Even in a skyship it could take them months. You don't want to let Jürgen be a statue for that long, do you?"

Kyle knew that Susie was right. The Zurans wouldn't be

able to decipher the second riddle any easier than the first. They needed someone familiar with Earth to help them. He sighed. He was tired and sore and hungry. And most of all, he wanted to make sure his dad was okay.

"Listen, Susie, they don't have just one more thing to find. They have three. Water and two others, fire and air, I guess."

"Water, fire, and sky, actually," Bozabrozy corrected him.

"Okay, water, fire, and sky. Let's say we help them find the water. Then we'll have to help them find the fire, and then the sky. Who knows how long that will take? Do you want to spend weeks or months flying around the world?"

"I guess you're right," Susie frowned. "But it sure would be fun to go for a ride in their skyship."

"We'll bring Jürgen back here when we've refleshed him," Bozabrozy promised.

"But the day's not over," Susie said. "We can still help them with the second riddle. We can go down to the visitor's center and use one of the computers to look up the answer to the riddle on the Internet!"

"Hey, that's a great idea."

"What is the Internet?" Barathrina asked.

Kyle paused for a moment, trying to think of a way to describe it to a Zuran. "It's like a giant library of all the knowledge in the whole world."

Bozabrozy's whiskers twitched. "And it is nearby?"

"It's everywhere, actually," Susie said. "But we can see it from the visitor's center."

"Miraculous! A library of all knowledge that is everywhere! And it has the answer to the riddle?"

"Well," Kyle hesitated, "not exactly. We can ask it questions to figure out the riddle. But we have to ask it the right questions."

"Excellent," Bozabrozy said. He rubbed his jaw, and then pointed at Kyle, Susie, and Barathrina. "You three can go talk to the Internet while we go back to the Windrunner. I'm sure Captain Machadaro has it repaired by now. We'll come back to pick up Jürgen and hopefully you will have a new destination by then."

"I like that plan," Barathrina said. "Except for the part where I go with them. I'm done trekking all over and under stone. I'll stand guard here with Joromwor and wait for you to get back with the skyship."

"Fine, fine," Bozabrozy acquiesced with a sigh. He obviously didn't want to argue any more.

"How long will it take you to get back here?" Susie asked.

"It won't take more than hour to reach the Windrunner. It will take it only five minutes to get back here."

"Okay, let's go," Susie said. "The fastest way is to climb down to the Hall of Records and take the trail from there."

Joromwor used the magical rope to lower the two children down to a trail in front of the unfinished Hall of Records. Kyle followed Susie down a long metal stairway to the Presidential Trail. Many tourists were still enjoying the national memorial. They calmly chatted and rested and snacked, completely unaware of the fantastic things going on around, and below, them.

Kyle couldn't believe all the excitement of the last twenty-four hours. Meeting aliens from another world, fleeing from a ravaging bear monster, delving deep underground and meeting a massive stone elemental! He smiled. Despite his initial misgivings about helping Bozabrozy, he'd never had so much fun on vacation before.

As they walked down the trail, Susie tried to call her brother again but he still didn't answer. She called her parents and asked them to come pick her up. She told them she had a great story about how much she'd done today. They hadn't heard from her brother, either. Johnny Five Eagles wasn't the most reliable person in the world, and they suspected he'd gone off with friends.

Susie and Kyle sped through the Grand View Terrace, Avenue of Flags, and Borglum Court. The milling tourists paid little attention to them. At the Information Center they found Ranger Deborah.

"Hi, Susie," Deborah said. "How was your hike?"

"Best ever!" Susie chirped. "Have you seen my brother?"

"No, I haven't." The ranger frowned. "I haven't seen him all day. He never caught up with you? He probably went to Rapid City to see a girl."

"My parents are coming to pick me up. Can I use your computer to surf the web?"

"Sorry, Susie. Our connection is on the fritz. But that new wireless network they put in is probably working. Do you have a laptop?"

"No," she said with a frown.

"Well, I guess you and your new friends can hang around the gift shop until your parents show up." Deborah smiled at Kyle. "Say, where's your other friend? Jürgen, was it?"

"He and his mom are resting over in the theater," Susie said quickly. "Thanks a lot!" And she pulled Kyle back the way they had come.

"What's the rush?" Kyle asked, stumbling along behind her.

"I saw a girl with a laptop! Maybe she'll let us surf on it."

Chapter 15

After stopping at Carver's Cafe to buy sandwiches and Sioux City Sarsaparilla, Kyle and Susie hunted for the girl with the laptop.

"There she is," said Susie, pointing from the Grand View Terrace down into the amphitheater, where a family sat about halfway down the terraced benches. Susie led the way and stopped next to a young girl typing into a bronze-colored computer pad.

"Hi! I'm Susie Five Eagles and this is Kyle Morgan. He's from Seattle. We saw you working on that laptop. I've never seen one like that before."

The girl looked up and smiled. "My name is Veeksha Das. These are my parents. We're from India." Her parents rose and shook hands with them, commenting on how nice the park was, before letting their daughter move off a few seats with her new friends. Veeksha continued. "The reason you haven't seen a laptop like this before is because it's not a laptop. It's a prototype. It's actually a kind of tablet computer, with a touch-sensitive screen. It hasn't been released to the general public."

Susie sat next to Veeksha. "Then how did you get one?"

"A few months ago I won the Annual International Pre-Teen Trivia Challenge. That was a very auspicious day," Veeksha said proudly. "One of the prizes was the chance to test a new tablet, and this is it." She handed the small computer to Susie, who ran her fingers over the bronzed housing.

"It's so pretty," Susie said. "What is this?" she asked, pointing to markings etched next to the keyboard.

"That says 'KnowPad' in Hindi," Veeksha said. "They let me name it."

"Wow, that's really cool. I've never named a new product. And it's so light!"

"Yes, it is the state of the art," Veeksha beamed. "It's waterproof, shockproof, heatproof, fireproof, coldproof, and dustproof. It's solar-powered and never needs to be plugged in. You can even use it underwater."

"Is it wireless?"

"Of course. I'm connected right now on the park's network."

"Ooh," Susie said. "Then maybe you can help us. We're trying to figure out a riddle."

"What kind of riddle?"

"The answer is a place."

"Please, tell it to me," Veeksha begged, obviously intrigued.

Where thirst scours the lands
And underfoot giant birds soar
Created and unearthed by ancient hands
From the beak it will pour

Veeksha said, "Does it mean somewhere in America? Or anywhere on Earth?"

"We don't know," Kyle said.

"The first line refers to a desert, of course," Veeksha said. "But thirst scours all deserts, so we have to figure out which one the riddle is talking about."

"Maybe one in Africa?" Kyle guessed.

"The last line doesn't sound like it refers to a place," said Veeksha, jumping ahead. "'From the beak it will pour.' What is it? A place like a desert isn't going to pour."

"Maybe the sand will pour?" Kyle suggested.

Veeksha frowned. "Maybe. Well, we'll get to the last line last because it is the last line."

"Er...okay," Susie agreed.

"Now, all we need to do is find a desert where giant birds soar underfoot. Hmmm..."

"Eagles are pretty big," Susie said.

"But they don't soar on the ground. What kind of bird soars on the ground?"

Susie shook her head. Kyle, however, suddenly remembered Jürgen and his trilobites.

"Pterosaurs! Dinosaur birds soar underfoot! As fossils, I mean. We're looking for a desert with fossils. I'm sure of it!"

Veeksha didn't agree. "Fossils are unearthed, but not really by ancient hands. They aren't created by ancient hands, either."

"Oh, right."

"I think the riddle is talking about an ancient monument or artwork in the ground created by ancient peoples. One with images of giant birds. It's pretty easy, really. We won't need to check the Internet for this."

"You know the answer?" Susie asked, shocked.

"Yes, I know the answer."

"Now you know how I felt when you got the first riddle so quick," Kyle said to Susie.

"The riddle is talking about the Nasca lines in Peru."

"What are those?" Kyle asked.

"They are giant drawings of geometric shapes and lines and animals all over the desert. I can show you." Veeksha tapped into her KnowPad and soon had several pictures of strange shapes drawn into the desert.

"You're really smart," Susie said. "That wasn't an easy riddle. I don't know anyone else who would have been able to figure that out."

"I did win a trivia competition."

"Okay, thanks, Veeksha," Kyle said. "Susie, we better get back."

Veeksha grabbed Kyle's arm. "Wait! You can't just get me to answer your riddle and then leave. You mentioned there was a previous riddle. What was it? Don't give me the answer."

Susie recited it for her. Within minutes, Veeksha guessed: "The old fire watchtower on Harney Peak. Although I don't know what 'the path descends between' means. Seems like the last line of each riddle doesn't really fit."

"That is amazing, Veeksha!" Kyle said. "How can you know so much about everything?"

"Well, the Nasca lines are quite famous. And, my father is an archeologist."

"But how did you know about Harney Peak?"

"Oh, we've been planning this vacation to America for a while. We've been visiting all the parks and memorials in the Black Hills. I've read up on the monuments at Mt. Rushmore and Crazy Horse, Jewel Cave, Wind Cave, the Needles, Harney Peak, and all sorts of things."

"You must read a lot."

"Yes, I do. I have hundreds of ebooks on my KnowPad. Plus, it has a dictionary, thesaurus, and several encyclopedias. Are there any more riddles? Those were fun."

"There will be two more, but we don't have them yet," Susie said.

"When will you get them? I'd love to help."

"I think the two we gave you are the only two we'll get," Kyle informed her. "The people that find them are leaving."

"Oh, that's too bad. Maybe you can e-mail them to me later."

"Sure!" Susie agreed. "That sounds like a–"

"Excuse me, Susie," said Ranger Deborah, who had walked up beside them. "Can you come with me? These gentlemen have news about your brother."

Three men in suits and dark glasses smiled at them.

"Who are you?" Susie asked. "And what do you know about Johnny?"

"My name is Reid Bannecker, Susie," said one of the men. He was tall and thin. "We've contacted your parents and they'll be coming along shortly." He turned to Kyle. "Kyle Morgan? Your dad is worried sick about you. You'll have to come along, too." He gently grasped the children's arms and urged them from their seats.

Susie, however, wasn't ready to go. "Wait, who are you? I don't know you. Are you the police or something? Why can't you tell me what's happened to my brother right now?" Her voice rose in volume and pitch.

Veeksha's father moved closer. "Excuse me, gentlemen. My name is Himesh Das. This is my wife and daughter. We have only just met Susie and Kyle, but I feel I must intervene on their behalf. Your behavior is frightening them. Perhaps you can begin by showing us some identification?"

"Of course, sir," Bannecker pulled a wallet from his pocket and unfolded it to reveal his badge.

Himesh Das examined it. "FBI? Thank you, Agent Bannecker. Now, can you explain what is going on here?"

"I don't really have time for that, Mr. Das."

"Hey!" someone yelled. "Look at that!"

"Oh, good heavens! What is it?" blurted someone else.

All around them, tourists shouted and pointed into the sky. Kyle looked up to see the Windrunner descending from above Mt. Rushmore.

CHAPTER 16

Kyle had been expecting a sleek metal spaceship, such as a rocket or maybe even a saucer-ship like something out of Star Trek. What he saw looked most like a wooden sailing ship, yet not like any sailing ship he'd ever seen before.

Yes, it had a wooden hull and white sails. But the sails billowed out from all parts of the ship, not just the top. Four of the largest sails radiated out from the bow of the ship – two above the hull and two below. They looked like parts of an umbrella thrust straight out of the bow of the ship. A huge vertical sail trailed off the stern, like a shark's tail. Two more sails flew from the sides of the ship, one on each side, like wings. Blue flags emblazoned with white wings fluttered from the masts. Several metal bulges protruded from the hull. A platform extended from the prow, in front of the umbrella sails. Kyle saw Bozabrozy standing there, waving down at him.

"Ahoy! Kyle!" the rascan yelled.

"What in blue blazes is that?" said one of Bannecker's associates. Mr. Das collapsed down to his seat, gaping at the ship. Mrs. Das stared, her hands on her cheeks. Veeksha's face was full of wonder.

"It's beautiful!" Susie giggled, jumped up and down, and waved back at Bozabrozy. "I hope we get to go for a ride!"

Commanding voices drifted down from the skyship as it maneuvered above the amphitheater. Kyle saw more Zurans crawling on the rigging, furling some of the sails. With their long furry tails and big ears, they looked like cat-men.

Many of the tourists cried out in panic.

"It's going to crash!"

"Look out!"

"Run!"

"They're monsters!"

The rush out of the amphitheater turned into a stampede.

"Move in! Move in!" Bannecker yelled into a small device in his hand. His two companions pulled out pistols.

Kyle tried to calm them. "Hey, don't worry, they're friends."

Several ropes descended from the Windrunner. Bozabrozy jumped over the side and climbed down on one of them.

"Get these children out of here!" Bannecker ordered. The two other men moved forward and grabbed Kyle, Susie, and Veeksha.

Kyle struggled against the iron grip of the man holding him. "No! What are you doing? Let me go!"

The skyship hovered a hundred feet above them, although the tips of the bottom masts were only twenty or thirty feet above the seats. Bozabrozy dropped to the ground between Bannecker's henchmen and the stairs to the Grand View Terrace.

"Let those children go!" he demanded.

"It's a Zuran!" Bannecker yelled. "Don't let it have the children!"

"What? No!" Kyle screamed as the man released him and aimed his gun at Bozabrozy. Kyle tried to disrupt his aim but failed. Three shots rang out and the rascan fell backward, clutching his chest.

Kyle ran to the rascan and knelt beside him. "Bozabrozy!" he stuttered.

"I don't feel very well," Bozabrozy moaned.

Bannecker pointed back up at the Windrunner. A couple

of the crew climbed on the low rigging. "Take out those two! We can't let the ship escape!" The two men opened fire on the ship.

"No! Don't shoot them!" Susie yelled, tears flowing down her cheeks. "They're not monsters!"

Most of the tourists had vanished, although a few remained at the edges of the amphitheater taking pictures or video. As the others fled, several more men dressed like Bannecker hurried into view. Some held machineguns, others had pistols.

"It's a Zuran ship!" Bannecker yelled. "Shoot anyone you see up there!"

Staccato reports of machinegun fire erupted in the amphitheater. The bullets hit the wooden hull but caused little damage. The crew, having seen the power of the firearms, hid out of view.

Except for one.

A spectacular Zuran stood at the railing of the ship. He wore loose trousers and a patch over one eye. Rusty orange fur, stunningly striped in black, coated his corded muscles. A long cat-like tail, ringed in black and orange and white, twitched behind him. Dramatic black swaths of fur splashed across his rusty face, framed in white along the jaw and around the eyes. His wide muzzle sported long, white whiskers. Terrifying fangs filled his huge mouth. He grabbed a rope in one clawed hand and leapt off the ship with a mighty roar.

At the same time, a huge lightning bolt shot down from the Windrunner, sending three gunmen and chunks of shattered concrete flying through the air.

Several dog-men in armor appeared at the railing of the ship, shooting smaller bolts of lightning from crossbow-like weapons. One hit an FBI agent, and he collapsed in convulsions.

The striped Zuran landed amidst a group of agents. He struck out repeatedly with enormous clawed hands, slashing and tearing.

"Retrieve Bozabrozy and the children!" called a screeching voice from above.

The rampaging Zuran sped toward the rascan, leaping from victim to victim as bullets zinged all around him. Lightning continued to rain down from above, forcing the gunmen to scatter and take cover.

The enormous warrior stopped beside Kyle and Bozabrozy. "I am Machadaro, captain of the Windrunner. You must come with me!" He took one of the dangling ropes and tied it quickly around Kyle's ankle.

"I can't believe you attacked those guys! They had guns and you only have claws!" Kyle said.

"Fortune favors the bold," the captain said simply, and lifted the boy. He waved to someone above him. The rope instantly went taut and the ground fell away very quickly. Kyle felt like he was plummeting, but upward into the sky. His baseball cap fell back into the amphitheater.

Machadaro tied another rope beneath Bozabrozy's arms. "Stay alive, rascan," he growled. "You'll soon be back on board."

Bozabrozy managed a weak smile as he, too, shot up into the sky.

The skyship captain turned to find Bannecker standing in front of Susie and Veeksha. "I won't let you Zurans use these children in your sinister plans!" He raised his pistol and fired.

But Machadaro was already pouncing. With a single swipe of his claws he tore through Bannecker's shoulder and chest. The man flew through the air and hit the wall of the terrace, collapsing in a bloody heap.

Susie and Veeksha stared in awe as Machadaro grabbed them both in one arm and caught a line from the ship. "Haul away!" The skyship captained roared, his voice filling the amphitheater. "Gustboxes wide open! Wingsails to maximum lift! Left full ruddersail!"

The Windrunner's crew scurried to follow their captain's orders and the ship gained altitude. The top sails filled with a strong tailwind. The skyship's tail sail pivoted sharply, and the wingsails tilted.

The agents stepped out from their cover, looking at the carnage wrought by Machadaro and the skyship's weapons. A dozen men lay scattered about the amphitheater, unmoving. Some limped or held broken arms, or squirmed on the ground with seizures. Others wiped at cuts on their faces from blasted stone and concrete. The amphitheater was scarred with large, smoking gouges. Rubble was strewn everywhere.

The Windrunner climbed more swiftly now, spiraling upward in front of Mt. Rushmore. The dying rays of the evening Sun gleamed red on the sails and hull.

Veeksha's parents crawled hesitantly from where they were hiding behind a bench. Mrs. Das cried as she hugged her husband, both of them watching the skyship. It sped away, carrying their only daughter with it.

CHAPTER 17

Machadaro climbed over the railing and put Veeksha and Susie down as gently as if they were newborn kittens. He then rushed off, roaring orders.

Veeksha stood beside Susie on the deck of the alien skyship. They stared in awe at the crew hurrying about their jobs. Most looked like humanoid cats – some multi-colored like tabbies, others all black or grey or brown. There were others that resembled dog-men, wearing armor and carrying crossbows. She saw one that looked like a raccoon, and another like a bear. And the captain! An enormous Bengal tiger-man dressed like a swashbuckler.

"I must be dreaming," Veeksha whispered.

"That's what I thought when I first saw them," Susie said, leaning over the ship's rail to look at the ground far below. "I can't believe we're really in a flying sailboat! Look, Mt. Rushmore is already far away."

Veeksha looked over the rail and saw the presidents getting smaller and smaller. She could barely make out the amphitheater. "But that's not fair! I don't belong here. Take me back! I want to go back to my parents!" She turned and looked around her for help, but none of the cat sailors or dog soldiers noticed her. They were tending the many needs of the Windrunner at full sail or keeping a lookout for possible pursuit.

"Susie! Veeksha! Over here!" Kyle was waving at them from near the stern. They rushed over to him.

"We're flying in a sailboat!" Susie said gleefully as she

ran up, but her smile quickly faded when she saw Bozabrozy lying in a pool of blood. He wasn't moving.

"I think he's dead," Kyle blurted out.

"Oh, no! What are we going to do?"

"You shall do nothing," said a hard voice behind them. The children turned to see a Zuran approaching. It wore a cloak of colorful feathers, and had dark feathers on its long curved neck. The short black feathers on its head were tinged with white. Black eyes beneath heavy brows stared at them.

Its sharp curved black beak opened and it spoke again. "I will take care of Bozabrozy."

From the folds of its robe it pulled out a slender vial. Kyle noticed that its arms were very long and very skinny, with much longer feathers on them. It reached out to the rascan with long fingers that ended in sharp talons.

"What are you doing?" Kyle asked as he moved away so the Zuran could kneel beside Bozabrozy.

"This one has much still to do on this quest," the Zuran said. "And so he warrants the healing touch of aquosia." It yanked apart Bozabrozy's punctured tunic to reveal fur matted with blood. "These wounds are dire. He'll need the lot of it."

The Zuran poured from the vial and the aquosia sloshed out, sparkling in the dying sunlight like no other water Kyle had ever seen. Clear and shining like the coldest mountain stream, the aquosia spilled onto Bozabrozy's chest. The air around them shimmered like sunlight piercing the waters of a tropical lagoon.

The Zuran poured the rest of the aquosia into Bozabrozy's mouth and then stood back. "This shan't take but a moment."

The whiskers on the rascan's face twitched. His ringed tail quivered. Kyle watched in amazement as the wounds on his chest closed. Bozabrozy sighed and lifted himself up onto his elbows.

"What were those weapons they were using?" he asked without preamble. "Terrible weapons they are! We could use a score of them on our quest."

"They're called guns," Kyle said.

"We don't have such things in Zura."

The bird-like Zuran helped Bozabrozy to his feet. "This world holds many wonders and perils, Bozabrozy. But we dare not be distracted lest we fail in our quest."

"Right, right," said the rascan, feeling his chest. "But our quest would be much easier with such weapons."

"That opportunity is lost to us," the Zuran said. Turning to the children, it said, "I assume this is Kyle Morgan. But you have two girls here instead of one as you reported. Which is Susie Five Eagles?"

Susie raised her hand. "I am! Nice to meet you! Bozabrozy told us all about the aeromagus leading this quest. I bet you're Savakala! He says you're an uburu."

"Quite right." The feathered bird-woman rose up to her full height, looking down at them. Even so, her long feathered cloak still brushed the timbers on the ship's deck. "I am an uburu, one of many types of feathered Zurans who rule the skies of our world. I am Savakala, Minister of the Sky, advisor to Emperor Exeverius, Soothsayer of the Imperial Augurium, artificer, aeromagus, magistrate, commander of this vessel, and leader of this quest."

"Oh, I thought Captain Machadaro commanded the Windrunner," Susie said.

Savakala's feathers bristled. "He is merely the captain! I am the emperor's official representative here, and none dare dispute it lest they suffer my wrath!"

Kyle pulled Susie away from the angry uburu. "Sorry! We don't know how things work on Zura."

"A wise young human," said Savakala with a nod. "Now, who is this one?" She reached out and ran a black talon over Veeksha's cheek. "No, do not speak," she said when the girl opened her mouth. "I know who you are. You are the fourth child. Your name is Veeksha Das, and I am very pleased that you are here." Her eyes sparkled darkly.

"But I'm not pleased," Veeksha objected. "I don't belong here. I was kidnapped by the tiger-man. I'm not with Susie and Kyle. I was just sitting at the park minding my own business when your sailboat showed up."

Savakala clucked amusedly. "This is no mere sailboat, Veeksha. The Windrunner is the fastest skyship in the Imperial Armada. And it is here at the behest of Emperor Exeverius himself for the greater good of all Zurans."

Veeksha frowned. "I…um…don't know what you mean, and I don't think that I really care. Could you please take me back to my parents now?"

"That is something I cannot do. You will play an important role in the things to follow. I have seen it."

Chapter 18

"Savakala can see the future," Kyle said, remembering what Bozabrozy had told him in the forest the night before. "She has visions of things to come."

The uburu laughed, and led the children along the deck. "Is that what Bozabrozy told you? Well, in a sense, it is true. True enough for his simple mind." Bozabrozy started to object, but Savakala waved away his protest and continued. "However, such a simplification is good, as it is most easily understood and accepted by young humans such as you." She ushered them into a cabin with a table, some stools, a bed, and a wide variety of strange objects on many shelves. Kyle saw feathered sticks, engraved rods, weapons, an empty hourglass, necklaces, clothing, and bottles of various sizes. He recognized Barathrina's Cloak of Humanity and Joromwor's Indomitable Armor and Sundering Bardiche. The room reminded Kyle of an antique shop.

"I don't care. I want to go back." Veeksha crossed her arms and stared angrily at the Zuran.

"A fire burns within you, Veeksha," Savakala noted. "It is a noble trait that will serve you well. Have you considered what you would lose if we return you to your mundane life down below? Imagine the wonders and knowledge you will gain onboard the Windrunner as we sail hither and yon, unearthing secrets and treasures never before seen by anyone from your world. By the end of our quest, you will help reshape your world into something unlike anything you could possibly imagine."

Veeksha, intrigued by the Zuran's poetic speech, did not respond immediately. Finally, she said, "What kind of knowledge?"

"Knowledge unknown by your greatest scholars," Savakala nodded. "Knowledge of the elements. Knowledge of quintessence and how to use it. You saw what the aquosia did for poor, dying Bozabrozy here." Savakala slapped at the rascan, who was inspecting the empty hourglass.

Savakala turned back to Veeksha. "What if you could find more aquosia on your world? It could be used to heal others. But only by those who have the knowledge. Come with us, for a time, and you could gain that knowledge."

"Actually, that doesn't sound too bad..." Veeksha mused. "How long will this quest thing take?"

"That we cannot know, Veeksha. First we have to solve the second riddle."

"Oh, I already did that."

"You did? What a smart little girl you are!" Savakala leaned in close. "What is the answer?"

"We have to go to Peru."

"Where is this Peru?"

"It's in South America," Kyle said. "A long ways south of here."

Savakala looked confused. "What is south?"

"It's a direction," Veeksha frowned. "Don't you know about compasses?"

"What is compasses?"

"A compass shows you which direction to go," Kyle said.

Bozabrozy glanced over his shoulder as he turned over the empty hourglass. "They mean a geodex," he surmised.

Savakala nodded in comprehension. "Ah," she said. "Now leave that alone!" The rascan reluctantly complied.

Savakala turned to Veeksha. "So, you have a fragment of Peru for us to use in our geodex?"

"You want a piece of Peru?" asked Kyle.

"How else will we set our course?"

"You could just fly south," Susie repeated.

"What is south?" Savakala said, annoyed. "Is it an island?"

"No. It's a direction."

"The direction to Peru?"

Susie smiled. "Yes."

"Well, basically," Veeksha corrected.

"How do we proceed in this direction without a fragment of Peru?"

"We use a compass, which shows which direction is south."

"How does it do that?"

"Some kind of magnet," Kyle said.

"Actually," Veeksha said like a teacher to ignorant students, "a compass is a magnetized pointer that aligns itself with the Earth's magnetic field."

Savakala and Bozabrozy just stared at her.

Veeksha sighed. "It's a little arrow that always points in one direction no matter where you are."

Bozabrozy clapped his hands and pointed at her. "See? I told you. A geodex."

"Then we shall give your compass to Machadaro," Savakala strode to the door and summoned the skyship captain. She glared at Bozabrozy, who was still fingering the hourglass.

"I told you to leave that alone!" she said, taking the glass from the shelf and putting it on the table. It was a large hourglass, at least a foot tall, with ornate legs of precious metals and studded with gems. But it was empty.

"Why doesn't that hourglass have any sand?" Susie asked.

"The magic in the Everglass is spent," Bozabrozy sighed.

Susie's eyes widened. "It's magical? What does it do?"

"It helped us get here," Bozabrozy said. "It can–"

Savakala interrupted. "Those who gaze through the

Everglass can see the past, the present, and the future."

Bozabrozy nodded. "Yes, right, that's what it does. Among other things."

Savakala scowled at the rascan. "Silence!"

"In any case," Bozabrozy added, "the sands are all spent and the Everglass is no longer of any use."

"You summoned me, Minister?" The captain's deep, rumbling voice startled the children. He stood in the doorway, glaring into the room with his one eye.

"Give Captain Machadaro your compass," Savakala told Veeksha.

Veeksha frowned "My compass is in my computer. I'll have to start it up."

Susie said, "You don't have to. I have a normal one." She pulled her hiking compass from her pocket and handed it to the captain.

"What do I do with this?" Machadaro frowned.

"That is the human's geodex," Savakala informed him. "It will point you to Peru, our next destination."

Machadaro nodded and turned to the door.

"Wait!" Veeksha grabbed his hand. "You have to go in the opposite direction that it points."

"Why? Is it broken?" Machadaro squinted at the compass and then shook it.

"No. But compasses always point north. That's the opposite of south. We want to go south."

"Toward Peru," Susie said.

Machadaro shook his head. "Why would you create a geodex that points in the wrong direction?"

"Do you mean your geodex always points to where you are going?" Kyle asked.

"It would be of little use otherwise. But I shall go where this one does not point, as you say." He winked at Veeksha as he left the cabin.

"Excellent," said Savakala. She rubbed her thin hands together, and returned to the table. "We sail for Peru."

"I'm still not sure I want to go," Veeksha said.

"After the storm starts, it is too late for little raindrops like you to vote," Savakala said. "We're on our way to grand adventure and arcane knowledge."

Veeksha did not look pleased, but Susie quickly piped up, holding out her cell phone. "Don't worry, Veeksha. We can call your parents on my cell phone and tell them what's going on and that you're safe. After I call my parents." The phone chirped as she opened it and punched the speed dial.

Savakala scowled. "What is this implement?"

"Cell phones are used to talk to people far away," Susie explained. "Mine also has texting and voice mail and a bunch of other stuff."

The Zuran waved her taloned hands in confusion. "I do not understand. Speak plainly!"

"My parents can use the phone to keep track of where I am. You know, in case I get lost or kidnapped or something." She grinned mischievously. "Kind of like I am now, I guess."

"Others can find you using that?"

"Hello?" said a voice over the phone. Susie smiled. "Oh, they picked up! Hi, Dad! Guess where I am! I'm in a flying ship with a bunch of–"

Savakala snatched the cell phone out of Susie's hand and threw it out a porthole.

"Hey! Why did you do that?" Susie ran to the window and looked out. She couldn't see the phone, only the darkening ridges of the Black Hills far below.

CHAPTER 19

"That wasn't very nice," Kyle said. "How are we going to tell our parents that we're safe and not to worry?"

"You do not understand," Savakala said. "Your world is not as safe as you seem to believe. Who do you think those men were down there? The men who attacked us and injured our crew with their weapons?"

"I think they were the FBI," Kyle said.

"I've not heard of them," Savakala said. "But their leader knew that we were Zurans. How did he know that?"

Kyle shrugged, but Susie said, "Maybe they're a paranormal investigation team."

"No, they are minions of Rakanian. He has enlisted the aid of an insidious group of humans."

"How do you know that?" Kyle asked.

"I have long known of Rakanian's sinister ambitions. His sweet tongue has tempted many an ear, and turned countless loyal subjects to rebellion. No doubt he has convinced your FBI to aid him in his intrigues," Savakala said grimly. "Rakanian is a deceiver, infiltrator, and corrupter. With these nefarious skills, he seeks to unite the magi against the beneficent rule of the emperor."

"What's a magi?" asked Susie.

"Magi are practitioners of elemental magic. A magus can use the refined quintessence in an artifact to bend the elements to her will."

"What does all that mean?" Kyle asked.

"Not all Zurans have the same ability with the

elements," Savakala explained. "Most can only use elemental artifacts as the artificer designed them. Others are magi. They can use refined quintessence, stored in receptacles called elequaries, to do magic limited only by their imagination and the type of quintessence. Mancers can do the same with raw quintessence that they absorb into themselves."

"That's what happened to Jürgen," Kyle said.

"Yes. He absorbed the geopsium directly into himself, but was unable to control it. Usually, quintessence must be collected and refined and crafted by skillful artifice into elemental implements."

"You mean like Joromwor's Sundering Bardiche?" Susie guessed.

Savakala nodded. "Exactly. Each such implement has a given purpose, ordained at its creation. The healing elixir I gave Bozabrozy was created from aquosia to heal injuries. The Sundering Bardiche was created from geopsium to cut through any material. Elemental artificers can mold quintessence into artifacts to perform specific wonders associated with the element."

Savakala took a large staff from where it leaned against the wall. It was made of some white wood. Large feathers dangled from the top. She tapped it on the floor and the feathers swirled around it. "And then there are elequaries, such as my Staff of the Sky. Elequaries hold refined quintessence. In this case, my staff is a repository of aethrial, the quintessence of the sky. As an aeromagus, I can manipulate the power within to invoke miracles of the sky."

"Like throwing lightning bolts," Susie said.

"Yes, just like that."

"Is that what Rakanian wants here on Earth?" Susie asked. "To use the quintessence for his magic?"

"He wants the primal quintessences," Savakala replied. "They are the first examples of a quintessence to appear. They appeared eons ago throughout Zura and multiplied.

They are now quite common. Zura is a world where magic reigns because of the prevalence of quintessence. That is what we use to create our skyships and weapons and all sorts of other wondrous things. But here on your world, the quintessence has not yet been freed from the four primal deposits. It is still limited to one instance of each."

"What does Rakanian want them for?"

"Power. With them, Rakanian can achieve dominion over your world. Then he could threaten Zura."

"If he has the FBI working for him, he's been here a long time," Kyle guessed.

Bozabrozy, who was trying on the scaly gloves, nodded in agreement. "If he has infiltrated your world, there is little time. We must hurry. Who knows how many enemies we have here?"

"Far more than we expected. But–" Savakala looked down at the three children–"at least we have three new and loyal allies."

"Four!" Susie said. "Don't forget Jürgen. You didn't forget Jürgen on the mountaintop, did you?"

"No," Bozabrozy said. "He is in the hold."

"Ah, yes, the unfortunate geomancer," Savakala said. "It was quite an adventure, I have heard, delving into those dark tunnels."

"It was amazing!" said Susie. "But Bozabrozy has some cool magic bottles that lit up the caverns."

"Yes, he does, doesn't he?" Savakala looked askance at the rascan. "And you have some still, do you not? You may give them back to me now."

"I might need them again," Bozabrozy said sadly.

"In which case I will give them to you." The uburu tapped the table like a parent demanding a dangerous knife from a disobedient child.

Bozabrozy approached and removed a few of his belts and pouches and placed them on the table. When Savakala continued to stare at him, he placed the remainder on the table.

"And the gloves," Savakala sighed. Bozabrozy removed the scaly gloves and put them back on the shelf.

"Why does everyone have to give you their magic stuff?" Kyle asked.

"I am the magistrate," Savakala explained. "I ensure that the emperor's elemental artifacts are used in accordance with his will."

"All those artifacts belong to the emperor?" Susie asked.

"All artifacts everywhere belong to the emperor. They are products of quintessence, and all quintessence is imperial property."

"And he just loans them out?"

"That's about it," Bozabrozy sighed.

"How does he keep track of them all?" Veeksha asked. "It sounds like a hard job."

"We magistrates regulate their creation, possession, and use," Savakala said.

"That doesn't sound very fair," Susie said.

"It is a matter of control," the uburu explained. "Imagine the chaos that would reign if anyone could do what they wished with such artifacts. Artificers creating whatever they wanted. Citizens defying the emperor. Magi with their elequaries waging war. Common rabble rebelling against imperial decree. Total anarchy! Only the emperor's wisdom protects us from such chaos. By restricting the use of artifacts, his dominion endures."

"I guess so," said Veeksha with a shrug.

Savakala eyed the children, "Do you have any artifacts?"

"No," Kyle said. "We've never even seen your magic stuff before today."

"Barathrina tells me you have magical sticks of light."

"Oh. Those are just flashlights. They're not magic."

"I will be the judge of that," the Sky Minister stated. "Place your pouches on the table. I will examine them later."

"You can't take our stuff!" Kyle objected.

"It is the emperor's will."

"Your emperor can't tell us what to do! We're Americans! Well, two of us are."

Savakala tapped her Staff of the Sky on the floor. Feathers swirled around it, and sparks jumped off the tip. "You will obey!" she shrieked.

Kyle cringed, slowly pulled off his backpack and put it on the table.

"That's better," Savakala said softly, sitting on a stool and pulling the pack toward her. Kyle noticed that her feet each had three large and vicious looking talons.

"Can I keep my backpack?" Susie asked. "It's got my food supplies. I won't be able to make any more Susie Snacks without it."

Savakala denied her and took her pack. "You will dine in the galley. Barathrina is an exceptionally fine cook."

Susie frowned. "Okay…"

"And you, young Veeksha, you must also give me your pouch."

Veeksha shook her head.

Savakala held out her taloned hand. "You must obey the emperor."

"Why? He's just some person far away."

"It is said the fates of emperors are borne on wings of destiny," Bozabrozy said, "and it is the fate of commoners to merely hear the rustle of the feathers passing overhead."

"Fate and destiny are the dreams of the weak," Savakala said. "The emperor's will is no dream, nor is he weak. Give it to me, Veeksha."

"I don't want to."

"I shan't be keeping it from you forever," Savakala cooed. "But, I must treat everyone equally to avoid the appearance of favoritism."

Bozabrozy coughed, but it sounded more like a laugh.

"That's enough from you, Bozabrozy! Come now, Veeksha. If you don't give it willingly, I shall take it by force."

Reluctantly, Veeksha gave the Zuran her pack. Savakala clicked her beak several times and put the pack on the table with the others.

"Today is a most inauspicious day," Veeksha mumbled.

"Now," Savakala said, striding through the door. "We had best go see what we can do about your geomancer friend."

She led them across the ship's deck and down into the hold. Between crates and sacks, Jürgen stood still and silent in the same petrified pose as the last time Kyle had seen him. Savakala examined the statue for several minutes before turning back to Kyle.

"Yes, I've seen this before. It's an adverse reaction that can afflict geomancers in two ways. First, as has happened to your friend here, they can be petrified the first time they absorb geopsium because they do not have the skill to control it. It is sometimes a temporary setback."

"Sometimes?" Kyle said worriedly.

"Yes."

"What's the other way?" Susie asked.

"Experienced geomancers can absorb so much geopsium over time that it corrupts them, and turns them into perilous creatures of stone, called geothropes. That is not what happened to Jürgen. He is merely petrified."

"You can unpetrify him, can't you?" Kyle asked.

"I could, if I were an aquamagus with an aquosian elequary," the uburu said. "But, that is not the case. Therefore, the only way to save him is to find more aquosia."

"And the only way we'll find more aquosia is to complete the quest," Kyle said.

"That is correct."

Kyle sighed. "Then we'd better hurry up and get to Peru."

CHAPTER 20

The Windrunner soared through the night skies far above America, heading south thanks to Susie's compass. The Rockies grew closer and closer as the skyship flew out of South Dakota, through Nebraska and Colorado, and over the Oklahoma panhandle. By the time Kyle woke late the next morning they were deep into Texas.

Kyle rolled out of the bunk and pulled on his shoes. Sleeping in a flying ship wasn't so different from sleeping in a regular sailboat. There was rocking and creaking and the sounds of wind, but no water sloshing against the hull. Veeksha's and Susie's bunks were already empty, but someone had left breakfast on the small table. Starving after a tiring day with little food, Kyle pounced on the bread and beef jerky. There was also a strange fruit, shaped like an apple with a thick yellow peel like a banana. He carefully opened it and took a bite of the crisp flesh. It tasted like banana, but with a hint of apple.

Washing it down with several long gulps from a bottle of juice on the table, Kyle went out to look for his friends. He found them quickly enough, sitting on coils of ropes.

"Hi," he said.

"Hi," Susie replied. "You sure slept a long time. We've been up for two hours."

"What have you been doing?"

"Watching the clouds going by and waiting for you." Veeksha seemed annoyed. "Do you always sleep so late?"

"Veeksha wanted a tour, but Bozabrozy said we'd have

to wait for you."

"But we didn't totally waste our time," Veeksha told him. "Savakala let me use my KnowPad this morning to show her and Machadaro where Peru is. I also read up on the Nasca lines and compared the Zurans to animals here on Earth."

"Savakala must be related to vultures," Susie said.

"Yes, she looks like a Eurasian black vulture."

"I wonder if there's a Zuran for every type of animal."

"Most of the crew are cat-people," Veeksha said. "Bozabrozy told us they're called mumbas. We've seen all sorts of them."

"They're really good at jumping around on the ropes and masts," Susie said. "I can't believe the way they leap around when we're up here in the clouds. One slip and they could fall!"

"We figure that the captain is descended from Bengal tigers," Veeksha smiled. "They're native to India and Bangladesh."

"Yeah, well, he's not too hard to figure out," Kyle agreed. "Can't hide those stripes."

"Joromwor must be a brown bear," Susie said. "Maybe even a Kodiak."

"And Bozabrozy is a raccoon," Kyle added.

Veeksha rolled her eyes. "Obviously."

"The soldiers are all dog-men – I mean canars – as far as we can tell," Susie said. "They spend most of their time below deck."

"But we've definitely seen a Rottweiler, Labrador retriever, bulldog..." Veeksha listed them off.

"Doberman pinscher," Susie contributed.

"What, no Chihauhau soldiers?" Kyle asked.

Susie laughed. "No, but quite a few German shepherds."

"Those are the kind that attacked us at our cabin," Kyle said.

"Rakanian has corrupted legionaries in the past,"

Bozabrozy said as he walked up. "He has no doubt brought many with him. All rested, Kyle?" The rascan patted him on the back. "You missed a great breakfast. Barathrina cooked us up a feast."

Susie rolled her eyes and licked her lips in delight. "Oh, yes, Kyle, you shouldn't have missed that. It was delicious. Scrambled eggs with bacon and sausages and hash browns. Delicious hot loaves of bread with melting butter. Fruits that tasted like apples, oranges, mangos, bananas, grapes, and bananas all mixed up together."

"Don't forget the strawpple juice," Veeksha reminded.

"I liked the grapple juice better," Susie countered.

"Let's not make the boy feel too bad," said Bozabrozy, waggling a finger. "He'll get supper tonight. So, are you ready for your tour of the ship?"

All three kids nodded emphatically, and Bozabrozy led them up to the poop deck at the stern of the skyship. Legate Joromwor stood there beside a large windlass. He wore a long tunic and pants. His magical armor and bardiche were still in Savakala's cabin.

"Because he is so strong, Joromwor takes turns on the ruddersail," said Bozabrozy, pointing off the stern of the ship where a slanted mast supported a vast triangular sail. "The ruddersail helps the Windrunner turn very quickly. If the captain wants to turn to port, he orders Joromwor here to pull the ruddersail over to port using the windlass. The same for starboard, but opposite."

"That's pretty simple," Veeksha said. "That sail is big."

"The bigger the ruddersail," Joromwor growled, looking at the three children like he wanted to eat them, "the tighter the turn."

"Joromwor is right," Bozabrozy agreed. "The Windrunner isn't only the fastest ship in the imperial fleet; it's also the most maneuverable. It can run rings around the battleships."

"But they can blast it to splinters with their cannon," the

bear man grumbled deeply. "This little ship is hardly more than a plaything. It wouldn't last a snap in a battle." And he snapped his fingers under Bozabrozy's nose.

"You'll have to pardon Joromwor's manner," the rascan said, pulling the children away from the grumpy urgra. "He was not pleased with being sent on this mission. He thinks sailing on anything less than a full battleship is beneath his dignity."

"Sky's truth, that is!" Joromwor roared after them. "And you can just keep those cubs away from me or I'll chew their bones for breakfast!"

Kyle shuddered at the urgra's hungry glare. The legate still reminded him of the urgra that shattered the cabin's front wall.

Bozabrozy led them quickly off the poop deck. The Windrunner had no masts rising up out of the main deck like sailboats on Earth. Instead, it had large, latticework hatches leading down to the hold.

"The Windrunner is a large swoop, which is a skyship with quadruple mainsails close to the prow, two topsails above the hull and two nethersails beneath the hull. It also has a pair of wingsails amidships, and a single, large ruddersail off the stern," Bozabrozy explained as he stepped to the ship's rail and pointed down at the starboard wingsail fluttering below. "The wingsails help control Windrunner's ascent or descent."

"Just like ailerons on a plane," Veeksha said.

"I don't know what those are," Bozabrozy admitted. "But maybe you can show me some day."

"What's that metal bulge?" Susie asked, pointing at a protrusion on the hull.

"That's the gustbox. There are four, one behind each mainsail."

"What do they do?"

"They hold the sky elementals that make the wind to fill the mainsails."

"There are sky elementals in there?" Kyle asked in surprise. "You mean like the stone elemental?"

"Yes." Bozabrozy then led them up to the forecastle. The two topsails billowed from masts that protruded from the bow. Beyond the mainsails, Captain Machadaro stood at the very prow of the ship.

"And here is the captain's deck," Bozabrozy explained. "From here the captain commands the ship."

Captain Machadaro turned, glaring down at his visitors from his imposing height. "I thought I told you not to bring them up here, rascan."

"Just giving them a quick tour, captain. Can't tour the ship without visiting the captain's deck."

Susie ran forward and leaned over the railing on the prow, with only the bowsprit beyond. Texas scrubland spread out far below her. "Wow! What a view!"

"What's this?" Kyle asked, looking at a thick wooden column that poked up out of the middle of the captain's deck. It rose to about five feet. Various metal tubes, bowls, and other strange devices protruded from it. Susie's compass rested on top.

"That's the binnacle," Bozabrozy explained. "It holds the captain's navigational instruments, such as the geodex."

Machadaro harrumphed and turned to gaze ahead of the ship while Bozabrozy explained the devices to Kyle.

Veeksha stepped up beside Machadaro and pulled on his pant leg. "What kind of Zuran are you?"

The captain glared down with his one good eye and bared his fangs a bit as he answered. "The best kind. A rasha."

"You remind me of the Bengal tigers in India," Veeksha smiled. "I always liked them."

Machadaro turned on her, roaring, "I am no tiger!"

Veeksha cowered and trembled. Bozabrozy stepped between them, saying, "No need to frighten the child, Captain! Savakala wouldn't like to hear that you're scaring our passengers."

"Don't lecture me, you conniving little deceiver. I am a rasha. I am not some mangy canar to be ordered about. Rasha are worth more than any other Zuran. We're worth a dozen sneak thief rascans like you. It would take a hundred feathered tyrants like Savakala to match just one of us!"

Bozabrozy held up his hand. "Captain Machadaro! Remember your place! No need to get upset in front of the children. If Savakala should hear you–"

Machadaro roared again. "If that feathered–"

But he was interrupted by an even mightier roar that shook the stout timbers of the skyship. Kyle grabbed the railing and watched as two AH-64 Apache attack helicopters buzzed by within a hundred feet of the Windrunner.

Chapter 21

"By the endless skies!" Machadaro rushed to the railing to watch the choppers pace alongside the skyship. "What are those?"

"Those are helicopters," Kyle yelled above the roar of the rotors. "I've never seen them up close like this before!"

"Are they ships of war?" Machadaro demanded.

"Oh, yeah! They've got machineguns and rockets." Kyle waved at the pilots, who he could see clearly in the cockpits.

"This world has the strangest and loudest skyships," Bozabrozy said. "They have no sails."

Machadaro turned back to the Windrunner and bellowed: "All hands on deck! Battle stations!"

"What?" Susie said. "You're going to fight them? I don't think that's a good idea."

"Yeah, I bet they won't attack us," Kyle said. "They're probably just going to watch us."

"I do not wish to be watched," said Savakala, striding onto the captain's deck. "Captain, continue your preparations for battle."

Machadaro turned to watch mumba sailors pull four strange looking cannon from compartments in the forecastle and stern castle. Canar legionaries rushed onto the deck.

"Get away from those cannon, you mangy dogs!" Machadaro yelled at the legionaries. "I told that cursed legate to keep his troops out of my way! They'll spoil the cannonade!"

"Shouldn't soldiers shoot the cannons?" Kyle asked.

"Those legionaries are merely infantry. They aren't cannoneers."

Savakala ignored the captain's irritation. "What sort of ships are those?" Feathers whirled round her Staff of the Sky. "They are made of iron?"

Kyle shrugged. "Some kind of steel, I guess. I don't really know."

"What weapons do they carry? Guns, you say? What are rockets?"

"Bigger than the guns the FBI used at Mt. Rushmore," Kyle nodded. "And rockets explode. One of them could probably blow up this whole ship."

Machadaro grunted. "The Windrunner is no battleship, to be sure. But her timbers are the finest geopsium-grown oak. They can withstand a terrible assault before breaking."

"I don't think you've ever seen the kind of damage a rocket can do," Kyle said worriedly.

Another helicopter neared, a UH-60 Black Hawk support chopper.

"Captain, order full ahead," Savakala said. "Their numbers grow and we must outrun them if we don't wish to be overwhelmed."

"All ahead full," Machadaro roared, and his orders were repeated along the length of the ship. The mainsails strained at the masts, the white canvas filling as the Windrunner gained speed. The three helicopters, however, kept pace easily, although the two Apaches moved away a hundred yards.

A voice from the Black Hawk boomed from a loudspeaker. "Attention! Attention! You will follow us to Fort Bliss army airfield. If you do not comply we will fire on your vessel."

Machadaro glanced at Savakala, who nodded. The captain leapt down to the main deck.

"Destroy that ship!" he ordered the port cannon crews. They spent only a moment positioning the cannon. There was no lanyard or fuse. Instead, one of the crew at each cannon pulled a mallet from his belt and hit the back of the weapon.

The muzzles erupted in flame and smoke, and two broiling balls of fire spat out toward the Black Hawk. The chopper pulled up and the fireballs arced away far beneath it.

"Stand down!" the chopper pilot ordered. "Stand down! Step away from the cannon or we will destroy them!"

While he spoke the two fireballs, instead of falling to the ground, flew up and around, homing in on the Black Hawk from the far side. The chopper's crew saw the fireballs too late. One slammed against the cockpit window and blazed there. The other found the open side door and flew inside, burning the gunner and filling the chopper with flame and smoke.

Machadaro smiled as the Black Hawk spiraled away from the Windrunner. The mumba cannoneers cheered.

One of the other choppers dove toward the Windrunner, its M230 30mm chain gun targeting the skyship's port cannon. The deck and railing around the first cannon erupted in splinters and chunks of wood as the explosive rounds tore up the ship. Machadaro and the two cannoneers dove away when the Apache fired on the second port cannon. Flames and smoke poured from the damaged hull of the Windrunner.

Savakala stood tall and resolute on the captain's deck as the two attack helicopters paced the Windrunner, one on either side.

"You shall not thwart this quest!" The uburu raised her feathered staff at the starboard Apache. A bolt of white lightning shot out with a thunderous crackle. It struck the hull of the Apache, cutting a long swath just below the cockpit and then up through the rear canopy before connecting with the rotor assembly. Sparks and smoke poured from the helicopter as it corkscrewed down and away from the Windrunner.

Savakala turned to the other side of the ship, where the second Apache swerved away. She sent another white bolt after the fleeing chopper, but the lightning only grazed the tail section. Even so, the chopper shook and quickly lost altitude.

"Why did you have to do that?" Kyle yelled, leaning over the rail to watch the helicopters fall. They only wanted us to follow them."

"Why would I want to follow them?" Savakala asked. "We have a quest to finish."

"But they could have helped."

"Like they helped at the mountain?" Savakala left the captain's deck, heading back to the main deck. "They are but more of Rakanian's minions."

Kyle followed the uburu. "Those are army helicopters. I don't think Rakanian is controlling the United States Army."

"You are young and easily deceived," Savakala clucked. "I have seen many things in my visions, and those skyships are agents of Rakanian."

"You can't know that," Veeksha said. "Maybe the army just spotted us and wants to talk to us."

"Yeah," Susie agreed, "they might even be able to help with your quest."

"If they knew of our quest they would most assuredly want the quintessence for themselves. Quintessence is a rare and valuable commodity, much rarer and more valuable here on Earth than in Zura. Anyone who controlled Earth's quintessences would have more power than you can imagine. No. Even if they are not doing Rakanian's bidding, I will complete this quest without their aid."

Machadaro met the group on the main deck. He had escaped injury, but others had not.

"Two of my crew are dead!" he roared. "And another injured! The port wingsail has been damaged, and one of the gustboxes. The elemental almost escaped."

Savakala spoke in a soothing voice. "Calm yourself, Captain Machadaro. We have defeated the enemy and they won't return. Our weapons are vastly superior and the crew will repair the damage."

"Actually," Kyle said, "you haven't seen all their weapons yet."

"No matter," said the uburu, shaking her staff. "I can make short work of their ships."

"Even so," Machadaro growled, "those skyships are faster than the Windrunner and they no doubt have many more of them. They'll be able to intercept us whenever they choose. They will have the upper hand. I can't outmaneuver a fleet of swifter ships in a foreign world."

Savakala paused, deep in thought. "You are right, of course, Captain. Continue on course and I will consider methods to confound them."

Machadaro shook his head. "I will not. We have been coursing straight since we left the mountain of four faces. We must change direction so as not to reveal our destination. Otherwise, they will arrive there first."

"Once again, you are right, Captain. Do what you must to ensure that we arrive at Peru first. I must retire to my cabin to prepare. I will require my full strength to prevent pursuit." Savakala turned back to the stern, her feathered robe flapping in the wind.

"Tend to the dead," Machadaro told the crew on deck. "Repair the gustbox and wingsail first. We must have full power and control as soon as possible." The crew hurried to obey.

Machadaro turned to Veeksha, bending down to stare at her with his amber eye, "And you, little girl, you will use your magic map to show me what is between us and Peru. I must find a way to fool our pursuers." He grabbed her shoulder and pushed her along to Savakala's quarters.

Bozabrozy called after him, "What shall I do, Captain?"

"You have no responsibilities on this ship, rascan,"

Machadaro replied without turning or stopping. "Hide somewhere. We'll call you out from under your rock when we need you."

Bozabrozy frowned. "It's always a pleasant voyage when he's the captain."

"What should we do?" Susie asked.

"Lunch seems to be in order. Unless Barathrina was killed in the attack."

CHAPTER 22

Barathrina survived, but the galley did not escape unscathed. When Bozabrozy, Susie, and Kyle descended into Barathrina's domain, they found her half-covered in flour. Her other half was drenched in strawpple juice. Broken jugs, dented pans, and a few shattered barrels littered the room.

"What in the endless skies happened out there?" Barathrina demanded as she bent this way and that, picking up spice bottles and looking for her other prized ingredients.

"A squadron of enemy skyships attacked us," Bozabrozy replied. "Machadaro and Savakala drove them off."

"That's all fine and good, but look what they've done to my galley! That barrel of flour exploded right in front of me! Look, I've got splinters all over my arm!"

"You fared better than other members of the crew." Bozabrozy began helping the grunk to clean up by righting a chair and sitting on it.

"Oh, my," Barathrina fretted.

"Two sailors were killed by a horrible weapon. Their bodies were torn asunder, much worse than your flour barrel."

Barathrina leaned against the wall, shaking her head. "It's a shame. I was hoping we'd finish the quest without battles and killing."

"That is a slim hope for a fat grunk," Bozabrozy said grimly. "Death is never a stranger with Savakala and Machadaro in command."

Barathrina snorted and then noticed Susie and Kyle. "Oh, dearies! Fare you well? Were you wounded in the battle?"

"No," they replied in unison.

"Well, come in, come in!" Barathrina ushered them into the galley and gave them two stools to sit at a small table. "Kyle, I left a cold meal in your cabin for you this morning. Did you find it?"

"Yes, thanks!"

"But you're still hungry, no doubt."

Kyle nodded.

"No need to worry," the cook said, grabbing a broom and sweeping away the mess. "Give me a few minutes to clean up and I'll get you something hearty and filling."

"You can get something for all of us," Bozabrozy interjected.

Barathrina scowled playfully at the rascan. "For all that you eat, Bozabrozy, I'd expect you to be twice as big."

"It's just your cooking, Barathrina. It's an unavoidable temptation."

Barathrina leaned over the table. "Listen to the sweet-talker. They say he could flatter the horn off a raging kerrod. Back in Zura, he's known across the endless skies as a great swindler. I still can't imagine why the emperor chose him for this quest. Maybe it's because he's so dashing in that hat and cape."

"Just cook lunch," the rascan suggested with a smile.

"Fine, fine. What would you like? Spiced roc leg soup, with veggies and rice? Or thick-sliced ham with poached eggs and toast?"

"Ham and eggs sound good."

"Same for me," Bozabrozy added.

Barathrina snorted pleasantly. "Coming right up!"

"What's a kerrod?" Susie asked.

"It's another kind of Zuran," Bozabrozy said. "They are huge grey lumbering oafs with big pointed horns on their snouts."

"Are there any here?"

"Storms and thunders, no!" Barathrina squealed. "They're even heavier than I am, and twice as clumsy. They're mostly in the Imperial Legions. They are fearsome juggernauts with thick hides and strong arms."

"If you ever get one angry at you," Bozabrozy advised, "just hide. They have very poor eyesight."

"But very good noses," Barathrina said. "Which Bozabrozy here knows well. Why, there's a funny tale about him trying to sneak past a kerrod that–"

"Hadn't you better mind the skillet?" Bozabrozy interrupted.

"–that I'll tell you dearies later," she finished. "Now, who wants to help me cook up lunch?"

Susie and Kyle eagerly volunteered, and spent the next hour in the galley, helping to clean up the mess, cooking, and eating.

For the remainder of the day they watched the cat-like crew repair the battle damage. They looked at the damaged cannon. To Kyle, they did not look like those on old pirate ships of Earth. These were much shorter and thicker, and could be aimed very high, even straight up. The shimmering metal surfaces were ornately carved with images of flames and infernos. Bozabrozy told them that a fire elemental was imprisoned in each cannon. When a cannoneer hit the bottom with a special mallet, the fire elemental inside discharged a piece of itself at whatever it could see through the end of the muzzle.

"Is that why the fireballs turned around and hit the helicopter?" Kyle asked Bozabrozy.

"Yes, each fireball retains a portion of the fire elemental's mind for a short time. So, it can fly and change course to hit the target."

"It's like a smart missile. Do cannon ever miss on Zura?"

"Yes. But not all of them are like the ones we have.

These are the pride of the Imperial Fleet. The emperor himself ordered them onto the Windrunner. These cannon are lighter and stronger and smarter, as you say, than most. Battleships usually don't have such weapons. But they make up for it by carrying many more that are even more destructive. Some battleships have dozens of them."

"But," Kyle asked, "the ships are made of wood and sails. Don't the fireballs catch them on fire pretty quickly?"

"Aye, that they do, unless the ship has sails made of materials grown with or seeped in pyrophyra. The sails of the Windrunner are made from flax grown in the imperial gardens and fertilized with pyrophyra. They are almost impervious to flame. The rest of the ship has similar strengths."

After dinner that night, Susie, Veeksha, and Kyle talked about what they had done.

"And after he changed course to head for the Gulf of Mexico," Veeksha said, "the Captain came back to Savakala's cabin and I showed him more maps. He wanted to see Mexico. He doesn't know the geography very much."

"You'd think think that they'd study and make maps from orbit before they landed," Kyle said. "Zura has strange astronauts, I guess."

"I think all of Zura is strange," Susie said. "But not in a bad way. They have skyships. They control the elements and can shoot lightning and fire. They can freeze things, and heal people with water. They have animal people. I wonder if some of the Sioux stories are a based on them? My granddad says that the spirits of the wild sometimes look like men wearing the skin of animals."

"I wonder if Savakala is right?" Kyle asked.

"About what?" Susie responded.

"About Rakanian controlling the Army."

"How can we know?" Veeksha said. "It won't do us any good to call her a liar. She can shoot us with lightning if we don't help her."

"Or just drop us off the ship," Kyle said.

"Or have Machadaro rip us to shreds like he did those poor men back at Mt. Rushmore," Susie recalled.

"I don't think Machadaro would do that," Veeksha said. "He's actually quite nice once you get to know him."

"Nice?" Kyle shook his head. "He seems mean and angry to me."

"No, he's not like that. I get the feeling that he doesn't really want to be here. He doesn't like Savakala or Bozabrozy and especially not Joromwor." She crawled into her bunk. "That's strange, too. Why would he be captain of a ship full of people he hates?"

"There's all sorts of things we don't know about the Zurans," Kyle lamented. "The only thing I know is that Savakala is the only one who can change Jürgen back to flesh. I have to help them find the aquosia."

"And I'll help you do that," Susie volunteered.

"And after that?" Veeksha asked. "We'll be standing in a desert in Peru. What's next?"

"I don't know."

"At the very least," Veeksha suggested, "we should get Savakala to agree to let us tell our parents that we're okay."

"Right," Kyle said sarcastically, "like she'd let us do that."

"I managed to tell my dad where we were on my phone," Susie said.

"Only because she didn't know what it was. I don't think she wants us talking to anyone."

"Doesn't that bother you?" Veeksha asked.

"Yes, but I have to help save Jürgen."

"We should still find some way to let our parents know we're okay," Veeksha insisted.

"If you figure out how to do that, let us know," Susie said, closing her eyes.

As the children nodded off one by one, a Lockheed C-130 Hercules military transport aircraft maneuvered into a parallel heading far above the Windrunner. The Air Force plane pulled ahead of the skyship and the rear door opened. Inside, a squad of commandos rose and moved toward the door in the green light of the jump indicator. They leapt out into the night. Reid Bannecker was the last man to leave. He pulled on his nightvision goggles and followed the elite commando unit out of the plane.

Chapter 23

Thanks to his nightvision goggles, Bannecker could see his target very clearly. The strange ship had everyone stumped. It flew against the winds and at speeds that belied its non-aerodynamic shape. It flew up to seventy miles per hour. The helicopter attack caused some damage, and it had slowed to half that speed. But the cat-sailors had repaired the ship quickly, and it sped up again only an hour ago.

If the ship kept its current southeasterly course, it would only be a matter of hours before it flew out into the Gulf of Mexico. That's why the wingsuited commando team was soaring down toward the vessel now. The children had to be rescued before the full force of an F-22 jet fighter squadron could be unleashed to prevent the ship from escaping.

Straightening his limbs, Bannecker leaned forward and plummeted toward the skyship. Thanks to fabric stretched between the legs and under the arms, the wingsuits enabled the five commandos and Bannecker to maneuver far more effectively than in freefall or with a parachute. With a bit of skill and luck, adjusting their velocity and angle of descent, they would land on the ship's rigging. Then all they had to do was climb onto the ship, avoid the crew, find the children, and leap off the ship with them.

It was a risky mission. Only if everything went smoothly would their plan succeed. To save the children, however, it had to be attempted.

He watched the five wingsuited commandos glide toward the ship. The first of them stretched out his arms and legs, the increased fabric area slowing him considerably. But when he neared the sails, he suddenly plummeted down and away from the ship.

"Sergeant Cox!" Captain Stearns shouted over the radio. "What happened?"

"There's a strange wind shear above the ship," Cox replied as he recovered far below. "It's like a space of dead air, some kind of bubble, about fifty feet from the ship."

"Change of plan," Stearns ordered calmly. "Approach to within eighty feet and then use your grapple guns to snare the rigging."

Another commando descended and fired a silent grapple gun. It tangled in the rigging of the starboard topsail. The commando then veered in toward the ship as the line silently pulled him closer. Suddenly, a chaos of wind currents buffeted him, and then the blasts from the gustboxes threw him into the sail. He caught hold of the rigging and managed to steady himself.

"Tough job, Captain," he said. "Way too many shears in here."

"We don't have a choice. We're coming in."

Captain Stearns and another commando successfully caught the rigging, but with just as much difficulty as the first. The last commando's grapple caught, but he was thrown around so much by the gustbox that his grapple line tangled around his left arm and left him dangling.

"Wegehenkel! Cut your line and get free!" Stearns ordered. The snarled commando obeyed and dropped away from the ship.

Finally, Bannecker approached and fired his grapple gun. It caught near Captain Stearns, who helped him get a firm grip on the rigging.

"We've lost two men," Stearns warned. "Quiet now, let's find those kids."

First, they all unzipped the wing fabric from their suits. They would use the compact parachutes in their backpacks to escape.

Bannecker followed the three commandos down the rigging. It was not an easy task. The strong gusts of wind that filled the sails also made crawling near them difficult. Bannecker looked down at the ship and into the wind. It seemed that the gusts were coming from metal protrusions on the side of the ship.

After several minutes of clambering along ropes and spars, Bannecker dropped onto the main deck of the ship. Captain Stearns crouched there waiting for him. Nearby, one of the dog-men lay on the deck, incapacitated by the commando.

Using hand signals, Stearns revealed where they'd sighted more of the crew. He led Bannecker toward the stern.

The skyship had been under constant surveillance since it blasted its way out of Mt. Rushmore. Satellites tracked its course and speed, while several spy planes aimed high-powered video cameras on it from multiple angles. With over twenty-four hours of footage, Bannecker had been able to examine the ship's exterior floor plan. He'd also identified the likely location of the children's cabin. The Zurans weren't keeping them locked up; they seemed to have free run of the ship. There was nowhere they could escape to. No sign of the German boy had been caught on film. Either he wasn't on the ship or he never came out on deck.

Stearns and Bannecker snuck to the stern castle and quietly stole through the door into a short passageway. They found three children sleeping inside the second cabin – Kyle Morgan, Susie Five Eagles, and Veeksha Das. There was no sign of Jürgen Schmidt. As Stearns closed the door behind him, Bannecker removed his night goggles and balaclava. He placed his hand lightly over the boy's mouth and whispered, "Kyle, wake up."

Kyle's eyes shot open in surprise and he tried to scream, but Bannecker held his mouth shut.

"It's me, Reid Bannecker. We're here to get you off the ship. Stay quiet, okay?"

Kyle nodded, and Bannecker removed his hand and similarly woke Susie and Veeksha.

"How did you get here?" Kyle whispered.

"That's not important," Bannecker pulled out small suits from his belly pack. "These are jumpsuits. Put them on, quickly. Where is Jürgen Schmidt?"

"He's in the hold," Susie answered. "But aren't you supposed to be dead? I saw Machadaro kill you."

"I recovered," Bannecker replied. "There's no time to answer your questions. We have to get out of here ASAP. Can you describe to me where Jürgen is?"

Kyle had not moved to put on the jumpsuit. "Why should I? You attacked Bozabrozy without warning. You shot him for no reason!"

"Keep your voice down," Bannecker ordered. "I'm not here to have a discussion. We're getting you off this ship. Put on this jumpsuit. Now!"

Kyle resisted. "Are you working with Rakanian? Why are you trying to kill the Zurans? They just want the quintessence."

Bannecker started. "What do you know about quintessence? Have the Zurans told you where to find some?"

Kyle shut his mouth defiantly.

"Your father would like it better if you told me what you know," Bannecker made one last appeal.

"You've got my father?"

"He's very worried about you. Come with me and you'll see him soon enough."

"No. I don't believe you. I'll help the Zurans find the aquosia and unpetrify Jürgen first."

Bannecker realized that Kyle wasn't going to cooperate, but there would be time enough to interrogate him once they were on solid ground. He clamped a hand over the boy's mouth and picked him up, heading back out the door. Stearns grabbed the two girls.

CHAPTER 24

"Phiel, Kilmer," Stearns called over his headset as they stepped into the passageway. "We have three targets. Prepare to exit."

"You take these three," Bannecker said to Stearns, "and I'll search the rest of the ship for the German."

"Roger that. Kilmer, Phiel. Confirm."

Stearns and Bannecker stepped onto the main deck and moved toward the railing.

"Stop!"

Stearns spun around to see Savakala standing atop the sterncastle. Joromwor stood beside him, holding two limp commandos.

"Let those children go," Machadaro demanded, stepping out from around a corner.

Stearns dropped the girls and raised his sub-machinegun, but Savakala was faster. A lightning bolt arced out and caught the commando in the shoulder, spinning him around to tumble over the railing.

Bannecker stood quite still as the giant tiger-man stepped forward and lifted Kyle from his grasp. After setting the boy down, the eye-patched Zuran glared down at Bannecker. "I remember you. You were at the mountain."

"We know what you're planning," Bannecker said defiantly. "We won't let you get away with it."

Savakala descended the steps onto the deck. "You have no idea what we are planning. And you know even less how to stop us. Thrice you have tried to do so, and each time you failed."

"We'll keep trying."

"No, you won't." Savakala patted Susie on the head. "You wouldn't want to harm the children. Your last attack was most gratuitous. Your weapons could have easily killed them. I suggest that you let us go about our business unmolested unless you want to explain to their parents how you killed them."

"You've invaded our territory, kidnapped children, destroyed government property, and killed our troops. You don't think we're just going to let you leave, do you?"

"Do not test my patience, human," Savakala warned. "You have only seen one small sampling of my power. I come from a realm where magic reigns like nothing you have seen in your world. I am a master of the skies and everything that soars within them. You would not wish to see the full extent of my fury unleashed."

"Then I'll just have to make sure you die," Bannecker said and pulled his sidearm from its holster at his side. Before the man could fire, Machadaro's sharp talons once again tore through Bannecker's flesh and bone, this time from his right hip up through his chest and ribs. The force of the blow catapulted him over the railing and onto the port wing sail. Bannecker lay there for a moment, but then slid off, leaving behind a dark streak of blood.

Savakala moved quickly to the railing to see the body disappear into the darkness below. Then he turned to Machadaro. "I told you I wanted one of them alive!"

"Your legate has two." Machadaro pointed at the two commandos the urgra was carrying down the steps.

"These humans are dead," Joromwor grumbled, throwing the men over the side of the ship.

"Alas," Machadaro shrugged, "it appears that your legate can't follow orders either."

Joromwor growled loudly, glaring at the rasha captain.

"You could have just wounded him," Savakala scowled

at Machadaro. "Must you kill everyone?"

"I'm a simple skyship captain. When an enemy attacks I respond boldly." Machadaro smiled, his fangs gleaming in the dim light. The two Zurans stared at each other for several long seconds.

"Without any prisoners to question, we cannot learn their plans," Savakala said. "Or can you guess what they will do next?"

"No. I do not know the minds of these humans. They could be planning anything."

"Few can see what darkness reaps in the depths of the night," Bozabrozy agreed, stepping onto the deck from the passageway.

"Bozabrozy is right," Savakala said. She turned to the captain and legate. "I don't have time to properly chastise either of you. It is clear that these humans will continue to molest us as long as they can track our course. I must begin the ritual at once."

"You are very wise."

The uburu scowled again. "It is time for me to once again use the Flagon of the Six Winds. Restrict access to the poop deck. I must concentrate. Maintain our current course toward the Gulf of Mexico. You will soon see the results of my incantations, so prepare for them. I will not have precise control, and the Windrunner must keep to the eye." She hurried into the stern castle.

"Aye, Savakala."

Joromwor showed Kyle the submachine guns he had taken from the commandos. "Do you know how these work?"

"Yeah. You aim this end at what you want to hit and pull this trigger. You only have so many shots before you have to reload."

Joromwor examined the gun, but it was far too small for his huge hands. His fingers couldn't even fit inside the trigger guard.

"And this?" Machadaro held out Bannecker's nighvision goggles that had fallen to the deck.

"Cool!" Kyle put on the goggles. "I've seen these in movies but I've never tried them before."

"What is it?"

"It let's you see in the dark," Kyle said, looking through the goggles, and then handing them back to Machadaro.

"All magical implements must be given to the magistrate," Joromwor grabbed for the goggles but Machadaro did not release them.

"Give me the artifact," Joromwor demanded, staring into the captain's one good eye.

"You have no authority over me, legionary," Machadaro replied evenly.

"Legate!" Joromwor growled, saliva dripping down his bared teeth. "You will address me by my proper rank!"

"As you will address me," Machadaro stated.

The two towering Zurans glared at each other for a long moment. Finally, Joromwor spoke slowly and clearly. "In the name of Savakala, envoy to Emperor Exeverius, and commander of this quest, give me the artifact, Captain Machadaro."

The rasha released the goggles. "Of course, Legate Joromwor." The urgra glared angrily at him for a moment longer before taking all the commando equipment to Savakala's cabin.

"He hates you, doesn't he?" Susie asked, and quickly added, "Captain."

"As I hate him."

"Why do you always have to kill that man?" Veeksha asked, referring to Bannecker. "Violence isn't always necessary."

"A dead foe is one less foe to worry about."

"Except that one. You've killed him twice now. Maybe he'll come back. Maybe next time you should talk to him."

"I care not for his words."

"What is Savakala going to do?" Kyle asked.

"She is going to summon the sky to defend us."

"What does that mean?"

"You will see soon enough," the rasha said. "And when you do, you will learn that our mighty minister does not make idle threats."

CHAPTER 25

It was not safe on deck while Savakala conducted her ritual. The captain ordered the children back to their cabin and told them not to come out until summoned. They went to the portholes to try to see what the aeromagus was going to summon.

Above them, alone on the poop deck, Savakala sat within an arcane design drawn with sparkling crystals that glittered like stars. She removed her cloak and spread her hands. Long feathers stretched out from shoulder to wrist. At full extention, her wingspan was more than twenty feet.

She pulled a large crystal bottle into her lap. A roiling mass of dark clouds and crackling energy strained within it. Long minutes rolled by and the uburu did not move, but her beak clicked occasionally as she muttered under her breath. Slowly, her feathers started to waft in a breeze. Several minutes later, a strong wind whirled around.

Finally, she stood and held the bottle above her head. The crystal trembled as the storm of haze and electricity tried to escape. With a shriek of command, Savakala uncorked the Flagon of the Six Winds and a thunderous boom shook the Windrunner. Clouds and wind and lightning spat out of the bottle.

When the last wisps of dark cloud had swept out, Savakala replaced the cork. She gazed into the night and knew the storm was forming. She stumbled over to the railing above the main deck, exhausted but with a long night of exertion still ahead.

"You," she said, pointing to a mumba sailor. "Inform the captain that the maelstrom will soon arrive." She returned to the diamond design and sat, chanting again and holding the Flagon of the Six Winds in her encircling arms. Another boom shook the ship.

"What was that? Thunder?" Veeksha asked, peering out the porthole. Dark clouds surrounded the ship.

"Do you think Savakala summoned a storm?" Susie asked. "Wouldn't that be cool to control the weather? You could make wind and snow and sunshine and rainbows."

"They do keep going on about endless skies," Veeksha said. "And Savakala is a sky magus. That must be her power. Lightning and storms."

"So, Bozabrozy is the water wizard," Susie said, "Joromwor is the stone wizard, and Savakala is the sky wizard. Who do you suppose the fire wizard is?"

"I bet it's Machadaro!" Veeksha said.

"We haven't seen anyone but Savakala actually do magic, though," Kyle noted. "Joromwor only has his armor and big axe. Bozabrozy used magic items, but he said he's not really an aquamagus."

"And we haven't seen the captain do or use anything magical," Susie said.

"That doesn't mean he's not a magus," Veeksha argued.

"I guess not. But all we know for sure is that Savakala is an aeromagus."

Veeksha frowned. She hoped that Machadaro would use some fire magic before the quest was over.

Eventually, they fell asleep again, and during the night the skies over southeast Texas darkened to roiling black clouds. The Windrunner soared straight into the eye of the storm and remained there, avoiding the worst of the turbulence and electrical storms. Even so, the crew was hard pressed to keep the ship aloft as they sailed out over the Gulf of Mexico, but they kept an east-southeasterly course thanks to Machadaro's navigation with Susie's compass.

Early in the morning, Kyle woke to find the ship sailing smooth and sure. Looking out the porthole, he saw the angry black clouds of a storm. He rushed out of the cabin and onto the main deck.

The Windrunner was completely surrounded by the storm. Dark clouds raged only a couple miles away. Lightning flashed constantly.

Kyle saw Bozabrozy on the forecastle with Machadaro and went to join them. "Did Savakala summon this storm?"

"What are you doing out of your cabin?" the captain demanded.

"Oh, er..." Kyle stuttered.

"I invited him," Bozabrozy said, lying for the boy, and Machadaro merely grumbled. "And yes, Savakala did summon the storm. It's an elemental maelstrom released from the Flagon of Six Winds. It's very impressive, wouldn't you say?"

"Yeah," Kyle said nervously. "Are there other winds in the flagon?"

"Yes, there are, clever Kyle. Savakala released the Storm Wind, an elemental maelstrom."

"What are the other winds?"

"The Swift Wind, the Returning Wind, and the Howling Wind."

"That only adds up to four," Kyle noted, "not six."

"Savakala already used up the other two," Machadaro said, still watching the clouds intently.

"Shouldn't you call it the Flagon of the Three Winds now?"

"No."

"Oh." Kyle looked at the dark clouds swirling around them. "Are we in the eye of the storm? I've never been in the eye of a storm before. I hope we don't get caught up in the bad parts."

"Don't worry." Bozabrozy pointed at Machadaro, who was giving commands to the feline crew. "This is why

Machadaro is here. He's the greatest sky captain there is. He'll keep us in the eye until we cross this gulf."

"What happens then?"

"It's all part of Savakala's plan. The maelstrom will cross the gulf, confusing Earth's skyships. When we near the peninsula, we'll sneak out of the storm and head overland to the other ocean. Meanwhile, the maelstrom will continue toward the large island at the gulf's mouth. As it diminishes, it will deposit some of the Windrunner's stores and repair stock, extra spars and canvas and the like, on the shores. Rakanian and his allies will think we crashed and died."

"The storm can carry that stuff?"

"Yes. Once we've lost our pursuers, we'll head to Peru."

Late in the day the Windrunner altered course and descended. Ahead, through a small break in the clouds, Kyle could see the green coast of the Yucatan peninsula. Huge waves hammered a long narrow island a few miles from the shore. A checkerboard of town blocks near one end was overwhelmed by seawater. Kyle hoped everyone had evacuated in time.

Machadaro expertly captained the ship through the narrow path between the clouds. The Windrunner passed over the island and toward the mainland, losing altitude as it did. As they sailed out of the eye of the storm, the winds picked up and the turbulence increased. Even Savakala's arcane dominion of the elemental maelstrom could not entirely protect the ship from the chaos. Machadaro fought the edges of the storm, trying to keep the ship on a southwesterly course and away from the lights of big cities.

When the children awoke the next morning they found the Windrunner coursing quietly over open sea. Very few of the crew were on deck, and those that were looked worn out from the voyage through the storm.

For Kyle and the other children, the dark journey across the Gulf of Mexico had seemed a long and boring day trapped, for the most part, in their cabin. Now, free to roam the ship in calm air, they found the sea passage even less exciting. They spent the hours watching the mumba crew and trying to identify the breeds of cats they resembled. Kyle wasn't too knowledgeable about cats, but Veeksha identified a few: Russian blue, Abyssinian, Maine Coone, and more.

They spent some time with Barathrina and Bozabrozy, learning about the various Zuran races. Canars were one of the most numerous, and most of the Imperial Legions were composed of the loyal and obedient dog-like soldiers, along with the horse-like buccan. The largest cities of the empire were populated by goatish hurkas, woolly baashi, grunks like Barathrina, and the limber mumbas, to name just a few. Feathered Zurans included the colorful nuri, ubiquitous pekkin, and regal rapten.

Susie grinned. "It sounds like a big Zuran zoo."

Barathrina shook her head in disagreement. "We are not zoo animals."

"Zurans are civilized creatures," said Bozabrozy. "But beyond the Imperial Isles lie vast regions of wilderness. They teem with all manner of beasts."

"Beasts?" Susie asked. "What kind of beasts?"

"About as many as you can count," Barathrina said. "Just ask Bozabrozy! He's told me tales of his adventures beyond the empire. Go ahead, tell them."

"Yeah, Bozabrozy," Susie pleaded. "What kind of beasts are there?"

The rascan began ticking off with his fingers. "Malafacles, blooderflies, stranglevines, frorsh, vores, griffs, many types of carnivorous plants–"

"Some of which bear fruit that is, ironically, quite tasty," Barathrina interrupted.

"Frenges, glims, shadowings, grievals, dragons, and more," Bozabrozy concluded.

"Dragons?" Kyle asked. "We have legends of dragons here."

"Dragons are not legends in Zura. They are a terrible threat to skyships. They breathe elemental fire, which can damage even the hardiest timber. They are perhaps the most perilous beasts for they eat quintessence of all kinds. The chaotic mixture inside them causes bedlam and calamity."

"And if you aren't careful, one might gobble you up," Barathrina added with a smile.

Even with Bozabrozy's wondrous tales of Zura, the hours of calm sailing in the warm tropical sun lulled the children and even some of the crew. Machadaro supervised the few remaining repairs, but of Savakala there was no sign. Apparently, the effort of controlling the elemental maelstrom had completely exhausted her and she slept in her cabin.

In the afternoon they sailed over the Galapagos Islands, and Machadaro ordered a new course to the southeast, with the help of Veeksha's KnowPad and Susie's compass. Soon, the islands disappeared behind, leaving only the Pacific Ocean spread out below them. The Sun sank off the Windrunner's starboard rear quarter.

They hadn't seen any sign of pursuit in the three days since Bannecker snuck onto the ship. After leaving the elemental maelstrom and crossing Central America they saw only a few ships. Machadaro kept the Windrunner hidden in clouds as much as possible, but Kyle suspected that they'd been spotted at least once. A fishing boat had changed course to run parallel to them until Machadaro found deep clouds to hide in.

Early the next morning, Kyle and Veeksha and Susie woke to the cry of one of the mumba crew. They rushed out to the main deck. The west coast of South America stretched along the horizon far off to port.

CHAPTER 26

The kids ran to the captain's deck to find Machadaro chasing away a canar legionary. "If I want a mangy cur like you on my deck, I'll send for one!" He turned back to the prow and raised a telescoping device of some kind to his eye.

"That's a neat spyglass," Susie said.

"It is a skyglass," he corrected.

"Oh, we call them spyglasses."

"You have such things?"

"Sure. Binoculars, telescopes, microscopes. All sorts of them."

"Your maps are quite accurate, Veeksha," the captain said. "I've never seen maps that were so detailed. We'll follow the coast and then head inland beyond the Paracas Peninsula, as you said. We'll reach your Nasca lines soon after."

Machadaro guided the Windrunner across the Peruvian lowlands. They soared over roads and farms and villages. They saw people far below them, gathering in crowds, no doubt watching the alien skyship. The sky captain ignored them, and the lines of the ancient Nasca civilization soon appeared.

"It looks more like a messy chalkboard than a desert," Kyle said as they stared down at the tangle of overlapping white drawings far below them. Lines seemed to stretch for miles, and the geometric designs and animal shapes were as big as football fields.

"It's not a desert," Veeksha corrected. "It's a pampa. It's like a desert except it's more of a tableland surrounded by valleys."

"How are the lines made?" Susie asked.

"They're cleared strips of ground," Veeksha said. "The ancient people removed the stones and piled them on either side of the strip. The stones on the surface are red but the ones underneath are whitish. By clearing off the top lay layer of rock, they made white designs in the ground like a giant chalkboard."

"How long have they been doing it?" Susie asked.

"The oldest ones were made over two thousand years ago," Veeksha said. "And the ancient people continued to make new ones for hundreds of years."

"What are they for?"

"No one is really sure, but it could have something to do with astronomy, genealogy, ancestor worship, underground aqueducts, foot races, communicating with gods, and even alien landing strips."

"Have any Zurans ever been here before, Bozabrozy?"

"If they have I've never heard tales of it."

"Where do we land?" Machadaro asked. "There are lines everywhere."

Savakala appeared from the stern castle. "The clues lie in the riddle."

Where thirst scours the lands
And underfoot giant birds soar
Created and unearthed by ancient hands
From the beak it will pour

"It's simple," Veeksha said confidently. "The last line tells us exactly where to look. From the beak it will pour. We only need to find the bird drawing."

"And where might that be?" Savakala asked.

"The animal drawings are grouped mostly at the north end," said Veeksha, pointing.

Machadaro nodded and returned to the captain's deck. Soon, the Windrunner soared near the northern end of the pampa. Susie quickly spotted the figure drawings on the ground. They were smaller than the trapezoids and lines they'd already seen, and there were many of them bunched on either side of a long wide line that ran from east to west.

"Look! There's a bird!" said Susie.

"And another one there!" Veeksha added. "And another!"

"That one over there could be a bird," said Kyle, "or some kind of bird-bug."

"There are a dozen of them," Susie said. "How do we know which one the riddle refers to?"

"We don't," Veeksha said. "The riddle isn't that precise. We should locate all the birds to see if any look promising."

Machadaro sailed the Windrunner lower over the pampa. It didn't take long to identify several of the bird drawings. They saw a hummingbird, pelican, chick, condor, two parrots, and other things that might have been birds.

"Where should we start?" Susie asked.

"If we start with the hummingbird, we can work our way east to the parrot and then the condor," Veeksha suggested.

"Let's go to the condor first," Kyle suggested.

"Why?"

"I don't know. It's just that hummingbirds and parrots aren't all that impressive, but a condor is pretty big and probably more important."

"It doesn't matter where we start," Susie said, "since we have no idea what to do, anyway."

"Okay," Veeksha said. "Let's check the condor first. Savakala will like it that way. A condor is a type of vulture."

A few minutes later the children stood on a platform descending from a hatch in the hull of the Windrunner.

Savakala and Bozabrozy stood beside them. Another platform lowered two canar legionaries armed with cutlasses and Joromwor in his Indomitable Armor and carrying the Sundering Bardiche. The platforms touched the rock-strewn ground with a sudden thump.

"Wow," Kyle said, "you can barely recognize the condor from the ground."

The others searched around, but all they could see were low mounds of stones stretching out in multiple directions. They assumed the nearest part was the beak.

"Even if we could see the condor," Veeksha said, "what would we do?"

Susie shrugged. "The riddle doesn't say. It just says 'from the beak it will pour'."

"How do we get it to pour?"

"No doubt we must conduct some kind of ritual," Savakala said, moving to the stones that seemed to mark the tip of the beak. "I will commune with the elements." She removed her cloak, sat on the ground and spread her deep black wings. Long feathers stretched out from her shoulders to her wrists and beyond. She brought her arms wide and then pointed them in front of her as she chanted.

"Wow!" Susie exclaimed, amazed at the uburu's enormous wingspan. "Your wings are beautiful!"

Veeksha stared in awe. "And so big! Look how long the feathers are."

Savakala did not reply. Joromwor stood nearby, keeping an eye on their surroundings.

"How long is this going to take?" Kyle asked. "It's really hot."

"Few are they who have power over time," Savakala said. "Be patient."

Kyle wiped his sweating forehead and squinted. He missed his baseball cap. "I'm not good at patient. Why would elemental water be in the middle of this desert?"

"Because this is where water is most needed," Veeksha

said. "'Where thirst scours the land.'"

"Do you suppose the ancient Peruvians found aquosia here?"

"It makes sense," Veeksha said. "The lines and animals could be markers of some kind to indicate where it is. One of the Nasca theories is that the lines point to underground springs or aqueducts."

"Didn't you say that one of the theories was that the Nasca lines were racetracks?" Kyle asked. "That's funny. Kind of like a NASCAR of the ancients. Makes sense. Nasca. NASCAR." He grinned.

"Very funny, Kyle," Susie frowned.

"What's NASCAR?" Veeksha asked.

"Car races in America," Susie answered. "He's trying to make a pun. Not a very good one, really."

"Well, we have to do something while Savakala clucks and mumbles," said Kyle.

Savakala's eyes popped open suddenly and she glared at the children. "What you can do is nothing! Most importantly, you can stop speaking. Either be quiet or go away."

Joromwor lumbered over to the children and shooed them off.

Kyle rolled his eyes and the children moved into the white beak of the condor. The drawing looked like it was hundreds of feet across. It was drawn from a single line, like a sharply curving path that wound back around itself.

"I think I'll walk around the whole condor and see how long it takes," Kyle stated.

"I'll go with," Susie agreed.

"Me, too," said Veeksha. "The riddle did say they soared underfoot."

The children started down the line of the condor's beak. They were soon walking back and forth along the bird's right wing feathers, then through the leg and claw and then into the tail. Other lines seemed to interrupt the condor's tail, and the kids took a while to decide which path to follow. Soon, though, they were back on track and going through the opposite claws and then the left wing. They stopped frequently to look at interesting rocks. About thirty minutes after starting their little trek, they approached the tip of the beak and the end of their walk.

Kyle, walking in front, could see that Savakala was still chanting. It didn't look like she had accomplished anything.

"Hey!" Veeksha cried from the rear of their little procession. "Look!"

She pointed at the path behind them. It looked like dew was forming on some of the rocks and sand. As they watched, the dewdrops increased in number and size until they started to pool together in small puddles. The puddles flowed together into pools, and the pools reached out to form a stream in the condor's lines. The stream trickled beneath Veeksha and Susie's feet and rushed up to stop right in front of Kyle.

"It's filling all of the condor!" said Susie. Across the desert, water was filling the animal design. "But it's stopping at you, Kyle. Quick! Run to the tip of the beak!"

Kyle sprinted the last dozen yards. When he leapt out of the line, the stream flowing behind him rushed around the corner and connected with the rest of the water. A single long water line glinted in the afternoon sun, like a condor-shaped moat.

"I told you I would devise a way to summon the water," Savakala bragged, standing up.

"You?" Veeksha scoffed as she and Susie ran up. "It wasn't you. It was Kyle. The water followed him around the path."

"How did you know that would work?" Susie asked Kyle.

Kyle shrugged. "I didn't. I just wanted to see how long it took to walk around the condor."

"Whoever summoned it," said Bozabrozy, stepping

148

forward, "the water is here. But it doesn't seem to be aquosia."

"How can you tell?"

"You will know aquosia when you see it."

"It sure doesn't act like normal water," Susie said. "Look over there. It's swirling and splashing and bubbling."

"You have a sharp eye," Savakala said. "This isn't aquosia or normal water. It is a water elemental."

CHAPTER 27

Everywhere the water splashed and bubbled and foamed. The Zurans and children watched as frothy waves collided at the point of the beak. The water blew upward like a geyser, showering them all in a cool spray.

"How can I help you?" asked a gurgling voice from inside the geyser.

Savakala pushed Kyle out of the way and stood before the elemental. "I have come for the aquosia!"

"It has been a long time since a Zuran has visited me," the water elemental said, "and I was curious. But it was not you who won the race. It was he." A squirt of water spurted out to hit Kyle right in the face.

"Hey!"

"He is merely a boy," Savakala said with a frown. "I am Savakala, sky minister and envoy of Emperor Exeverius. You will deal with me."

The geyser shot up into the sky another fifty feet, falling back into the moat with a raucous splashing. "You have not bound me, Zuran. I am free, and I will not transact with you."

"That is preposterous!"

The elemental shot out a powerful jet of water that hit Savakala in the chest and sent her sprawling. Joromwor rushed over to help her rise.

"I never did like those feathered Zurans," the water gurgled. "They think they're so much better than everyone else because they can fly. Step forward, boy."

Kyle tentatively scooted a little nearer to the elemental.

"Um…my name is Kyle Morgan."

"Closer! Don't fear the spray."

Kyle moved to within a few feet of the geyser. A fine mist wafted around him and heavier drops showered on him from above.

"How can I help you?" the water elemental asked.

"Actually, we really do need aquosia, if you have any. My friend, Jürgen, has been turned to stone by geopsium and aquosia is the only thing that can make him normal again."

"How can I help you?" it asked again, but the geyser suddenly stopped spurting, the water stopped falling, and the moat settled down to a tranquil pool.

Veeksha stepped up into the mud beside Kyle. "That's not what I expected to happen," she said.

"Did you insult it or something?" Susie asked.

"No, I just asked it for the aquosia."

"That's what Savakala did and she got blasted." Veeksha looked back at the soaked uburu. "I guess you were lucky."

Kyle clenched his fists at his sides. "Great! Now we'll never get the aquosia."

"Wait!" said Bozabrozy, looking into the pool. "There! There is aquosia in the water."

The children peered into the clear water. One bit of it looked purer. Kyle didn't know how to explain it. The best he could do was: "Yeah, I see it. It looks more…watery."

"It's really strange," Susie said.

"Let's get it!" Kyle reached into the water and grabbed the aquosia. It flowed through his fingers.

Veeksha laughed. "I knew no one else had thought it through. We're going on a quest to collect magic water and nobody brings anything to hold it in. Well, I did!" Veeksha pulled a mug from beneath her jacket and handed it to Kyle. "I got it from Barathrina."

"Thanks, Veeksha! You really think ahead." He turned back to the pool and dipped the mug into the water. The aquosia flowed away from it. Kyle tried to catch it but it always flowed out of the mug. "I can't catch it!"

"Give me that!" said Savakala, still dripping wet. She yanked the mug from Kyle's hand and tried to scoop up the aquosia. She, too, failed. "What is this trickery? Bozabrozy, you are the aquamagus, what is wrong here?"

Bozabrozy took the mug from Savakala and fruitlessly tried to catch the aquosia. "It seems the water elemental does not want us to have it."

"So, it's teasing us?" Savakala seethed. "Curse that elemental to the depths of the bottomless skies! Capricious! It's just as I've said. The only thing water elementals enjoy more than babbling is tantalizing!"

"But, the water is still here and the aquosia stays in this area," Veeksha noted. "It could flow away and make us chase it."

"Yes, as I said. Caprice and tantalization. Foul, bedeviling elemental!"

Veeksha shook her head. "No, I don't think so. I just think we aren't doing it right."

"What do you mean, Veeksha?" Susie asked.

"The last thing that the water elemental said was 'How can I help you?' But, it didn't get an answer before it collapsed. I think it's still waiting for an answer."

Kyle had a flash of insight. "Another riddle?"

"Yes, why not?" Veeksha said. "Remember what you told me about the stone elemental? You said that it repeated 'What do I want?' a couple times. Then Jürgen gave it the fossils. It was like a simple riddle with a hard answer. I think that the water elemental's 'How can I help you?' is another riddle like that one."

Susie nodded. "The stone elemental wanted something in return for the geopsium. What would a water elemental want?"

"The stone elemental wanted more stone," Kyle said. "Maybe this one wants more water?"

"I don't think so," said Veeksha. "They didn't ask the same question so the answer wouldn't be the same. We have to examine the water elemental's question."

"'How can I help you?'" Kyle quoted. "It can help us by giving us the aquosia."

"I don't think it's that easy," Bozabrozy said. "I doubt that the answer to the riddle is the substance we desire."

"It can help us by unpetrifying Jürgen?" Susie suggested.

"Would the water elemental be expecting an answer that is specific to our quest?" Veeksha asked. "Maybe the question is more generic."

"What do you mean?" Susie said.

"Maybe it's not asking how it can help us, specifically. Maybe it's asking how water can help."

"It can turn a desert into an oasis!" Susie chirped, and took the mug to catch the aquosia. It continued to elude her. "Drat. That's not right. It can make plants grow or help wash cars or fill balloons or make fountains or help salmon spawn." With each guess she tried to scoop up the magic water but each attempt failed.

"Hey!" Kyle said, looking around. "We're in a desert!"

"Your powers of observation are astounding," Savakala scoffed.

Kyle glared at the Zuran. "No, we're missing the point. We're in the middle of a desert. How can water help us in the desert? By making us not thirsty!"

Veeksha's eyes widened and she smiled. "Yes! That must be it."

Susie pushed the mug back in the water and said, "You can help us when we drink you!" The aquosia still did not cooperate.

Everyone frowned.

"Why isn't it working?" Susie asked.

Kyle suddenly realized what had to be done. "The only way we can get the aquosia is by drinking it."

Veeksha slapped her forehead. "Brilliant! Why didn't I think of that?"

"I'm going to drink you!" said Susie. She thrust the mug into the water again, but to no avail.

"No," said Kyle, kneeling beside her. "Someone has to drink the aquosia from the pool."

Veeksha put a hand on Kyle's shoulder as he bent down. "Wait, Kyle! Jürgen turned into stone when he touched the geopsium. What if you turn into water? You'll seep away into the ground."

Kyle leaned back, realizing she had a great point. At least turning into stone left a statue of you behind. A statue that could be picked up and moved and stored. Getting turned into water was a thousand times worse. Kyle didn't want to just wash away.

He looked up at Bozabrozy. "Is that true? Will I turn into water?"

Savakala answered. "It is possible. However, the only reason that your friend absorbed the geopsium is because he is a natural-born geomancer, able to be one with the rock. At his most basic level he is attuned to stone, but his first encounter with geopsium overwhelmed him."

"Well, what if I'm a…water-mancer?"

"Aquamancer. That is…unlikely," Savakala said. "Even if you are, aquosia is much more forgiving than geopsium. Aquosia heals and soothes. It is pure water, and your body already has much water in it."

"What does that mean?"

"Even if you are an aquamancer, it is not likely that you will liquefy. Perhaps."

Kyle frowned. "Great. Just great."

"It's the only way to save Jürgen," Bozabrozy reminded him. "And, often, risks must be taken for important tasks."

"Yeah, I know." Kyle paused, staring down at the

aquosia. It hovered in the water so near and tantalizing. All he had to do was bend over and sip from it. If he did it he could save Jürgen.

"You can do it, Kyle," Susie said. "You'll be okay. And you'll save Jürgen. You'll be a hero!"

Kyle laughed. "I never really wanted to be a hero."

"You don't have to do it," Veeksha cautioned. "It's dangerous. You could die. Is it really worth it? We can get help for Jürgen from doctors and scientists. Or geologists, I guess."

"The only sure way to save Jürgen is with aquosia," Savakala stated flatly. "Nothing your smart little friend here says can change that."

Kyle nodded, but his hands shook has he leaned over. He put his lips to the surface of the water and watched as the aquosia flowed right to his mouth. He drank.

CHAPTER 28

The aquosia tasted like nothing Kyle had ever experienced before. The quintessence touched his lips, making them tingle. Then it flowed into his mouth, and his tongue shivered at the sweet coolness. He let it pool in his mouth and slide down his throat. The pleasantly cool feeling spread out through his body as the aquosia flowed through him. His entire body felt cool in the desert sun. He had never been so refreshed.

As he drank, the water elemental spoke one last time:

Fires thrust it up from the sea
Ringed by watchful faces, tall and stony
Follow the path of the birdman's test
Reach for the sky from the lofty nest

"Another riddle!" said Susie, clapping her hands in delight.

"Are you all right, Kyle?" Veeksha asked.

He turned to look at his friends. Everyone and everything appeared to have a faint wavy blue tinge, like he was looking at them underwater with the waves casting strange shadows.

He jumped up. "I feel…great!"

"You don't feel like you're going to wash away?"

"Nope! I feel very cool and refreshed. It's like I just jumped into a cold stream after walking through the desert."

"Good," Bozabrozy said. "We'd better get you back up

to the ship before anything unfortunate happens."

"Unfortunate? But he looks okay and feels okay."

"We don't know how long that will last. Also, if you want to save Jürgen, we need to get back up there quickly."

"We must first solve the new riddle," Savakala stated.

"We don't have time to figure it out here and now," Bozabrozy said. "We must get Kyle to the ship to heal his friend. We can work on the riddle later."

"Yes, of course. Let us return to the ship." Savakala said, retrieved her cloak, and led the way back to the ship. Veeksha lingered behind, using the mug to collect some of the water as it seeped away into the ground. She also wrote something in the mud.

"I don't understand why we need to hurry," Kyle said as they neared the Windrunner hovering a hundred feet above the desert.

Savakala rolled her eyes. "You drank the aquosia. That usually means its magic will be used on you, healing any ills you may have." She saw Veeksha loitering in the mud. "Quickly, girl! Back up to the ship." She hurried to catch up.

"But I'm not sick," Kyle objected.

"Even if you are not sick, the aquosia will make you feel better. You said it yourself. You feel invigorated, do you not? Better than you have ever felt before?"

"Yes!"

"That's what quintessence does to you," Bozabrozy interjected. "All the different kinds of quintessence, when used or touched, imbue feelings of exultation and power. It does not last forever, however."

"But I don't want this feeling to end!" Kyle complained.

Savakala placed a hand on his shoulder. "Calm yourself, boy. This is your first taste of aquosia. You may enjoy this euphoria, but steel yourself against its impending departure."

Kyle stepped on to the platform with the others, and the crew above cranked a windlass to bring them back up into the ship. Kyle did not want the exhilaration of the aquosia to go away. How could he keep it?

They made their way to the hold and the statue of Jürgen.

"How does Kyle unpetrify Jürgen?" Susie asked.

"Place your hands on him and imagine him once again as flesh," Savakala instructed.

"That's it?" Kyle asked. "Nothing to chant? No magic words?"

"No. If you have the power to heal him, only your will is required."

"What do you mean, if I have the power to heal him? You said this would work."

"If we had brought the aquosia back in a container and poured it over Jürgen, it most definitely would have worked," Savakala said. "However, the aquosia is within you now, and you must command it."

"Just by imagining it?"

"Imagination is a powerful ally," Savakala nodded. "With it, and a bit of quintessence, great deeds can be done. You must concentrate hard on the image in your mind. Do not lose heart if nothing happens immediately. It may take a while to convince the aquosia to act."

Kyle moved up to Jürgen and put his hands on the statue's shoulders. In his mind, he pictured Jürgen as his normal, pudgy self.

CHAPTER 29

Susie pointed at Kyle. "There's dew in your hair!"

Indeed there was. Drops of water formed on his hair and clothes, and soon it streamed down his arms and through his hands and onto the Jürgen statue. A thin sheet of water spread over it, melting away the statue's stone and revealing Jürgen's skin beneath. Within a few seconds, Jürgen stumbled back against the bulkhead, gasping and drenched.

"Jürgen!" Kyle exclaimed, glad to see his friend back to normal. He began wringing the water out of his sleeves.

"Wow!" said the German boy, wiping water from his face. "I couldn't move! I've been stuck down here forever! Hey, are you a bird Zuran?" He stared at Savakala.

"I am Savakala, leader of this quest, and an uburu," the aeromagus replied and then turned to Bozabrozy. "Tell the captain to sail immediately."

"Where are we going?"

"We were seen by many people on our way here," Savakala said. "Until we can decipher the new riddle and determine our next destination, we must keep moving lest Rakanian's minions find us."

Veeksha beamed. "Oh, I've already figured out the new riddle."

Bozabrozy looked at the little girl. "So quickly?"

"A new riddle?" Jürgen shook his head. "What's going on? Where are? What's happened?"

"Silence, boy," Savakala ordered. "What is the answer to the riddle, Veeksha?"

"The next destination is Easter Island," Veeksha said.

"Who are you?" Jürgen asked her.

"Oh, hi," the Indian girl smiled. "I'm Veeksha Das. So nice to meet you."

"I'm Jürgen Schm-"

"Enough!" Savakala interrupted. "Where is this Easter Island?"

"Tell Machadaro to sail straight out to sea," Veeksha said. "I'll show him the place on my KnowPad."

Savakala nodded to Bozabrozy, who rushed up to the main deck. "You truly are a font of knowledge, little one. Come with me to my cabin and explain how you solved the riddle."

"Isn't any one going to tell me what's going on?" Jürgen pleaded as the uburu and the girls left.

"I'll tell you while we dry ourselves off," Kyle offered as everyone else left.

In Savakala's cabin, Veeksha explained to the aeromancer and Susie how she had determined the answer to the new riddle.

"The first two lines," Veeksha said, "were enough to identify the location. 'Fires thrust it up from the sea' is an obvious description of an island formed by volcanic activity. But there are thousands of islands like that around the world."

"And you know all of them?" Savakala asked.

"Of course not. But the second line, 'ringed by watchful faces, tall and stony,' must refer to Easter Island. It has lots of ancient monuments, huge stone-carved faces, along its coast. Easter Island is very famous for its cultural heritage and archeology."

"Why do you know so much about these places, Veeksha?" Susie asked.

"I read a lot."

"And what do the last two lines mean?" Savakala asked.

Veeksha turned back to her KnowPad, scanning the

encyclopedia entry for Easter Island. "'Follow the path of the birdman's test' probably refers to the cult of the birdman. It was some kind of government or religion in ancient times. Every year, the people chose a new leader, called the birdman, by sending young men on a test. They had to swim through shark-infested waters to a nearby islet to find the first egg of the season. The one who did earned the right to rule the island for the next year."

"It was a test of stamina and resolve, then," Savakala mused. "They were obviously wise people to venerate birds for the kingship."

"It sounds more like luck to me," Susie said. "Escaping sharks and finding an egg? It's just like hunting for Easter eggs. It's pretty much the lucky ones who find the most. I wonder if that's where they got the name for the island. Easter Island because they hunted for eggs?"

Veeksha smiled. "No. It was named Easter Island because it was discovered on Easter day in 1722 by a Dutch explorer named Jacob Roggeveen."

"Wait," Susie said. "How can someone discover an island that already has people on it? The people who lived there must have discovered it long before he got there."

"That's a good point," Veeksha agreed.

"Back to the riddle," Savakala said. "It seems obvious enough what the last two lines mean. The third line means we must go to this birdman islet. The last line means we must ask for the aethrial from a high nest."

"Don't forget," Veeksha warned, "that the stone and water elemental also had their own riddles. The stone elemental asked 'What do I want?' and the water elemental asked 'How can I help you?'"

"You think that the next elemental will do the same thing?" Susie said.

"It's a pattern. Do elementals on Zura ask questions before giving away their quintessence?"

Savakala breathed in deeply. "Not all elementals have

quintessence to give away. They are chaotic and unpredictable beings. Normally, you cannot guess how one will act. They are wild creatures that one must deal with carefully and on an individual basis."

"That doesn't sound like the elementals we've met," Susie said. "Ours have been pretty cooperative."

"Elementals on Earth must be different from those on Zura," Veeksha said.

"It would seem so, yes," Savakala agreed. "You are a very wise girl, Veeksha."

"We all know some stuff," Susie said. "I figured out the first riddle."

"So did I," Veeksha said. "And I solved the second and now the third!"

"Well, you didn't give me a chance to try," Susie griped.

"Now, now, children," Savakala held up her hands. "This is not a competition. We are all in this quest together. We all have contributions to make."

"I'll just keep solving the riddles," Veeksha said. "I bet I get them all."

"Next time give the rest of us a chance," Susie pouted.

"So, Veeksha," Savakala asked. "What is this Easter Island?"

"It's an island all alone in the Pacific Ocean. Very remote. More than a thousand miles from anywhere. Well, actually, there are a few islets along the coast."

"Are there many people there? Is your army there?"

"No, I don't think so. Not many people there at all."

"How many is not many?"

"I'm not sure. I can look, though." She checked her computer. "According to this, there are about four thousand inhabitants. Plus however many tourists happen to be there."

"Tourists?"

"The people that go there to see the monoliths. There are hundreds of them."

"Hundreds of tourists?"

"No hundreds of monoliths. Giant stone carvings of faces. Here, I'll show you one." Veeksha clicked on a picture of one of the monoliths to enlarge it, and then showed the Zuran. "They're called moai."

Savakala leapt back with a shriek, then struck out and knocked the KnowPad to the floor. Her feathers ruffled wildly. "What are those doing here?"

CHAPTER 30

Susie stood up. "Why did you do that?"

Savakala stared at the fallen computer. "Did you say moai? The island is populated with hundreds of moai?" She nearly spat out the words.

Veeksha picked up the KnowPad and examined it for damage. "Yes. What's the matter? Don't you like them?"

Savakala regained some of her composure and pulled her wings back under her cloak. "Thank you for explaining the riddle to me. I must tell Machadaro."

"Okay," Veeksha said. "I'll show him the map so he can chart a course."

Savakala spun around as she neared the door. "No! I must confer with him first. Speak of these monoliths to no one else, and do not show the pictures to anyone. Moai are perilous and deceitful. I will return." She opened the door, but then stopped. She turned and held out a demanding hand. "Give me the tablet."

Veeksha complied and Savakala tossed it up on a high shelf. "Now, out!" She roughly ushered the girls out of the room and locked it behind her before rushing off toward the prow. Kyle and Jürgen had to jump out of the way to avoid her in the passageway.

"What's her problem?" Kyle asked. Both he and Jürgen were much dryer.

Veeksha shrugged. "She got upset about the statues on Easter Island. She kicked us out of her room."

"Then let's go back to our cabin," Kyle suggested.

"I wonder why she doesn't like the statues," Jürgen said, when they flopped down in their cots. "They're just big stone faces, right?"

"Yes. They're called moai."

"Moy?"

"No. It's pronounced 'mo-eye'. The people who lived there carved them, many hundreds of years ago. Nobody knows for sure what they were for. They cut them out of the slopes of the volcano and then stood them on the coast."

"So now we're going to Easter Island? Cool."

"These riddles are sending us all over the world," Kyle said. "South Dakota, Peru, the Pacific Ocean."

"It's very exciting!" Susie agreed. "I wonder where the last quintessence will be?"

Kyle, Susie, and Veeksha told Jürgen everything that had happened since he was turned to stone. He had been aware only of what he had heard in the hold. He was surprised that the helicopters had actually shot at the Windrunner.

"I wondered what all that shooting was. Didn't they know we were here? They could have killed us!"

"That's what Bannecker said when he tried to kidnap us," Susie said. "He said they couldn't risk another attack while we were still on the ship."

"Machadaro ripped up Bannecker twice," Jürgen said. "I wonder how he survived."

"You think he's still alive?" Kyle asked.

"He had a parachute," Susie said.

"What was it like, being a stone statue?" Veeksha asked Jürgen.

Jürgen smiled. "At first I couldn't see or hear or feel anything and I couldn't move. It was like being all tied up underwater in the dark. But after a while I started to see and hear things a little."

"You could? Why didn't you tell us you were okay?"

"Oh, I couldn't talk. I tried, but I couldn't. And I could

165

only barely move the tips of my fingers. I didn't even know I could do that at first. But for days I had nothing else to do. So I tried and it worked!"

"Do you think you could have walked around eventually?"

"Oh, yeah! It got easier the more I tried. Being made of stone is like...like...being powerful, I guess. Even though I couldn't move, I felt really strong and indestructible. I still do now."

"I know what you mean," Kyle agreed. "I drank the aquosia and it feels amazing. I feel like nothing can stop me."

"I heard the Zurans say I was a geomancer," Jürgen said. "I guess you are one, also."

"No, I'm an aquamancer. It's the aquosian version of a geomancer."

"Oh. Well, I sure like the geopsium."

"It can't be as good as the aquosia."

"It's better!"

"I don't think we'll find out unless we find more of each and try it out," Kyle said.

"Savakala said that elemancers weren't common," Veeksha mused. "But the first two people they found turn out to be an aquamancer and a geomancer."

"So?" Jürgen asked.

"What if it's not a coincidence?" Veeksha said. "What if they knew you were elemancers and that's why Bozabrozy came to you?"

"I thought he just picked the first cabin he found," Kyle shrugged.

"They must have known what you are."

"How could they know that?" Susie asked. "Do they have a mancer-detector?"

"Or they could have been watching you," Veeksha said. "Did you hear the water elemental say that it's been a long time since he'd seen a Zuran? They must have been here before. Bozabrozy said that Rakanian has been on Earth for a while. Maybe others have as well. And, if they have, they could have been spying on you."

"But," Susie said, "you're forgetting that Savakala can see the future. Maybe her visions led her to Kyle and Jürgen."

"I guess that could be," Veeksha said. "There's something I don't like about Savakala."

"I don't think anyone likes her," Kyle said. "Except Joromwor."

"She's too bossy," Susie said.

"Machadaro isn't much better," Kyle noted. "He likes to tear people apart."

Veeksha defended the big rasha. "Only when he's attacked! Remember that Bannecker and his agents shot first."

"Oooh, does someone have a crush on the tiger-man?" teased Jürgen.

"No. I just think he's defending himself."

"He could at least try to talk first," Kyle said.

"Too bad we can't talk to anyone. It would be nice to let my parents know I'm okay," Susie said, looking out the porthole. "Hey, why are we sailing up into the mountains?"

The other kids joined her at the porthole. Mountains loomed around the Windrunner.

"This isn't right," Veeksha said.

CHAPTER 31

The kids ran to the captain's deck. "Why aren't we going out to sea?" Veeksha asked Machadaro. "Easter Island is west, not east."

The rasha grinned, baring his sharp teeth. "Many will have seen us visit the Nasca lines. The man who tried to take you from the ship will hear of it. We must use more misdirection."

"You think Bannecker is still alive?" Kyle asked.

"That is his name? He clearly has a supply of aquosia, probably a gift from Rakanian. They used it to save his life before. They will do so again." Machadaro peered through his skyglass at the terrain ahead. "Next time I will rip off his head to make sure he can't be healed."

Susie cringed. "Do you really have to do that? It's not very nice."

"Yes, I really have to do that."

"But," Kyle said, "you're trying to avoid meeting him again by heading in the wrong direction, so some Peruvians will see us fly up into the Andes and report it. Then we'll turn around and sneak through some remote valleys and out to sea. That's your plan, right?"

Machadaro nodded. "Indeed."

"Why is Savakala scared of the monuments on Easter Island?" Susie asked.

Machadaro lowered the skyglass and growled, baring his teeth. "I don't have time to explain that. I must find a hidden course to get us out to sea unnoticed. Leave me!"

The children recoiled, startled by the rasha's angry response. They didn't wait to be told a second time.

"What got into him?" Susie asked.

"Those Easter Island statues really scare the Zurans," Jürgen said. He glanced back at the captain, marveling at his great size and dramatic stripes. "I wouldn't think that a tiger-man could be scared."

"Let's ask Bozabrozy about them."

The children found Bozabrozy at the stern of the ship, talking to Joromwor.

"Hello," the rascan said as they walked up. "How does it feel to be back to normal, Jürgen?"

"Different," Jürgen admitted. "Even though I'm not a statue any more I still feel stiff. But it's not a bad stiff. It's more like I feel strong and unbreakable."

"Geopsium has that effect," said Joromwor. "You will feel like that until the geopsium is gone."

"What?" Jürgen was surprised. "What do you mean, gone? It's going to go away? I don't want it to go away!"

Bozabrozy swished his ringed tail. "Quintessence does not last forever. Every time it is used to empower some magic, it diminishes."

Jürgen smiled. "I can use it to do magic? What kind of magic?"

"As an elemancer," Bozabrozy explained, "you can do wondrous things. With the right training and practice, you can do much more than a simple geopsium artifact can do."

"Can you teach me?"

"I know little about geopsium."

"Will you teach me?" Jürgen asked Joromwor excitedly.

The urgra laughed at the boy's impatience. "The elements have him."

"It is that way with all who suddenly feel the power of quintessence," Bozabrozy agreed.

Jürgen pressed on. "Will you teach me how to use it?"

"No."

Jürgen frowned. "Why not?"

"I do not wish to," Joromwor said with a scowl.

Kyle asked Bozabrozy, "Does that mean you won't teach me magic, either?"

"If I had time, yes, I could teach you," said the rascan. "It is a long and difficult process to learn magic. Not to mention dangerous. If you make a mistake you can become a thrope."

"But Kyle cured Jürgen almost instantly," Susie said.

"Yes, yes, he did. And that was quite amazing. However, aquosia is not a dumb liquid. It sensed that Jürgen was petrified and knew what had to be done. Aquosia is the quintessence of soothing and healing. It is one thing to do something obvious and aligned with an element's primal nature. It is another thing entirely to make it do something unexpected and unlikely."

"Like melt glass or freeze a door," Kyle said, remembering the magic items Bozabrozy had used back at the cabin in South Dakota.

"What can geopsium let me do?" Jürgen asked.

"It can make you impenetrable and give you power over stone," Joromwor said.

Jürgen jumped up. "Hey! Maybe I could use it to control the moai! They're made of stone."

Joromwor suddenly froze and stared at the German boy. "The what?"

"The moai on Easter Island," Jürgen repeated. "A moai is a big stone statue of a face."

The urgra grunted in surprise. "One of those resides on this Easter Island?"

"Not one," Veeksha said. "Hundreds."

"Thunder and storms!" Joromwor grunted. "This is dire news."

"Why? What's wrong with them?" Kyle asked.

"They're evil stone elementals," Joromwor said. "They spread lies, foment rebellion, and attack the empire."

"But you have this skyship," Jürgen said. "You can attack them from way high up."

Joromwor ignored the boy, directing his comments to Bozabrozy and shaking his heavy head in disappointment. "An entire island full of them? And we seek quintessence there? This ship cannot stand against hundreds of moai."

Kyle watched the huge urgra, that towering mass of fur and muscle, fang and claw. He didn't think anything could scare such a ferocious beast. And the moai had a similar effect on Machadaro and even Savakala, a powerful aeromagus who could throw lightning bolts and summon hurricanes.

"Why is everyone so afraid of them? Can't Savakala destroy them with lightning?"

"They are stone elementals," Bozabrozy repeated. "Savakala is an aeromagus. Moai are one of the few things that ruffle her feathers. The elements of stone and sky are diametrically opposed."

"Zura was created when sky and stone clashed during the Cataclasm," Joromwor said. "Whenever opposed elements battle the result is chaos and tumult."

"Moai are powerful elementals," the rascan said, "and none too friendly."

"None too friendly?" Joromwor growled. "They are furious and belligerent! I won't set foot on an island of moai. The Imperial Legions fought them at the Gates of Tanniser. It was only by the inexorable might and dreadful sacrifice of the Legions that we defeated them." He fingered the stone hanging from the leather thong around his neck. "I lost many friends that day, and I wear this moai shard so that I shall never forget."

"The Zuran moai might be terribly dangerous," Veeksha said, "but Earth moai are just statues. They don't do anything. In fact, most of them are toppled and lying face down in the dirt."

"Trickery!" Joromwor said. "It's a trap. We should avoid

the place."

"We must go there if we want the last two quintessences."

"We'll never survive."

"Savakala will find a way," Bozabrozy insisted, but Kyle thought he could see doubt and worry on the rascan's face.

For hours the Windrunner flew through the western valleys of the Andes. Using her KnowPad, once again loaned to her by Savakala, Veeksha showed the captain maps of South America, Easter Island, and the two thousand miles of empty Pacific Ocean between them. He shook his head back and forth.

"This will be a difficult leg of the journey," the skyship captain said. "Just a small mistake to the left or the right and we'll miss such a tiny island."

"But, you can use the compass," Veeksha suggested.

"Yes, it will help us. But it is not precise enough. I am not familiar with your world nor the magic of your compass."

"Can't you navigate by the stars?"

The rasha paused. "How would I do that?"

"You find a star over your destination and follow it."

"Your ships can do that?" Machadaro mused. "That is a powerful talent. The stars tell us nothing in Zura. They are never in the same place. Following a star does not help us find anything."

"Your geodex can help you find islands, right?"

"We need a stone fragment from the island to use the geodex. It is useless to us without a fragment of Easter Island."

"What if you had a piece of a moai?" Veeksha said. "They're made of stone, aren't they? And they're on Easter Island."

Machadaro spun around. "Do you have a piece?"

"No," Veeksha said, and Machadaro's face fell. "But Joromwor has a piece of a Zuran moai. Maybe Earth moai

172

and Zuran moai are close enough that it will work."

Machadaro's tail twitched as he looked up at the sky, thinking. Then he rushed past her, shouting, "They are!"

Joromwor, who was operating the rudder sail, watched as the captain approached the stern.

"Do you have a moai fragment?" Machadaro demanded without preamble.

"Aye, that I do," said the urgra, fingering the amulet around his neck. "And hard won it was. The blood of the Legion paid for this shard."

Machadaro held out his hand. "Give it to me."

The urgra bristled and straightened, shaking his head. "I think not."

"I won't have insubordination on my ship. I command you to give it me!" the captain repeated. Two mumba sailors in the rigging paused to watch.

"No," Joromwor said quietly, his eyes narrowing. "This shard is mine. It's the recompense I claimed for my lost brothers of the Legion. It was won by fang and claw and blade. That's the only way you will take it from me."

Machadaro stared menacingly at the urgra. Both Zurans bared their fangs.

"So be it," Machadaro said eagerly and leapt at Joromwor's throat.

Chapter 32

The roars of the two Zurans echoed across the Andean canyons through which the Windrunner sailed. Flocks of birds leapt from their perches at the mighty screams of battle. Veeksha watched in horror as fang and claw ripped and bit and tore.

Mumba sailors gathered in the rigging to watch the battle, more intent on the fate of their captain than tending the ship. Canar legionaries soon gathered as well, barking support for their commander.

Machadaro's claws dug deep into Joromwor's shoulder and he pulled close to the urgra, trying to sink his long fangs into his throat. Joromwor tumbled onto his back and pushed the captain over his head. Already bleeding from numerous wounds, the two warriors leapt to their feet and sprang at each other again. More sailors gathered, and canar legionaries poured from below decks.

Joromwor tossed the captain onto the main deck and rushed down the stairs after him.

The ruddersail waved unattended and the Windrunner's starboard nethermast scraped a cliff. The ship lurched, sending everyone tumbling along the deck. Two mumbas rushed to the rudder windlass to prevent a wreck.

Kyle ran out from his cabin as Joromwor leapt onto the main deck. Machadaro immediately sprang at the urgra, knocking him into the stern castle. Kyle scrambled away from the towering combatants just in time. They struggled and tore with bestial fury. Fur and blood flew through the air. The sailors and soldiers hissed and screamed and barked and yelped, cheering for the captain or the legate.

Machadaro and Joromwor jumped apart and circled each other in the middle of the main deck.

"Give me that shard," Machadaro demanded.

The urgra growled ferociously. "This ship needs a new captain."

Machadaro roared, slashing out with his claws.

Susie and Jürgen ran out to join Kyle. "What's going on?"

"Mutiny!" Kyle shouted over the yells of the crew and the roars of the fighters.

The commotion attracted Savakala, who stepped out from the stern castle. "Cast them to the bottomless skies for the fools that they are!" she cursed.

"Stop them, Savakala!" Veeksha screamed.

"That I shall," the uburu said. She bore the Staff of the Sky, and it spoke with thunder and lightning that struck both fighters. They flew across the deck and slammed heavily into the forecastle. Even that did not temper their fury, for they jumped at each other again.

"Stop this!" Savakala screeched, and sent a thicker lightning bolt at Machadaro. It struck him in the shoulder and spun him around like a top. He collapsed in a heap. Joromwor pounced on him and pulled his head back. He roared as he lowered his fangs to the captain's throat.

"Joromwor!" Savakala screamed. The shrill call hurt Kyle's ears.

The urgra stopped and looked up at the uburu. "You are an Imperial Legate!" she shouted. "You will obey! Release him!"

Joromwor scowled and looked at the defenseless rasha. "Let me finish this!"

"No! He has a task to perform, as do you!"

Disgusted, Joromwor pushed Machadaro's face roughly to the deck and then stood up. "As I said when we embarked, no rogue pirate should be giving orders to the Legion!" The canar legionaries yipped in agreement.

"You don't take orders from him," Savakala said. "You take orders from me. I command at the behest of the emperor. He chose the best skyship captain for this venture. Until our quest is complete, Machadaro remains captain. Is that clear?"

Joromwor stood over the rasha. The legionaries waited expectantly to see what the massive urgra would do.

Savakala stepped closer, waving her staff under Joromwor's snout. "Is that clear?"

"Machadaro remains captain," Joromwor acquiesced, wiping blood from his eyes. "Until our quest is complete and I slake my vengeance with his blood."

"Good." Savakala straightened up and called out to the rest of the soldiers. "And that goes for the rest of you scurvy dogs! Begone! Disperse!" The canars turned away. "Joromwor, get back to the ruddersail."

"Aye, Savakala." Joromwor bowed slightly and moved off.

"Wait!" called Machadaro, slowly pushing himself up. Blood matted his fur in many places. Smoke drifted from his charred shoulder, and his arm hung limp. His eye patch was gone, torn off in the battle, revealing an empty socket and a terrible scar. He stood and steadied himself, then walked over to Savakala and Joromwor. He held out his hand to the urgra. "Give me the shard."

"No," Joromwor growled, breathing deeply.

"Did you not hear Savakala's command? I am the captain."

"What shard?" Savakala asked.

Machadaro pointed. "His amulet is a moai fragment. We can use it in the geodex to lead us to Easter Island."

Savakala's eyes bulged and she stared at the amulet. "Is that true, Joromwor?"

"Yes, but I won't give it to him."

"He fears the moai," Bozabrozy called down from the poop deck.

Joromwor roared, his teeth bared and dripping with Machadaro's blood. "Fool! A coward imagines more cowardice in others! Speak not of what you do not know, rascan! It is the Legion that bears the brunt when battles rage. We do not shirk our duty. Nor do we blindly cast our lives aside in hopeless endeavors. My small force on this vessel is no match for hundreds of moai."

"Give him the shard," Savakala ordered. "Now."

Joromwor grasped the amulet tightly in his fist and held it there.

Savakala scowled. "It will be returned to you. Without it, we might seek the island for days."

"I do not wish to find the island," Joromwor said.

"That is not your decision to make," Savakala said. "Do you wish to doom our quest?"

"The moai have doomed this quest."

Savakala bristled furiously and shoved her staff against Joromwor's throat. "The moai will not impede our quest. You forget that we have the sky as our ally, while they are confined to an island. We can avoid them easily enough."

"Our skyships proved vulnerable at the Gates of Tanniser."

Savakala took a deep breath. "I grow weary of this. You are a legate bound by the emperor to obey my commands. Relinquish the fragment or I will incinerate you and take it from your ashes."

Joromwor snarled, looking back and forth from the sky minister and the sky captain. Finally, he yanked the amulet, snapping the leather thong, and dropped it into Machadaro's hand.

"I will kill you," he stared into the captain's eyes.

"You have tried that more than once," Machadaro replied, "and failed."

Joromwor stomped back to the stern.

"And you, Captain," said Savakala, "should have come to me first. I would have obtained that stone for you and we could have avoided this entire spectacle."

Machadaro shook his head. "The emperor made me captain of this ship. I must retain authority or morale and discipline will suffer."

"I doubt your battle with Joromwor has improved morale or discipline," Savakala sneered. "This quest is far from over. You will obey me until we see its end."

"And when it is done you and Joromwor will kill me," Machadaro said.

"When the quest is complete, you will take us back to Zura, your freedom won."

"When the quest is complete," said the rasha, "freedom will be the least of our worries."

CHAPTER 33

Later that day the Windrunner sailed silently across a stretch of deserted Peruvian coastline and over the Pacific Ocean. Veeksha stood on the captain's deck with Machadaro. The captain's wounds had been cleaned and bandaged, and he seemed well on the way to recuperation. He had replaced his lost eyepatch.

Veeksha suspected he had taken a healing potion. "I thought there wasn't any more aquosia on the ship, Captain."

"Perhaps."

"I thought everyone had to give her all their magic? It's the emperor's law."

He winked at her. "You will find that some do not obey."

"Why don't you use a potion to heal your eye?" Veeksha asked.

After a moment's pause the captain replied, "I lost it in battle with a dire elemental. Such wounds cannot be healed, even with aquosia."

"That's too bad."

"I have grown accustomed to it."

Veeksha changed the subject. "How long until we reach Easter Island?"

"By your maps, if we don't run into foul weather, we should sight it in the morning the day after tomorrow."

Veeksha looked at the binnacle. Joromwor's moai shard rested in the geodex, the pointer indicating a straight and sure course to Easter Island. "It is most auspicious that the moai on Zura and the moai here are similar enough to work in the geodex."

Machadaro curled his tail around his leg. "Yes," he grunted.

"Will Joromwor really try to kill you when the quest is finished?"

"If not before."

"Are you really a pirate?"

"Indeed."

"Why are you captain of an imperial ship?"

Machadaro sighed. "That is a tale long enough to fill more than one book."

Veeksha smiled as she stood beside the towering rasha, watching the last of the sunset. "I think we have a lot of time."

Machadaro squinted in the sparkling light. "You will know the story one day. But today is not that day."

"What about tomorrow?"

"Tomorrow is not that day, either," Machadaro said with a grin as he looked down at the Indian girl. "You ask a lot of questions."

"My father says to never stop asking questions. He says knowledge is like a flame and facts are the wood. Only by asking questions, or burning the wood, can you find the secrets within. With enough flames you have a fire, and fire is wisdom. The flames go out if you stop asking questions."

"You will be a fine scholar some day."

"Maybe. I think I might want to be a sky captain. Or a pirate."

"There are not many books on a skyship," Machadaro pointed out.

"You don't need books to ask questions. Anyway, libraries and books have old questions. New questions are out there," she said, indicating the horizons, "waiting to be asked."

"And when you've sailed the endless skies and asked your questions, what then?"

"I'll write the answers in a book and put it in a library for others to read." Veeksha laughed, and Machadaro smiled.

The next day, the vast and placid Pacific Ocean extended in every direction, unblemished by any hint of land. The Windrunner's four mainsails billowed in the bluster of the gustboxes. Good weather and smooth sailing spurred the ship on. Even so, the hours passed slowly. Too slowly for Jürgen.

"I had enough waiting when I was a statue. We don't have anything to do on a sailboat. Just sit around and get in the way and watch the water. It's boring. The same in every direction. The only thing different is the clouds."

"So watch the clouds," Kyle suggested. He was thinking about his dad, that he was probably very worried. And angry. At first, Kyle hadn't wanted to go with the Zurans. But, now that he had the aquosia, he was happy he had. The quintessence made him feel powerful. He wondered how powerful he would be if he found more aquosia. Jürgen felt the same way about the geopsium. If things went on like this, the aethrial and pyrophyra would end up in Susie and Veeksha.

"What if Susie and Veeksha are elemancers?" he blurted.

"You mean like us?" Jürgen asked from the railing.

"Yeah." Kyle thought it through. "The first two quests pretty much happened the same way. We found the elemental but it would only give the quintessence to one of us. It wouldn't give it to a Zuran. And when we got it we found out we were elemancers."

"Yeah, that's true."

"So, there are four of us and four elements. Two elements left and two girls. I bet one of them is a fire-mancer and the other one is a sky-mancer."

Jürgen nodded in agreement. "Does that help us?"

Kyle hesitated. "I'm not sure. It must, somehow. It can't help Savakala or Rakanian. They want the quintessence for themselves."

"I still don't understand why Savakala wants it," Jürgen said. "She already has sky quintessence in that staff of hers. And they're always telling us that there's lots of quintessence on Zura."

"Let's ask her," Kyle suggested.

"You think she'll tell us?"

"No, not really. But Machadaro might. They don't like each other."

The boys went to the captain's deck, but found only the first mate, who told them Machadaro was in his cabin. They were soon knocking on the captain's door, and entered when he responded. They found Veeksha and Susie inside.

"Hi," Susie said. "We're telling the captain stories about Earth. Did you know that ancient Egyptian gods had human bodies and animal heads? Reminds you of Zurans, huh?"

"Except that Zurans don't have human bodies, they have Zuran bodies," Jürgen said. "With fur and tails and claws."

"There are lots of myths on Earth about anthropomorphized animals," Veeksha said.

"Anthro what?" Kyle asked.

"Anthropomorphism. It means animals that have human characteristics. You know, like werewolves or minotaurs."

"Or Bugs Bunny," Susie added.

"Susie was saying how lots of Native Americans believe in spirits that take the form of animals. And the Nasca people worshipped animals, otherwise they wouldn't have drawn them in the desert."

"And Veeksha says that there are gods with elephant heads in India," Susie added.

"What's your point?" Jürgen asked.

"Maybe Zurans or something like them visited Earth

long ago. Maybe ancient people thought they were gods and worshipped them."

"Is that true, Machadaro?" Kyle asked. "Did Zurans visit Earth long ago?"

"I'm no historian. I'm just a skyship captain. Ask Savakala about myths and legends."

"Joromwor knows something about myths and legends," Kyle said. "He mentioned something called the Cataclasm. What's that?"

Machadaro grabbed a skin bag hanging from the wall and poured some ale into a mug. "That's what some believe created the world of Zura. I've never put much effort into thinking about the past."

"You think about the future, instead?" Veeksha asked.

The captain drank deeply from his mug. "The past and the future are best left to historians and seers. I concentrate on the present. I can do something about the present."

"You can do something about the future, too," Susie said. "Everything we do can change the future."

Machadaro laughed. "You sound like a Kalakaran."

"What's a Kalakaran?" Susie asked.

"Foes of the empire. They are proud but have too many kings who cannot agree." Machadaro gulped from his mug. "Some of them believe that the future is set and cannot be changed. Others believe that the future is random and beyond our ability to control. Still others think that we control the future by our actions today."

"What do you believe?" Veeksha asked.

"I have not yet decided," he sighed. "I'm just a lone sailor lost in a tumult far beyond my control. I have a simple task, to pilot this vessel. Past, present, or future, it's not my place to shake the pillars of history. That is for others. That is for Savakala and her ilk, the skylords of the empire. They have the power."

"Is that what Savakala wants the quintessences for?" Kyle asked. "To do something about the future?"

Machadaro laughed. "You've been with us all these days and you still don't know what this quest is about?"

The children shook their heads.

"Bozabrozy told you nothing?"

"Nothing definite," Kyle admitted.

"Savakala wouldn't want me to reveal what's really behind the quest."

"We won't tell!" Susie said. "Please?"

Machadaro frowned and gulped more ale. He opened his mouth to speak, and then closed it again, looking out the porthole.

"Please, Captain?" Veeksha begged. "We just want to know what is going on."

The captain sighed and looked down at the young Indian girl. "It's best you do not know."

Kyle was getting angry. "Why not? Why do adults never want to tell kids stuff? Why not just answer our questions?"

The rasha leaned forward and growled at the boy, "Answers are perilous and terrible things."

"We can handle it," Kyle insisted.

"I think not." Machadaro stood and opened the door to his cabin, ushering the children into the passageway. "Begone. You will know more than you wish by the time this quest is done."

Chapter 34

"Grumpy tiger, isn't he?" Jürgen said after they had left the captain's cabin. "Hey, I'm hungry. Let's go down to the galley and get some lunch from Barathrina."

"You're always hungry," Susie noted as the four of them headed down into the ship.

"I can't help it. I didn't eat the whole time I was a statue."

Veeksha glared at Kyle. "The captain wasn't grumpy before you came in. If you wouldn't push him like that he wouldn't get angry."

"I'm just trying to find out what's going on," Kyle said with a shrug.

"Well, he's much more cooperative if you're nice to him," Susie said.

"Okay, okay. I'll let you two work on him," Kyle said to Susie and Veeksha. "Did you find out anything before Jürgen and I got there?"

"No, we just told him about Earth," Veeksha said. "He likes stories about Earth."

"They make him sad, though," Susie added. "Don't you think, Veeksha?"

"Yes. I wonder why that is?"

"I don't think he's the happiest tiger-man sky-pirate captain around," Kyle suggested as they walked into the galley. Barathrina stood near the oven, cooking. A few mumba sailors and canar legionaries sat at separate tables, occasionally growling and hissing at each other. Bozabrozy munched at a table by himself.

"No kidding," Susie agreed. "He's moodier than my cousin."

"I doubt that you two would be all sunshine and little white flowers if you had to work with Savakala and Joromwor," Veeksha said.

Kyle and Jürgen looked at each other. "But, we do have to work with them," Kyle said.

"Oh, just shut up!" Veeksha commanded and plopped down on the bench next to Bozabrozy.

Barathrina walked over to their table. "What can I get you, dearies?"

"Everything!" Jürgen requested enthusiastically.

"I'm starting to think you have a bottomless stomach," Barathrina said with a laugh, "just like me."

"Your food is so good!"

"Okay, I'll fix up some lunch for all of you," she said and went back to the stove.

"I wonder how that oven works," Jürgen said. "It's not hooked up to anything electric."

"Oh, she told us while you were a statue," Susie responded. "There's a fire elemental inside."

"Really? I thought you said that Savakala keeps all the magic stuff in her cabin."

"Not all of it," Bozabrozy said around a mouthful of strawpple. "Barathrina has a lot of kitchen magic. The stove, and heating pots, and freezing buckets."

"That's how she keeps the meat from going bad," Kyle said. "The freezing buckets use magic aquosia to keep everything frozen."

"Well, whatever she does, she sure knows how to cook." Jürgen grinned. "I bet she's a cookomancer."

"Bozabrozy?" Veeksha said.

"Yes, Veeksha?"

"Why do Machadaro and Joromwor hate each other so much?"

"Oh, there's always been competition between the Imperial Armada and the Imperial Legion, between sailors and soldiers. Each thinks they're the best. But with Machadaro and Joromwor, it goes a lot further. Bad blood that's been brewing for a long time."

"Is Joromwor really going to kill Machadaro?"

"Oh, he'll try, of that I'm sure," he said. At Veeksha's horrified expression he added, "But don't you worry about the captain. There's an old Zuran saying: sky captains never die, their spirits just keep sailing far across the wild blue yonder."

"That rasha's spirit won't be sailing anywhere after this quest is done," Joromwor growled from the door. The canar legionaries rose from their benches and stood at attention. The legate entered the galley and sat at a table with his soldiers. The mumba sailors, their ears back, left without saying a word.

"He sure knows how to plunge a room into gloom, doesn't he?" Bozabrozy whispered to the kids.

With the imposing bulk of the urgra so near, the children lapsed into an uneasy silence. Fortunately, it was soon broken by Barathrina carrying out a huge tray of food, steaming and aromatic.

"Here you go, my piglets," she said, putting a heaping plate in front of each.

Veeksha pushed the plate away. "Oh, no meat for me. I'm a vegetarian."

Barathrina leaned back, staring uncomprehendingly at the young Indian girl. "You keep saying that. What does it mean?"

"I don't eat animals."

Joromwor turned around and glared at Veeksha. "What do you mean, you don't eat animals?"

"I don't eat any meat," she replied quietly, not looking at the urgra.

"You don't eat meat? What kind of silliness is that?

Anything worth eating is meat. There's nothing better than a succulent haunch of beef. And bacon. How can you not eat bacon?"

"I don't think we should eat cows or pigs."

Joromwor guffawed loudly. "If we're not supposed to eat cows or pigs, why are they made out of food?"

Veeksha sighed and looked askance at the urgra. "It's a sign of respect. There's no reason to eat animals. It's cruel to eat animals."

"You sound like a dandelion-eating loppin. Dumb cattle don't deserve respect! They exist to be eaten. And I have many reasons to eat them. Starting with these!" He bared his mighty fangs. "Do you think these are for eating potatoes?"

Veeksha turned to face the urgra, glaring at him angrily. "Actually, based on the study of their molar teeth, and their behavior observed in the wild, scientists believe that bears are evolving from an omnivorous to an herbivorous diet. You actually might find potatoes quite tasty."

"Especially French fries with lots of ketchup," Jürgen piped in.

"Do I look like a bear to you?" Joromwor roared. "I am no stupid beast! I am an urgra! And if I choose to devour pigs or cows or chickens or anything else, I will do so. I won't have some insolent human cub dictate my fare. And if you try, perhaps I will see what you taste like!" He glanced at Jürgen. "With ketchup!" He rose and stormed out of the galley, followed by his canar soldiers.

"Gee, Veeksha," said Susie, patting her on the back. "You sure know how to put him in a good mood."

"Yeah," Jürgen moaned, "thanks a lot! I was going to ask him how his magical axe was made. I bet he won't tell me now."

"What's ketchup?" Bozabrozy asked.

CHAPTER 35

"Land ho!" yelled a mumba from his perch on the bowsprit the next morning. The children ran to the captain's deck to find Machadaro and Bozabrozy already there. Machadaro peered through his skyglass at the ocean. The children looked but saw nothing beneath them except the Pacific Ocean and lots of puffy clouds.

"Are we there yet?" Jürgen asked.

Bozabrozy pointed. "No. It's over there, near the horizon."

Kyle squinted but still saw nothing. "Is it behind a cloud?"

Lowering the skyglass, Machadaro said, "Aye, at times."

"Great!" Jürgen said. "When do we land?"

"We don't," grunted the captain.

"If we don't land, how are we going to get on the island?"

"Savakala will tell you."

The Windrunner soon approached within a few miles of Easter Island. It looked tiny and alone in the immense ocean, a little triangular piece of land surrounded by an endless sea. Well, almost alone. There were a few even tinier islands clumped near one corner. Machadaro sailed the ship around, using the skyglass to search every shore and hill.

Savakala appeared. "And?"

"It is true," said Machadaro, handing the skyglass to the uburu. "There are hundreds of moai. Most of them are toppled, but some are upright."

Savakala used the skyglass for long minutes. "We cannot descend into such a multitude. We must send the children alone."

"I don't know why you are so afraid of the moai," Veeksha said. "They're just statues. They don't speak or move or attack or do anything. Maybe on Zura they do. But here they're just lifeless monuments."

"I do not believe you," Savakala stated, then turned to Machadaro. "Take us far above the island, as we planned." The captain shouted orders to the crew and the Windrunner ascended.

"What are we going to do there?" Veeksha asked.

"You must retrieve the aethrial," Savakala explained. "But neither Kyle nor Jürgen can touch it." She looked at Susie and Veeksha. "It must be one of you two."

"It won't turn us into air like it turned Jürgen into stone?" Veeksha asked.

"It is even more forgiving than aquosia," Savakala said. "You already breathe in the sky. You can easily breathe in aethrial."

"Okay," Susie said dubiously. "How will we get down there?"

"You will jump."

"Jump?" Kyle exclaimed. "On ropes, or something?"

"No," Savakala said, "with these." She brandished her staff, plucked three small feathers from it, and gave one to Veeksha, Susie, and Kyle.

"Are those magic feathers?" Veeksha asked.

"Of course," the uburu replied. "Clasp it firmly in your fist and jump off the ship. You will float down safely to the island."

"Where's mine?" said Jürgen with a worried look. "Aren't I going with them?"

"Yes, but these feathers won't work for you," said Savakala. "You have geopsium in you. It will negate the air magic in these feathers. Aethrial and geopsium do not mix well."

"Then how will I get down there?"

"Jump."

"Jump? Without magic to save me?" Jürgen looked over the side of the ship at Easter Island many thousands of feet below. "You're crazy!"

"As I said, you have geopsium coursing through you. You cannot be harmed by stone."

Jürgen looked at her in confusion.

"Let me demonstrate," Savakala said. She stepped to the railing beside Jürgen. "Do you see the island down there?"

Jürgen leaned over the railing and looked. "Yeah, so?"

Savakala reached down and grabbed Jürgen's legs. Before anyone else could do anything, she pulled Jürgen up and tossed him overboard. The boy plummeted earthward, screaming and gyrating.

The other children rushed to the railing. "Why did you do that?" Kyle demanded.

"He won't be harmed."

"He won't be harmed? We must be two miles up! The fall will kill him!"

Savakala smirked. "It's not the falling that kills you. Anyone can fall for eternity and come to no harm. Well, until they die of thirst. It's not until you land that you actually get hurt."

"Well, Jürgen is going to land!"

"Yes, on an island. Made of stone and sand and rocks. Jürgen cannot be harmed by stone or sand or rocks. He'll land, but it won't harm him."

"Really?" Veeksha asked. "That's very interesting."

Kyle calmed down a bit. "But...you could have told us before you threw him over the side."

Savakala shrugged. "He'll learn more by discovering it himself."

"You're a maniac," Kyle said.

"You'd best follow him. You don't want him wandering

around alone down there," Savakala suggested.

Susie climbed up onto the railing, holding a line for support, the magic feather in her other hand. "Come on, everyone! This will be fun!" And she jumped off the side. She fell, but as slowly as a bird feather, wafting in a breeze. She squealed in delight.

Veeksha watched her descend. "She's all right! She's floating!"

"Of course. I have no reason to lie to you."

Veeksha climbed onto the railing, holding the rigging tightly. "I'm still not sure about this."

"You don't need to be sure." Savakala walked up behind Veeksha and pushed her roughly off the ship.

Kyle leaned over the railing as Veeksha screamed, but only for a moment. As she wafted gently down, her expression changed from terror to wary delight. "It works! Kyle, it works! Come on!"

Kyle turned back to Savakala. "How do we get back on board?"

The uburu pulled the Flagon of the Six Winds from beneath her cloak. She uncorked and upended it. A short, slender white stick fell out into her hand. "When you have retrieved the aethrial, hold hands altogether and break this bone. A Returning Wind will bring you to me." She gave Kyle the bone and recorked the Flagon. It was very light and felt hollow. It had carvings of birds on it, and reminded him of the scrimshaw art created by whalers.

Kyle put the bone in his pocket. "Do you have whales on Zura?" he asked. "Why would you use whale bone for flying magic?"

"You are too stupid to understand," Savakala scoffed.

"You're not a very nice person," Kyle said. "You enjoyed throwing Jürgen and Veeksha over the side."

"They would not obey."

"Why do you always get to tell everyone what to do?"

"I wield great magic, and magic reigns supreme. Go.

Now." She pointed to the side of the ship.

Kyle looked at Bozabrozy. "Good luck," the rascan said.

Kyle nodded and climbed over the railing. He looked down. Far below lay Easter Island. He saw Susie and Veeksha still wafting downward, but there was no sign of Jürgen. Kyle squeezed the magic feather in his hand and took a deep breath. He let go of the railing and toppled away from the Windrunner.

Chapter 36

It didn't feel like falling. Not at all like jumping off the cabin roof at Mt. Rushmore. Kyle imagined it must be what a floating leaf or feather felt like. Above him, the Windrunner sailed off. Bozabrozy still watched and waved. Kyle waved back.

He turned onto his stomach and looked down. Veeksha was several hundred feet below him and off to his right. Susie was even farther away, toward one of the three large hills on the island. Kyle realized that, unlike Jürgen who fell straight down, he and the girls were drifting this way and that. Savakala had said nothing about how to control the magic feathers.

Kyle had seen movies about skydivers. He remembered that they tucked in their arms and straightened their legs to maneuver. He tried to do the same. It felt like he was falling a little faster, but his descent was still uncontrolled. He put out his arms like wings and tilted and twisted. Still he couldn't make himself fall toward Veeksha or Susie. He tried swimming in the air, but that didn't help either and he probably just looked silly.

After several minutes of strange gyrations and positions, he finally decided that there was nothing he could do to land where he wanted. He just relaxed and let the magic feather decide.

Eventually, he landed on the side of a hill as softly as if he had stepped off a bus. Kyle could no longer see the Windrunner. He guessed that it had snuck behind a cloud during his fall. He opened his hand and the magic feather disintegrated into dust and the slight breeze blew it from his hand. Kyle supposed that each feather was only good for one fall.

From where he stood, the island looked like a hilly grassland. Below him was a dirt road cutting across an open field, and beyond that a white sandy beach and a small grove of palm trees. A row of moai stood on a stone platform nearby. He started off down the hill. It was only a few hundred feet to the beach, and he paused at the line of tall moai. Seven of them stood there, in varying stages of dilapidation. Four had huge stone blocks on their heads. Two were missing their heads entirely.

"Hey!"

Kyle thought he heard someone calling. He looked behind him through the trees, but didn't see anyone. It looked like there might be some buildings on the other side.

"Kyle! Over here!"

The voice was coming from the ocean. Kyle walked out onto the deep beach. Up ahead he could see a wide hole. Getting nearer he saw a head sitting on the sand. It was Jürgen's head!

"Jürgen!" Kyle ran up and knelt beside his friend's head. "What happened? Who cut off your head?"

Jürgen frowned. "What are you talking about? No one cut off my head!"

"But where's your body?"

"Attached to my neck and buried under the sand!"

"Oh!" Kyle laughed in relief. "Sorry. I totally spaced."

"Can you dig me out, please?"

"Yeah, sure," Kyle said and started digging the sand away from Jürgen's head.

"I saw you floating down from the Windrunner," Jürgen said as the sand flew. "It sure took you a long time to get down here. Those magic feathers work really good." Kyle nodded, and Jürgen continued. "But I hit the beach so hard I

195

sank up to my neck!"

"I can see that."

"Why didn't I die?" Jürgen asked.

Kyle explained what Savakala had told him about Jürgen being immune to damage from rocks.

"But this is sand," Jürgen pointed out.

Kyle shrugged. "Rock, sand, stone, it's all the same to geopsium, I guess." He had Jürgen's arms free now, and the German boy helped dig.

"That's really cool," Jürgen said. "I wonder if I would be crushed by falling boulders? Wait! What about swords and spears and stuff like that? Do you think they would hurt me? They're made out of metal. Minerals, I mean. I wonder if I'm immune to all minerals? Then bullets wouldn't even hurt me."

"Who knows? But do you really want to find out?" Kyle asked, taking a break from digging and wiping his forehead. He could see the top of Jürgen's fat stomach. "You sure are buried in there."

"Yeah, I can't move my legs at all."

"Hey, maybe you can move the sand away from you using the geopsium," Kyle suggested.

"How can I do that? No one will teach me how to do magic."

"No one taught me how to use the aquosia to unpetrify you. All they said was just imagine it."

"You think that would work for me?"

"It couldn't hurt to try. They're just grains of sand. If it doesn't work, we'll keep digging."

"Okay," Jürgen agreed. "What do I do?"

Kyle stood up and moved away. "Just imagine the sand digging itself up around you."

"Okay." Jürgen closed his eyes and squinted hard. After several seconds of intense imagining he opened his eyes to find himself still firmly lodged in the sand. "It didn't work."

"Did you imagine the sand being dug up? You didn't

feel anything?"

"Yes, I did. And, no, I didn't."

"I was hoping that would work," Kyle said, sitting down.

"Well, aren't you going to help dig some more?"

"I'm thinking."

"I just tried thinking and it didn't work. I don't see how you thinking is going to get me out of this."

"When I unpetrified you, I imagined you as your normal self, flesh instead of stone. I imagined the result I wanted."

"So?"

"So maybe, instead of imagining the sand digging itself out, you should imagine yourself standing on top of the sand."

"Or you could just help dig me out."

"Just try one more time," Kyle insisted.

"Okay." Once again, Jürgen scrunched up his face and imagined. This time, however, he pictured himself standing on top of the sand.

Kyle watched happily as Jürgen rose slowly out of the sand, as if he was being pushed from below. When his feet appeared he stopped. Sand spilled out of his pockets.

Jürgen laughed. "It worked!"

Kyle jumped up and clapped his friend on the shoulder. "Cool!"

"This elemental magic stuff doesn't seem so hard." Jürgen swatted the sand from his clothes. "Maybe we don't need lessons from the Zurans to use it."

"Maybe not," Kyle agreed. "But Bozabrozy said it was dangerous. If we try it on our own, who knows what will happen. We could become one of those thrope-things they talked about."

"How hard can it be? You saved me pretty easily," Jürgen said. "We didn't get the dangerous elements like sky and fire. It's not like we're going to burst into flame or electrocute ourselves. You might get wet and I might get dusty."

They walked along the beach to a small knoll. A single moai stood on the remains of a stone platform. Rocks lay strewn about in the short grass.

"It sounded worse than that," Kyle said. "Besides, without knowing any magic you survived the fall from the ship."

"Yeah, that is pretty cool," Jürgen agreed, sitting down on the platform and leaning his back against the moai. "But, wouldn't it be cool to be able to do that and shoot lightning bolts and fireballs?"

"I never thought of that. I wonder if you can absorb all the different kinds of quintessence."

"We should try it with the next one we find," Jürgen said. "I'll do it."

Kyle sat down next to his friend. "I don't know. That might not be a good idea. Savakala said we shouldn't do it. Stone and sky are opposites. The magic feather wouldn't work on you because you have geopsium in you."

"So?"

"So I bet if you tried to grab the aethrial it would react badly with the geopsium in you."

"Don't worry," Jürgen scoffed. "This is magic. Nothing bad will happen."

"Look at what happened to you the first time you touched quintessence. You turned into a statue!"

"But I feel much better now." Jürgen hit his fists on his chest. "I bet I could absorb the sky and fire quintessences, no problem."

"Do not mix the elements," said a deep, grumbly voice behind them, and the ground trembled.

Jürgen and Kyle jumped up and spun around to see who had spoken.

CHAPTER 37

"Who said that?" Kyle called out.

The moai standing before them moved. The mouth opened, the lips parted, and the deep voice came from within it. "I did."

"A talking moai!" Kyle said.

"Wow!" Jürgen said. "But Veeksha said they don't move or talk."

"I have never been so close to primal geopsium," the moai said.

"Oh, yeah, that's me," Jürgen said.

"Where did you come by it?" the statue asked.

"I got it from a stone elemental in South Dakota."

"I do not know that place."

"What are you?" Kyle asked.

"I am Kamo-Kikamo, guardian of Rapa Nui." The moai leaned back, as if trying to stand taller.

"What's Rapa Nui?" Jürgen asked.

The moai frowned. "You stand upon it and you do not know its name?"

"He means the island," Kyle said. "Easter Island must be Rapa Nui."

"Yes, the land upon which you stand is Rapa Nui."

"Do you always talk to people?" Jürgen said.

"No," Kamo-Kikamo said. "I have not spoken since the birdmen conquered Rapa Nui."

Kyle gave Jürgen a significant glance. "Who are the birdmen?" he asked the moai.

"The invaders. The destroyers."

"I'm guessing you don't like them very much," said Kyle.

"No!" Kamo-Kikamo's voice thundered across the beach. "Long did we moai protect the lands and people of Rapa Nui from the birdmen. We watched the land and whenever we saw a birdman we stoned it until it lay broken and lifeless. Then they corrupted the people, and tempted them to their ways. The birdmen convinced them to blind us. Without our eyes, we could not see them unless they touched the ground. This they did not do. They stayed in their skyships."

Kyle and Jürgen looked at each other. "Skyships?"

"The birdmen worshipped aethrial, sylphs, and all things of the sky," Kamo-Kikamo explained. "They flew on their wings and in the ships they built. They always looked down on stone and water and fire. They believed themselves greater than all else because they always flew above. They believed themselves to be the eternal lords of the world."

"Lords of our world? Earth?" Kyle asked. "But they're from Zura. Why would they want to be lords here?"

"Zurans seek dominion over all."

"The Zurans were here that long ago?" Jürgen exclaimed.

"Why would they want dominion over a tiny little island in the middle of the ocean?" Kyle asked.

"To hide their aethrial," the moai said.

"They hid aethrial here?" Kyle said.

"Curse them for the villains they are," Kamo-Kikamo spat, and pebbles showered the boys. "They sought all the quintessences. When they found the primal aethrial they came here to hide it while they sought the others."

"Why would they hide it? Why didn't they just keep it?"

"Aethrial is very hard to possess. It always seeks its freedom. They bound a sky elemental to Moto Nui to guard the aethrial."

"What's Moto Nui?" Jürgen asked.

"The small land across the water," Kamo-Kikamo spun and faced west. "Beyond Rano Kau."

"He means another island," Kyle guessed. "Probably one of those small ones we saw nearby."

Jürgen nodded, and then spoke to the moai, "Would you mind if we took the aethrial?"

"Rocks and boulders!" the moai rumbled deeply. "If you take the primal aethrial all moai will wake and rejoice!"

"The moai are just sleeping?"

"The primal aethrial weakens us with its presence. It wearies us. If it were to leave we could awaken."

"So," Jürgen said, "we can take it and it won't bother you?"

Kamo-Kikamo smiled. "All the moai of Rapa Nui will be in your debt if you take the vile aethrial away."

"We'll do our best," Kyle said.

Kamo-Kikamo looked at Jürgen. "Thank you, young geomancer. May the geopsium within you keep you safe and protected. But beware! Do not touch the aethrial. Chaos reigns when quintessences combine. Especially those that are opposed. Stone to sky, water to fire. Do not mix them lest you suffer turmoil and madness."

"Oh, okay, if you say so," Jürgen said despondently.

Kamo-Kikamo spun again to face southwest. "Follow my nose to the end of Rapa Nui. You will stand on the edge of the crater of Rano Kau. Nearby you will see three small lands: Moto Kau Kau, Moto Iti, and Moto Nui. On Moto Nui will you find the sky elemental and the primal aethrial. Take it far from here."

"Don't worry, we will," Jürgen promised.

"Go now," the moai suggested. "Go and free Rapa Nui and the moai."

Kyle and Jürgen walked away from Kamo-Kikamo, and the moai's face slowly froze into its previous enigmatic expression.

"So, now we know it's the aethrial that's here," Kyle said as the pair walked across the beach toward the southwest, heading toward the palm trees. "This riddle is easier than the last two. We're getting directions!"

"Yeah," Jürgen agreed. "But how are we going to get to the other island. We'll need a boat."

"First, we need to find Susie and Veeksha."

"I bet Veeksha will have an idea about how to get there. She's pretty smart."

They walked in silence for a few minutes before Jürgen spoke again. "I wonder why you can't mix aethrial and geopsium?"

"Weren't you listening to the moai? It causes chaos."

"But I'm learning how to control the geopsium. I bet I could learn how to control the aethrial."

"But not at the same time."

"Maybe I can control them in short little bursts?"

"I don't think there is any such thing as short, controlled bursts of chaos."

They left the beach and walked through the palm grove toward a dirt road on the other side. An old Land Rover approached.

"Uh oh," Jürgen said, "I bet it's a park ranger. What should we tell him?"

"Um...that our parents left us here while they walked around?"

The Land Rover stopped and the passenger door opened. Susie and Veeksha jumped out and came running toward them.

Jürgen grinned, and ran with Kyle toward the car, shouting, "Hi! Guess what? We know where the aethrial is! We spoke to a moai and it told us it's on Moto Nui!"

Susie was shaking her head and waving her hands. "No, don't!" she said.

"What's the matter?" Kyle asked, but then he saw Reid Bannecker step out of the car.

Chapter 38

Bannecker smiled as he walked toward them. "Hi, boys. You get around, don't you?"

Kyle and Jürgen stood slack-jawed as the man walked over to them. He wasn't limping. He wasn't wearing a sling. He didn't look injured at all!

"I saw the girls falling from the skyship and picked them up before coming to find you. How are you? Not hurt from the fall, I hope?"

Jürgen pointed at the man. "You're supposed to be dead!"

Bannecker grimaced and rubbed his chest. "Yes, that tiger-man packs a wallop with those claws."

"Machadaro is not a tiger-man," Veeksha insisted. "He's a rasha."

Bannecker nodded. "I'll have to remember that the next time we meet."

"How did you survive?" Kyle asked.

"Not the same way you kids did. I was wearing a parachute."

"But Machadaro clawed your guts out," Kyle said. "Blood was everywhere. Just like at Mt. Rushmore. You should be in a hospital, at least."

"After spending several days with the elementally-powered Zurans," said Bannecker, cocking an eyebrow, "I think you can guess how I healed my injuries so quickly."

"You have aquosia," Veeksha stated.

"Your father isn't wrong when he says you're a bright

young girl, Veeksha," Bannecker said.

"You spoke to my father?"

"All of your parents are very worried about all of you. But now that you've escaped from the Zurans, we can reunite you. After we get the aethrial, of course."

"What aethrial?" Kyle asked.

Bannecker smiled. "Jürgen should learn to look before he speaks. You're here on another quest for quintessence. The aethrial, as he just said. No need to deny it. I can help you find it."

"We don't need your help."

"Come on, Kyle. Why don't you trust me? I've only been trying to rescue you from the Zurans. I would think you would be grateful."

"The first time you showed up you shot Bozabrozy for no reason," Kyle said.

"No, that's not quite true," Bannecker disagreed. "I did have reason. He and his bear-man and dog-man friends attacked you and your father. They demolished a good part of your cabin. You were kidnapped and your fathers were nearly killed. I had to prevent more attacks. That's why we shot Bozabrozy. He and his friends are a dangerous threat."

"Bozabrozy isn't a threat. He didn't attack us. The urgra and canars that attacked our cabin were minions of Rakanian. He's the bad guy. He's the enemy of Bozabrozy."

"Really?" Bannecker said. "We have reports from people around Mt. Rushmore who saw a raccoon-man talking with a bear-man in the vicinity of your cabin."

"That's not true!" Jürgen said. "Bozabrozy was fighting them! Rakanian is the bad guy!"

"And who is this Rakanian?" Bannecker asked. "Is he on the ship?"

"No," Susie said. "He's not on the ship. He's your boss. He's infiltrated the government and is trying to get the quintessence so he can take over the world!"

"Strange that I haven't heard of him before. What does

he look like?"

The kids looked at each other and shrugged. "How should we know? We've never seen him."

"He's working from behind the scenes," Susie asserted. "Like a criminal mastermind."

Bannecker held up his hands. "Listen, we don't have to discuss this now. You're safe. You can sort things out when we get back to the States. You don't have to worry about those dangerous Zurans any more."

"It's Rakanian and his minions that are dangerous."

Jürgen pointed an accusing finger at Bannecker. "And you're a minion!"

"No, I'm not. I work with numerous governments around the world. I'm not a threat. I'm here to protect."

"Protect what?"

"Protect Earth from Zurans. There are many things you don't know. Shall we go into town so I can explain it all to you?" Bannecker jerked a thumb back at the car.

"We aren't going anywhere with you!" Kyle said defiantly.

"What are you going to do, then? Walk across the length of Easter Island, swim across shark-infested waters to the jagged cliffs of Moto Nui, and crawl around looking for the aethrial? Imagine how much easier that would be if an adult were with you to help. Do you have any money with you? Enough to rent a boat and guide?"

Kyle looked at the ground. "No."

"If I wanted, I could report you to the local authorities. You have no passports, no record of having come to the island legally. You have no parents or guardians with you. If anyone caught you here you would spend the rest of your time sitting in the police station."

"He does have a point," Veeksha admitted.

"And, he could just throw us in the car if he wanted," Susie added.

"He couldn't throw me around," Jürgen said proudly.

"I've got geopsium."

"Listen," Bannecker said, "after we find the aethrial I'll fly all of you back to the States and reunite you with your parents. What do you say, Kyle? Jürgen?"

CHAPTER 39

Jürgen kicked the dirt defiantly. "I want to finish the entire quest. We won't get a chance to find the pyrophyra."

"There's more of this quest?" Bannecker asked.

"We aren't telling you anything more," Kyle stated firmly, glaring at Jürgen. The German looked away abashedly.

Bannecker smiled. "Your father says you have a stubborn streak. Maybe you can tell him when we get back. But first of all, how about we all get in the car and I'll take you into town for a late breakfast?"

Veeksha and Susie moved to comply, but Kyle stood still.

"It's over, Kyle," Bannecker said. "Being kidnapped can be a very traumatic experience. There are psychological impacts that can confuse you, mix you up about who your friends and enemies are. Come with me, get some food, and I'll answer any questions you have. Then I can get your dad on the phone and you can tell him you're all right."

Veeksha walked up to Kyle. "That sounds like a very good idea. I'm hungry."

"What should we do, Kyle?" Jürgen asked.

"We don't have much choice," Kyle said, his shoulders sagging. "Everything he says is right. We can't get the aethrial without his help."

"Are you sure?" Jürgen asked.

"Yeah. Aren't you hungry? We should go." He winked at his friend. No one knew that he had the magic scrimshaw in his pocket, but he hoped Jürgen would go along.

"All right," Jürgen relented.

The children piled into the car and Reid Bannecker drove away from the beach and palm trees.

"What can I tell you first?" he asked.

"How did you know we were on Easter Island?" Kyle asked.

"Where did you get aquosia?" Jürgen asked at the same time.

"Why do you have to protect Earth from the Zurans?" Susie added.

Bannecker smiled. "Hold on, hold on, one at a time. I'll start with you, Kyle. That flying ship is an amazing bit of otherworldly technology, but it's not invisible. We had it under constant surveillance until that strange storm appeared in the Gulf."

"It's a skyship called the Windrunner," Jürgen corrected.

Bannecker nodded. "When the Windrunner flew into the storm we lost it. That storm was very strange. Not only because it was moving in the wrong direction but also because of the massive electrical disturbances and temperature fluctuations within it. They interfered with our surveillance equipment. That storm will have meteorologists talking for decades."

"That was Savakala's whole plan," Susie said. "To get away. She summoned the storm from the Flagon of the Six Winds."

"Yes, we assumed it was a ploy to throw us off their trail. We found debris on the coast of Cuba that matched the Windrunner. But, there wasn't enough for the entire ship. We assumed it was a ruse. Even so, we weren't able to locate you again until reports came in from Peru."

"What kind of reports?" Kyle asked.

"Of course, you wouldn't know this since you've been on the ship for several days, but the arrival of the Zurans in their skyship is news all over the world since tourists took pictures and video of them at Mt. Rushmore."

"Why didn't you take the cameras and make the people shut up?" Jürgen asked. "Isn't that what always happens?"

"Unfortunately, that is not as easy as it is in the movies. There were too many people and too much photographic evidence. Pictures and video were on the Internet in a matter of minutes. When the Windrunner flew over more densely populated areas, the news showed live video. Unfortunately, the chopper battle over Texas was also caught on film."

"Wow," Susie said. "That must have freaked people out."

"Along with the descriptions of the Zurans as ferocious werewolves, it caused a panic."

"They're not werewolves!" Susie exclaimed.

"No, they're not. But that's the easiest way to describe them, don't you think? Bipedal dogs, tigers, and cats? That doesn't get as much attention as ferocious werewolves. Or were-raccoons."

Veeksha frowned. "Does anyone really believe that?"

"When there are photographs and video, dead government agents, shattered cabins, frozen park rangers, and kidnapped tourists? Of course."

Susie leaned forward from her seat in the back. "Frozen park rangers? What frozen park rangers?"

Bannecker looked at the girl in the rear view mirror. "Your brother, John, was found in the forest near the park, frozen solid in ice."

Susie's hand went to her mouth. "Oh, no! Is he okay? Where is he? Did Rakanian do it? We have to go back!"

"Don't worry, Susie. He's okay and we'll get you back to see him," Bannecker promised. "There are photos of him on the news, and more." Bannecker shook his head. "There's a video of Machadaro attacking me at Mt. Rushmore that they play over and over. 'Alien Weretiger Kills U.S. Agent.' Another video shows two army helicopters being shot down. People got very scared. When the storm appeared from out of nowhere, they got terrified. Lots of people have died. 'Weather-controlling aliens attack Gulf!' was one of the headlines. Some people even started blaming them for other disasters, like Hurricane Katrina."

"It's all Savakala's fault!" Veeksha cried. "She's the one who summoned the sky elemental to do it. Why couldn't she just talk instead of summoning a storm?"

"We can't explain the actions of aliens we know little about," Bannecker said. "But the human reaction was predictable. People panicked and ran out to buy up supplies and guns. Scared people had arguments. Arguments turned into scuffles. Scuffles into riots. The National Guard was called in to calm things down."

"Did that work?"

"As the days passed with no further sightings or storms, things did calm down a little. But the damage has been done. Most people believe that Earth has been invaded by aliens who intend to conquer us."

"Why didn't the Peruvians attack us when they saw us?" Kyle asked.

"We convinced the Peruvian government not to. As we learned over Texas, the skyship is very dangerous. Plus, the Zurans had you on board as hostages."

"We weren't hostages," Susie said, but with little conviction in her voice. "We were just trying to help them. And get Jürgen unpetrified."

"Unpetrified?"

"I got turned to stone when I melded with the geopsium!" Jürgen exclaimed with a grin. "I'm a geomancer."

"Really? You'll have to tell me all about that over breakfast," Bannecker said. "Anyway, we didn't want to destroy the Windrunner with the four of you on board."

"But the helicopters shot at us," Veeksha said. "They could have killed us!"

"Yes, I'm sorry. The pilots responded excessively. That's

why we tried another way with the commandos. We were hoping to get you off the ship quickly and quietly." As he spoke, Bannecker took a curved turn to the right onto a dirt road, Camino A Anakena, that paralleled the airport runway. Looking out the window, Kyle saw several groups of people talking excitedly and pointing up into the sky. He guessed that the Windrunner's arrival at Easter Island was causing a big stir. "When the commando raid failed, it was decided that no further attacks would be made unless the ship attacked, or you landed."

"We landed at the Nasca lines and you didn't attack," Susie said.

"No, you were only there a few hours and that wasn't time enough for us to get forces down there to strike. But we had you back on satellite surveillance, and we saw you head out to sea. We've been watching ever since."

"And you just guessed that we'd stop here at Easter Island?" Kyle asked.

"Not really. Someone left us a message in the mud in Peru."

"What?" Jürgen blurted. "Who would do that?"

"Someone who understands the gravity of your situation," Bannecker replied. "I think you don't appreciate what it means to be kidnapped by aliens and taken thousands of miles from home. Your parents sure do. And, fortunately, Veeksha understands what kind of worry and pain that can cause."

Susie looked at Veeksha. "You? You left him a message in the mud? You told him where to find us?"

Veeksha looked down at her knees, but shook her head. "I didn't tell him. I left a message for my parents telling them I was okay and where we were going. I had to tell them. They're my parents."

Jürgen stared angrily at Veeksha. "You traitor! How could you do it?"

"I love my parents! They're very worried! I had to let

them know I'm okay!"

"And they do know, Veeksha," Bannecker said. "I told them myself. They are very happy to have gotten word from you. It was a great relief to them."

"But now we're caught by him," said Jürgen, pointing at Bannecker. "He'll turn us over to Rakanian!"

"No, I won't turn you over to anyone. You should all be thanking Veeksha. She helped rescue you from the Zurans."

"Some of us don't want to be rescued," Jürgen insisted, crossing his arms and looking out the window.

"Don't be too hard on Veeksha," Bannecker said. "Don't you want to talk to your parents? Let them know you're still alive, at least?"

"Yes!" Kyle agreed. "Can we do that?"

"Yes, you can." Bannecker pulled into the parking lot of the Manutara Hotel. "I can answer the rest of your questions and you can call your parents. But first, what would you like for breakfast?"

Chapter 40

Jürgen and Kyle had French toast with lots of syrup, bacon, hash browns, fresh fruit, and juice. Susie had an omelet and Veeksha had cereal and a sliced banana. While it was being prepared, Bannecker let each of them contact their parents. Thanks to his comforting words and promises, their parents soon felt much better. In just a day or so, he told them, they'd all be reunited back in the United States.

"You should see the kitchen on the Windrunner," Jürgen bragged while he poured syrup on his breakfast. "All sorts of exotic food. They have fruit that's a mix of normal fruit. Rasples, strawpples, grapples, and more, also."

Bannecker smiled. "I guess they like apples." He drank coffee and ate a bagel. They talked about their adventures and finding the geopsium and aquosia. He told them about the history of quintessence on Earth. Many years ago, molecular biologists had discovered aquosia as an unexpected and rare component of the pure water they were using for experiments. Later, and equally surprisingly, other scientists discovered geopsium while creating synthetic diamonds.

"Both substances caused quite a stir," Bannecker said. "Scientists still aren't sure what they are or how to fully exploit them. Luckily, we have been able to process aquosia into a few useful elixirs." He took a packet out of his pocket and pulled the Velcro cover off, revealing a row of small vials, each containing a clear liquid and marked with a bit of colored tape. He handed the packet around to the kids.

"To answer one of your earlier questions, the vials with light blue tape can heal all but the most devastating physical injury. That's what I used to heal the wounds the rasha gave me."

"Savakala used some stuff like that to heal Bozabrozy after you shot him," Susie noted.

"What do the other vials do?" Jürgen asked.

"The yellow one is a truth serum. The purple one can actually bring someone back from the dead."

"Wow!" Susie exclaimed. "Why aren't they marked? They just have blank tape on them. What about the green, orange, red, and other ones?"

"I don't want the wrong people to get their hands on these," Bannecker said, taking the packet back and replacing it in his jacket. "Some of them are dangerous. So, I just use colored tape and only I know what they're for. But I will tell you something the orange one does. It unfreezes park rangers."

"That's what you used on my brother?" Susie asked.

"Exactly."

"So he's okay now? He didn't get frostbite and lose any fingers or toes, did he?"

"No, no, he's perfectly fine and waiting for you back home."

"How did he get frozen?" Jürgen asked, helping himself to another three slices of bacon.

"We're not exactly sure," Bannecker said, "but I would guess that aquosia was involved somehow. Synthetic aquosia sometimes randomly cools down, and has even frozen."

"Bozabrozy had a key he used to ice our door shut in the cabin."

"Maybe Bozabrozy froze your brother, Susie," Veeksha suggested.

"Why would he do that?" Susie asked. "He's on our side."

"We don't know he did it," Jürgen said. "I bet Rakanian has a bunch of artifacts, also. It was probably one of his minions that got your brother."

"There's no harm done, whoever did it," Bannecker smiled. "He's fully thawed out, thanks to the aquosia."

"Synthetic aquosia," Veeksha mused. "I never would have thought that technology could duplicate magic water!"

"As a famous author once said, any sufficiently advanced technology is indistinguishable from magic." Bannecker took a sip of coffee.

"You mean Arthur C. Clarke," Veeksha said. "I've read his stories."

Banner smiled. "And I think he would agree that just because the Zurans appear to use magic doesn't mean their powers aren't technological in nature. Imagine what the Native Americans first thought about guns."

"Thunder sticks!" Susie said.

"Do you have synthetic aethrial or pyrophyra?" Veeksha asked.

"No, we don't," Bannecker said. "Unfortunately, we haven't figured out how to simulate elemental sky and fire. We've tried many experiments with pure oxygen and flammable gases, but no luck so far."

"Well," Veeksha said, a spoonful of Fruit Loops waiting outside her mouth, "at least you have two of the four elemental quintessences."

"What are quintessences, really?" Jürgen asked.

"That is a huge topic of top secret discussions. Once we're back in the States you'll learn more. There are many scientists that will have lots and lots of questions for you."

"You said you'd answer all our questions," Jürgen reminded him.

"That I did. But that could take a long time, since you're such smart and inquisitive kids. Wouldn't you rather get off to Moto Nui and collect the aethrial as soon as possible?"

"Yeah!" Susie said. "I wonder what it looks like?" She

turned to Veeksha. "What do you think pure sky looks like, Veeksha?"

"Invisible, I guess," she replied. "Cloudy? No, clouds are water vapor, more like aquosia. Maybe it's lightning, like from Savakala's feather staff."

After breakfast they went back out to the Land Rover. Two tall, beefy men joined them in the parking lot, and spoke to Bannecker for a few minutes.

"What are we going to do?" Susie whispered while Bannecker was distracted.

"I have a plan to get away any time we want," Kyle replied, making sure that Veeksha wasn't close by. He didn't know if he trusted her any more.

"So we shouldn't believe him?" Susie said. "He's telling us a lot."

"Not enough," Jürgen said. "I still don't trust him."

"Let's go along with him for now," Kyle said. "Once we find the aethrial, we'll escape."

"How do we do that?" Susie asked.

"Savakala gave me a magic whale bone that will fly us back to the ship."

Jürgen's eyes popped wide. "Can I see it?"

Bannecker was walking back toward them. Kyle shook his head. "Not now."

"The boat is waiting," said the agent. "Ready to go?"

Chapter 41

The main harbor on Easter Island was in the town of Hanga Roa, only a few hundred feet behind the Manutara Hotel. They drove to the dock, and the other two agents followed in another Land Rover. A smiling fisherman waited for them and helped them onto his boat, talking happily in Spanish. One of the other agents joined him at the helm.

The fishing boat maneuvered out of the harbor, pulling a small inflatable dinghy, and was soon motoring south along the cliffs. The southern tip of Easter Island was an extinct volcano named Rano Kau and the cliffs swiftly grew taller and more treacherous as they neared.

"You never said why you need to protect Earth from the Zurans," Susie reminded Bannecker.

"It's simple enough," the agent replied. "We suspect that Zurans have visited Earth for millennia with mysterious if not terrible results."

"I knew it!" Veeksha said.

"What's the big deal about them coming to Earth?" Jürgen asked.

"They seek to enslave and destroy," Bannecker said. "We believe that they've had contact with numerous cultures in the past. We think they were the instigators of the cult of the birdman here on Easter Island, for example. They probably caused the clan wars here, and possibly had a hand in the ecological damage that deforested the island and doomed the people to enslavement and starvation. They were probably involved with Nasca culture in Peru, considering some of the animal glyphs there. Many cultures have beast-headed men in their mythology."

"Like ancient Egypt," Veeksha said.

"That's the most obvious example, yes," Bannecker agreed. "But there are others."

"Why do you think they're here to hurt us?"

"We captured one of them in New Mexico sixty years ago."

"You did?" Susie said. "What was he like?"

"A dog-man," Bannecker said. "We learned a bit about Zura from him. They need our quintessence to save their world. They aren't willing to ask for our help. Instead, they want to take it by force and won't let anyone get in their way."

"Why don't you just let them take it?" Susie suggested. "If you don't try to stop them, maybe they won't hurt anybody."

"Elemental quintessence is very powerful," Bannecker said. "If they perceive us as weak, they'll take more. What if they want humans for slaves? Or for food? Maybe they'll come back and strip-mine the Earth. We have to stop them, and learn more about quintessence and how to use it. We can't let technologically advanced invaders trespass and murder without retaliation."

"Oh," Susie said. "I didn't think of that."

"Why don't you use diplomacy?" Veeksha said.

"We've tried that. They don't want to talk."

The fishing boat didn't take long to travel a few miles to the three small islets close by the southern tip of Easter Island.

The first was Motu Kao Kao, a lonely sea stack that looked like the tip of a gigantic spear sticking dozens of feet out of the sea. Kyle could see black and white sea birds nesting and flying around its height. Their squeaky calls filled the air.

The next island, Moto Iti, looked like part of Moto Nui until the fishing boat moved past it. Then Kyle could see a narrow and dangerous looking channel between the two.

"How do we get onto that?" Veeksha asked, looking warily at the rocky shoreline of Moto Nui.

"The rubber dinghy," said Bannecker. He and the other two agents helped the kids into the small boat. One agent accompanied them, while the second stayed with the fisherman. The landing was not as treacherous as they expected. Bannecker found a relatively calm section and the other agent jumped ashore with a line and pulled them up onto a wide rock.

"Moto Nui!" Bannecker yelled over the cacophony of the large number of birds. "Not many folks have set foot here."

"I don't think we're supposed to be here, either," Veeksha said. "This is probably protected land. Like a wildlife sanctuary."

"I hope we won't be here long, otherwise we'll go deaf from the sound of all these birds," Bannecker said. He led the way up the rocks, deeper into the island. "Let's find the aethrial quickly. Where do you think it is?"

Kyle looked over at Veeksha. "You're the riddle master."

Veeksha repeated the riddle they had received from the water elemental in Peru:

Fires thrust it up from the sea
Ringed by watchful faces, tall and stony
Follow the path of the birdman's test
Reach for the sky from the lofty nest

"The first two lines led us to Easter Island," she said. "The third line led us here to Moto Nui. The last line, I think, means we should find a bird's nest."

Susie nodded. "Seems like it could be a good hiding place for a piece of pure elemental sky," she said, checking the ground around her. There were many clumps of twigs and grass scattered nearby, some with birds nesting in them. "I don't think we'll have a problem finding nests."

"How do we know which nest is the right one?" Kyle asked.

"Look for a lofty nest," Veeksha said. "Maybe it's a nest near the cliff."

"Let's walk around the edge," Bannecker suggested. "But be careful. It's a long fall to the water."

"I don't see any eggs," Jürgen noted as they walked. "Are we looking for eggs?"

"I don't know what we're looking for, exactly," Veeksha admitted.

It didn't take them long to walk around the island. They found several nests near the cliffs.

"Which one is it?" Bannecker asked.

Veeksha shook her head and frowned.

"I think it's here!" Susie called. She stood on a rocky outcrop near the north end of the island, overlooking the narrow channel between Moto Nui and Moto Iti.

"Why do you think it's this one?" Veeksha asked when she joined Susie. The nest looked old and deserted.

"I think it's the highest nest on the cliff side," Susie said, looking around. "I don't think any of the other nests are higher up, do you?"

Kyle squinted and kneeled down. "It's hard to tell."

"It's a good place to start, I guess," Jürgen said. "What do we do now?"

"Reach for the sky," Veeksha said.

"That's what cowboys say," Jürgen laughed.

"Maybe we should jump up as high as we can?" Kyle suggested. They all stood on their toes or jumped and reached up.

Susie pointed. "Look! The birds are watching us!"

It did seem like the birds soared closer as they reached up to the sky. Several swooped past only a few feet above their heads.

"What kind of birds are those?" Kyle asked, still reaching up.

"Sooty terns," Veeksha answered. "I read about them. They're very common in tropical regions."

"That one likes Susie," said Jürgen, pointing to a tern as it hovered on the updraft of the cliff, apparently watching Susie.

"Hi!" Susie smiled, and held out a hand to the bird. It drifted in closer and landed on her palm.

"Wow!" Jürgen said, moving forward.

Bannecker held him back. "Better not scare it away."

"Mere humans can't scare me," the bird squawked, and turned to Jürgen. "But you're full of geopsium. Go away!"

"It talks!" Kyle said.

"I don't want to go away," Jürgen said.

"The bird must be a sky elemental!" Veeksha guessed. "He doesn't like being around you, Jürgen, because you have all that geopsium. You better go to the other end of the island."

Jürgen stared angrily at them. "I won't do that! I want to see what happens! I was stuck as a statue while all the other stuff was happening! I don't want to miss this, too!"

The tern hovered away from Susie and screeched at Jürgen. "Go! Now!"

"Please, Jürgen?" Susie pleaded. "If you don't go it might not help us."

Bannecker nodded to the other agent, who stepped up to Jürgen and pulled him away from the cliff.

Jürgen resisted and shouted, "Leave me alone! No! I don't want to!" The agent finally picked him up and carried him away over his shoulder. "This isn't fair!"

With Jürgen hidden from view by rocky outcroppings, the sooty tern alit once more on Susie's outstretched hand. It tilted its head to look up at her. "You need help?"

"Yes," Susie smiled. "We're on an elemental quest.

We're looking for the aethrial."

"The aethrial is here for the Zurans," the tern said. "They defeated the stony sentinels. They captured the aethrial. They hid it here. They bound me to guard it. Humans can't have it."

"But we're helping the Zurans," Veeksha said. "They brought us here."

The bird hovered up in the air and wheeled about in a wide circle. "I see no Zurans. Where are the Zurans?"

"They're up in a skyship somewhere around here," Kyle said, gazing into the sky.

Susie pointed. "There!" Peeking out of a puffy cloud, the Windrunner momentarily appeared a couple miles away. "There it is! A Zuran named Savakala is on board. She wants the aethrial."

The sooty tern chirped and flew off, heading for the skyship. The children watched it go.

"What do we do now?" Kyle asked.

"Maybe it's going to talk to Savakala?" Susie said.

"We'll wait," Bannecker said. "It'll take the bird a while to get over there."

But the sooty tern swooped back in only moments.

"Zurans are there," it said and soared down toward Moto Iti. After a few moments, it came back and hovered beyond the cliff. It held an egg in its beak. Susie reached out to take it, but the bird retreated several feet and let go of the egg. It floated in midair, barely moving.

"Where is it?" the tern said, and flew away. The egg remained hovering out of reach, bobbing slightly in the wind.

"Where is it?" Susie called after the departing bird. "Do you mean it's in that egg?"

"How are we supposed to get that?" Kyle asked.

Jürgen hurried up behind them, a bit out of breath. "What did I miss?"

"How did you..." Bannecker looked around for the

other agent. "Where's Tatman?"

Jürgen jerked his thumb. "He's over there. I got away from him."

"You kids stay here and don't do anything," Bannecker ordered. "I'm going to check on Tatman and then get some rope from the boat. Maybe we can catch the egg." He rushed away.

"How did you get away from that guy?" Susie asked Jürgen. "He was huge!"

Jürgen smiled and looked at Kyle. "I used the stone magic! The geopsium. I just thought about getting away and the ground opened up and swallowed him!"

"What?" Kyle shouted. "Is he okay?"

Jürgen shrugged. "I don't know. The ground closed up over him."

"Oh my gosh!" Susie said. "That's terrible!"

"We have to save him!" Veeksha said.

"Is that the aethrial?" Jürgen asked, pushing past them and looking at the egg hovering several feet beyond the cliff edge. "What are we supposed to do? Jump for it?" He looked down at the water below. Waves crashed and sprayed over numerous rocks.

"We can't worry about that now," Kyle said. "We have to go get the agent back out."

"So he can drag me away again?" Jürgen shook his head. "Let's get the aethrial first."

"We can't," Susie said. "We'll be smashed on the rocks if we jump."

"I won't be," Jürgen said. "I'm immune to rocks." He moved several feet back from the edge.

"What are you doing, Jürgen?" Kyle asked him worriedly.

"I'm going to get the egg," He jogged in place, his stomach jiggling.

"You can't do that, you'll be killed!" Veeksha said.

"No, I won't. I fell from the skyship and hit the beach

and wasn't hurt. This cliff is nothing compared to that. No problem."

"No!" Kyle ordered, trying to push Jürgen back. "You have to go get the guy out of the ground first."

Jürgen paused and glared at him. "Don't push me, Kyle. I could put you in the ground, too."

Kyle looked in surprise at his friend, too shocked to speak.

Jürgen's voice softened. "This is the right thing to do. It makes sense. I'm the only one who can safely get the egg."

"I can't let you do it," Kyle said. "The aethrial won't mix with your geopsium. Something bad will happen."

"You can't stop me," Jürgen said, and pushed Kyle aside. He ran toward the edge and leapt from the cliff.

CHAPTER 42

Instead of flying out from the cliff, Jürgen plummeted like a stone. He collided with an outthrust rock then slammed onto a large wet boulder.

"Oh no!" Veeksha screamed.

They watched as Jürgen stood up and stamped his feet in anger. Unfortunately, he slipped and toppled into the sea.

"Jürgen!" Susie shouted. "What are we going to do?"

"The fall didn't seem to hurt him at all," Veeksha said, amazed. "I thought he was going to crack his head open."

"Why isn't he coming back up?" Susie asked. "Does he know how to swim?"

"Yeah, I think so," Kyle said.

"What if he can't swim with all that geopsium in him?" Veeksha asked.

"You're right," Susie said. "Rocks don't float, they sink!"

"He'll drown!"

"What do we do?"

Kyle ran along the edge of the cliff. "I have to find a way down there! Maybe I can save him."

"I don't see any path," Veeksha searched. "It's all just sheer cliff!"

"You'll have to jump, Kyle!" Susie said. "If the geopsium protects Jürgen from getting hurt by falling on rocks, maybe the aquosia in you will protect you from getting hurt by falling into the water."

Kyle paused and looked down. "But I could hit a rock."

"Just aim away from them," Susie said.

"That doesn't seem too easy," Kyle worried.

"While you're thinking about it, Jürgen is drowning," Susie said.

Kyle nodded and ran back and forth along the cliff edge, looking for a wide space of rockless sea below him. He found a likely spot. But what if there were rocks hidden beneath the water? He wasn't protected from rock like Jürgen. He wasn't even sure he was protected from water. It was a long fall.

"Kyle!"

His legs trembled. He didn't have a magic feather to slow his fall.

"Hurry!"

Kyle clenched his fists and willed himself to jump. Nothing happened. He remained unmoving at the edge.

"We don't have time for this!" Susie moved behind Kyle. "Sorry," she said, and gave him a big push.

"No!" Kyle screamed as he fell. Fortunately, he had chosen a good spot and landed in the water without bouncing off the rocks like Jürgen.

"I can't believe you did that!" Veeksha said to Susie.

Kyle barely felt the water when he hit. He slipped peacefully into the sea like he might slip into a pleasant bath. Bubbles swirled around him, and the swell of the waves felt like a soothing hand. He looked around and discovered he could see quite a distance underwater. Sharp rocks sloped away from Moto Nui. Between the two small islands, rough water bubbled in the narrow channel. He saw Jürgen struggling far below him. He was sliding deeper beneath the sea.

Kyle swam toward him at amazing speed. He felt like a fish shooting through the water. In an instant he was beside his friend. Jürgen's face was red and his eyes were wide and fearful. Kyle grabbed him under the arms. He hoped he could lift him. To his surprise, when he kicked off the two of them shot upward. He broke the surface like a dolphin, and both of them vaulted five feet in the air. Kyle carefully pulled Jürgen onto a large flat rock at the base of the cliff.

Jürgen lay unmoving on the rock. It looked like he wasn't breathing. Kyle remembered his sixth grade first aid training and tilted Jürgen's head back, then began pushing on his chest. A fountain of water erupted from Jürgen's mouth and he began coughing and sputtering and struggling.

"Jürgen! You're okay!" Kyle said happily. "I thought you drowned."

Jürgen rolled onto his side and spat out some more water. "I did, also."

"Well, I'm glad you're okay," Kyle said.

"Me, too." Jürgen sat up. "I'm sorry I acted like that up on the cliff. It was a bad idea and I shouldn't have treated you that way."

Kyle smiled. "It's okay. You were just excited."

"Yeah," Jürgen said, "but I really wanted that aethrial. The geopsium is so cool I thought the aethrial would be even better."

"Hey!" Bannecker shouted from above. "Are you two all right?"

"Yeah!" Kyle shouted back. "We're fine."

"You just stay there," he called. "We'll come around and get you with the dinghy."

"Okay!"

"How are we going to get that little egg with a rope?" Susie asked Bannecker at the top of the cliff.

"Good question. It's too far out there to just tie the rope around someone and have them jump. They'd get hurt falling back against the cliff."

"I think I could jump out that far and grab it," Susie said.

"Grab an egg while you're falling?" Veeksha said. "You'd break it and then break yourself." She pointed at the rocks.

"I've jumped off cliffs before."

"This high?"

"No," Susie admitted. "But how else are we going to get it?"

"Maybe the fisherman has a net on a pole?" suggested Veeksha.

Susie shook her head. "I don't think that would work. This is the sky quintessence. I bet it won't let you just grab it from the edge of the cliff. I bet someone has to jump. The bird said "where is it?" That probably means the only way to get it is over there." She pointed at the floating egg.

"That's really dangerous," Veeksha said. "More dangerous than getting the geopsium or the aquosia."

"Maybe the aethrial will meld with me like the other stuff did with Kyle and Jürgen," Susie speculated. "Maybe after I grab it I won't fall."

"Before we try anything," Bannecker said, "I have to get Kyle and Jürgen. I also have to find Tatman. I have no idea where he is."

"Jürgen said he was–" Veeksha started to say, but Susie interrupted her.

"Jürgen said he tricked Tatman into looking for him. He's probably walking around in the maze of rocks. We'll wait here until you find him."

"Yes, wait here. Don't do anything foolish like the boys did. They're both lucky to be alive."

Susie gave him her best smile, the one she used on her parents when they got too protective. "Don't worry, Mr. Bannecker, we'll stay here."

"Okay, I'll be back in a bit."

"Why did you lie to him?" Veeksha asked after the man left.

"We can't trust him with the aethrial. We have to get it first."

"So someone has to jump and grab the egg?"

"Don't worry, I'm not asking you to do it," Susie said.

228

"I've jumped into lakes before. It's fun. You can go catch up with Mr. Bannecker."

"Okay."

"No use waiting," Susie said, and moved several feet away from the edge.

Veeksha stepped aside and Susie ran toward the edge. She leapt off the cliff and sailed out to the egg, grabbing it easily in both hands. It was light and empty, like an Easter egg. It cracked as soon as she touched it.

Chapter 43

The egg crumbled, crushed in her hands. Susie plummeted down and crashed into the water. The impact stung like someone had slapped her across the whole length of her back and legs. She opened her eyes underwater to see a riotous storm of bubbles spiraling around her left hand, in which she held the shards of the broken egg. The bubbles churned around her hand and snaked up her arm. They slid around her neck and swarmed her face. She couldn't see through them, but felt the air sliding into her mouth. She could breathe! Underwater!

She giggled and heard herself quite clearly.

She felt the bubbling around her head, and then something whispered in her ears:

> In the eternal city's ancient heart
> The burnt stone immures the spark
> Between two of seven hills it burns
> Eons it has starved, for food it yearns

The final riddle! Susie grinned happily. She had the final riddle all to herself. Now she could solve it before Veeksha did. All she had to do was find an eternal city. But what did that mean? Maybe it meant an old city? Or ancient? She wondered which one it could be. She didn't know very many ancient cities. But, then, how old did a city have to be to count as ancient? She knew that some cities in South Dakota, like Deadwood, were founded in the Old West.

They were more than a hundred years old. Was that old enough?

"I guess you're okay," Kyle said.

Startled out of her concentration, Susie saw Kyle floating in the water in front her. She could hear him perfectly despite the water. "Let's get back to Jürgen," he said, and pulled her along with him. He moved swiftly through the water, barely kicking or paddling.

"You did better than I did," Jürgen said as he helped to pull her up on the rock.

"Everyone did better than you did," Kyle laughed. "Are you okay, Susie? Did you get the egg?"

Susie held out her hand and opened it. Only a few shards of the egg remained, the rest had washed away.

"Where's the aethrial?" Jürgen asked. "Did it meld with you?"

"I think so. A lot of bubbles went into my mouth."

"Hey, you're not wet!" Kyle exclaimed. It was true. Susie had climbed out of the sea as dry as a bone. Her dark hair waved in the wind.

"Wow!" she said. "That's amazing."

"The aethrial must have dried you," Jürgen said. "Like a hair dryer."

"Weird," Kyle said.

"What should we do now?" Susie asked. "I have the aethrial and the next riddle. But should we help Bannecker or the Zurans?"

"You have the next riddle?" Kyle asked. "What is it?"

"We can talk about that later," Susie said, wanting more time with the riddle herself. "First we have to decide what we're going to do."

"I think Bannecker is lying," Jürgen said. "He hasn't given us any proof of anything he's said."

"But he let us talk to our parents. And have the Zurans proven anything to us?" Kyle said. "They act strange."

"Why should we be surprised that aliens from another

231

planet act weird?" Jürgen said. "You Americans act weird to me, sometimes, and you're from the same planet. I think."

Kyle smiled. "I guess you're right. This is so confusing. I don't know who to trust."

"So we help the Zurans?" Susie asked.

"I guess so."

Jürgen smiled. "Great! Let's go!"

"What about Veeksha?" Susie asked.

"She's a traitor," Jürgen said. "She told Bannecker where we were going. She wants to go back to her parents. I say we leave her."

Susie nodded. "She does want to go back. She never wanted to come along in the first place."

"Yeah, let's leave now," Jürgen insisted.

"No, we can't," Kyle disagreed. "First, you have to go back and save Bannecker's friend."

"Oh, yeah. Right," Jürgen said. "Are you sure?"

"Yes, of course! You can't leave him trapped underground. You don't want to be a murderer, do you?"

Jürgen looked aghast. "You think it could kill him? I thought he'd be in a cave or something and just have to dig his way out."

"Well, if you don't know, we better find out," Kyle insisted.

The inflatable boat appeared around Moto Nui. Bannecker maneuvered it closer and Veeksha threw them a rope. When the boat neared the three kids jumped in.

"Is everyone okay?" Bannecker asked after he had motored away from the cliff into more open water.

"Yeah, we're all fine," Susie answered.

"You're not even wet," Veeksha said to Susie.

"I think it has something to do with the aethrial."

"Do you have the egg?" Bannecker asked.

Susie stared at him. "I accidentally crushed it."

Bannecker swore. "Do you have the aethrial?"

The kids exchanged glances, but no one spoke.

"Come on," Bannecker demanded. "This is no game. Those Zurans are up to no good and unless you level with me I can't be sure to stop them."

Still the children did not speak.

"Fine," Bannecker said, guiding the boat back around to the other side of Moto Nui. "If you won't confide in me, I'll draw my own conclusions. Susie is completely dry, minutes after jumping into the ocean? I'd say she has the aethrial."

"Yes, she has," Veeksha said.

"Only one of you trusts me? Maybe that's to be expected. I am a stranger, after all." He looked down at the children in turn. "But without your help, I won't be able to save your Zuran friends."

"What do you mean by that?" Kyle asked.

"Simple, really. We can't allow the skyship to return to populated areas. They've already killed hundreds of people with that storm. While you were on board, we couldn't risk harming you. But, now we can use whatever force is necessary to disable or destroy the ship."

"What force?" Veeksha asked, concerned for the Zurans.

"Unless you help me find a non-violent solution to the Zuran invasion," Bannecker said, "we'll use powerful missiles to blow up the Windrunner. I doubt very much that any of the Zurans will survive an attack from a naval missile barrage."

"No!" Veeksha yelled. "You can't do that! They aren't here to harm anyone!"

Bannecker steered the boat up to the rocks of the island and jumped out with the rope. He pulled the boat up on shore, and the children disembarked.

"Really? Did they tell you that? Because, if they did, they lied. Kyle and Jürgen can tell you. Their parents were attacked in their cabin. It's only luck that they weren't harmed. Several of my agents were killed or seriously injured at Mt. Rushmore. Helicopters were destroyed, crews killed. Your rasha friend tried to kill me twice. The storm they conjured killed hundreds more. And they've caused such a panic around the world that riots are breaking out and normal people are turning on each other."

Tears started to flow down Veeksha's cheeks. "It can't be…"

"None of that would have happened if you hadn't attacked them," Jürgen said.

"And we wouldn't have attacked them if they hadn't invaded," Bannecker said. "They should have contacted us first, and asked for our help. Instead, they suddenly appeared deep in our territory and refused to talk."

"I guess they could have been more diplomatic," Susie agreed.

"No!" Jürgen said angrily and pointed at Bannecker. "He's the bad guy! He's the one who shot first. He's just trying to trick us. The Zurans just want the quintessence. Nothing more."

Bannecker grabbed Jürgen by the arm. "I'm getting fed up with you, Jürgen! You've been brainwashed by those Zurans. But I can't deal with that now. I have to find Tatman. Where is he?"

"Stop pushing me around or I'll bury you, too!" Jürgen yelled.

"Jürgen!" Kyle said. "Stop it! Just get the guy out from underground before he dies."

"Not until this guy lets me go."

Bannecker released him. "Your father wouldn't like this attitude of yours, Jürgen."

"You don't know my father. You're only his kidnapper!"

Bannecker rolled his eyes. "Enough of that! Where is Tatman?"

Jürgen stomped over to an area of stony ground and pointed down. "Down there."

"I don't see anything," Bannecker said, looking at the bare stone.

Jürgen knelt down and touched the ground. Cracks

widened and pulled apart with a grumble. Everyone jumped back as a deep rocky pit opened at Jürgen's feet. At the bottom stood the agent, looking up at them.

"Thank goodness he's alive," Kyle breathed.

"Tatman!" Bannecker said, smiling. "What happened?"

"The kid made the ground open up and I fell in."

Bannecker looked at the boy. "That's a neat trick, Jürgen. Where'd you learn to do that?"

Jürgen smiled. "The geopsium gives me lots of powers. I bet I could probably turn you to stone."

"Jürgen!" Kyle said. "Quit being a bully!"

Jürgen looked at Kyle. "I just want him to know that we're not pushovers."

"I understand that," Bannecker said. "But do you really want to use those powers against people? You'd be an outlaw and never see your family or friends again."

"I could go to Zura with the Zurans," Jürgen said defiantly.

Kyle shook his head. "Jürgen, you don't mean that."

"Be careful what you wish for, Jürgen," Bannecker said. "I doubt that a visit to Zura will be anything like solving riddles and traveling to tourist attractions."

"Hey, are you going to get me out of here?" the man called from the pit.

"Just a sec," Bannecker said. "You kids stay here while I get the rope. We can discuss everything on the trip back to the States." He hurried off to the boat.

"You didn't really mean what you said, did you, Jürgen?" Susie asked.

Jürgen looked at her, a bit surprised. "I was just trying to scare him. We can't let him get away with telling those lies about the Zurans."

Kyle didn't know if he believed Jürgen's explanation. He had seemed so intense when he made his threats. Kyle wondered if the geopsium had other effects than just the magic that Jürgen had invoked.

"We better get back to the Windrunner," Kyle said, motioning the three other children to come closer.

"Is that what we've decided to do?" Susie asked.

"How else do we save the Zurans?" Kyle said. "We either have to do what Bannecker says or go back and be hostages. Unless you can think of something else?"

Jürgen and Susie didn't have any other solutions.

"We can't trust Bannecker," Jürgen said.

"I guess not," Susie agreed reluctantly.

"Veeksha?" Kyle asked.

"No, I don't think so. But I don't really trust the Zurans, either. We don't know what they're planning."

"They can't do anything without the quintessence, right?" Susie asked. "It ended up in each of us. I bet the fire quintessence will end up in Veeksha. They can't do anything with it while we have it."

"That's true," Jürgen agreed. "And I wouldn't give it to them, even if I could."

"Okay," Susie said. "Let's go back."

"But how are we going to do that?" Veeksha asked, confused.

Kyle smiled. He took out the scrimshaw and handed it to Susie. "Here, you use the magic bone, Susie. You're the aeromancer. Everone hold hands." He grabbed Susie's free hand, and then Veeksha's, who grabbed Jürgen's.

"What do I do now?" Susie asked.

"Break it."

"What are you kids doing?" Bannecker said as he walked up with the rope.

Susie snapped the scrimshaw bone in half.

CHAPTER 44

A vortex of dust and debris blew up around the children. It lifted them off the ground, Susie rising quickly and giggling in the wind. Kyle and Veeksha also rose, but Jürgen's feet stayed planted firmly on the ground, a human anchor. The wind rushed around him frantically, but could not lift him.

"It can't lift Jürgen because of his geopsium," Kyle yelled above the noise of the wind.

"Maybe I can help!" Susie said, and maneuvered down until she could reach Jürgen. She grabbed his arm and then pointed herself back up. They started to rise.

Bannecker rushed up and grabbed Jürgen's legs. "You aren't going anywhere!"

All five of them, the children and Bannecker hanging from Jürgen's legs, rose up.

"Let go of me!" Angrily, Jürgen wrenched a leg free and rammed his foot hard into Bannecker's hands. The man still held on. Jürgen tried again, and this time his legs transformed into stone. With a sickening crunch, Jürgen broke Bannecker's wrist. The agent screamed in pain and lost his grip, falling forty feet back onto the harsh stone of Moto Nui.

"Good riddance," Jürgen yelled, "you creep!"

The children flew into the sky, moving away from Moto Nui and Easter Island. They could see the Windrunner high above them. The sky elemental carried them straight for the Zuran ship.

"Look at the island!" Susie said. Down on Easter Island, many of the moai were lifting themselves to stand once again after centuries of repose.

"Do you think they'll attack the Windrunner?" Veeksha asked.

"They can't," Kyle said. "They don't have their eyes. Without them, they can only see what's on the ground."

A few minutes later they landed on the deck and the elemental gusted off, never to be seen again. Machadaro, Bozabrozy, and Savakala stood before them.

"Top gustboxes full open," the sky captain roared to his crew. "Wingsails to maximum lift. We must get away from this isle!"

The uburu watched Susie's hair and clothing flap in a strange wind. Her avian eyes sparkled happily and she rubbed her taloned hands together. "You have found the aethrial. Excellent!"

Jürgen rushed forward. "You're in danger. Bannecker was on the island. He said that there are navy ships ready to shoot you down!"

"He lives again?" Machadaro growled. "It seems he has a good supply of aquosia."

"He has synthetic aquosia," Jürgen said. "They want to kill you all."

"What is synthetic aquosia?"

"Man-made aquosia. They can make aquosia, instead of just finding it."

Savakala jerked back, amazed. "Your world is truly a magical realm. To create quintessence from naught is an ultimate power indeed."

"Where are these ships that threaten us?" Machadaro demanded.

"I don't know," Jürgen said. "But they don't want to let you get back to populated places."

"When will they attack?"

"They won't," Veeksha said, "as long as we're on board.

They don't want us harmed. They think we're your hostages."

"Yes, it would be difficult to destroy the Windrunner," Machadaro said, "without using overwhelming force that would kill everyone on board."

"Then we're okay," Susie said. "We can go to the next place and they won't bother us."

"Where is the next place?" Savakala asked.

"We don't have the riddle," Veeksha lamented.

"Oh, I have the riddle," Susie said triumphantly. Veeksha stared at her in surprise.

"Good!" Savakala clucked. "Where does it lead us?"

Susie frowned, but did not respond.

"Where must we go for the pyrophyra?"

Susie looked at her feet and mumbled.

"Speak up, child!"

"I don't know," she said sadly.

"What do you mean, you don't know? You have the riddle, do you not?"

"Yes."

"But you don't know the answer. Well, don't keep it to yourself. Tell it to us so we can solve it."

Susie sulked. "I just haven't had time to figure it out yet, you know? I only got it a few minutes ago and I haven't been able to think about it much. I've been trying to remember all the old cities."

"Enough! Just tell us the riddle," Savakala squawked.

Susie sighed, glancing sideways at Veeksha, who she worried would solve the riddle instantly. "Okay, here it is." She recited:

> In the eternal city's ancient heart
> The burnt stone immures the spark
> Between two of seven hills it burns
> Eons it has starved, for food it yearns

Savakala straightened and tapped her beak with a taloned finger.

"Well? What is the answer?"

"You expect us to figure it out in five seconds?" Jürgen laughed.

"Yeah," Susie agreed, "give us some time."

Savakala did not respond. She silently looked down her beak at Veeksha. The young Indian girl hadn't said a word since the riddle was revealed. Slowly, she looked up at the uburu and they stared at each other for several long seconds.

Susie scowled. "Oh! You don't know the answer already, do you, Veeksha? That is so not fair! How come you always get them so quickly?"

"She's a brainiac." Kyle smiled. "You do know the answer, don't you?"

Veeksha nodded.

"Then tell us," Savakala demanded, "so we can depart before we are attacked."

Veeksha looked at Susie. "But I want to give her a chance to guess it."

"We don't have time for childish games," the aeromagus said. "Just tell me. Now!"

Susie took Veeksha's hand. "It's okay, Veeksha. You can tell her. I'm not going to get the answer. I can't even guess the first line."

"Are you sure?"

"Yes, go ahead," Susie urged, even though everyone could tell she was disappointed.

Veeksha looked up at Savakala, who stood with arms folded, staring expectantly at the child.

Chapter 45

"Rome," Veeksha said. "We have to go to Rome."

"How do you know that?" Susie asked.

"The first and third lines of the riddle point to Rome," Veeksha said proudly. "The first line mentions the eternal city, and that's a nickname for Rome. And Rome is famous for having seven hills."

"Oh," Susie said, frustrated. "I didn't know that."

"Where is this Rome?" Savakala asked.

"Halfway around the world," Veeksha answered.

"Is that far?"

"I'll have to check my KnowPad to be sure, but it's many thousands of miles."

"That will take many days," Machadaro noted. "Many days of being followed by your strange skyships. Bannecker might be waiting for us there. Unless you call up another maelstrom to fend them off."

"There was but one storm wind in the Flagon of the Six Winds," Savakala lamented.

"That's good," Kyle said, glaring angrily at Savakala, "because your last storm killed a lot of people!"

"Yes," said Savakala with a nod. "Elemental maelstroms do not concern themselves with the plight of the tiny beings below them. They exist to storm and rage and thunder and scour the land with their fury."

"Then why did you summon it?"

"Our quest is more important than the lives of a few humans," Savakala said. "Our quest will save our entire world."

"It wasn't a few humans," Kyle said. "It was hundreds."

Bozabrozy frowned. "I'm sorry to hear that, Kyle."

Savakala sighed. "If I could have averted such loss of life, I would, of course, have done so. I was forced to act by the repeated attacks of Rakanian's minions. It is at his feet, not mine, that those lives lay."

"Getting back to the problem at hand," Machadaro said. "I don't wish to be harried by the Earthling skyships. They will devise new schemes to thwart us."

"The Flagon still contains two winds," Savakala said. "The Swift Wind, I think, will serve us here, although I am loathe to release it."

"Since we're on the last leg of the quest," Machadaro said, "perhaps you should."

"Perhaps. Come, Veeksha, you and Machadaro and I will review the journey to Rome on your magical tablet. Then I will decide if the Swift Wind is the best method to get us there."

The three returned to the main deck more than an hour later. Veeksha had shown them where Rome was, and also done more research on the riddle. She still wasn't sure what some of the lines meant.

Jürgen, noticing Savakala's Flagon of the Six Winds, asked, "What's in the bottle?"

"A way to greatly increase our speed to Rome," the uburu replied.

"Another sky elemental like the one that brought us back to the ship?" Veeksha said.

Savakala nodded. "Simply put, yes. However, this one is vastly more powerful and perilous."

"Not like the elemental maelstrom, I hope?" Susie asked fearfully.

"No. This elemental is called a sylph," Savakala explained. "The Windrunner already has a sky elemental bound to the bowsprit, parting the air in front of us so the ship can sail more swiftly. But the sylph will create a sylph stream, a tunnel in the sky, and push us through at amazing speeds. Like a stream."

"Won't we get blown off the ship by the winds?" Veeksha asked.

"That is why it is perilous. The sylph is a capricious being, like all sky elementals. Unless it is rigidly dominated, it will fly off to wherever it wishes and take us with it. Fortunately, this is not the first time I have commanded one of them."

"How long will it take to get to Rome?" Jürgen asked.

"A day or more, perhaps."

"Great. More sitting around on deck twiddling our thumbs."

"This time you must stay in your cabin," Machadaro said.

"Why?"

"Because the sylph is not infallible," Savakala said. "Over such a long journey there will be times when gusts will wash across the decks. You could be blown off the ship quite easily."

"How will the crew handle the ship?"

"Very carefully," Machadaro said grimly.

"The crew is accustomed to such peril," Savakala said. "And their captain is very skilled. You need not fear, if you stay below decks."

Jürgen frowned. "I guess it's okay if it's only until tomorrow."

"You'd best go to your cabins," Machadaro ordered as he headed toward the captain's deck.

Veeksha followed him. "But I want to stay with you."

The big tiger-man shook his head. "I must remain at the prow and watch for the landmarks you described. I must also command the crew and give Savakala course corrections. I will be on deck. It will be too dangerous for you."

"It will be dangerous for you, too!"

Machadaro smiled. "It will take more than a simple sky elemental to slay this rasha. Fear not. I will still be standing on the captain's deck when we fly over your eternal city of Rome."

"Promise?"

"I promise."

"Machadaro!" Savakala yelled. "Get to the captain's deck and prepare the ship. Veeksha, go to your cabin. Now!"

"I don't like Savakala," Veeksha whispered to Machadaro.

"Very few of us do," the rasha agreed. "Now off with you. I will see you tomorrow."

Veeksha reluctantly followed her friends to their cabin.

"The last leg of the quest!" Jürgen clapped his hands together. "I wonder what the fire elemental will look like. Hopefully, it will be as cool as the stone elemental and not as boring as the sky elemental."

"Hey!" Susie objected. "What was wrong with the sky elemental?"

"It was only a bird," Jürgen scoffed. "I was expecting a tornado, at least."

"I like birds," Susie said.

Jürgen smiled. "I figured that, Susie Five Eagles."

"At least she doesn't go around killing people," Veeksha said.

"I didn't kill anybody!" Jürgen said.

"That man could have suffocated in that pit," Veeksha said.

"And Bannecker could be dead after that fall," Susie pointed out.

"I don't think so," Jürgen said. "He has aquosia. He'll be fine."

Someone knocked on their door, and a moment later Bozabrozy stuck his whiskered nose into the room. "How are you faring?"

"Great!" Jürgen replied. "This really is a fun quest."

"Except for boring elemental birds," Susie noted.

"Has Savakala summoned the sylph yet?" Kyle asked.

"She has started the ritual," Bozabrozy said, sitting down on a stool. "It will be only a short time before it appears and whisks us on our way."

"What are you going to do on the trip?" Susie asked him.

"Stay below decks, as ordered," he said with a smile. "Just like you."

"What will happen after we find the fire quintessence?" Jürgen asked. "What's it called again?"

"Pyrophyra," Bozabrozy said. "It is perhaps the most dangerous of the four quintessences. Savakala will know what to do after we find it."

"I bet Veeksha melds with the pyrophyra," Jürgen guessed.

"I agree with you, Jürgen," Bozabrozy said. "And that is why I have come to talk with her."

"Talk with me?" Veeksha asked. "Why?"

"At Machadaro's request. He bade me to educate you on the dangers of pyrophyra."

"Can't he just tell me himself?"

"If he could, he would. He has grown quite fond of you over the…" Bozabrozy paused, but then hurried on, "…over the last several days. He will be busy until we reach the city, and he does not want you to encounter the pyrophyra unwarned."

"What's so dangerous about the stuff?" Kyle asked.

"Of all the elemental quintessences, pyrophyra is the most destructive. Fire can burn skyships and cities and forests and Zurans and humans quite easily. Pyrophyra is even more powerful, and primal pyrophyra is more powerful than that."

"That doesn't sound good," Kyle said. "Maybe Veeksha shouldn't even get near it."

"That's not fair," Veeksha said. "All three of you have quintessence. Why can't I?"

"No one is saying that you can't," Bozabrozy said. "I'm only here to tell you what dangers you face. The pyrophyra hungers for fuel, anything that burns. Don't let it consume you."

"What does that mean?" Veeksha asked, suddenly less certain about the prospect of getting near the stuff.

Susie looked aghast. "You don't think it will burn her up, do you?"

"Unfortunately, that is a possibility," Bozabrozy said. "Just as Jürgen was petrified by the primal geopsium, so, too, might Veeksha be incinerated by the pyrophyra."

The children stared at him, mouths agape. Kyle finally spoke. "I think maybe we should skip the last quest, don't you?"

"Savakala would never allow that," Bozabrozy said.

"We can't let Veeksha die!" Susie exclaimed.

"Who says I'll die?" Veeksha said. "I won't die, will I, Bozabrozy?"

Bozabrozy stared at her. "No, of course not. Well, actually, yes, you might. If you do not master the pyrophyra immediately, it may overwhelm you. You could die a most painful death."

Veeksha sat down, eyes wide.

"Aren't you supposed to try to make her feel better, instead of worse?" Kyle said.

"Machadaro wants her to know the full menace that she faces."

Susie sat next to Veeksha and hugged her. "You don't have to do it, Veeksha. You can't risk it."

"There are ways to minimize the risk," Bozabrozy said. "There is Kyle."

"Me?" Kyle looked surprised. "What can I do?"

"You are melded with primal aquosia, the opposite of pyrophyra. You can use the power of aquosia to subdue the pyrophyra."

"How do I do that?"

"The same way you helped Jürgen, by imagining it."

Kyle frowned. "That's really helpful."

"When the time comes," Bozabrozy said, "you can use the aquosia to stem the fires."

"That's it?" Susie asked.

"I'm afraid so."

"What if she decides not to have anything to do with the pyrophyra?" Jürgen asked. "I can get it instead."

Bozabrozy looked at the boy. "A noble gesture, to be sure. But you already have geopsium within you. You don't want to mix it with pyrophyra."

"Why not? It's not the opposite of stone. Don't geopsium and pyrophyra get along?"

"Combining quintessences is a dangerous game," Bozabrozy warned. "Chaos erupts when the elements mix. If you were to absorb geopsium and pyrophyra, there is no telling what catastrophe might occur."

"It's better than letting Veeksha get burnt up," Jürgen insisted.

"We can't be sure of that," Bozabrozy said. "No, it's best to let Veeksha do it. I'm sure she is strong enough to control its raging fires. Aren't you, Veeksha?"

She did not answer.

CHAPTER 46

Shortly after the rascan left, the wind grew outside. The ship lurched forward and the children guessed that they had slipped into the sylph stream.

"I can't tell how fast we're going," Jürgen said, looking out the porthole. "We're too high up and it's only water down there."

"I wish we would go slower," Veeksha said. "I wouldn't mind taking longer to get there."

"Why didn't they tell us this before?" Susie asked. "It's not fair to make you risk your life."

"They can't make her do it," Kyle reminded them. "And I don't think she should do it. Let one of them meld with the pyrophyra."

"Yeah, let that Savakala do it," Jürgen said and laughed. "Fried chicken!"

"She's an aeromagus," Susie said. "She'd be mixing elements."

Kyle pondered how they had found the previous quintessences. "Don't you think it's strange that Savakala keeps letting us do all the melding?"

"She's not letting us," Jürgen said. "She didn't have a choice with the geopsium. She wasn't even there. Joromwor tried to get it, but the stone elemental wouldn't give it to him."

"And the water elemental didn't like her at all," Susie said. "It blasted her away. It would only give the aquosia to you."

"And the Zurans wouldn't even get close to Easter Island," Veeksha said. "So they had no chance to get the aethrial."

"I guess that's all true," Kyle agreed. "But it's still weird that it keeps happening like this."

"It just seems like bad luck for them," Susie said.

"Good luck for us, then," Jürgen said. "I like having the geopsium. I can turn to stone. I can fall from anywhere and not get hurt. I can make the ground open up."

"And why wouldn't the Zurans want those powers?" Kyle asked. "They can only use their artifacts to make magic. They'd be a lot more powerful if they melded with quintessence."

"They can't," Veeksha said. "They aren't elemancers."

"But they have the magical elequaries," Kyle insisted. "Savakala said her staff can hold quintessence."

"That's true," Susie agreed. "Why don't they grab the quintessence with that?"

"Maybe they can't."

"If the four of us have the quintessences, what are they going to do then?" Kyle said. "If they need the stuff to save their world, what good is it going to do inside us?"

"They'll have to take us to Zura!" Jürgen said happily.

"I don't want to go to Zura," Kyle said. "I've had enough of Zurans. They're too different."

"And too mean," Susie said. "Only Bozabrozy is nice."

"Machadaro is nice!" Veeksha said.

"Nice to you," Susie said. "Not so nice to the rest of us."

"You guys don't think going to another planet would be cool?" Jürgen asked. "Seeing all the species of Zurans? Trying out all the alien food? It would be like…like…like a big party of nothing but Zurans and Zura!"

"Like a Zurapalooza," Susie laughed.

"What's that?" Jürgen asked.

"Nothing," Susie said. "I just made it up. It's like a big concert that my dad went to once."

"I'd like to go back to my parents," Veeksha said.

"Me, too," Kyle agreed.

"Yeah," Susie said. "I miss them and my brother."

"I miss my parents, too," Jürgen said. "But they wouldn't think twice about a chance to go to Zura."

"If you want to go to Zura, you can," Susie said. "Just don't expect us to go with you."

"Yeah," Kyle agreed. "Once we have all the quintessence, we'll have the upper hand. They'll have to do what we say if they want us to cooperate."

"But what will they want us to do?" Veeksha wondered. None of them could answer that.

"What does the rest of the riddle mean, Veeksha?" Susie asked, changing the subject. "I can't figure it out." And she recited the riddle.

> In the eternal city's ancient heart
> The burnt stone immures the spark
> Between two of seven hills it burns
> Eons it has starved, for food it yearns

"I think the ancient heart means the ruins of the Roman Forum," Veeksha said, "which is near two of Rome's seven hills."

"What's the Roman Forum?"

"It's a bunch of ancient ruins of shrines, government buildings, and monuments."

"There must be a fire elemental there," Jürgen said. "There's been an elemental at each of the three other places. We probably have to bribe it like we did the stone elemental."

"That's what the last line means, I bet," Kyle agreed.

"That should be easy," Susie said. "A fire elemental just wants to burn things. We can bring some wood with us."

"That's a good idea, Susie," Kyle complimented her.

"What does immure mean?" Jürgen asked.

"It's another word for imprison," Veeksha said.

"The pyrophyra must be locked up," Susie said.

"By a burnt stone," Jürgen said. "What does it mean burnt stone?"

"Maybe some kind of lava or magma?" Kyle guessed. "Is Rome near that volcano that exploded a long time ago?"

"You mean Mt. Vesuvius," Veeksha said. "And, no, Rome is not near it. Vesuvius is a hundred miles away."

"Are there any volcanoes in Rome?" Susie asked.

"No."

"Then what does 'burnt stone' mean?" Jürgen said.

"Maybe it means a kiln, or an anvil?" Kyle guessed.

"Oh," Veeksha said. "You could be right. It might not literally mean a burnt stone. That might just be poetry that means something else."

"What else could be burnt stone?" Kyle asked. "Lava? Magma? Obsidian? Pumice?"

"What happens when you burn stone?" Susie asked.

"Stone doesn't burn," Jürgen replied. "It just gets all covered in soot."

Veeksha smiled. "That's it! It means black! Burnt stone is blackened!"

"So?"

"When I was researching the Roman Forum with Savakala, I noticed something called the Lapis Niger. It's Latin for Black Stone."

"Wait a minute," Susie held up her hands. "You speak Latin?"

"A little," Veeksha sheepishly replied.

"What makes you think the Black Stone has something to do with our riddle?" Kyle asked.

"The Lapis Niger was found in one of the oldest shrines in the Roman Forum. It was found in the Vulcanal. That's the shrine to Vulcan, the Roman god of fire!"

Jürgen clapped his hands together. "That's it! A burnt stone in the fire shrine. You did it again, Veeksha!"

"Good job, Veeksha!" Susie hugged her.

"I should have figured it out immediately. I feel so stupid."

"Now we know where the pyrophyra is," Kyle said. "But should we even try to get it?"

"We should," Veeksha said, taking a deep breath. "But I'm scared."

"We'll be there to help you, Veeksha," Susie promised.

"That's right!" Jürgen agreed.

"We sure will," Kyle said. "Where is this shrine?"

"It's buried under the Forum."

Jürgen grinned. "Buried? No problem. I can dig it up with my geopsium powers."

"You shouldn't do that," Veeksha warned. "This is a valuable historical site, full of ancient architecture and culture. You'd ruin it."

"Ruining the ruins?" Jürgen laughed. "How else are we going to get to it?"

"I don't know."

"Don't worry," Jürgen said. "I'll just open a little hole and close it back up when we're finished, just like it was."

"Can you do that?" Susie asked.

"Of course," Jürgen said confidently. "I'm a geomancer."

"We'll need rope to climb down," Kyle said.

"And wood to feed the elemental," Susie added, and they made plans to collect their supplies for the adventure.

The Windrunner flew eastward and the sun set swiftly behind them. Sailing through the sylph stream, they crossed over the west coast of South America. A few hours after that, the skyship shot out over the Atlantic Ocean.

Machadaro remained on the captain's deck, only taking short breaks after long hours. He watched Susie's compass as the Windrunner coursed northeast. By the time the coastline of Portugal came into view, the rising sun glared in Machadaro's eye. The Mediterranean Sea sped by swiftly beneath them. The islands of Malta and Sardinia came and went. Finally, the Windrunner flew over the Tyrrhenian Sea. Machadaro ordered the first mate to tell Savakala that the sylph could be released. The children, long since awake in their cabin, tumbled forward with the sudden decrease in velocity.

"Hey!" Jürgen complained, spilling strawpple juice all over his shirt.

"We must be in Italy!" They hurried to the captain's deck to find Machadaro standing tall and strong. Under an overcast sky, the Windrunner sailed the last few miles above the Tyrrhenian Sea between Sardinia and the Italian peninsula.

"Are you okay, Machadaro?" Veeksha asked.

"Of course," said the tiger-man. He pointed at the coast. "Does that look like Italy to you?"

The kids rushed to the railing.

"I wouldn't know," Veeksha said. "I've never been there."

"I have," Jürgen said. "That's it, all right. And that's Rome over there!" He pointed to the left.

Machadaro looked through his skyglass and then shouted orders to the crew. The Windrunner turned toward the Eternal City.

"Look!" Susie pointed. Two jet fighters flew toward them, engines roaring.

CHAPTER 47

"Roll out the cannon!" Machadaro roared.

"Do you think they're going to attack us?" Susie said.

"Bannecker said they didn't want to attack while we were on board," Kyle reminded her.

"Maybe they changed their minds," Jürgen said.

"Bozabrozy!" Machadaro yelled. "Fetch Savakala. We'll need her lightning to fend off those skyships." The rascan rushed off.

"Look!" Veeksha said. "They're circling."

It was true. The jet fighters did not approach the Windrunner. Instead, they curved around the skyship, at least a mile away.

Machadaro grinned, his sinuous tail waving. "It seems they have learned their lesson." He turned around and bellowed out to the crew. "They're too frightened to attack! They've heard of the Windrunner's bite!" The crew cheered. "But, just in case, keep your stations at the cannon!"

Bozabrozy returned. "Savakala is too weak to battle. We have only the fire cannon to defend us."

"It matters not," Machadaro said. "They do not wish to fight."

Kyle watched as they neared Rome, the Eternal City, a sprawling metropolis of white and brown and yellow buildings with red tile roofs. From the coast it stretched many miles inland to the foothills of the Appenine Mountains.

"Now it is up to you, Veeksha," Machadaro said.

"Where is this Forum we must visit?"

"It's several miles up the Tiber River, near the Coliseum," she replied.

"That river there?" Machadaro pointed.

"Yes. There is an island in it some miles up. We should be able to see the Forum when we see the island."

The Windrunner sailed only several hundred feet above the ancient city. Kyle looked down. He could see the streets and parked cars. But…

"Where are the people?" he asked.

"I don't see any people, either," Jürgen said, staring down.

"That's strange," Veeksha said. "Millions of people live here."

"All the cars are parked. The roads are empty."

"Look over there," Susie pointed. "There's something moving."

Machadaro used his skyglass. "Strange wagons." He handed the glass to Kyle. "What are those?"

Kyle could easily see tanks grouped in an open area. The turrets swiveled to follow the Windrunner.

"Um…those are tanks. They're war machines."

"They have cannon?"

"Oh, yeah. Big, bad monster cannons."

"There are more over there," Susie said.

Machadaro nodded. "Bannecker does not make the same mistake twice. His previous aerial assault failed, and so he keeps his skyships at a distance merely to watch us. His stealthy strike at night with elite warriors failed, so now he prepares a ground force to stop us."

"How did he know we were coming to Rome?" Veeksha asked.

"He is crafty, with a world's resources at his beck and call. If this city of Rome is as ancient and important as you say, it would be a simple guess to name it as our destination based on our course."

"We'd better leave," Veeksha suggested. "They could have all sorts of tanks and soldiers waiting for us."

"We are near the end of the quest," Savakala spoke in a weak voice. She hovered onto the captain's deck, her feet inches above the planking, the feathers of her magical cloak fluttering.

"Wow!" said Susie. "You're floating on air! Does that cloak let you fly?"

Savakala ignored her. "We shan't be frightened off by a few puny human warriors and their cannon."

Kyle frowned. "I don't think there will be only a few of them. And they aren't puny."

Joromwor strode onto the deck, towering beside the uburu, wearing his Indomitable Armor and carrying the terrible Sundering Bardiche.

"Expecting a war, legate?" Bozabrozy asked.

"We won't win the pyrophyra without a battle, mark my words," Joromwor replied. "They have had long to prepare. But they have not faced me."

Kyle shook his head. "I don't think armor and a big axe will be much use against tanks."

"Silence, boy!" Joromwor growled. "Your work is nearly done. I would have thought you eager to finish it and flee back to your parents."

"Is that the island?" Machadaro interrupted.

Veeksha turned to look over the rail. The boat-shaped Tiber Island was clearly visible below, as was the Coliseum. Between them, several blocks of ruins and monuments marked the Roman Forum.

"Yes, that's the island. Do you see that open area by the domed building? That's the Forum. We should land there."

"It shall be done," said Machadaro, smiling at her. He yelled orders to the crew.

Jürgen leaned over the rail. "I wonder where everyone is?"

"I bet they evacuated the city," Kyle said.

"The whole city?" Susie said, surprised. "Millions of people?"

"They fear the wrath of Zura," Savakala boasted. "They are wise."

The Windrunner circled around the dome of the Temple of Concord, flew over the blocky building called the Curia Julia, and then hovered over the rubble and ruins of the Forum.

"I am too spent to aid you in recovering the pyrophyra," Savakala said. "Joromwor, you and the captain will accompany the children."

The rasha looked surprised. "You want me to join the landing party? Why?"

"We don't need his help," Joromwor objected, obviously upset at Savakala's lack of trust in him and his legionaries. "He cannot compare to me and my legionaries."

Savakala cackled. "Perhaps you don't recall your previous battles against him."

"Luck," Joromwor scoffed. "He could not stand against me claw to claw."

Veeksha moved next to the captain. "Machadaro wasn't losing until Savakala hit him with lightning!"

"That's right," Jürgen agreed. "That wasn't a fair fight. Two against one is cheating."

"I would have slain him without Savakala's interference," Joromwor claimed.

"You have yet to prove that boast," Machadaro growled. The two stared at each other.

Savakala rolled her eyes. "Enough of this rivalry! We have a quest to complete. The captain will accompany you to the Forum and help retrieve the pyrophyra. He certainly knows more about pyrophyra than you do, legate."

Joromwor ground his teeth but said nothing.

"I do know about pyrophyra," Machadaro agreed. "And so I will need the Burning Blade."

Joromwor's eyes widened. "You can't give him the

sword. He's far too dangerous with it."

"So," Bozabrozy said with a laugh, "if equally armed, you're no match for him?"

The urgra spun around and growled at the rascan. "Shut your muzzle, pest! I'll not endure your jibes. The Burning Blade is an elequary!"

"So it is," Savakala agreed, looking at the captain, "and I doubt your need for it on this short landing."

"You do not doubt the need," Machadaro countered. "We both know that the pyrophyra will be guarded by a fire elemental, just as the other quintessences were guarded by elementals."

"What of it? Those elementals were dealt with easily enough."

"Not according to the children," Machadaro said. "The stone elemental almost killed your urgra, and the water elemental doused you."

"And yet, no lasting damage was sustained."

"Fire elementals are far more dangerous and unpredictable than stone and water and sky," the rasha stated.

"As are you," Savakala said softly. She turned away, thinking.

"You can use an elequary?" Veeksha asked the captain. "Does that mean that you're a pyromagus?"

Machadaro nodded.

"I knew it!" Veeksha said gleefully, and turned to Jürgen. "See? I told you. He's a powerful fire wizard!"

"He has quite a reputation," Bozabrozy said. "You might even say he's a legend."

Joromwor snorted.

Savakala asked, "What assurance do I have that you will return the sword to me when you are done?"

"You have my word as captain of this ship."

"The word of a pirate and spy and traitor is worth nothing," Joromwor scoffed. "His betrayals are infamous."

"And yet," Savakala said, "he has proven himself honorable many times." She lapsed once again into silent contemplation.

Machadaro shook his head in disgust. "You are a poor leader, Savakala. All this talk and debate. Stop talking! Stop debating! Make a decision. Give me the blade, or do not. Fortune favors the bold, and without fortune, this quest will fail."

Kyle expected the uburu to bristle at the insult, but Savakala merely narrowed her eyes and slowly said, "The captain will disembark with the rest of you. I shall give him the Burning Blade so he may contend with the fire elemental."

Joromwor opened his mouth to object, but Savakala stopped him with a gesture. "If the captain does not relinquish the weapon immediately upon his return, you may kill him."

Joromwor smiled.

Chapter 48

Moments later, Savakala returned from her cabin with a large curved blade, ornately decorated and glowing like a hot coal. Machadaro took it, smiling.

"Too long has this languished in your cabin," he said.

"All the emperor's property resides with the magistrate," Joromwor said.

"This blade is mine," Machadaro said as he strapped a scabbard to his belt and sheathed the weapon. "I paid an eye to win it, in distant skies you would quail at braving."

"That's heresy!" Joromwor growled. "All quintessence is the emperor's!"

"All quintessence that he knows about." Machadaro winked at Veeksha.

"Spoken like a true pirate!" the legate snarled. He turned to Savakala. "Mark my words, his loyalties lie not with us. He cares only for himself."

Savakala sighed. "You have told me that before, and I've marked your words. But, as you well know, everyone on this ship is united in our desire to save Zura. The captain included. If he does not help us, Zura is lost. Is that not right, Captain?"

Machadaro frowned, but nodded.

"And, Veeksha," Savakala said, "here is your magical tablet, in case you require its knowledge to win the pyrophyra." She handed the girl her backpack.

"Thanks!" said Veeksha, quite surprised.

"Hey!" Jürgen objected. "That's not fair. What about our

backpacks? Why does she get her stuff and we don't get ours?"

"Of course. I have dealt with children before, and I am familiar with your petty jealousies," Savakala said, waving to two legionaries behind her. They bore the other three children's backpacks, and gave them back to their owners.

"Wow!" Susie exclaimed, taking her backpack. "When did you get nice all of a sudden?"

Jürgen's eyes widened. "I can't believe you just said that out loud."

Susie clapped a hand over her mouth, abashed.

And so, with everyone fully equipped, the captain led the children below decks to the platform room. Jürgen carried a bundle of wood under his arm and Kyle had a rope looped over his shoulder. Mumbas turned the windlass and lowered them down to the Forum, first Joromwor and several canar legionaries, heavily armed and armored, then the children and the rasha. Bozabrozy slid down a rope, smiling and waving.

Machadaro knelt down beside Veeksha. "Listen to me, little one. I did not expect Savakala to allow me to disembark with you. Since she has, I shall collect the pyrophyra. It is far too dangerous for you."

"How can you collect it? You're not a pyromancer, are you?"

"No, I am merely a magus. However," he said, patting the sword at his side, "the Burning Blade is an elequary, and it can collect pyrophyra within it. It will also protect me from the peril of a fire elemental."

"Really?" Veeksha smiled in relief. "So I don't have to touch the pyrophyra?"

The captain smiled back. "No, you do not."

"That's good," said Susie. She gave Veeksha's shoulder a squeeze. "I was really worried that you'd get burned up."

"So was I."

"That's an awesome sword," Jürgen said. "Can it do

261

anything else?"

"It can do many things."

"Where did you get it?"

"Beyond the Grinding Isles on the far side of the Bosikor Expanse." The captain held up his hand when he saw Jürgen open his mouth again. "No more questions."

They stepped off the platform and into the Eternal City of Rome.

"Wow," Susie said, spinning around. "I've never seen so many ancient ruins in one place before. Well, actually, I've never seen any ancient ruins in person before."

"Haven't you ever been to Europe?" Jürgen asked. "Ruins are everywhere in Europe."

"No."

"Me neither," Kyle said, gaping at the architecture. "I've only been to Canada. This is cool."

Jürgen laughed. "Americans sure love collapsed buildings. I guess it's because you don't have any history like we do."

"Hey!" Kyle objected. "We have history! What about Paul Revere and cowboys and…um…the Civil War…"

"A couple hundred years can't really compare to thousands," Jürgen said proudly.

"Well, at least we have…Devil's Tower!" Susie spouted.

Jürgen shook his head and smiled. "Nope. Geologic formations can't be used in a history duel. I win."

"Enough," Joromwor interrupted while his legionaries spread out warily. "No jabbering while an army threatens to attack us. Where do we go now?"

"Over there, in front of the Curia Julia," Veeksha said, checking her KnowPad and leading the way. Everyone followed her through scattered stacks of stone and fallen pillars to a blockish brick building. She walked across a narrow sward of short grass and onto a stone path until she stood looking at the Curia Julia on her right, squat and powerful and ancient, and the towering Arch of Septimius

Severus on her left.

Susie gaped at the white marble monument of three imposing archways with ancient Latin text engraved across the top and weathered friezes carved between four columns below. Bozabrozy ran his hands over the ancient stone. "There are similar monuments in Azuria."

"We're not here to gawk at ruins," Joromwor said. "Where is the pyrophyra?"

Veeksha tore her gaze from the impressive historical structures and looked around the plaza, comparing it to the map on her computer screen. "This area is called the Comitium and the Vulcanal lies beneath it. We're looking for black marble that covers it."

"Like that?" Susie said, pointing to a small area hemmed in by a low stone wall and a black metal railing. Irregular black and gray stones covered most of the ground inside but left some earth exposed. A narrow stairwell led down nearby, but it was also blocked off by the fence.

"This must be it. It's in the right place."

"The pyrophyra is beneath these stones?" Bozabrozy leapt over the railing and knelt to look.

"Yes."

Joromwor strode up and tore the fence from the ground.

Veeksha screamed, "What are you doing? You can't do that! That's vandalism!"

"Yeah," Susie said, pointing. "We can use these steps!"

"That tunnel is far too small for me," Joromwor said, raising the Sundering Bardiche. "I will make a larger hole."

Veeksha interposed herself between the urgra and the black paving stones. "I won't let you do it! You'll be destroying history!"

"So be it," Joromwor said.

"Hey!" Jürgen said, hurrying over to Veeksha. "I can use my geopsium powers to make a hole and then close it back all nice and neat."

"Foolish human," the legate scoffed. "You haven't the

training to work such magic."

"Let the child at least try," Bozabrozy said. "It will be a good test for a young geomancer."

"Stand aside, whelps!" Joromwor demanded, but Susie and Kyle joined their friends to block his efforts.

"Arguing with a child is the province of a fool," said Machadaro, smirking at the sight of four tiny humans standing resolute before the towering urgra. "It will be quicker to let him try. When he fails, you can laugh at his folly and get on with it."

Joromwor scowled at the sky captain.

"You're wasting precious time, Legate, with an enemy so near."

Joromwor stepped back, sneering. "You have until the count of ten before my bardiche cleaves this stone."

"You'd better hurry, Jürgen," Kyle said, stepping aside.

Jürgen dropped his bundle of wood and knelt at the edge of the fenced area. He touched the ground and it bulged. The paving stones slid apart and away. Beneath, larger stone blocks folded up and back, sliding and tilting over one another to stack neatly around the perimeter. Jürgen's forehead furrowed in concentration as the stones obeyed his will and revealed the ancient pit.

Chapter 49

"Hah!" Susie laughed and pointed at Joromwor. "You were wrong! He did it!"

The legate growled but said nothing.

They gazed down into the Vulcanal. Within squatted three short blocks of stone and what looked like a column. Near one of the platforms was a stele inscribed with ancient text.

"That's it," Veeksha said.

"What do we do now?" Jürgen wondered.

"Free the spark," said Machadaro, who leapt into the pit and placed his massive paws on the stele.

"Wait, Machadaro!" Veeksha yelled, and pointed at her KnowPad. "You have to be careful! It says here that the stone is cursed."

"If curses are all that stand between me and the pyrophyra, then so be it." His mighty thews rippled beneath his fur. With a grunt and a growl he toppled the stele from the platform, revealing a cavity beneath, deep and dark.

"What do you see?" Joromwor demanded.

"Naught but darkness," Machadaro sighed.

"What? That can't be right. The pyrophyra must be there," Veeksha said.

"Wait…" Machadaro bent down to gaze deeply into the cavity. "There…is a spark."

A tremor ran through the ground around them. Machadaro threw himself away from the cavity just as a geyser of flame erupted from it. A terrible blast of heat washed over the Comitium, sending everyone stumbling backwards. Machadaro leapt out of the pit, his fur smoking. Jürgen rolled away across the stone walkway, trying to pat out his burning clothes.

"Jürgen! You're on fire!" Kyle rushed over to his friend. He slapped his flaming clothes and a huge spray of water splashed all over them.

"Thanks, Kyle," Jürgen said.

"No problem," Kyle wiped the water from his face. Both of them were drenched.

Susie laughed. "It looked like you both got hit by a giant water balloon." She and Veeksha were unharmed by the fiery blast. Veeksha hurriedly replaced her KnowPad in her pack, hoping to protect it from any further explosions. The Zurans were not injured and even Machadaro, who had been in the pit where the fire was hottest, was barely singed. He stared at the inferno filling the pit.

"I think we freed the fire elemental," Susie said in awe.

The fire churned and pulsed and waved. Its crackling roar pounded their ears like a crescendo of incendiary doom. Within the howl they could hear a voice, like none they had ever heard before. A voice that sizzled and crackled and popped.

"Who has freed me at their own doom?" it asked.

Machadaro strode bravely forward, holding the Burning Blade before him, apparently oblivious to the scorching heat. "I did. And for that I demand the boon of your pyrophyra."

A gout of flame spurted out at Machadaro, but he did not flinch.

"You do not belong here or now, Zuran," the elemental said. "I shall give you nothing. I shall not give my treasure to anyone!"

"You would not reward your liberator after so many centuries?" Machadaro growled.

"The reward you shall suffer is the curse placed upon the lock of my prison. The Romans feared my wrath, and rightly so. I have ravaged their precious city before, and thanks to you I shall do so again. For that, you shall forfeit your life to their ancient vengeance."

"NO!" Veeksha screamed and ran to Machadaro, hiding from the elemental's heat behind his legs. "He wasn't supposed to free you. I was!"

The elemental blazed with an intense light. "Then you must thank him for saving you from endless woe."

"You can't do this to him!" Veeksha pleaded.

"It is not I who do this, but the curse laid down so long ago."

"But it should have been me!" she cried.

"And why would you wish to free me, small one?"

"For the pyrophyra," Veeksha said.

"Freeing me would not have earned you the pyrophyra."

"What price do you ask for your treasure?" Machadaro demanded.

"There is no price," the fire elemental sizzled. "The pyrophyra is mine and mine alone."

Everyone cringed as another wave of heat spread over them.

Bozabrozy shook his head sadly. "Did I forget to mention that fire elementals are greedy? They want everything for themselves."

Machadaro squinted into the heat. "If you will not give it to us, then we shall take it."

The elemental crackled and sputtered, and Kyle realized it was laughing. "Who shall brave my inferno?" it said.

"I shall!" Machadaro strode forward against the heat, Veeksha still hiding behind him. The elemental grew hotter as its flames changed from orange to yellow. The rasha's pace slowed, and he had to shield his face with his arms, even as he held his sword before him. His fur smoked and singed. Flames rippled along the Burning Blade, and the rasha pressed forward.

The fire elemental pulsed with a great wave of intense heat. Machadaro toppled backward as flames washed over the Comitium. When they receded Veeksha stood alone before the elemental.

"That puny sword cannot protect you from my flames. Nothing can! The pyrophyra is mine! Who shall take the pyrophyra? Who?" The elemental laughed.

"Veeksha," Machadaro called, "I cannot help you. The elemental is too powerful for the Burning Blade to control. You must take the pyrophyra yourself!"

Veeksa didn't move. She cowered, trying to protect herself from the heat, but it was too much. It felt like her hands and face were burning. "I can't! I'll get burned up," she whispered. She hurried back to Machadaro.

"No! Cowardly child!" spit Joromwor, striding up to stand beside Machadaro. "Do not fear the elemental. Go take it. It cannot hurt you!"

"The human body was not intended to be set on fire!" she yelled angrily at the urgra. "Why don't you go get it?" Joromwor looked away, unwilling to do so.

Machadaro put his big hands on her shoulders. "Little one, I know you are afraid. Do not be. You are a pyromancer! Just as your friends did with the other quintessence, you will absorb the pyrophyra and master it. Yes, it will burn, but that burning will give you strength. So go. Go take it! Be brave!"

She turned around. Peeking through her fingers she saw a smaller geyser of white flame at the heart of the elemental. It shone and flickered and beckoned. The pyrophyra. But it seemed so far away and her hair was already scorched. She took a few steps forward. The smell of her burnt flesh filled the air. Her hair caught fire and she stumbled to the ground.

Cold hands grabbed her shoulders and she felt a wash of the coolest, purest water splash all over her. She turned to see Kyle crouching over her, and a sheet of water protecting them both.

"It looked like you could use some help," he said with a smile.

The heat still pounded them, but Kyle's protective sheet of water soothed the pain.

"Quick," Kyle said. "I don't know how long I can do this. Can you go get the pyrophyra now?"

Fear still masked Veeksha's face, but she nodded. They rushed forward through the blaze. Flames licked at them, but the aquosia inside Kyle continued to defend them against the infernal onslaught.

When they reached the edge of the Vulcanal pit, the elemental exploded again with a blast of heat and fire. It pushed Kyle and Veeksha back.

"It's too much!" Kyle said, as steam poured off them. "I can't hold it off much longer!"

"I can't do it!" Veeksha moaned.

Joromwor pounded his Bardiche on the ground in anger. "The child lacks the courage to go forward! Both of them will be incinerated. The quest is doomed!"

"Not while I yet breathe," Machadaro said and rushed forward. Gouts of flame shot from the elemental, but were deflected by the Blade. Even so, before he reached the children his fur smoked.

"I am here!" he yelled to the children as he knelt beside them.

Veeksha looked up in relief and crawled up to hug him around the neck. "Save us! It's too hot! Get us away!"

"I'm sorry, little one," Machadaro said, "but, you must take the pyrophyra when you near it!"

"I'm not going any closer!" Veeksha wailed.

"Yes, you are." The rasha stood, pulled her from his neck, and threw her at the heart of the fire elemental.

Veeksha screamed.

She had no time to be surprised, angered, or disappointed at Machadaro before the pain hit her. Once again her hair caught fire, and her clothes, too. Just as the

269

pain of her burning flesh registered in her mind she saw the pyrophyra. She reached out and touched it. The power of the pure elemental quintessence of fire incinerated her instantly.

Chapter 50

The elemental fumed with another wave of heat and fire. Kyle felt the protective water evaporating from his body and he realized he was going to die just like Veeksha.

But he didn't die. The heat subsided, and he opened his eyes to see the fire elemental shrinking. In mere seconds it was only four or five feet tall, sputtering atop the cavity that had been its prison.

Machadaro, his fur smoking and charred, helped Kyle to his feet. "How do you fare?" asked the tiger-man.

"I'm okay, I guess."

Susie ran up to Kyle and hugged him. "Are you burnt?"

"No, no, I'm fine."

"You're alive!" said Jürgen, smiling and slapping him on the back. "I can't believe you ran into the fire like that."

"Yeah," Susie agreed. "You saved Veeksha!"

"Until the captain threw her into the fire and killed her!" Kyle said angrily.

"She is not dead," Machadaro said hopefully. He gazed at the smaller elemental.

"What do you mean?" Kyle asked.

"He means I'm not dead," the elemental said, much more quietly than before.

The three kids stared in surprise.

"Yes, it's me. Veeksha," the fire said in barely more than a crackling whisper.

"The pyrophyra turned her to fire just like the geopsium turned me to stone," Jürgen said.

"And she can no doubt be returned to normal in the same manner," Bozabrozy said as he approached.

"Right," said Kyle as he realized what he must do. He scrambled down into the Vulcanal and stood before the fire. He reached out with his hand.

"You must embrace the flame, Kyle," Bozabrozy called from the edge of the pit.

Kyle wrapped his arms around the fire. At first it was terribly hot, but it didn't burn him. Soon he could feel Veeksha materializing in his grasp. A few seconds later she stood next to him, unburned and unharmed, and the fire was gone.

"Thanks, Kyle!" she said with a concerned look. There were sparks in her eyes.

"Come over here, you two," Machadaro said, "and I'll help you out."

The rasha pulled them easily from the pit. He stared intently into Veeksha's eyes. "I see you have the pyrophyra, and with nary a blister."

She pointed an accusing finger at him. "You threw me in! After you said it was so dangerous! You said I could have been killed!"

"And yet you were not. The quest did not fail."

"But I trusted you! I thought you were my friend!"

"Never trust a pirate," Joromwor said. "But in this case, his gamble proved wise."

"He gambled with my life," Veeksha said angrily.

"When you know him better you will learn that he will gamble anything for his own ends."

"It wasn't too great a gamble," Machadaro said to Veeksha softly, almost apologetically. "We all expected you to be a pyromancer."

Veeksha frowned, only slightly mollified. In any case, she was feeling much better. Much less frightened. In fact, she felt full of energy and power. A burning passion filled her chest, and spread through her limbs, making her fingers

272

tingle. She looked at the captain. "Your fur is all burned. Are you okay?"

"It will take more than a fire elemental to send my spirit sailing across the yonder." He smiled. "Now, let's get back to the Windrunner."

"What does it feel like, Veeksha?" Jürgen asked as they walked toward the ship. "The geopsium makes me feel all slow and stiff, but in a good way, somehow."

"My insides are all warm," Veeksha said slowly, feeling her stomach. "Hot, even. Kind of like when you take a spoonful of cold medicine. No, probably more like a whole bottle."

"You turned into fire," Susie said. "I was so scared for you!"

"It was probably no different than when I was turned to stone," Jürgen said.

"Except she was on fire!" Susie repeated emphatically. "I think that might be more painful than turning to dirt."

"I wasn't dirt! I was stone. There's a big difference."

"Yes, it was terrible at first," Veeksha said to interrupt Jürgen's complaints. "It hurt a lot. It was burning me. But I think that was the fire elemental. Without Kyle's protection, it would have burned me to a crisp. Even with his water powers, it still hurt. But when I grabbed the pyrophyra it seemed to die. Or give up. It wailed and moaned and begged."

"It spoke to you?" Machadaro asked.

Veeksha hesitated. "Yes, um... It said it didn't want to die. I didn't even know that elementals were alive."

Machadaro laughed. "Of course they're alive. They are as alive as you or me. What else would they be?"

What Veeksha did not reveal was that the elemental, while sputtering away to nothing, had secretly given her another riddle. A fifth riddle!

The ancient and perilous riddle

Stand betwixt the paws in the middle
Sacrifice four treasures to the sand
Then descend to the shrine most grand

They now had all four quintessences, so why did they need another riddle? She didn't know. But she was sure that if she revealed the fifth riddle, it would lead to another journey to another distant place and delay her reunion with her parents. She decided to keep it secret, so the quest would end and she could go home.

"I thought elementals were ghosts or spirits or something," Veeksha said to change the subject. "How can something that doesn't breathe or have blood or a heart be alive?"

"We asked the same question about the stone elemental," Susie said.

"You humans have a very limited definition of life," Machadaro said. "To be alive does not require blood or a heart."

Bozabrozy interjected, "I would argue that elementals do breathe. Fire elementals certainly breathe, for they cannot exist where air does not. Sky elementals breathe constantly, for they are air itself."

"What about water elementals. You can't breathe underwater," Jürgen argued.

"What about fish?" Kyle asked.

"Oh, yeah, right."

"The only thing to understand," Bozabrozy concluded as the group neared the ship's platform, "is that there are many forms of life. Humans, Zurans, and elementals are but three."

"It's strange to think of a pile of rock or pool of water as alive," Kyle said. "Even if they talk and move."

"I don't think it's so strange," Susie said. "My grandfather spoke to the sky and the rivers and the rocks."

Jürgen laughed. "Yeah, but did they ever speak back?"

"He said they did."

"Back up to the ship," Machadaro ordered as he held out his hand to Veeksha. "We'd best be on our way."

"What's that?" Veeksha pointed at something dangling from the rasha's shoulder. It was a small plastic tube, caught in his fur.

Machadaro looked at the object in surprise. He plucked it from his arm and held it in the palm of his hand. "I know not," the rasha said, confused.

Kyle looked closer and saw that the plastic tube had numbered lines on the side. A needle protruded from one end, while a colored tuft decorated the other. "It looks like a syringe..."

"It's a tranquilizer dart!" Susie yelled.

"Where did it come from?" Jürgen said, looking around.

"It is a weapon?" Machadaro asked.

"Yes," Susie explained. "It's used to capture animals alive."

"Bannecker!" Kyle said.

"He must be nearby!" Jürgen agreed.

Machadaro tossed the dart aside while scanning the Forum. "Quickly! Onto the platform! We must hurry back to the..." He stumbled to his knees, and the children saw four more darts in his back.

Canars spread out around the children, hoisting their shields to protect them. Joromwor roared angrily, pushing the children onto the platform.

Bozabrozy tried to help but he wavered on the edge of the platform. A tranquilizer protruded from his chest. "I seem to have found another of those darts," the rascan said.

Chapter 51

Bozabrozy stumbled forward and fell to the ground as two more darts hit him. Kyle leapt off the lift to catch him. The rascan was unconscious. Kyle pulled out the tranquilizer darts and turned back to Joromwor.

"We're under attack!" the urgra roared. "Recall the lift! Legion! To battle!" He grabbed Bozabrozy and Kyle and tossed them roughly onto the platform. Darts ricocheted off the urgra's armor.

"Come on, Machadaro!" Veeksha yelled as the platform rose. "We have to get back to the ship!"

Machadaro struggled to his feet and held the Burning Blade in both hands. Fire surged from the sword and flames engulfed the rasha, rippling over his fur and clothes. He roared as the power of pyrophyra conquered the tranquilizers. Joromwor roared beside him and they charged off into the ruins, followed by the canar legionaries.

"What are they doing?" Veeksha screamed. "Come back!"

Strange subdued thumps sounded from the Forum below them.

"What are those?" Jürgen asked, watching as grappling hooks, trailing long cables, arced up toward the Windrunner. Several flew above the ship, but others quickly tangled in the rigging. Blue-helmeted soldiers fastened the lines around pillars and other large chunks of rubble.

"They're trying to capture the ship!" Kyle exclaimed.

The gustboxes slammed open. The topsails billowed.

The Windrunner sped forward and upward, causing the lift to lurch and swing. Susie tripped on the unconscious rascan and rolled off the platform, barely managing to catch one of the ropes. She dangled far above the Forum.

Kyle grabbed her arm. "Hang on, Susie!"

A jolt shook the Windrunner as it struggled against the steel cables. Some hooks slipped free and the cables tumbled back to the ground. Others tore rigging from the masts, but more held fast. The ship listed sharply and shuddered.

Veeksha clung to a line with all her strength as the lift swung wildly. "This is not good."

Jürgen smiled, barely bothering to hold on. "It's not too bad for me."

"Jürgen!" Kyle yelled. "Help me get Susie!"

"Right!" Jürgen took a step to help but lost his footing and toppled off the lift, giggling. He dropped through the air, striking the top of towering columns of the Temple of Saturn, and fell to the hard stone of the portico. Jumping up immediately, he waved back at them, completely unhurt.

"He's all right," Susie sighed in relief as she dangled from the rope.

"Don't worry about him." Kyle grimaced as he tried to pull her up. "Just get back up here!"

Susie looked at him and smiled. "I don't think I need to do that." She let go.

Kyle yelled in shock as she fell, but she didn't fall very fast. Her descent was like a feather wafting on the wind.

"Don't worry about me," she giggled as she drifted downward. "I have the aethrial. Just take care of yourself and Veeksha!"

Kyle crawled over to Veeksha. "Jürgen and Susie are okay."

"I saw," she replied. "But I don't think fire or water will protect us if we fall."

"Yeah, I think you're right."

The Windrunner was losing its battle against the

restraining cables. The gust boxes filled the topsails but the ship did not gain any more altitude. It flew in a circle, getting more and more tangled in the lines. Fortunately, the lift continued to ascend and so far remained free of grapples. Kyle looked up to see several mumba sailors operating the windlass while others tried to prevent the lines from tangling.

Lightning suddenly arced from the ship down to the ground. Evidently, Savakala had found enough strength to fight. Canar legionaries fired their shocking crossbows at the soldiers below.

Sailors grabbed Kyle and Veeksha as the lift rose into the hull of the ship. The children rushed to the main deck, where fire cannon spat flaming missiles at the Roman Forum. Sailors ran back and forth with axes and swords, trying to cut the stout cables that prevented the ship from ascending.

Kyle ran to the rail to see the homing balls of flame bursting amidst squads of blue-helmeted soldiers. The Roman Forum was now a swarm of activity. Soldiers in urban camouflage ran amidst the ruins, securing more cables to keep the Windrunner from escaping. Tanks and other military vehicles sped down the surrounding roads. Several attack helicopters circled at a distance.

"Machadaro! Machadaro!" Veeksha called. Far below, she could see the flaming form of the sky captain leaping into battle with the human soldiers securing the cables. The mighty rasha dodged through the ruins. His Burning Blade cut down the enemy. He effortlessly tossed them aside and tore cables from the rubble to which they were secured.

On the others side of the Forum, Joromwor and his canar legionaries lumbered through the ruins in their heavy armor, wielding swords and axes and spears against the guns of their enemy. Soldiers fired more tranquilizer darts at them, but the needles could not penetrate their armor. The mighty urgra cut a bloody swath through the soldiers with

278

the Sundering Bardiche. With each swing of the mighty weapon, he drew closer to the cables that restrained the skyship. Joromwor's blade sliced through the nearest as if it were string.

Kyle gaped at the battle raging below. "I can't believe it. They're actually winning!"

Veeksha smiled. "They're freeing us!"

Below, the blue-helmeted soldiers retreated from the ferocious Zurans. Fireballs and lightning bolts showered the Roman Forum, filling it with a storm of flame and sharp rocks. Machadaro, Joromwor, and the legionaries moved from cable to cable, cutting or ripping them loose from their moorings. In mere minutes, most of the cables dangled freely from the Windrunner, and the skyship began to ascend.

"Hey! We can get away!" Veeksha said.

"But where are Jürgen and Susie?" Kyle asked, scanning the carnage below.

"And Machadaro!" Veeksha stared into the ruins. "How will they get back on the ship?"

A tank rolled into view from behind a building. The turret spun and the barrel pointed directly at the skyship.

Chapter 52

The tank emitted a thunderous boom and at the same instant Kyle and Veeksha were thrown from their feet. The ship listed and they slid across the deck. Sailors and legionaries screamed and yelled and pointed. The starboard wingsail fell away from the ship. In its place was a gaping, smoking hole in the hull.

Savakala appeared beside the two children. There were large splinters in her leg, her feathers were ruffled, and her magical cloak was missing.

"Swiftly!" she shrieked. "Go hide in my cabin. You must not be harmed."

The aeromagus struggled to the captain's deck and saw the tank moving near the Temple of Saturn. She thrust forward the Staff of the Sky and several arcs of lightning pounded the metal shell of the tank, but the attack had little effect.

"Joromwor!" Savakala screeched loudly. "The iron wagon! Destroy it!"

The urgra and his legionaries were already jogging across the ruins toward it. As he ran up to the Temple of Saturn, the tank's turret spun toward him and its machinegun opened fire. Bullets bounced off the Indomitable Armor, but the force of their impact pushed Joromwor off course. He scrambled around the massive pillars of the temple even as the canars behind him fell to the tank's gunfire.

Shards of stone flew around the urgra as he hid behind a

pillar. The staccato reports of the machinegun sounded like a thunderstorm. Joromwor hefted the Sundering Bardiche and jumped out from cover. Bullets hammered him, but his armor did not yield. Dauntless, he ran to the outermost pillar and struck it with his blade. With another slash a wedge of stone fell away. The notched column, unable to sustain the weight of the huge lintel above it, collapsed. Joromwor fled the Temple of Saturn as three of the ancient pillars, towering dozens of feet high, toppled onto the tank. Chunks of stone weighing several tons each crushed the turret, bent the cannon barrel, and shattered the armor. An instant later the tank exploded violently in a huge ball of flame.

Savakala crowed in triumph. "We are free! Joromwor! Machadaro! Return to the –"

A heavy rumble drowned out her voice and she turned to see an attack helicopter moving closer. She ran to the prow of the Windrunner, spread her dark wings, and leapt off the ship. Soaring over the ruins of the Roman Forum, Savakala sent bolt after bolt at the helicopter, striking it several times. It spun out of control and crashed into the Curia Julia.

Landing on the precarious remains of the Temple of Saturn, Savakala caught her breath and surveyed the battle. Human soldiers scurried throughout the ruins of the Roman Forum, most of them running from the savage ferocity of Captain Machadaro and his Burning Blade, or fleeing the resolute fury of Legate Joromwor and his Sundering Bardiche. Helicopters crashed, tanks exploded, and the Zurans pressed their advantage. The aeromagus cackled in glee and sent lightning bolts at the weak humans.

The only problem that faced her now was the Windrunner. The attacks had considerably damaged the skyship, and it would require extensive repairs. She had to prevent any further harm to the ship. Despite her fatigue, she leapt from her perch, large wings beating and carrying her high, to hold the human skyships at bay.

Joromwor growled happily as Savakala soared upward to meet the human onslaught. There was a reason that the feathered ruled Zura, and that was their unrivaled mastery of the skies. As the emperor often crowed, he who controls the skies, controls Zura. That doctrine no doubt held sway on Earth as well. With her Staff of the Sky, and the aethrial within it, Savakala blasted the noisy yet fragile human ships. Strangely, the skyships were not shooting at her, then Joromwor realized that they did not want to kill Savakala. They wanted her alive.

So it was with little surprise that Joromwor saw one of the skyships shoot a huge net at the uburu. The net opened wide and enveloped her, wrapping tightly as heavy weights constrained her wings. The skyship swooped away, pulling the captured aeromagus behind it. She sent lightning bolts in wild directions, her aim spoiled by the constricting net.

"Savakala!" Joromwor roared, and sprinted after the skyship. He rounded a corner and smashed into a group of soldiers. He jogged on, ignoring them and their useless weapons. Another tank rolled into his path, spitting ineffectual bullets.

With a grim smile, Joromwor charged the tank. He chopped off the barrel with a short swing from the Sundering Bardiche. With another slash, he cleaved the front of the hull to expose a very startled driver. He yanked the soldier out and threw him aside like a doll. Bending into the interior of the tank, he roared violently. The remaining crew cringed in terror.

"Joromwor!" called a voice behind him.

The legate turned to see Reid Bannecker and a pack of soldiers a block away.

"You!" the urgra snarled. "You are the architect of this attack! Where are you taking Savakala?"

"The same place you're going," Bannecker replied, and nodded to his soldiers. They threw small objects at

Joromwor that spurted thick smoke when they landed.

Joromwor strode through the roiling gas toward Bannecker. "Twice has that incompetent rasha killed you. And twice he has not killed you enough. I will kill you until you are dead."

"More gas," Bannecker said calmly as Joromwor charged them. The soldiers hurried to comply, throwing more grenades and filling the narrow lane with fumes. Still the towering mass of impending death lumbered toward them.

"More gas, you fools!" Bannecker yelled, and pulled on a mask. He began throwing his own gas grenades.

Joromwor rushed through the gas cloud and crashed into the soldiers, scattering them with his bulk. Without even a swing of his blade, the soldiers fled. Only he and Bannecker remained in the cramped street filled with fumes.

"You have courage, human," Joromwor said, coughing. He towered above Bannecker, almost within striking distance. "Perhaps I will make this quick." He stepped closer, but stumbled slightly.

Bannecker held two grenades in his hands, pointing the spewing gas at Joromwor's head.

Joromwor stood directly before him and raised the Sundering Bardiche. "So it ends…" the urgra said, preparing to strike. But the blow never fell. The blade slipped from his fingers and he collapsed to the cobblestones, unconscious.

The grenades sputtered their last wisps, and the sleeping gas dissipated. Reid Bannecker bent down and removed the sleeping urgra's helmet.

"You should beware strange lands and strange weapons, legate," said Bannecker with a grin. He spoke into his headset, "Target Yogi is down. Repeat. Target Yogi is down. Report on the status of other targets."

"Target Thunderbird is down. Target Bandit on alien ship," came the reply. "Target Hobbes status and location unknown."

"What?" Bannecker yelled. "What was his last position?"

"Target was last seen behind the Curia Julia."

"What do you mean, last seen?" Bannecker said angrily, pacing down the deserted street. "Can't a battalion of armed troops keep track of one giant flaming tiger-man waving a sword?"

"We've suffered heavy losses, sir. The tight streets here make it difficult to fully exploit our superior numbers."

"I don't want excuses!" Bannecker demanded. "I want that rasha found and captured!"

"Yes, sir!"

"Send a recovery team and cage to my location."

"Yes, sir!"

Shaking his head in frustration, Bannecker walked back toward Joromwor. Only a few wisps of sleeping gas remained, so he removed his mask.

Something growled behind him.

Bannecker spun around. Machadaro leapt out a window into the street. Flames covered his fur, but did not burn him. He brandished the Burning Blade.

CHAPTER 53

Kyle saw Savakala captured in the net and dragged away by the chopper. He watched as Joromwor gave chase and disappeared around a corner.

"I don't see how he can catch a helicopter," Kyle said. The Windrunner shook again and splinters of wood showered around them. The chopper squadron, despite the heavy losses they had suffered from Savakala's bolts, continued to attack. The Windrunner fought back. Fireballs soared through the skies, wreaking carnage on the remaining choppers. The Zurans caused considerable damage, but enemy reinforcements continued to pour into the battle.

"They're killing the Zurans!" Veeksha said, watching as legionaries and sailors fell to the machineguns and explosions.

"Can you help them?" Kyle asked.

"How? I'm just a little kid!"

"You have the pyrophyra now. You're a pyromancer. You can shoot flames!"

"I don't know how to do that."

"You just have to imagine it," Kyle said. "Just point at them and shoot fire."

"I can't do that! Why don't you do something? You've had the aquosia a lot longer than I've had the pyrophyra."

Kyle frowned. "I don't think aquosia is used for attack that much. It's more for healing."

"Then start healing the Zurans," Veeksha suggested as

the ship rocked again.

"We're in the middle of a battle. You have to fight back!"

Veeksha shook her head. "They're just trying to help us. To rescue us. I don't want to hurt them."

"If you don't do something the Zurans will all die," Kyle shouted over the roar of gunfire. "Machadaro will die!"

Veeksha screamed, "This isn't fair! Whatever I do, someone gets hurt!"

"If you do nothing, we'll be hurt. We'll be killed if the ship crashes."

Gunfire from the choppers split the topmast into chunks and splinters. It toppled toward the captain's deck.

"Look out!" cried Kyle. He pushed Veeksha back onto the main deck just before the mast slammed down. The huge timber sheared through the already damaged decking. The mast and captain's deck fell away from the ship and crashed into the ruins.

Gunfire raked the deck, focusing on the cannon. The crew scattered to avoid the hail of bullets. Two of the cannon toppled off the ship through the shattered railing.

"Look!" Kyle pointed. One of the choppers launched a missile. It struck the Windrunner's stern and the explosion sent the ruddersail cartwheeling to the ground. The Windrunner shuddered and began losing altitude.

"I think we're going to crash," said Veeksha. She trembled as she clung to the ship's railing.

Chapter 54

"What are we going to do?" Veeksha yelled.

"Hang on!"

The Windrunner slammed into the three columns of the Temple of Castor and Pollux. A shudder went through the ship as it careened around the columns, sending one toppling. The stern spun around and crashed into another ruin. The Windrunner hit the ground with a heavy shock. The port wingsail spar snapped.

Kyle and Veeksha were thrown onto the port uppersail. Luckily for them, the sail still billowed and broke their fall. They slid down the white canvas and landed in a heap right next to the ship.

"Are you okay?" Kyle asked.

"Yes, I think so. How about you?"

Kyle nodded and he and Veeksha picked their way through the smoking wreckage until they were free of the tangled mess.

"I don't think it will ever fly again," Kyle said sadly.

Susie ran up from out of the rubble and hugged Veeksha. "Oh, my gosh! I can't believe you survived!"

"Neither can I," Veeksha agreed. "I thought you might have died when you fell."

"Nope! I just floated to the ground," said Susie with a smile. "I tried to fly, but I don't have the hang of it yet."

"Where's Jürgen?" Kyle asked, looking around.

"Right here." A nearby pile of rubble rolled away and the German boy stepped out of it.

"Where have you been?"

"Using my geomancer powers to help!" Jürgen said excitedly. "I've been making walls to block off streets and pits to trap soldiers."

"Have you been doing the same thing, Susie?" Kyle asked.

Susie frowned. "No. I don't know how to use the aethrial very well."

"Where are the Zurans?" Jürgen asked.

"Savakala was captured by the helicopters," Kyle said.

"And Bozabrozy?"

"He was on the ship when it crashed."

"We should go find him," Susie suggested. "Maybe your aquosia can wake him up."

"Good idea!" Kyle moved toward the wreckage.

"Wait," Veeksha said. "What about the captain? Has anyone seen him?"

"Last I saw, he was burning his way through the soldiers and cables that were holding the Windrunner," Jürgen said.

"But where is he now?"

CHAPTER 55

"Aquosia won't save you this time," Machadaro growled.

"I don't need saving," Bannecker said, looking around the deserted street at the empty canisters of sleeping gas. He had only two left, and these he pulled from his combat harness as he slowly backed away from the rasha.

Machadaro stalked the man. "Your poison darts did not thwart me," he growled. "Do you think you will fare any better with your poison gas?"

"If not, I have other tools at my disposal."

"None that will prevent me from chopping you into little charred morsels." Machadaro's sword surged with a wave of flames that spread up his arms and added to the fires that coated him.

"Killing me won't save you, or the rest of your crew. How can you defeat an entire army?"

"I'll worry about that after you're dead." Machadaro roared and leapt to attack. Bannecker pulled the pins on the gas grenades and threw them. The captain easily swatted them aside. He swung the Burning Blade down on Bannecker's head.

But Bannecker's head wasn't there. The man dodged aside in the nick of time and scrambled over to Joromwor's prostrate form. He picked up the heavy Sundering Bardiche just as the rasha struck another blow. The Burning Blade bounced off the geopsium haft of the urgra's huge weapon.

"That won't help you." Machadaro snatched away the

Sundering Bardiche and threw it aside. He swung his sword a third time, but once again Bannecker was not there to suffer the blow. The man snatched up Joromwor's helmet and held it in front of him.

Machadaro grinned, and his tail twitched. "Good. You're going to fight." He lunged forward, striking repeatedly with the Burning Blade, but Bannecker deflected the blows with the Indomitable Armor helmet. The impact of the pyrophyra in the sword and the geopsium in the helmet produced huge splashes of multi-colored flames and sparks.

"You are a quick one," the rasha complimented the man.

Bannecker smiled grimly. "So it would seem."

Machadaro's attacks could not get past Bannecker's deft defense. Even so, the power of his onslaught forced the man to stumble backwards. With a growing rage, the captain pressed his advantage, striking with all his might and speed, exploiting his greater size and strength to keep Bannecker unbalanced and retreating. The constant blows from the Burning Blade showered flames and sparks around them, and the Indomitable Armor helmet glowed red from the searing heat. Finally, under a flurry of attacks, Bannecker tripped over some rubble and fell. The smoking helmet spun from his grasp.

Machadaro pounced immediately, reaching down to grab Bannecker and sink his fangs into the man's jugular. But Bannecker rolled aside with amazing speed and jumped to his feet. Machadaro swung the Burning Blade in a wide arc, but his target dodged aside.

The rasha's eye narrowed. "You are too quick for a mere human. You have an elemental artifact!"

Bannecker tipped his head and smiled. "If you say so."

"It won't help you. The Burning Blade rages with pyrophyra." Machadaro held the sword in two hands and it pulsed with flames. "It shall make me quicker than any talisman you possess."

Bannecker did not wait for the Zuran to complete his magic. He turned and ran, yelling orders into his headset. Machadaro bounded after him. The chase sped through the streets of Rome, down the Via Tribuna di Tor de 'Specchi and onto the Vicolo Capizucchi. Machadaro frequently closed to within striking distance, but Bannecker was too quick to catch. The man ducked beneath trucks, jumped over cars, crashed through windows, fled through cafes, and even sped across rooftops. Always Machadaro followed a hair's breadth behind, swift and furious, a wake of flaming destruction behind him.

Bannecker turned onto a shaded street that ran along the river, running as fast as he could toward a bridge. Machadaro assumed the foolish human was going to leap into the water in an attempt to save himself. The rasha grinned. The water would protect Bannecker from the flames of the Burning Blade, but there was no protection from his fangs and claws.

Machadaro chased Bannecker onto the bridge to Tiber Island. Unfortunately for the man, a semi trailer truck blocked his path, and he scrambled to get into the open back doors. Machadaro closed the gap between them, and the Burning Blade slashed across Bannecker's back with an upward stroke, catapulting him far into the empty trailer amidst a spray of sparks.

"Geopsium armor!" Machadaro roared. "That won't save your neck from my fangs!" He sprang into the trailer and rushed toward the prostrate man. Before the rasha could reach his prey, Bannecker leapt out a small opening in the side of the trailer. An instant later, the doors behind Machadaro slammed shut.

"Fool!" Machadaro yelled. "I'll easily burn my way out of this!" He hacked at the wall with the Burning Blade. The thin metal paneling sheared away easily, and the rasha peeled it back, revealing heavy bars beneath. Machadaro slashed at them, but immediately realized they were made of geopsium, and resistant to his attacks. He roared furiously, ripping more of the thin metal sheeting away from the cage of bars that trapped him. Soldiers ran onto the bridge.

"The bars are a geopsium alloy," Bannecker said, smiling. "You won't be burning through those."

"As a living flame, I don't need to burn through them," Machadaro growled. "I'll walk through them." He invoked the magic of the Burning Blade and the flames that coursed over his body intensified and deepened.

Bannecker ran forward, yelling and waving at the soldier driving the truck. "Now! Now! Now!" The driver hit the accelerator and the truck lurched backward, crashing through the bridge's stone railing. The trailer fell into the Tiber River and Machadaro's swelling flames were snuffed as he disappeared under the swirling waters.

Bannecker ran to the edge of the bridge and spoke into his headset. "Get the divers into the water and attach the cables! Call in the chopper. We need to raise the cage as soon as he's unconscious. I want him alive, understand?"

Men in wetsuits appeared at the waters edge and dove in. A Sikorsky S-64 Skycrane thundered over head, lowering its cable.

Bannecker watched from the bridge. Everything was going just as he had planned. Three of the primary targets – codenamed Thunderbird, Yogi, and Hobbes – were captured and soon to be en route to the airport. The last, Bandit, was no doubt still tranquilized in the skyship. According to reports, many of the Windrunner's crew and legionaries had been captured. A few had escaped into nearby neighborhoods, but the alien dog-men and cat-men would be rounded up soon enough.

It was a near perfect operation, except for the collateral damage. No doubt the Italians would be furious over the destruction of their Roman Forum. Bannecker smiled. A barrel of synthetic aquosia would be more than enough to soothe their wrath.

Bannecker waited until the helicopter raised the geopsium cage from the Tiber River. Within, the bedraggled rasha lay unconscious yet alive.

Now he only needed to collect the children.

CHAPTER 56

The Windrunner was a jumbled mess on the inside as well as the outside. Spars and timbers jutted at odd angles and squirming into the ship was difficult. Eventually they found the unconscious rascan under a pile of debris in the hold. With a lot of effort they cleared away the timbers and crates. Kyle knelt next to Bozabrozy, placing his hands on his chest.

The rascan's eyes popped open.

"Hi," he said. "What happened?"

"You were hit by tranquilizer darts," Susie told him.

"I seem to be all better now." Bozabrozy jumped to his feet. "Thanks, Kyle."

"Not a problem."

"Now you can help us rescue Savakala," Susie said courageously.

"And find Machadaro," Veeksha said anxiously.

"And repair the ship," Jürgen said hopefully.

"The ship is damaged?" Bozabrozy asked, looking around the mess in the hold.

Jürgen nodded. "It crashed."

Bozabrozy's eyes widened. "We're marooned? Where is Savakala?"

"Captured by the army."

"Then we have no time to lose!" The rascan rushed across the slanted floor and out of the hold, followed by the children.

"Where are we going?"

"To Savakala's cabin to get my things," Bozabrozy said. They hurried through the ship and were passing the galley when they heard a squeal.

"Dearies! Dearies! Don't leave me here!" Barathrina cried from under a pile of wood and fruit.

"Are you all right?" Jürgen asked the grunk. He ran to her and helped her get out from under the debris.

"No, I'm not all right!" Barathrina snorted angrily as she stood. "Look at this devastation! My beautiful ovens and ingredients, destroyed! The galley is ruined. Ruined, I say! Tomatoes crushed. Eggs broken. Spices scattered everywhere. There won't be any cinnamon buns for tomorrow's breakfast!"

"We've got more important things to worry about than your buns," Bozabrozy interrupted. "We're marooned. The Windrunner won't fly again soon. Come with us!"

"What? We crashed?" Barathrina asked, obviously growing even more dismayed. "Where are we going?"

"To get my implements."

"Savakala won't like that."

"She's been captured."

"Oh, my!"

The door to the uburu's cabin had been shattered and the interior was a shambles. Bozabrozy dove into the mess, scrounging for anything he could find. He stuffed numerous items into his pouches and bandoliers.

"Tsk, tsk, tsk," Barathrina shook her head. "Savakala won't like this. Won't like this at all." Even so, the grunk spied her Cloak of Humanity amidst the jumble and retrieved it.

"I doubt very much if she'll ever come back," Bozabrozy said sadly, lifting the shattered remains of the Everglass from the floor.

"What are we going to do?" Barathrina asked.

"Surrender," Veeksha suggested. "It's the best thing to do."

"She's right," Kyle agreed. "You can't escape. You'll be found easily. There's nowhere for Zurans to hide in Rome."

"But I bet a human could hide somewhere." Barathrina donned her cloak and as it settled on her shoulders, her form shifted to that of a fat woman.

"That doesn't help Bozabrozy," Kyle said.

"I'm sorry about that," said Barathrina, backing out of the cabin, "but I don't want to be caught by that evil Bannecker."

"Where are you going?" Bozabrozy asked. "You want to spend the rest of your life hiding amongst humans?"

"Everyone needs a cook." Barathrina waved to them and hurried away.

"Shouldn't you try to stop her?" Jürgen asked.

Bozabrozy continued to stuff items into his pouches. "Me? Stop a lumbering mass of terrified grunk blubber? I don't think so. She's made her choice. I hope she escapes. Now don't just stand there with your mouths open, take some of this." He brought over an armful of items and pushed them into Jürgen's and Kyle's packs, then he dove back into the mess.

The kids started scrounging around in the debris. Kyle found Bannecker's nightvision goggles. Smiling, he stuffed them into his backpack.

"We can't spend all day on this," said the rascan, stuffing a final item into a pouch. He led the way out of the cabin and into the passageway.

"Where are we going?"

"We need to get out of here, find a place to hide, and consider our options." He hurried out of the passageway. Bannecker stood on the slanting deck, waiting.

CHAPTER 57

"You don't have any options," Bannecker said as they emerged. He raised a gun and fired several tranquilizer darts into the rascan.

"Not again." Bozabrozy rolled his eyes and collapsed.

Kyle bent down to help him but Bannecker held him back. "Let him sleep, Kyle. It's best for all concerned if the Zurans stay sedated."

"What are you doing here?" Jürgen demanded. "You always show up at the worst times!"

"Or the best times," Bannecker countered, "depending on your point of view. For instance, I was able to prepare for you when I arrived in Rome. Because of that, I've captured your four Zuran friends. They are alive instead of dead."

"You captured Machadaro?" Veeksha asked.

"Yes. And the urgra and Savakala. They're all being transported to a park nearby where we can load them onto helicopters." Several soldiers appeared who removed Bozabrozy's pouches and fitted him with handcuffs.

"What are you going to do with them?" Kyle said.

"We're taking them all to a secure facility, away from prying eyes," Bannecker said. He looked around at the Windrunner. "It is quite amazing that they were able to cause so much damage and trouble with a wooden sailing ship."

Susie looked sternly at Bannecker. "Why did you attack us like that? You killed some of the Zurans!"

Bannecker glared at the young girl as he led them off the

ship and back into the ruins of the Roman Forum. "Don't take that tone with me, young lady! You were all kidnapped and brainwashed by these cute and cuddly alien animals. In the meantime, they've destroyed property, killed hundreds of people, and terrorized the planet. So you can just follow me and do as I say."

"What if we don't want to go with you?" Jürgen planted his feet firmly and crossed his arms.

"I don't have time to debate this with children," Bannecker said, and beckoned to a nearby soldier. "Sergeant, take them to the choppers and wait for me."

"Yes, sir!" The soldier stepped up to Jürgen and tried to push him along but the boy did not move. He smiled. His feet were rough and stony, and seemed to be melded with the marble block on which he stood.

"I'm not going anywhere!" Jürgen stated adamantly.

Bannecker looked at the children. Veeksha's eyes blazed with defiance, Susie's hair waved angrily, and Kyle stared at him coldly.

"You can't boss us around anymore," he said. "We have quintessence inside us. And we can use it."

"So it would seem," Bannecker agreed. "What do you want?"

"We want to go with Machadaro and make sure you treat him fairly!" Veeksha said.

"Is that what all of you want?" Bannecker asked and the children nodded. "But what about your parents? Don't you want to go back to them? See them again?"

"Oh," said Kyle in sudden surprise, and then guilt. He'd forgotten about his parents.

"I will see them soon enough," Jürgen said. "I will go with the Zurans."

"And the rest of you don't mind delaying your reunions with your parents? If you don't return to them now, who knows how long it will be before you see them again?"

"My mom and dad will understand," Susie said. "They

wouldn't want you to hurt the Zurans, either."

"All right, all right," Bannecker consented. "You can come with me. But," he added, as smiles spread across their faces, "you have to do what I tell you, when I tell you."

Jürgen took a step forward as his foot faded back to normal flesh. "As long as we can stay with the Zurans, we'll do what you say."

"As long as you don't hurt them," Susie added.

"And you let us see that they're okay," Veeksha added.

"Yes, we can do that," Bannecker said. "Follow this soldier to a helicopter and we'll get going."

Soon, the children were on board a Chinook helicopter with Reid Bannecker and four large cages that held the unconscious Zurans. Veeksha looked sadly at the soggy rasha captain, wishing she could free him. Heavy manacles restrained his hands and feet. Four soldiers sat nearby, their tranquilizer guns aimed at the Zurans.

"So that's what wet tiger smells like," Jürgen said.

Susie elbowed him in the stomach. "Don't be mean."

Veeksha turned to Bannecker. "Do you have to keep him locked up like that? It's demeaning."

"That creature is a lethal terror, even without his flaming sword," Bannecker said. "He killed many of my men and I'm not going to let him harm anyone else."

"He wouldn't harm anyone if you didn't keep attacking him," Susie said.

The slim agent shook his head. "Listen, kids. You've spent several days with these creatures and you've come to like them."

"We don't like Savakala," Jürgen objected.

"Be that as it may," Bannecker continued, "from your point of view I can see how I may seem vicious and uncaring. However, I've gone to great pains to capture them alive. And if you'd take a moment to think about it, you might begin doubting the motives and methods of your Zuran 'friends'."

"They didn't start it," Veeksha said. "You did."

"No, that's not correct. The Zurans attacked the boys' parents and kidnapped you. You were captives and I was trying to free you."

"We weren't captives," Jürgen said. "They were protecting us from Rakanian."

"More of this Rakanian," Bannecker said. "Has anyone ever seen him? How do you know he even exists? He could be a bogeyman they conjured up to scare you."

"It wasn't a bogey-man who attacked our cabin," Jürgen said.

"Actually," Kyle said, "they did kind of kidnap Veeksha. She didn't want to go."

"It hasn't been that bad," Veeksha said hesitantly.

"These Zurans are from another world, with technology that far exceeds our own," Bannecker said. "And they have a nefarious, unknown purpose. Is it merely resources they want, the quintessence? Or is it conquest and destruction? We can't trust them. You can't trust them."

"Sir, we're ready for takeoff," the chopper pilot yelled back into the compartment.

Bannecker nodded. "Okay, kids. Buckle up. It's going to be noisy. It'll take a couple hours to get to Sigonella where we'll switch to a plane." He took a few steps toward the cockpit, then paused and turned around. "Remember our deal. Don't try to release the Zurans. Even if you help them escape, we'd just mobilize even more soldiers and tanks and jets and helicopters. The next time we fight, they probably won't survive. Do you understand?"

Veeksha frowned, Susie pouted, Jürgen nodded, and Kyle said, "We won't do anything, if you don't."

"It's a deal," Bannecker agreed and went to the cockpit.

"Do you think we can trust him?" Susie asked.

The helicopter's engines roared before anyone could answer.

CHAPTER 58

The Boeing CH-47 Chinook helicopter rose from the Circus Maximus, a long and wide grassy park that had been a center of spectacle during the ancient Roman Empire. Kyle looked out the window at the ruined ruins of the nearby Forum. The Windrunner still smoldered near the crumbling Curia Julia. Several columns had fallen during the battle. Other structures were damaged. Flames and smoke rose from some of the buildings nearby. He doubted very much that the Italians would fondly remember the Zurans' visit to the Eternal City.

Several other Chinooks fell into formation around them, carrying more captured Zurans. Fighter jets preceded them through the skies, and attack helicopters paced them. Rome swiftly fell behind as they flew south over the Tyrrhenian Sea toward Sicily. On their left, the Italian coastline gleamed in the sunshine, winding roads and picturesque seaside villages passing by quickly.

After an hour and a half, the aircraft flew over the north coast of Sicily and skirted the eastern slopes of Mt. Etna. Ahead, Naval Air Station Sigonella sprawled southwest of the city of Catania. As the Chinooks landed, Kyle could see numerous airport vehicles and troops approaching.

"All right," Bannecker said, "you kids stay with me. We'll be in the air again in twenty minutes."

"Where are we going now?" Kyle asked as they jumped out of the helicopter onto the tarmac.

"There." Bannecker pointed at a nearby plane, a C-20

Gulfstream III jet.

Soldiers rushed forward, guiding cargo trailers to each of the Chinooks. They pulled the cages out of the helicopters and onto the trailers.

"The cages won't fit in that plane," Jürgen noted as they all neared the Gulfstream.

"Of course not," Bannecker said. "The Zurans are going in that." He pointed to a huge plane which sat nearby. Soldiers pushed the cage containing Bozabrozy up through the aft cargo doors.

"You promised that we'd be going with them!" Susie protested.

"The planes will fly in formation to the final destination," Bannecker replied calmly. "That is a Boeing C-17 Globemaster III cargo plane. It's loud, it's uncomfortable, and it's going to be full of those crates." He pointed as a line of cages formed near the back of the plane. Each crate contained a Zuran. "You've just spent two hours in a noisy chopper. Wouldn't you prefer to spend the next two hours in something more comfortable?"

"How do we know we can trust you?" Veeksha asked.

"You'll be able to see the Globemaster during the flight. If I try to trick you, you can use your elemental powers to make the pilot do what you want. I'm betting a fireball would scare him pretty good."

Veeksha was surprised. She didn't want to hurt anyone, but she realized that being able to create fire from nothing could be very persuasive.

"Come on, Veeksha," Kyle said, mounting the steps to the Gulfstream. "He's given us his word. We should trust him. For now."

The rest of the kids followed Kyle into the plane, and threw their backpacks into a corner. The interior was very nicely appointed, and they quickly sat down in the comfy seats. Kyle realized that it had been several days since he had a chance to rest in something so cozy and snug.

"Let's get this thing in the air," Bannecker told the pilot as the door closed, and then turned to the kids. "Would you like something to eat or drink? Juice, perhaps?"

"Yeah, that would be great!" Jürgen said eagerly.

"Food and drink are back there," Bannecker pointed as he dropped into a seat. Jürgen scuttled off. "Be quick. You want to be buckled up when we take off."

"We never get to eat before taking off on airline planes," Jürgen called back from the food cupboards. "They always make us stay in our seats until the light goes off."

Susie looked out the window as the Gulfstream taxied across the tarmac. "Where are we going this time, Mr. Bannecker?"

"Cairo."

"Cairo?" Susie said gleefully. "You mean like in Egypt? I've never been to Egypt. Imagine all the cool stuff we'll see!"

"Lots of sand," Kyle guessed.

"Maybe we'll get to ride camels!" Susie postulated.

Jürgen sat down and passed around bags of crackers. "I rode a camel once. Or was it an elephant?"

"You don't know which it was?" Veeksha asked.

"Well, it was either a camel or an elephant."

"Don't you know how to tell them apart?" Kyle asked incredulously.

"Of course I do."

"One is huge and grey with a trunk," Susie explained, "and the other is tall and tan with a hump."

"I know that!" Jürgen reiterated.

"And camels spit at you," Kyle noted.

"How can you mistake a camel for an elephant?" Susie asked.

"It was a long time ago," Jürgen said, annoyed. "I was very young."

The others laughed as the Gulfstream sped down the runway and took off.

"Don't let them get you down, Jürgen," Bannecker consoled. "You'll forget all about it once you see the pyramids."

"We're going to see the pyramids?" Susie squealed in delight.

"And the Sphinx," he nodded.

"That is so cool! Can we climb the pyramids?"

"They don't let tourists do that anymore," Bannecker said.

"That's not fair," Susie sighed unhappily.

"We can always bribe someone," Jürgen suggested. "Lots of people like being bribed."

"Why are we going to Cairo?" Kyle asked Bannecker. "Is that where your secure facility is?"

Bannecker smiled. "Yes, it is. But that's only one reason we're going there."

"What are the other reasons?" Susie asked.

"Veeksha knows," Bannecker said. The Indian girl had been very quiet.

Three sets of young eyes turned on Veeksha in surprise.

Veeksha looked at Bannecker. "I do?"

"Of course," Bannecker said. "The Sphinx is the answer to the riddle the fire elemental gave you, is it not?"

"How do you know about that?" Veeksha demanded in astonishment.

Chapter 59

"I haven't told anyone the riddle!" Veeksha said. "How do you know it gave me one?"

"Actually," said Bannecker, smiling like the snake that caught the mouse, "I didn't know. I guessed."

"What?"

"He tricked you, Veeksha!" Kyle said.

Veeksha glared at the man. "Hey! That's not fair!"

Bannecker held up his hands. "Don't get upset."

"The fire elemental gave you another riddle?" Jürgen asked Veeksha. "Why did it give you another riddle? And why didn't you tell us?"

"Yeah, we have all four quintessences." Susie counted off on her fingers. "Jürgen has the geopsium, Kyle has the aquosia, I have the aethrial, and Veeksha has the pyrophyra. We're all done."

"Maybe the Zurans didn't tell you the truth," Bannecker suggested.

The children looked at him in shock.

"Their motives have always been a mystery, don't you think?" Bannecker continued. "Yes, they told you they were looking for the quintessence. But why? To save their world? How? Did they ever go into detail? It doesn't sound like they did. And now we discover that the four elements – stone, water, sky, and fire – are not the end of the quest. Why didn't they tell you that?"

"Maybe they didn't know," Jürgen suggested.

"You don't think Savakala knew? The Minister of the

Sky and an all-powerful aeromagus. She didn't know the full extent of the quest?"

"Maybe we don't have enough quintessence yet," Jürgen pondered. "Maybe we need to get more. Kyle found the aquosia in the desert in Peru. Maybe there is more of it in the deserts of Egypt, also."

Veeksha moaned. "How long are we going to do this?"

"That doesn't make any sense," Kyle mused. "Why would we need more quintessence?"

"Maybe the Zurans need a lot of it." Susie said. "How can they save an entire planet with just what we have in us?"

Bannecker said, "I think you're letting the Zurans trick you into believing something that may not be true."

"What's that?" Kyle asked.

"Perhaps there are not only four elements."

The children sat dumbfounded.

"You see, we've been tracking and investigating Zurans and elemental quintessences for quite a long time." Bannecker leaned back in his seat, the children in rapt attention. "We found some of their artifacts, and they confounded our scientists. For instance, thin armor that is stronger than thick sheets of steel."

"What else did you find?" Susie interrupted.

"I'll tell you the whole story sometime," Bannecker said, "but let's keep on track now. The Zuran we captured in New Mexico gave us information that helped us understand the quintessence we had discovered in the pure water and synthetic diamonds. And we learned from the Zuran that there was also pyrophyra and aethrial. But the scientists had no idea how to synthesize it."

"You told us that before."

"Yes. But I didn't mention that some of our scientists theorized that there were more than four elements. They had no idea what they could be, but they didn't believe that there were only four quintessences. In Nature, if there is one

306

of anything, there are almost always many more. Definitely more than just four."

"So, when did you first suspect that the Zurans were looking for more than four quintessences?"

"When I found out you were going to Rome to find pyrophyra."

"I don't understand," Susie said. "How did you know we were going to Rome?"

"My spy on the Windrunner told me."

Chapter 60

"A spy!" Jürgen exclaimed. "You had a spy on board?"

"Yes, we did."

"Who is it?" Susie asked.

"It's Veeksha!" Jürgen pointed at the Indian girl. "She told him about Easter Island. I bet she told him about Rome, also."

"I didn't," denied Veeksha. "I swear I didn't."

"Who else would have done it?" Jürgen insisted.

"Why, all four of you, of course," said Bannecker, pointing at each of them.

"What's that supposed to mean?" Susie asked.

"It means that I planted a listening device on each of you while we were on Easter Island. We could hear everything you said."

Jürgen reached into his pockets, searching for the device.

"Oh, you won't find it," Bannecker said. "Surveillance technology is far more advanced than what you see in the movies or on television. You'd be surprised what we can hide a microphone and transmitter in these days."

"That's how you knew Veeksha got a riddle from the fire elemental!" Kyle exclaimed. "You heard it."

Bannecker frowned. "Actually, no. The bug stopped working while Veeksha was transformed into fire. It wasn't until she returned to normal that it started working again."

"Then how in the world did you guess that there was another riddle?" Susie asked.

"Yeah," Jürgen agreed, "that's impossible."

"Not impossible, just highly improbable. Unless I know something that you don't."

"Like what?"

"There is an ancient temple hidden deep beneath the Sphinx. In this temple are pre-Egyptian hieroglyphic carvings of Zurans and quintessences."

"I've never heard of a temple under the Sphinx," Jürgen said

"We've kept it a secret."

"How did you find it?"

"That doesn't matter. It only matters that we did and that it was related to Zurans."

"But," Kyle said, "that doesn't mean the riddle would lead there."

"No, it doesn't. We won't know for sure until Veeksha tells us the fire elemental's riddle."

"Why didn't you tell us before?" Susie asked the Indian girl.

Veeksha looked at the floor. "I didn't want to go on another quest. We've been all over the world for days. I miss my parents. I want to go home. If I didn't tell anyone about the new riddle, then we wouldn't have to go after it."

"Oh!" Jürgen stood up and pointed a finger at her angrily. "That is so not fair! You can't decide that kind of stuff yourself!"

"Calm down, Jürgen." Bannecker pushed the German boy gently back into his seat. "Veeksha is very close with her parents, and they are worried. She just wants to go back to them. Don't you want to go back to your parents? Don't you miss them?"

"Yeah, sure I do," Jürgen said. "But I want to see and learn everything I can about the Zurans."

"And you will. But first let's hear the riddle." Bannecker looked at Veeksha.

"I wasn't sure what it meant when the elemental first told me," Veeksha began, "but I figured it out on the helicopter ride. It is the Sphinx. It fits."

"Tell us the riddle!" Susie demanded.

"Here it is," she said, and began to recite.

The ancient and perilous riddle
Stand betwixt the paws in the middle
Sacrifice four treasures to the sand
Then descend to the shrine most grand

The children pondered the riddle for a few seconds, while Bannecker smiled knowingly.

"How does that mean the Sphinx?" Jürgen asked.

"The first two lines," Veeksha responded.

"Yeah," Susie interrupted. "The Sphinx has paws. And the riddle of the Sphinx is ancient and perilous."

"What's the riddle of the Sphinx?" Kyle asked.

"It's the most famous riddle in history, supposedly asked by the Sphinx of Thebes to allow passage into the city," Veeksha explained. "It strangled and devoured anyone who couldn't answer correctly."

Jürgen shuddered. "Remind me not to go to Thebes."

"But what was the Sphinx's riddle?" Kyle asked.

"Which creature walks on four legs in the morning, on two legs in the afternoon, and on three legs in the evening?"

"I've never heard that before," Jürgen said.

"I guess the most famous riddle in history isn't actually too famous," said Kyle with a laugh. "What's the answer?"

"Man," Bannecker replied.

"Why man?"

"A baby moves on all fours, an adult walks on two legs, and old people use a cane, or three legs."

"Oh, I see," Kyle said.

"What about the other two lines of the fire elemental's riddle? What do they mean?"

"The last line, 'Then descend to the shrine most grand', is obviously a reference to the temple beneath the Sphinx,"

Bannecker said.

"And the third line? 'Sacrifice four treasures to the sand'."

"Simple," Veeksha said, "we have to sacrifice a bit of each of the four quintessences to reach the temple."

"Well done, Veeksha," Bannecker congratulated her.

"Why do we need to do that?" Kyle looked at Bannecker. "I thought you already found the temple."

"Yes, we did. But we didn't get there from the Sphinx. We have a tunnel under the desert leading to the temple from a secret base a few miles away."

"That's good," said Jürgen with relief. "We don't have to sacrifice any quintessence."

Bannecker disagreed, "Actually, we will. We need to know if anything special happens when the entrance described by the riddle is used."

"Why? If you can already get there, why should we waste geopsium?"

"The temple is quiet and dark. Scientists have pored over every inch of it and can't tell us any more. Perhaps by unlocking the official entrance, other parts of the temple will be revealed."

Jürgen shook his head. "I don't think that's worth the cost. Geopsium is too valuable to waste as a key to a door that we don't need to open."

"You don't have to worry, Jürgen," Kyle said. "Bannecker has synthetic geopsium he can use instead of yours. Right?"

Bannecker nodded. "Yes, that's true. We have sythetic aquosia, too, of course. And now that Veeksha and Susie have pyrophyra and aethrial, we should be able to open the door."

"And then what happens?" Susie asked.

Bannecker shrugged.

CHAPTER 61

Two hours later the Gulfstream and Globemaster touched down at Cairo International Airport, the second busiest airport in Africa. Bannecker's two planes were given priority descent and taxied to a private terminal. The kids exited the Gulfstream as military personnel swarmed the Globemaster and unloaded the cages of Zurans. Veeksha started walking toward them but Bannecker called her back.

"The crates are being loaded into those trucks, Veeksha. Our ride is over here." He pointed to a Hummer parked nearby and then held up his hands to forestall her objections.

Veeksha ignored him and walked swiftly to the crates. Everyone followed her, and the children watched the Zurans being unloaded.

"Is this all of them?" Kyle asked.

"All that we captured," Bannecker said.

Kyle watched canars, mumbas, urgra, rasha, rascan, and uburu disappear into the trucks. He did not see a grunk. Apparently Barathrina had escaped into Rome. She wouldn't fight, that was for sure. If she wasn't captured or killed, she'd probably end up working at a restaurant. He smiled, happy that at least one Zuran wouldn't spend the rest of her life in captivity.

"Satisfied?" Bannecker asked. "We'll be driving along with the trucks for a while but they'll head off toward the secret base. We'll go straight to the Sphinx."

Veeksha acquiesced without argument. The kids

climbed into the back of the Hummer. Bannecker got in the front and told the driver to get going. Soon they were heading west on Ring Road, a major avenue that encircled Cairo. Kyle sat silently, wondering what would happen at the Sphinx. Susie watched the sights of Cairo whiz by.

"Look at all the spires and domes. It's so pretty!"

"Cairo is a very impressive city," Bannecker agreed.

Soon enough, the looming peaks of the Pyramids of Gizeh peeked over the buildings of Cairo. Suddenly they drove out from what seemed like an ordinary neighborhood and the enormous Pyramid of Khafre loomed before them.

"Wow!" Kyle and Susie said together.

"It's so close to the city?" Susie was surprised. "The pyramids always seem so alone in the desert in the movies."

"Well, those are just movies, Susie," Bannecker noted. "I've learned that movies and books take quite a bit of artistic license to make things more dramatic."

Susie sighed. "I don't know. I think it would be pretty dramatic to wake up every day and see the pyramids in my backyard."

The Hummer took a couple more turns and pulled into a parking lot full of buses and vans dropping off and picking up tourists. The driver stopped the car and got out, as did Bannecker.

"All right, folks, this is it. Just a short walk."

"I can't believe that I'm actually here!" Susie said as the kids exited the car, pulling on their backpacks. "It seems like yesterday that I was in my house in South Dakota watching TV. The only foreign country I've ever been to is Canada."

"Canada doesn't really count," Kyle said. "It's right next door and not very foreign."

"What foreign countries have you been to before?" Susie demanded.

"Just Canada," Kyle sheepishly admitted.

"Well, they don't have stuff like this there," Susie said.

"Neither does America," Jürgen pointed out.

"I wonder how they built these things so long ago?" Susie said as she gawked. "How could primitive people do such things? I mean, they didn't even have tractors or bulldozers."

"Did the Zurans help them?" Kyle asked. "I bet they did."

"Naturally," Jürgen agreed. "They probably had a geomancer. They couldn't do this without magic."

Veeksha was perturbed. "Why does everyone think that ancient people couldn't build enormous monuments themselves? Just because we can't figure out how they did it without our machines, or magic–" she shot Jürgen a glance "–doesn't mean they didn't. The pyramids' existence proves that they did. Our inability to determine how they did it says more about our own intelligence than it does theirs."

The three other kids looked at her.

"You're strange," Jürgen finally said.

Bannecker smiled. "No, she's passionate and wise. Now, I'd love to spend the rest of the day listening to the four of you argue about ancient alien astronaut theory versus indigenous ingenuity, but why don't we figure out the last riddle, instead?"

"Sure!" Jürgen shouted and ran ahead, pulling his backpack on. "I have no idea what she was talking about anyway. Come on! Last one there is a *dummkopf!*"

"What's a *dummkopf?*" Veeksha asked.

"You are, if you don't start running," Kyle called back to her as he chased after Jürgen and Susie.

Veeksha looked up at Bannecker, shrugged, and ran after the others. The government agent spoke into a mike in his hand and then followed.

The kids raced along walls of giant stones toward the Sphinx, seated regally in front of the giant pyramid of Khafre. They passed tourists and guides who barely noticed the excited children. Kyle soon ran ahead of the huffing and puffing Jürgen and descended to the level of the Sphinx. He stared at the ancient monument. The paws were double his height, made from neatly stacked large stones of brown and tan. The head towered far above him, cracked and worn.

"He doesn't have a nose," Susie said as she ran up beside him.

"There's a legend that Napoleon blew it off with a cannon," Veeksha said, joining them. "It had a beard, too. Long ago."

Jürgen heaved himself up to them, breathing hard.

Susie smiled. "Guess you're the *dummkopf*." Jürgen frowned.

"What do we do now?" Susie asked. They looked at the Sphinx. The two paws thrust out from the body, hemming a narrow area between. An altar or pillar, about their height, stood between the paws. Beyond that a small courtyard-like area of packed sand led up to a blank grey stone at the base of the Sphinx's chest.

"We put the quintessence on the sand in there," Kyle guessed.

"Do you know how to do that?" Susie asked.

"Nope."

"Come on," Jürgen said, walking into the small courtyard. "It can't be that hard. I bet once we do it that wall there opens up to reveal stairs leading down."

Bannecker walked up to them. "Hold on now, kids. Don't do anything without me."

"Do you know what we should do?" Veeksha asked him.

"Haven't a clue. But 'betwixt the paws in the middle' is pretty clear. We won't accomplish anything out here." He and the other kids joined Jürgen in the courtyard.

"It's quiet in here," Susie observed.

"And very sandy," said Jürgen. He bent to pick up a handful.

"This is a desert, after all," Veeksha said.

"I wonder how we sacrifice the treasures?" Susie said.

"We've got time to figure it out," Bannecker informed them. "This seems to be the end of the road. Nothing to do now but this."

"What do you think?" Susie asked Kyle, who was staring upward.

He pointed. "I think we're going to find out very soon."

They all looked up to see the head of the Sphinx bend down and stare at them. Its mouth opened and it spoke. "What travels on four legs in the morning, two in the afternoon, and three in the evening?" Its voice boomed across the Gizeh Plateau, shuddering sand, stone, and pyramid alike.

The kids stared in awe as the echoes of the enormous voice dwindled away.

"Man!" they all yelled at once.

The Sphinx nodded. "And Men may pass."

Veeksha shrieked and everyone turned to look at her. She was sinking in the sand. Kyle tried to run to her but he was already knee deep.

"Quicksand!" Susie yelled. "Help!"

All four children were now buried to their waists in the sand. Bannecker rushed between them, his feet planted firmly atop the ground. He grabbed Veeksha and tried to pull her up.

"It worked! It worked!" Jürgen laughed as he disappeared into the ground.

Veeksha continued to scream even as Bannecker failed to save her. In mere seconds, the children were gone, swallowed alive by the ancient sands of Egypt.

CHAPTER 62

Kyle took a deep breath just before his head was pulled under the sand. He suspected that they would all soon be safe and sound in the underground temple Bannecker told them about. But it never hurt to be prepared.

He could feel the sand as he slid past, scraping his clothes and exposed skin. He felt like he was tumbling in the Earth, with his arms and legs flailing like he was being thrown about in surf near a beach. Instead of being cool and wet and liberating, however, this was dark and dry and hot and suffocating.

Sand scratched against his face, pushed into his nose, and even got between his clenched lips. He had no idea how much time was passing, but his chest ached from holding his breath and he was getting dizzy. He started to worry that he would suffocate.

Maybe the Sphinx wasn't sending them to the temple. Maybe it was killing them! The Sphinx was made of stone, so it was probably some kind of stone elemental. Maybe it only wanted geomancers to reach the temple far underground. No doubt Jürgen would reach it safe and sound. He couldn't be hurt by a fall onto stone or sand. He probably couldn't be smothered by it either.

Why couldn't the Zuran temple be underwater in Hawaii or something? Then Kyle could have survived the submarine journey instead of dying of asphyxiation in the bowels of the Earth.

Finally, Kyle could hold his breath no longer. He

involuntarily opened his mouth to gasp at air that wasn't there. Sand poured in...

And he was poured out of the sand onto a stone floor, coughing and spitting and wheezing. It was pitch black with darkness. He could hear others struggling for breath nearby.

"Jürgen?" he wheezed. "Susie? Veeksha?"

"Right here, Kyle," Jürgen replied with no trace of labored breathing.

"Me, too," Susie said chirpily.

A little squeal amidst a flurry of rasps and coughs sounded a lot like Veeksha.

"What's wrong with you guys?" Jürgen asked, crawling over to the noises. "Are you okay?"

"No," said Kyle. He finally caught his breath and sat up. He reached out and felt Jürgen's arm. "We almost suffocated!"

"You guys couldn't breathe?" Susie asked.

"No," Kyle replied. "You could?"

"Yes. I guess it's because of the aethrial."

"And my geopsium helped me, also," Jürgen said.

"Doesn't sound like Veeksha's pyrophyra did any good," Kyle said, listening to Veeksha's continued gasps.

"Or your aquosia," Jürgen added.

"I found her," Susie said from the darkness. "Come on, Veeksha, spit it out. Try to breathe slower."

"Where are we?" Jürgen asked.

"We must be in the hidden temple Mr. Bannecker told us about," Susie guessed.

"Why is it so dark?"

Kyle pulled off his backpack and searched blindly until he found one of his glow sticks. He broke it and the soft glow illuminated their surroundings.

They sat on the floor of a wide corridor. The light barely reached the two walls. Behind them, it looked like the ceiling had collapsed. A pile of sand blocked off the corridor. Opposite that, the light-stick's glow yielded to darkness.

Jürgen stood up and touched the nearby wall. "It's made of big stone blocks, like the Egyptian ruins around the Sphinx."

Kyle helped Susie bring Veeksha to her feet. "Are you okay?" he asked.

Veeksha spit out more sand and wiped her mouth. She nodded.

"Someone has been here," Jürgen said. He pointed at a large lamp on a tripod with a power cord extending into the darkness. He flipped the switch, but the light did not come on. "I wonder why it doesn't work?"

"Maybe the cord isn't plugged in," Kyle said.

"You'd think they'd have the lights on for us."

"Maybe no one knows we're here yet," Susie suggested.

"Yeah, they won't know until Mr. Bannecker tells them," Kyle said.

Veeksha finally spoke. "Where is Mr. Bannecker?"

They looked around but he was nowhere to be seen.

"I don't think he was sucked down here with us," Susie said. "He was trying to pull Veeksha out of the sand."

"He wasn't sinking," Kyle replied. "I don't think the Sphinx brought him down here."

"Why not?" Susie said. "The Sphinx said that 'Men may pass'."

"Then why are you here?" Jürgen asked.

Veeksha rolled her eyes. "Men with a capital 'M', as in human."

"Oh."

"I don't think that had anything to do with it," Kyle said. "The riddle said to sacrifice four treasures. Each of us has one of the quintessences. Bannecker didn't."

"Good point," Veeksha agreed. "But do we still have our quintessence? Or did the Sphinx take it?"

Jürgen's eyes widened in horror. "I hope not! I don't want to lose my geopsium! I still feel like I have it."

"How could you not have it? You could breathe in the

sand."

"Or," Veeksha said, "the Sphinx might have taken it once it dumped us here."

Jürgen walked over to the sand pile, stuck his hand into it, and closed his eyes. The sand swirled and congealed and formed a shape. Moments later, a grand sandcastle stood resplendent before them.

"*Neuschwanstein!*" Jürgen said gleefully, staring at his creation of the famous German castle.

"Okay, we still have our quintessence," Susie said. "What next?"

"Only one way to go. Up the corridor," Kyle said, pointing into the darkness. He led the way along the slightly upward slope of the hallway, following the power cable from the lamp. It wasn't long before they emerged into large space and onto a platform that fell away into darkness in front of them.

"End of the road?" Veeksha asked.

Kyle held the glow stick as high as possible, but its feeble light could tell them no more about the chamber they had entered.

"Helloooo!" Jürgen called into the darkness. His voice echoed back to him. "Cool!" he responded.

"How do we get off this platform?" Veeksha wondered.

"We could just follow the power cord down the stairs," Susie suggested. Indeed, the cord wrapped around the corner, where it connected to another tripod light before following wide steps that led down from where they stood.

They had started down the steps when Veeksha stopped and grabbed Kyle's arm. "What's that?"

In the distance before them were two gouts of flame.

CHAPTER 63

Another flame appeared near the first two, and another, and another. The flames continued to erupt, each one nearer than the last. The kids had retreated back to the corridor when Kyle realized what the flames were.

"They're lighting up the room."

Calling the gigantic chamber a room was an understatement. Balls of flame spontaneously appeared at various heights throughout the hall. Huge bonfires appeared high up near the ceiling. Within a few heartbeats, the enormous space was bathed in the warm light of dozens of flames.

"Wow!" Jürgen gasped. "The flames just float in the air!"

They stood on a wide platform on one side of the huge chamber, some distance above the floor. Other stairs led to other platforms. Thick pillars of various shapes supported the ceiling. Between four daises on the floor below was a huge circular mosaic of irregular and colorful tiles.

"That's pretty," Susie said, heading down the steps again. "Let's go down there."

As they descended the stairs, they could see that most of the surfaces were decorated with geometric designs, pictographic shapes, and lines. There were lots of squares, diamonds, circles, and triangles. Kyle noticed that the pillars had similar shapes. The nearest platform was circular, and the other three were square, triangular, and diamond-shaped. The lines on the walls and pillars were either straight or wavy or jagged. Pictographs of animal-headed man-shapes appeared here and there.

"I wonder why no one else is here?" Veeksha said as they reached the bottom. Amidst all the strange and ancient architecture were numerous unlit tripod lamps. Tables, garbage cans, crates, and chairs were scattered in clumps here and there. On the tables were coffee cups, papers, pop cans, donuts, apples, pens, notebooks, computers, and other electronics.

"Maybe it's lunch time?" Jürgen suggested, his stomach growling. He walked over to a table and took a bite from a donut. "It's kind of stale."

"Hey, you guys," Susie called. She was admiring the floor. They joined her to observe that the huge mosaic was composed of tiles of four different shapes and colors and many sizes, arranged in a geometric pattern that created a giant circle. At four equidistant points on the edge of the giant circle, the tiles formed shapes about six feet across.

"Whoever made this place sure liked squares, circles, diamonds, and triangles," Jürgen said.

"Each shape is always the same color," Veeksha noted. "Red triangles, green circles, blue diamonds, and grey squares."

"It probably means something to the Zurans," Susie guessed.

"Look over there!" Kyle pointed to a far wall, beyond the triangular dais. The wall between opposite sets of stairs was damaged. Rubble was strewn to either side of a large metal ramp that descended from a modern metal door.

"That must be the door to the tunnel that leads to Bannecker's secret base," Kyle said.

"Where is he? Shouldn't he be here by now?" Veeksha asked.

"Seems like someone should be here," Susie agreed. "Would they leave this place unguarded?"

"It only has one entrance. They probably guard the other side. I bet they don't want too many people knowing about this place."

"What are we supposed to do now that we've found it?" Jürgen said.

"Aren't we done?" Veeksha asked. "We have all the quintessence. We solved all the riddles. What more is there to do?"

"Did we solve the last riddle?" Kyle asked.

"We found the temple," Veeksha answered.

"Maybe there is another quintessence here," Susie guessed. "But I don't know how to find it."

"I guess we should go find someone and tell them we're here," Kyle suggested. They walked up the ramp to the steel door.

"That button probably opens it," Jürgen said, pointing at a panel beside the door.

Before they could get to the panel, the door opened. Bannecker stepped into the room, a little out of breath. Behind him, the children saw a long tunnel. "Sorry I'm late, but I was expecting to get here the same way you did."

"Hi," Jürgen said. "You missed a fun trip through the sand."

"That wasn't fun," Veeksha objected.

Bannecker stared around the room, ignoring their comments. "Amazing! The eternal flames are ignited. How did you do that?"

Jürgen shrugged. "I don't know. They just came on when we got here."

"Why are they called eternal flames?" Veeksha asked. "They weren't on before we got here."

Bannecker smiled. "Right you are, Veeksha. Perhaps we translated the writings incorrectly. I'm guessing, however, that your presence had a lot to do with them coming to life."

She nodded. "Because I have the pyrophyra."

"Yes. You probably have some kind of control over them." Bannecker was almost gleeful as he strode down the ramp toward the mosaic. "Nothing else has happened yet, I hope?"

"Is something supposed to happen?" Kyle asked.

Bannecker looked back at the boy and grinned. "That's the question, isn't it, Kyle? Is something supposed to happen? And, if so, how do we make it happen?"

"You don't know what this place does?" Veeksha asked. "It's not very smart to turn something on when you don't know what it does."

Bannecker laughed. "Cautious, aren't we, little Miss Das? I haven't been able to determine much about this temple of elemental mystery. Even with the help of very talented scientists."

"Scientists?" Susie said.

"Yes. All sorts of them. Archeologists, linguists, cryptologists, Egyptologists, physicists. From all over the world."

"Are they coming now?" Kyle asked, looking toward the metal door. He'd never met a bunch of scientists before, and wondered if they would all be wearing white lab coats.

"They won't be joining us for a while," Bannecker said. "I wouldn't want to overwhelm you with endless questions from over-excited geniuses."

"Veeksha wouldn't mind," Jürgen said. "She's a brainiac."

Veeksha frowned at Jürgen, then turned to Bannecker. "I'm surprised they didn't demand to be here for this."

"Well, they aren't in a position to demand. I let the various nations send experts, and swore them to secrecy, of course. I couldn't decrypt the mysteries of this place myself. It's a very perplexing place. Perplexing for them, too, it seems."

"So, what?" Kyle asked. "You sent them on vacation? Their governments let you do that?"

Bannecker smiled. "As a matter of fact, they do. You'd be surprised what kind of cooperation you can get when you're the only one capable of turning synthetic aquosia into the cure for plagues, wounds, and even death."

"You can do all that?"

"Of course! How do you think I get access to all that wonderful military equipment and personnel?"

"By bribing them?"

"Yes. The Italian government wouldn't have let me destroy the Roman Forum without a barrel of aquosia as compensation. They'll take it and try to figure out how to make the various elixirs that I have been providing to governments around the world. But, none of them will figure out how to turn aquosia into anything other than a simple healing potion."

"It's not very nice of America to keep all that knowledge secret," Veeksha said.

Bannecker smiled. "Oh, I'm not American." He turned to the door to see several armed soldiers pushing in a wheelchair holding a restrained and struggling Savakala.

CHAPTER 64

"Ah, yes, the guest of honor," Bannecker said. "Right over there, sergeant, by the mosaic."

Savakala glared at Bannecker, but could not speak. A leather strap clamped her beak shut.

Susie ran up to the Zuran while other soldiers rolled in some crates. "Why are you being so mean to her?"

"I thought you didn't like her?" Bannecker asked. "You told me she wasn't very nice."

"She isn't," Susie agreed. "But that doesn't mean you have to strap her down like that. It's cruel and sad."

Bannecker shrugged. "The Zurans are a threat and I must take precautions. That beak of hers is sharp and could take someone's hand off. And she wouldn't stop squawking. It was very annoying."

Soldiers rolled in three more chairs, each with another Zuran chained in tight: Bozabrozy, Joromwor, and Machadaro.

Veeksha yelled in dismay to see the sky captain. She ran up to him. "Machadaro, are you hurt?"

The rasha stared menacingly at Bannecker. "Not nearly so much as that human will be."

"Those are geopsium chains," Bannecker said. "I don't think you'll be getting free."

"I will kill you," Machadaro threatened.

"Oh, shut up," Bannecker replied. "You've tried three times and failed."

Kyle didn't like the way Bannecker was treating the

Zurans. He had agreed to treat them humanely, but this could not be called humane. And Kyle was bothered by other things that Bannecker had said. He knew a lot more about Zurans and the quest than he had originally admitted. Who was he?

"If you're not American, why are you in the FBI?" Kyle asked.

"Oh, that is a common deception I use when in the United States. It helps put you people at ease. Most of you are quite fond of the FBI and submit to their requests like puppies at the heel."

"We're supposed to do what they say," Susie said. "They're like the police. They're protecting us."

"If you're not an FBI agent, what are you?" Kyle insisted.

"I work for myself."

"But you had army helicopters and jets and soldiers," Jürgen argued.

"Yes, bought and paid for with the healing powers of synthetic aquosia and the protective qualities of synthetic geopsium."

"You can buy armies and air forces and navies with that stuff?" Jürgen said.

Bannecker nodded. "Wouldn't you pay anything? You have the quintessence in you, so you know what it can do for you. Geopsium alloys coat Air Force One and geopsium fibers are woven into the president's suits. Aquosian elixirs have saved numerous senators from inoperable cancers. That, I can assure you, is more than enough for the Congress to comply with my requests. And your celebrities pay me millions for the potions I concoct for them to look young."

"But enough of this." He motioned for his soldiers to close the door and remove the strap from Savakala's beak. "Time to get some answers from the prophet herself."

"I am no prophet," she said, "but I can foresee your fate for abusing the emperor's minister in this manner!"

Bannecker laughed. "Do tell. You make the most subtle threats."

"The results of my threats will not be subtle."

"You know, I could go on sparring with you until the world crumbles." Bannecker bent down and plucked a feather from the Zuran's head. "But we have business to conduct."

He strode out into the middle of the mosaic, spinning around with his arms held out.

"Here is the great mosaic and the end of your quest. Look! All sorts of glyphs rife with elemental icons. There, the four symbols of the elements. Square, diamond, triangle, circle. Here, four elemancers bearing the four elemental quintessences! I'm betting that their presence is required to summon the four elementals. Four symbols, four platforms, four elemancers, four Zurans, four elements. Am I on target, minister?"

Savakala glared.

"Yes, well, you'll need to speak sooner rather than later. You see, I don't know exactly how to summon the elementals. But you do." He bent close to the uburu. "You will tell me what I want to know."

"I will die before I let you possess such power," Savakala said.

Joromwor finally spoke, as he struggled at the geopsium chains that held him in the chair. "Harm the minister and I will kill you."

Bannecker waved a dismissive hand. "Yes. Of course. Blah blah blah."

"This is my quest!" Savakala squawked. "This is my duty! Emperor Exeverius sent me to find the quintessence. No one else shall use it."

"Yes, that I know. The emperor sent you to locate the children, collect the quintessence, find this temple, and finally to summon and commune with the elementals. It's the summoning part that I'm not sure how to accomplish.

My scientists tell me that the platforms and the mosaic are the focal points of this temple, and that it contains many references to the elements, humans, and Zurans. I must assume that the children and you Zurans are integral to the summoning process."

"I am not concerned with your assumptions," the uburu said.

"Come now. You must realize that I will get you to talk, or one of your allies." Bannecker waved a hand at Joromwor, Bozabrozy, and Machadaro.

"Fool!" Savakala spat. "Do you think I would entrust the secret of the summoning process to anyone else? I alone possess that knowledge."

"Good, good," Bannecker smiled. "I had hoped you would. Now, if you please, give me that knowledge."

"I will tell no one, let alone a human." Savakala clamped her beak shut.

"Oh." Bannecker stepped back. "Would it help if I wasn't human?"

He unbuttoned his jacket and took it off, followed by his geopsium armor vest, and then his shirt. Beneath that he wore a short cape tied at his neck. He unclasped the cape and cast it aside.

And he changed.

Chapter 65

Reid Bannecker's hair fell out. His skin deepened to a greenish tinge as scales appeared along his back and arms, and then spread over his whole body. He collapsed to the floor as his legs fused into a tail that lengthened and spread out behind him. His head flattened, and his facial features disappeared into a reptilian snout. Black, soulless eyes stared at Savakala, and a forked tongue darted from a lipless mouth.

Veeksha shrieked, and they all stared aghast at the snake creature coiling where Bannecker had stood. The thing's head was at least as high as a man's, and the thick and muscular tail looped behind at least thirty feet. The thing had two scaly arms.

"Rakanian!" Machadaro shouted in surprise.

"Yes." Rakanian dipped his serpentine head at the rasha in a parody of a bow. "So nice to see you again."

Jürgen gaped in awe. "*Unglaublich*! A snake Zuran! What kind of Zuran are you?"

"A sleesh," Rakanian hissed. "And we are very dangerous." He bared sharp fangs and they dripped with venom.

Veeksha cowered behind the sky captain's chair, staring up at the reptilian Zuran like a cornered mouse. "I don't understand this. Where is Mr. Bannecker?"

A long stuttering hiss escaped the Zuran's mouth. It could have been laughter. "Stupid humans. You are dupes and fools. I have always been Bannecker, since I arrived here long ago."

"But, you were so…human," Susie said. "And you know everything about Earth. How could you trick us like that?"

"I have fooled a long line of warlords, kings, generals, scientists, intelligence agencies, and presidents. Humans create technological marvels but they are completely oblivious and vulnerable to magic. As they shall soon learn."

Kyle tried to figure out what this meant. Bannecker had been the alien villain all along, infiltrating governments and controlling them through bribery and deception. Now Rakanian stood in the elemental temple with, apparently, everything he needed to fulfill some insidious plot. But at least there was one thing Kyle was sure about.

He confronted Rakanian. "We're not going to let you get away with this." Susie stepped up next to him. Jürgen clomped over beside his friends, his stony feet pounding the floor of the temple. Veeksha joined them.

"Before you make any idiotic attempt to thwart me and unshackle your Zuran friends, you might remember that I have a squad of soldiers with machineguns pointed at you."

The children looked around the edges of the room where twenty soldiers were indeed covering them with their weapons.

Rakanian slithered to the crates his soldiers had brought in. "Let's see what they recovered from the wreck of the Windrunner." Opening a crate, he pulled out a piece of Joromwor's Indomitable Armor and strapped it to his forearm.

"I'm immune to bullets, *dummkopf*!" Jürgen rumbled happily.

"Your friends are not," Rakanian said, strapping on more of Joromwor's armor.

"I can heal anyone you hurt," Kyle said. He noticed that the armor shrank to fit Rakanian's smaller physique.

"Are you sure?" Rakanian asked. "These soldiers are not using normal bullets."

"What do you mean?" Susie asked.

"I've had decades to integrate elemental magic into your modern technology." He donned the Indomitable Armor breastplate. "The bullets in those guns aren't mere lead. They are geopsium, laced with my venom and augmented with aquosia."

"So?" Jürgen said, his voice cracking from uncertainty.

"First, this means that the bullets will hurt you, Jürgen, despite your stony protection." Rakanian snaked over to another crate. He pulled out the Sundering Bardiche and let it fall to the floor. Then he took out Machadaro's Burning Blade and belted it around himself. "Second, my venom is quite powerful, and much more so with aquosia enhancing it. Kyle cannot counteract it."

"He lies!" Joromwor shouted, straining against his geopsium chains. "Don't believe him. He's just stalling for time. Attack! Now!"

"And third, even if I was lying, Susie and Veeksha have no protection even against normal bullets. They would be the first to die."

"Don't listen to him," Savakala urged. "He is a liar, a deceiver. You must free us!"

"Me? A liar and deceiver? What about you, sky minister? And your friends here?" He waved a hand at the other Zurans. "Bozabrozy, for example, the friendly and helpful rascan. Funny, harmless Bozabrozy. Did you know, Kyle, that he has deceived you from the moment he met you?"

"What are you talking about?"

"He didn't rescue you at your cabin."

"He helped us get away from your minions!" Jürgen said, defending the rascan. "You sent an urgra and canars after us."

"Really? I sent an urgra and canars after you? Do you see any urgra or canars here?"

"You're hiding them," Susie accused.

Rakanian laughed. "If I had Zuran allies on Earth, don't you think I would have them here at the culmination of my plans?"

The children said nothing as they looked back and forth between the sleesh and the other Zurans.

"No, all my Zuran allies are dead. I am the last survivor." He pointed at Joromwor. "There sits the urgra that broke into your cabin. Legate Joromwor and his canar legionaries attacked you and your parents."

"Why would they do that?" Kyle asked.

"To scare you! To imperil you! So Bozabrozy could rescue you. Fear is a great motivator. It forces one to act. And act you did, running out into the night, away from your parents and their wise counsel."

Kyle frowned.

"If you don't believe me," Rakanian said, "ask them."

"Don't believe Rakanian's lies," Savakala said. "You have the power of the quintessence in you. Stop him, now!"

"It's a well-known fact that Rakanian has turned some Zurans from the emperor," Joromwor growled. "It was just such villains that attacked you at the cabin. He has tricked canar and urgra legionaries to follow him. He has tricked other Zurans. Not to mention Machadaro. Those two have known each other a long time. When Rakanian was king of the pirates, Machadaro served him."

"Joromwor!" Savakala ordered. "Be silent, you fool!"

"Is it true, Machadaro?" Veeksha looked into his eye. "You haven't been tricking us this whole time, have you?"

The captain looked down at the little Indian girl. His troubled face contorted, with whiskers shaking and ears laid back. He did not speak.

"Is it true, Bozabrozy?" Kyle asked.

The rascan shook his head. "No, of course not." He looked at Kyle, and then he nodded. "Okay. Well, yes. A bit."

"Fool!" Savakala shrieked. "What are you doing? Don't

tell such lies!"

"They are not lies," Rakanian said triumphantly. "It is true. Savakala and these others have used you to collect the quintessence. They are not your friends. You should not protect them."

Kyle shook his head. "Maybe not, but why should we let you do what you want?"

"If you don't, my soldiers will open fire."

Kyle looked at the girls. Susie's aethrial wouldn't protect her like Jürgen's geopsium. Veeksha's pyrophyra would not heal her like Kyle's aquosia.

"So," Rakanian said, donning Savakala's feathered cloak of flying, "do you want the girls to die?"

"No," Kyle said, placing a hand on Jürgen's shoulder.

"We can't let him get what he wants," Jürgen said.

"We don't have a choice."

"We do have choices," Susie said. She turned to look at the soldiers. "All of you! Why are you doing this? Why are you helping an alien? He's an invader! You should be protecting us and shooting him."

The soldiers did not respond.

Rakanian laughed. "You are a clever girl, aren't you? But you would need a lot more than a pathetic speech to turn my men against me. I handpicked them as my personal bodyguard. They know the value of quintessence. Many of them are over a hundred years old, but my aquosian elixirs have kept them young. Would you turn against someone who gave you immortality?"

Susie did not reply.

"Good. Now, if you children would be so good as to stand over there by those tables, I will deal with the sky minister."

Reluctantly, the children moved to obey.

"So, back to Savakala," Rakanian sighed, taking the Staff of the Skies out of a crate. "What will it be, Minister? Will you tell me how to summon the elementals?"

"Never!"

"You know you can't complete your quest if you are dead?"

"My death won't get you the answer."

"Are you sure about that?" Rakanian thrust the staff at Savakala. Lightning arced between the staff and the uburu's wings, crackling and burning. The bolt seared off a wide swath of Savakala's wingfeathers. Her shrill scream echoed throughout the chamber.

"You monster!" Susie yelled at Rakanian.

"Don't worry, Susie," Rakanian said. "I won't send her spirit flying far across the wild blue yonder yet. Oh, sorry, my mistake. She's not a skyship captain. I wonder what happens when a sky minister dies? Where does her spirit go?"

Savakala glared at her tormentor. "Your threats don't frighten me."

"I don't need threats," Rakanian said. He retrieved the elixir packet from his jacket and pulled out a vial marked with yellow tape. "That was just a gratuitous demonstration. I have no qualms about using force to get what I want, Savakala. If that method happens to kill you, I can bring you back to life with aquosia. First, however, I'll try this truth serum I've concocted." He dangled the vial in front of his captive. "I've tested it on humans and it works well enough. Other than some unsightly side effects. It's time to test it on a Zuran. Unless you tell me how to summon the elementals."

Savakala shook her head.

"Have it your way." Rakanian grabbed Savakala's beak but she jerked free of his grasp and bit down on his hand. Her sharp beak sank deep into his scaly flesh. The sleesh screamed in pain and tried to pull away. Two soldiers rushed forward and pulled Savakala's beak open, freeing Rakanian's hand.

"Keep her mouth open!" the sleesh ordered, his hand

dripping blood on the floor. He pulled another vial from the packet. "I'll force feed her this serum as soon as I've healed my hand."

"We have to do stop him!" Susie whispered to the others as Rakanian tended to his injury.

"How?" Jürgen asked.

"I don't know!"

"I do," Kyle said. The other children looked at him expectantly.

Chapter 66

"How?" Susie asked.

"I have a plan," Kyle said. "Jürgen can create a fortress around us like the sand castle. Except it will be made out of thick stones." He pointed at the floor, which was made of slabs of stone.

"Won't their magic bullets get through?"

"Hopefully not, if he makes the walls really thick."

"I will," Jürgen emphasized.

"Then Veeksha will turn off the lights."

"She can do that?" Susie said.

"She turned them on, so she can probably turn them off."

Veeksha was obviously surprised at the suggestion. "I don't know if I can do that."

"I know you can," Kyle said encouragingly. "Jürgen can move rocks. I bet putting out fires is even easier for you."

Veeksha nodded, cheered by Kyle's enthusiasm. "Okay, I'll try."

"But then we'll be in the dark. What good is that?" said Susie.

"Yeah, we won't be able to see," Jürgen noted.

"I will," Kyle said. "I'll use these." He pulled Bannecker's night vision goggles from his backpack. "I'll run to the crate over there. I saw the Flagon of the Six Winds in it. I'll break it."

"Break it!" Veeksha said, astonished that Kyle would suggest such a thing. "The winds in that bottle created a hurricane!"

"Hopefully, the wind will cause a distraction, then Jürgen can sneak out and use the Sundering Bardiche to free the Zurans."

"That's a good plan," Jürgen agreed.

"What do I do?" Susie asked.

"Control the wind. Make sure it attacks Rakanian and his soldiers."

"Can I do that?"

"I hope so."

The soldiers succeeded in shoving a thick iron bar into Savakala's mouth, forcing her beak to remain open. Rakanian hissed in delight as he watched the healing elixir close the wound on his hand. He was preparing to use the truth serum when he noticed the children whispering amongst themselves. Kyle was wearing goggles, while Jürgen was kneeling with his hands on the floor.

"What are you doing?" the sleesh hissed.

Jürgen smiled and stone walls rose up around the children. An instant later the elemental temple plunged into impenetrable darkness.

CHAPTER 67

Everything looked green through the goggles. It was a little disorienting. Despite this, Kyle leapt through a gap Jürgen had left in the stone fortress and ran to the crate. He grabbed the Flagon of the Six Winds and raised it over his head.

Long coils wrapped around him, and Rakanian yanked at the bottle. Kyle clung tightly to it, but was lifted from the ground as Rakanian's long snaky body constricted him.

"And just what were you going to do with this, Kyle?" Rakanian asked, smiling down at him through another set of night vision goggles.

Kyle grimaced in the suffocating grip of the snake-man. "Stop you!"

"Unlikely."

Holding the Flagon of the Six Winds in one hand, Kyle wrapped his other arm around Rakanian's scaly body. Even as he imagined it, ice and frost spread from both his hands, flash-freezing the bottle and Rakanian's body. Snowflakes swirled around them. The chill spread from the Flagon of the Six Winds into Rakanian's hand and arm and through the coils he had wrapped around Kyle.

"Bothersome whelp!" Rakanian screamed, dropping the Staff of the Sky. "When I rule I shall burn the brand upon you!" He yanked the Burning Blade from the scabbard at his side. Fire burst from it, and then coursed down his arm and across his body, pushing back the rime.

"You see? No childish ploy will thwart me!"

The searing flames did indeed thaw Rakanian's body and protect him from freezing in place. But the flames also spread up his arm and onto the crystal flagon. When the intense elemental heat struck the elementally frozen bottle, it exploded.

CHAPTER 68

Razor sharp crystal shards cut into Kyle's flesh and he screamed even as Rakanian collapsed backward. Kyle fell from the Zuran's loosening coils. Blood poured from the boy's arm, but only for a moment before the aquosia within him expelled the crystal fragments and sealed his cuts.

An ear-shattering shrieking filled the temple. The last elemental in the Flagon of the Six Winds, the Howling Wind, flew free with bluster and rage.

Kyle held his ears against the excruciating noise. Rakanian flailed in obvious torment. His soldiers fared even worse. Most had dropped their guns and collapsed to the ground in agony.

"Turn on the flames!" Kyle yelled, but he doubted that Veeksha could hear him over the noise. He stumbled back to Jürgen's stone fortress where Veeksha and Jürgen squirmed on the ground holding their ears. Susie knelt beside them, apparently unaffected by the noise.

"Susie! The bad guys are down," Kyle said. "Veeksha needs to turn on the fires!"

Susie looked up into the darkness and nodded. She said something, but Kyle couldn't hear her. "I can't hear you, Susie! The wind is too loud."

Susie held her hands to her face, forming circles around her eyes with her thumbs and forefingers. Then she held out her hands. Kyle understood, and gave her the goggles. She put them on and then leapt into the air.

She laughed in exultation. She was flying! Actually

flying! Like Superman! The aethrial obeyed her! It didn't take any effort at all. She soared around the towering pillars of the elemental temple, immune to the sonic ravages of the Howling Wind. Rakanian and the soldiers writhed and screamed in pain on the floor. The captive Zurans strained against their chains in anguish.

The Howling Wind churned along a chaotic path through the chamber, knocking over tables and scattering papers behind it.

"Quit your screaming, you baby!" Susie yelled, hoping the unleashed sky elemental would listen to her demands.

The howling somehow changed into a voice. "Dare not to command me, even with your aethrial! I shall never stop screaming!" To prove its point, the elemental let loose a terrible, undulating screech that made even Susie cringe.

"You're hurting everyone in the room!"

"It's not my fault that I was released from one prison into another. Trapped, I am, in this tiny space!"

"This room is huge," Susie argued.

"Not for one who has enjoyed the endless skies of Zura."

"I know how you can get back to the skies," Susie yelled.

"How?"

Susie flew down to the metal ramp and pushed the button that opened the door. She pointed up the corridor through which Bannecker-Rakanian had entered.

"Up there! It leads outside!"

Susie felt a prolonged gust of wind rush past her. As the air current died down to nothing, the howling dwindled to a distant whisper, and then vanished altogether.

"What? Not even a thank you?" Susie called up the hallway.

"Elementals are renowned for their ingratitude," Rakanian said as the room flooded with light.

Susie turned to see the sinuous Zuran slithering up behind her, Burning Blade in hand.

CHAPTER 69

After Susie took the goggles, Kyle found another glow stick in his backpack. In its soft light he could see Jürgen and Veeksha still suffering from the noise. Kyle cupped his hands around Veeksha's ears. Her spasms eased immediately and she smiled. Kyle reached over and touched Jürgen. The healing powers of aquosia relieved his pain just as quickly. They rose to their feet as the howling faded away.

"Turn the lights back on, Veeksha," Kyle said as he ran out of the stone fortress. "We have to save the Zurans before the soldiers recover."

The flame lights came to life in great gouts that threw blazing brightness throughout the temple. Kyle saw Rakanian wrapping his thick coils around Susie near the metal door.

"Veeksha! Over there!"

"Leave her alone!" Veeksha yelled. A ball of flame erupted from her outstretched hands, zoomed straight at Rakanian and hit him in the head. Momentarily startled, he relaxed his coils and Susie escaped into the air. Veeksha looked in surprise at her smoking hands.

"Thanks, Veeksha!" shouted Susie.

"Good work!" Kyle yelled as he ran to the Sundering Bardiche. He tried to lift the massive weapon, but it was too heavy. "Jürgen! Help me!"

Jürgen, his flesh coarse and grey like rock and stone, easily picked up the weapon and went to the Zurans.

"Fools!" Rakanian yelled as he dodged more of Veeksha's fireballs. Kyle turned to respond to the villain, but saw that he was speaking to his soldiers. "Use your healing potions!"

The soldiers were lying in collapsed heaps on the ground, moaning and bleeding from their ears. Some of them responded to Rakanian's command by pulling small vials from their pockets and drinking the elixirs within.

"Hurry up, Jürgen!" Kyle yelled as he placed his hands on Joromwor's ears, healing him. The urgra sighed as the pain subsided. Kyle rushed to the next Zuran.

Jürgen hefted the Sundering Bardiche and brought the blade down on the chains binding the legate. Sparks flew as the blade sank into the links. They did not break. Jürgen tried again and again, finally severing the geopsium chain. Joromwor leapt up, grabbed the weapon from Jürgen, and charged Rakanian.

"No!" Machadaro yelled. "Free us first!"

The legate ignored the sky captain. Rakanian turned to face the urgra's onslaught. The Sundering Bardiche swept down onto the Indomitable Armor, knocking the sleesh backward with the force of the blow. But the armor did not yield.

"Have you forgotten the power of your own armor?" Rakanian asked.

Joromwor indicated Rakanian's long body, unprotected by the magical plating. "The armor doesn't cover all of you!"

"But I also wear this cloak," Rakanian said, and soared into the air, feathers fluttering on the Cloak of Flying. Infuriated, Joromwor swung the Sundering Bardiche, but the villain was well out of reach.

"Get me out of these chains," Bozabrozy pleaded after Kyle healed his ears.

"How? Joromwor took the Bardiche."

"I put the Everkey in your backpack."

"Really?" Kyle searched in his pack and found the icy

key. He inserted it into the padlock and turned it. The chains fell to the floor.

"Free the others," the rascan said, throwing off his chains and jumping toward the crates.

"Me next," Machadaro snarled, and Kyle obeyed. The furious sky captain leapt at the recovering soldiers.

Kyle unlocked Savakala's chains and cast them aside. Despite having healed her ears, Kyle didn't think she looked well. Singed feathers lay scattered around her.

"You look really bad," he said.

"Rakanian will soon look worse," Savakala groaned.

"This might help," Bozabrozy said and handed her the Staff of the Skies.

As the uburu grabbed the magical elequary, her spirits lifted. She took a deep breath and raised her head high. She stared fixedly at Rakanian.

Chapter 70

The elemental temple shuddered in a raging chaos of flame, flying rocks, and lightning. Rakanian soared through the air, Burning Blade in hand, dodging from pillar to pillar to avoid being struck by elemental attacks. Veeksha continued to throw fireballs at him, Jürgen hurled large stones, and Savakala used the Staff of the Sky to send gusts and lightning after him.

Joromwor, unable to reach the sleesh, wrought havoc on the soldiers, hewing them down with the Sundering Bardiche. Machadaro used his bare claws to accomplish the same task. The soldiers counterattacked with grim yet futile resolve.

Susie Five Eagles watched the fighting from a high corner. She saw Veeksha shooting flames and Jürgen lobbing large stones he pulled from the floor. Kyle turned soldiers into icy statues. But not even Savakala could strike the speedy Rakanian. With the Cloak of Flying, he easily avoided harm by using the pillars for cover.

Susie imagined him being hit by lightning. A bolt arced from her hand. Amazingly, Rakanian ducked out of the way in the same instant. Spotting Susie near the ceiling, he darted through the air and wrapped her in his coils again.

"This time you won't be so lucky," Rakanian hissed in her ear as she struggled. "You children have caused me far too much trouble."

"You can't do anything to any of us," Susie said. "You need us alive."

"True. But there are ways to kill you slowly." He bared his fangs close to her face, and Susie cringed from his dripping venom.

With that threat, Rakanian flew down from the roof, holding the Burning Blade close to Susie's throat. He surveyed the carnage the Zurans had wrought.

"I didn't really expect my men to last long against your fury," he said.

"Come down and face it yourself," Machadaro said.

"I think not. Now drop all your weapons."

"Why?" Savakala said. "The boy can heal her of any wound you inflict."

Rakanian laughed. "Oh, if only that were true. I have spent many years augmenting my venom with synthetic aquosia. My bite is the deadliest curse on any world. It cannot be cured with aquosia."

"Aquosia heals people," Kyle said. "It's not a poison."

"Speak not of what you do not know," Rakanian warned. "Through my artifice I have created elixirs that restore the dead to life! Do you think I cannot turn aquosia to other purposes?"

"Is that true?" Veeksha asked Savakala.

"Of course not. Nothing can defy the healing powers of aquosia."

Bozabrozy crept out from behind the pile of crates. He once again wore many of his belts and pouches. "Actually, there are fiends whose bite cannot be soothed with aquosia."

Rakanian hissed. "You see? I do not make idle threats."

"Even so, you need her alive."

"And she will be alive, for a time, after I bite her. Her death will not be a quick or pleasant experience."

"He is bluffing," Joromwor growled to Savakala. "If his threat were real, he would have already bitten her."

"Does this look like a bluff?" Rakanian sank his envenomed fangs into Susie's shoulder.

CHAPTER 71

Susie screamed as the fangs punctured her flesh.

"No!" Veeksha cried.

"And now you have precious little time," Rakanian said. "Summoning the temple elementals is the only way to save her now."

A burning feeling seeped from Susie's shoulder down her arm and into her neck and chest. She had expected the venom to make her faint or at least groggy. Instead, it heightened her senses and made everything clear and precise. Unfortunately, the clearest sensation was the pain in her shoulder, which continued to grow. But she felt more aware than she ever had before. She looked up at Rakanian as he gloated at the Zurans below them. She vividly observed the individual scales on his face, the individual drops of her blood on his fangs and lips. The feathers on the Cloak of Flying fluttered, but they were so clear she could have counted each one of them. Firelight glittered off the cloak's crystal clasp at his neck. Susie reached out, yanked off the clasp and threw it away.

"What?" Rakanian yelped in dismay. Unfettered, the Cloak of Flying flew from his shoulders and he fell to the floor. Susie, freed from his enveloping coils by his surprise, floated down near the mosaic.

Machadaro and Joromwor pounced on the fallen villain. Rakanian fought back with the Burning Blade. At first, the combination of his lightning reflexes, magical sword, and Indomitable Armor gave him the upper hand. But when

Savakala struck him with a thick bolt of lightning, electricity coursed through his body, his coils jerked spasmodically, and the sword spun from his grasp. He skittered across the floor to collapse amidst a pile of his defeated soldiers. He rose unsteadily.

Machadaro pounced, his long fangs sinking deeply into the villain's throat. The sleesh's coils wrapped around the rasha, constricting tighter and tighter. The pair rolled across the floor as they battled, fur and scale, coil and claw. Machadaro kept his jaws clamped tightly on Rakanian's throat, but the coils squeezed tighter. After long seconds of struggle, both Zurans collapsed to the ground, unmoving.

"It seems you will not have a chance to slake your vengeance," Savakala said to Joromwor.

Joromwor nodded silently.

Veeksha cried, barely able to look at the fallen rasha. Susie hugged her, the pain from her snakebite forgotten in her sorrow.

Kyle looked at the tangle of scales and fur. It had been an epic struggle, long overdue. After repeated attempts, and at the cost of his own life, Machadaro had finally slain Bannecker-Rakanian.

Or had he? The scaly tail moved!

"Lookout! Rakanian's still alive!"

As the coils unwound, Savakala pointed her Staff of the Sky and Joromwor raised the Sundering Bardiche.

An imposing striped shape rose up from the carnage. Machadaro lifted his head to the ceiling. The temple reverberated with his terrifying roar of victory.

"Machadaro!" Veeksha screamed in joy, but loyally remained by Susie's side.

Joromwor retrieved the Burning Blade and returned it to its owner.

"You fought well," the legate said.

"As did you," Machadaro replied, taking his weapon.

"We shall still clash when this quest is done," Joromwor

said. He retrieved his Indomitable Armor from Rakanian's corpse and strapped it on.

"Fools!" said Savakala. She stepped up behind them and whispered, "Restrain yourselves, and obey me. All the elements are at hand. Soon I shall have the chronum and Zura shall endure. After that, you can tear each other to flinders. Until then, do as I have instructed and say nothing to the children."

Chapter 72

Veeksha and Jürgen sat close at hand as Kyle pressed his hands against Susie's snakebite.

"Does it feel better?"

"No," Susie replied, gritting her teeth. "It burns! It burns! Ow!"

"The aquosia isn't working," Veeksha cried.

"What do we do?" Jürgen asked. "How do we save her?"

Kyle looked at the uburu. "Is it true, what Rakanian said? That the elementals can save her?"

"Yes."

"How do we do that?"

Savakala pointed. "Place her on the diamond on the edge of the mosaic."

The children helped Susie to her feet and quickly moved her as instructed.

"Now, each of you stand on the other shapes," Savakala directed. "Jürgen to the square, for stone. Veeksha to the triangle, for fire. Kyle to the circle, for water."

As the children obeyed, Savakala pulled herself wearily onto the diamond-shaped platform outside the mosaic, near Susie. Joromwor mounted the square platform, and Machadaro the triangular.

"Bozabrozy!" Savakala screeched. "Take your place!"

The rascan hesitated and looked at the children.

"Hurry, Bozabrozy," Kyle pleaded. "Or Susie will die!"

"But there is something–"

"Silence!" Savakala interrupted. "We have little time. Take your place. You know the consequences if we do not complete the summoning."

Bozabrozy mounted the circular platform.

"Ready? Now!" Savakala shouted, and then each of the Zurans acted.

The uburu tapped the diamond platform on which she stood with her Staff of the Sky. Sparks scattered and a cyclone swirled around her.

Machadaro scraped the triangular platform with this Burning Blade. Flames burst forth around him.

Joromwor swung the Sundering Bardiche and sank it deeply into the square platform. Fissures and cracks spread through the stones, scattering rubble.

Bozabrozy pulled a small vial from inside his slouch hat and dropped it. It shattered on the circular platform with a huge splash of water.

Instantly, each of the children felt a pull from the mosaic shape beneath their feet. It seemed to Kyle as if gravity suddenly doubled. The shapes started to glow. The children collapsed to their hands and knees.

Veeksha felt something wrenching her insides. The warmth she had felt since absorbing the pyrophyra cooled.

"No!" Jürgen yelled. The rough stone texture faded from his forehead, and then his face. "It's pulling the geopsium out of me!"

"No!" Susie screamed. She, too, sensed the quintessence leaking from her body into the glowing blue tiles beneath her. Her waving hair and clothes slowly calmed.

Kyle felt the cool aquosia seep from him and into the tiles. "Is this what's supposed to happen?" he angrily asked Savakala. "How will I heal people without the aquosia?"

"Silence," Savakala replied. "I must concentrate."

The glow from the tiles beneath the children's feet flowed to all the tiles in the mosaic. Red, blue, green, and grey light shimmered from the floor, each color covering a quarter of the mosaic. With a sudden flash and rumble, the children were thrown across the temple floor.

"It's gone! It's gone!" Jürgen cried as he looked at his normal skin. "The geopsium is gone!"

"Don't worry about that!" shouted Kyle. "We have to save Susie." He ran to the girl, who with Veeksha's help was struggling to rise.

"She is not doing well," Veeksha said.

Strange things happened on the mosaic. A miniature cyclone spun above the diamond, a geyser spewed from the circle, an inferno raged in the triangle, and a pile of boulders tumbled on the square.

"We Zurans demand that you obey our will!" Savakala yelled. The whirlwind descended to touch the mosaic.

"Why should I obey an aeromagus?" rumbled the stone elemental.

"Because I stand on your summoning dais and I command you," Joromwor ordered. The stone elemental stopped tumbling.

"And I command you," Machadaro said forcefully to the fire elemental.

"And I, you," Bozabrozy said quietly to the water elemental.

"What is your will?" the four elementals said as one.

"Unite!" the Zurans replied.

The four elementals moved out of their respective places toward the center of the mosaic, where a geometric design of all four shapes glowed with an intense light.

Kyle watched as the elementals neared each other at the center of the mosaic. "Wait!" he shouted. "I thought you said you couldn't mix the elements! I thought that would cause chaos!"

"And so it shall," Savakala agreed, cackling with delight.

The four elementals collided at the center of the temple.

CHAPTER 73

Fire blackened stone, sky blew water, stone crashed down on sky, water steamed on fire. As they collided, each element altered the other in a furious maelstrom of smoke, mist, dust, steam, mud, and lava. The chaotic mixture roiled in the midst of the mosaic.

"Our triumph is at hand!" Savakala cheered.

"What's going on?" Susie said through clenched teeth.

Jürgen gaped at the sight. "The elements are all mixed up. *Unglaublich!*"

Kyle ran to the diamond platform where Savakala stood. "Make it save Susie!"

"First it must reveal the final quintessence." The uburu stared in wonder at the madness storming before her.

"What is it?"

Savakala glanced down at Kyle for but a moment. "Chronum!" she revealed. "Now be gone! I must conquer the quadrimental and bind it to my will." The sky minister turned back to the mosaic. "Quadrimental! I have collected the four quintessences. I have geopsium, aquosia, aethrial, and pyrophyra. I have sacrificed them to summon the elementals. I commanded the elementals to unite, giving you life. As your creator, I now order you to obey!"

The massive quadrimental churned and rumbled and spun. A part of it coalesced into a recognizable shape. A face.

"It looks like the Sphinx," Veeksha yelled.

"I am Savakala, sky minister of Azuria! I have tamed

dragons and the skies obey me. I was sent by the emperor to claim the prize."

"You are Zuran!" the quadrimental roared. A spray of magma and fire blasted at Savakala. The uburu leapt away from the platform and avoided the burning rock, but flames enveloped her and she crashed to the ground, her feathers ablaze. Shrieking in pain and terror, she waved the Staff of the Skies and a vortex sucked the air away from her, extinguishing the flames. She struggled to her feet, charred and smoldering and nearly featherless.

"Your plan doesn't seem to be working," Bozabrozy called to Savakala, eyeing the quadrimental warily as it churned in a terrible fury.

"It will do our bidding! It will reveal the chronum!" Savakala stumbled around the mosaic, keeping a good distance away from the quadrimental. "Joromwor!"

The legate nodded grimly and turned to the quadrimental. He bellowed loudly and waved the Sundering Bardiche over his head. "I am Joromwor. Legate of the Emperor's Legions. I defeated the moai at the Gates of Tanniser. I command you!"

"You are Zuran!" Bolts of lightning arced from the quadrimental, striking Joromwor and throwing him off the platform into a pillar. Stunned, he fell to the floor but arose with a struggle, his Indomitable Armor etched and charred.

Savakala squawked angrily, then signaled to the sky captain.

"Give me the chronum!" Machadaro demanded from the triangular dais.

"Who are you?" the quadrimental asked, spinning to face the rasha.

"I am Machadaro! Sky Captain of Zura! I bear the Burning Blade that I wrested from the darkness beyond the Grinding Isles."

"You are Zuran!" The quadrimental lurched and a geyser of needle-sharp icicles spat out. Machadaro was ready for the attack and flipped backward. The icicles shattered on the empty platform.

Savakala turned to Bozabrozy, as did everyone else in the temple.

Bozabrozy looked at Savakala with wide eyes.

"Command it!" she insisted. "We must have the chronum."

Bozabrozy shook his head. "Not me!" He jumped off the circular dais and scurried away from the mosaic.

"Coward," Joromwor growled in disgust.

Kyle ran after the rascan. "It's the only way to save Susie."

The rascan stopped and grabbed Kyle by his shoulders. "Do you think Savakala will let you use any of the chronum? She needs it all for her own ends. She won't spare a second of it for Susie."

"Why not?"

"It's the only way to save Zura," Bozabrozy whispered, "or so she believes."

"What is chronum?"

"It is the quintessence of time."

"How can that save Susie?"

"Can you not imagine a way that dominion over time could save her?" Bozabrozy asked.

"Yes!" Kyle smiled, and ran up onto the circular dais.

"Kyle!" Veeksha yelled. "What are you doing?"

"Saving Susie."

CHAPTER 74

"I'm Kyle Morgan!" he yelled at the raging quadrimental. "I... um... unpetrified Jürgen! I'm from Seattle!"

"Why?" the quadrimental snarled, sparks flying from the boulders that tumbled at its base.

Kyle hesitated, unsure what to answer. "Why what?" he finally said.

"WHY?" the quadrimental repeated loudly.

"It's another riddle," Veeksha yelled to Kyle.

"Just like the other elemental riddles," Jürgen said.

"But what could it want for an answer?" Veeksha pondered. "It hasn't told us anything else. Maybe it's some kind of philosophy question."

"It did tell us something already," Kyle said. "At least, it asked us something. It asked the Sphinx's riddle."

"It didn't ask us that, the Sphinx did."

"But look at the face. They look the same."

"Maybe it wants to know why the answer was 'Man'," Veeksha guessed.

Kyle nodded. "That must be it. It wants to know why man walks on four legs in the morning, two in the afternoon, and three at night."

"Because he gets older," Jürgen said. "Babies crawl, adults walk, and old people use a cane. It's how old they are! Their age!" He yelled at the quadrimental: "Age!"

The quadrimental did not respond.

"I thought that would work," Veeksha said with

358

disappointment.

"It should have worked," Jürgen said.

"I know the answer!" Kyle said. "Humans age, but why do they age? Because time passes. The answer is 'time'! Time!"

"Look!" Jürgen pointed. "It's doing something!"

The quadrimental spewed elemental debris in a frenzied torrent, spinning and undulating. It reared up and struck the ceiling. Tiles and sand poured down as it struck again and again. Finally it stopped and a gleaming orb descended from a hidden alcove.

The orb glimmered like midnight stars and morning dew. It floated down in front of Kyle. He was enthralled by the kaleidoscope of subtle colors that reflected from its liquid surface.

"Kyle! Lookout!" Veeksha yelled.

Kyle jerked out of his reverie in time to see Savakala on the platform with him, reaching for the chronum above them.

"No! That's mine!" Kyle cried.

Savakala pushed him aside. "Be gone! You do not possess the knowledge to control time. It is a dangerous quintessence. More dangerous than the others. Impossible for one as untrained as you to control." As the uburu's fingers grasped for the chronum, a spray of rocks struck her in the chest and knocked her backward off the dais.

"No chronum for you!" the quadrimental stated. It then watched intently as Kyle reached up toward the magical substance.

The chronum was about the size of a soccer ball, but not solid. It didn't look like liquid or gas, either. It was something outside his experience, an inexplicable substance, mysterious and new and ancient and perilous. He grabbed it.

It felt like… change. It felt like it changed him. It changed his surroundings. In an instant he saw the elemental temple as nothing but stone and sand and earth, then he saw Zurans and human slaves cutting and digging as if in fast forward, until the temple appeared in its current grandeur. Then, he floated high above two mountaintops but the ceiling of the temple still towered over him. The cool breeze above the mountains vanished and Kyle was back in the elemental temple, with Susie expiring across the room.

Kyle jumped off the dais and ran to her. Everyone else, including the quadrimental, seemed to be moving much slower. Kyle realized that the chronum was speeding him up. Joromwor ran toward him in slow motion, roaring. Kyle knelt beside Susie, Veeksha cushioning her head.

Kyle took Susie's hand and placed it on the chronum. As he imagined the terrible instant when Rakanian had bitten her, everyone started moving backward! He watched as the events of the past few moments transpired again, but in the opposite direction like a movie on rewind.

"Yes!" He laughed gleefully. Soon, he would return to the time before Susie was bitten, and he could do something to stop Rakanian.

But the time reversal slowed, and he found himself stopped at the point when the four elementals were summoned. Susie was still poisoned! He didn't go back far enough! He shook the chronum, but it did nothing. The chronum was not obeying him.

Time moved slowly forward again. He watched as his previous self and the others stood on the mosaic and their quintessence was drained.

He looked at the corpse of Rakanian, lying amidst his fallen soldiers, his throat torn by Machadaro's fangs. Smoke curled where Savakala's lightning had scorched him. If he still had his aquosia he could heal Rakanian and learn how to save Susie.

Aquosia!

Kyle ran to the table where Rakanian had used his packet of elixirs. He moved swiftly, much faster than everyone else. Time, it seemed, was on his side again. The table was knocked over, but scattered on the floor around it he found several vials of different sizes, labeled with different-colored tape. He found a blue vial, but it was empty. Another was smashed. And another. He spotted the purple vial. Bannacker said the purple vial could bring someone back to life. He hurried to Rakanian's body sprawled atop a pile of rubble and soldiers. Kyle poured the elixir into the sleesh's open mouth.

Nothing happened.

Kyle shook the sleesh. "Come back to life! I need to know how to save Susie!"

Rakanian's tongue quivered, his eyes opened, and he coughed.

"You have revived me," he hissed softly and at the same time-speed as Kyle. There was barely any strength left in him. "As I knew you would."

"How can I save Susie from your venom?" Kyle demanded.

Rakanian's tongue quivered. "With the anti-venom, of course."

"Where is it?"

Rakanian's sinister eyes stared at the quintessence in Kyle's hand. "You have the chronum. Give it to me and I will give you the anti-venom."

Kyle shook his head. "You have it on you? Where?"

"It is in this room. With all the elixirs."

"I'll go find it!" Kyle stood, but Rakanian weakly held his arm.

"There are many elixirs," Rakanian hissed, "all marked in code."

"Which one is it?"

"The chronum," Rakanian held out a hand.

Kyle looked around. Everyone else was still moving in slow motion, and occupied with the elementals. Only Rakanian moved at his speed. He had no one to help him.

"I'll just give her all the potions."

Rakanian shook his head. "There are poisons. Give her the wrong potion and she dies instantly."

"I can't trust you," Kyle said. "You're a liar!"

"Then she dies…"

Kyle yelled in frustration. He had to find the anti-venom and administer it to Susie.

"Of course," Rakanian said, "you could give the chronum to me and try to get it back later. I'm sure the Zurans would help you fight me again. They want it for their own nefarious purposes."

"What purposes?"

"If you let them have the chronum you will find out. Give it to me instead."

"What are you going to use it for?"

"To travel through time, young fool. I will use it to conquer Earth and rule it."

"So why would I give it to you? It was stupid to tell me that!"

"My dominion over Earth will be far kinder than what Savakala plans."

"What's that? Tell me, or there's no chance of you getting the chronum."

"She wants to destroy Earth so Zura can have the quintessence."

Kyle laughed. "How can she destroy Earth?"

"She will give the chronum to the quadrimental and then order it to cause an eruption of quintessence that will shatter this world in a terrible armageddon. New and frightful elementals will be born, and an elemental war will wash over, under, and through the world. Geopsium will cause earthquakes, aquosia will cause tidal waves, aethrial will cause storms, pyrophyra will burn through civilizations, and shards of chronum will destroy the past, present, and future. When it's all over, she will collect the quintessence for Zura."

Kyle remained silent.

"You would be wise to decide quickly." Rakanian's voice sounded a bit stronger.

"Why? I have the chronum. I can control time."

"Do you? Time is a difficult element to master. If you wait too long, it will inexorably march forward. It will spring back to equilibrium like a rubber band." Rakanian's tail twitched, his sinewy coils squirmed.

Kyle stepped back. "I don't know what to do."

"To save Susie, you must give me the chronum."

Kyle watched as Susie was knocked off the mosaic by the summoned elementals. He was catching up with his proper time. He had to make a decision. But how could he decide when each choice ended in disaster?

"You have but one choice," Rakanian said, slithering into a sitting position as the revivifying elixir coursed through him. "You brought Susie into your elemental odyssey, and it will be your fault if she dies. If she had never met you, she would not be in danger. You have to save her, or her blood will be on your hands."

He was right. The fate of the world was too terrible and significant for Kyle to decide. But he could save one person. He could save Susie.

"Here!" He handed the chronum to Rakanian. "Now where is the anti-venom?"

The sleesh's coils quivered and his tongue trembled as he took the fifth quintessence. "It is in a vial marked with orange tape. Be quick! We will soon be pulled back to your time."

Kyle ran back to the mess he had searched earlier. Green tape, red tape, brown tape, black tape. None of the vials had orange tape. Rakanian lied!

But wait! What was that? Lying tranquilly amidst the rubble was a single vial wrapped in orange tape.

Kyle reached down, but time instantly sped forward and he was pulled away. In the blink of an eye, he was back in his proper time, kneeling beside Susie, but without the anti-venom!

Chapter 75

Susie whimpered as Rakanian's venom wracked her with severe pain.

"What are you doing, Kyle?" Veeksha asked. "She's dying!"

"Where's the chronum?" Jürgen demanded. "You had it a second ago."

Before Kyle could answer, Joromwor lifted him into the air and briefly examined him. "What have you done with the chronum?

Kyle cringed before the urgra's huge fangs.

"I have it!" said Rakanian from nearby, laughing and holding the chronum above him.

"What?" Joromwor bellowed. "You're alive! And you have the chronum? How?"

"The boy!" Savakala spat the words. "The boy altered the past."

Joromwor turned back to Kyle. "Ungrateful whelp! I'll bite your head off!"

"He is nothing," Savakala shrieked. "The chronum! Take the chronum from Rakanian. I must repair the damage the boy has done to history or we are all doomed!"

Joromwor threw Kyle aside and charged Rakanian. Shaking his head in fury, Machadaro once again sprang to attack his enemy. But the sleesh evaded them as if they were moving through mud.

Rakanian laughed. "With the chronum, I am invincible!"

Savakala threw a bolt of lightning, but it missed as the

villain dodged aside. "You cannot control raw chronum."

Rakanian sped behind a pillar. "I can feel its power. It is pure and primal. I am the greatest artificer Zura has ever known. I will use it as I would an artifact. It is a natural elequary. How else did the boy use it? It will soon submit to my will."

"Quickly!" Savakala ordered Joromwor and Machadaro. "You must wrest the chronum from him before he can master it."

Kyle sat up. His entire right side hurt from where Joromwor had thrown him against a pillar. But at least the angry urgra was now battling Rakanian, and so wouldn't bother with a powerless child.

Powerless!

Kyle realized he was exactly that. And foolish! He'd stupidly obeyed Savakala, at the cost of all their quintessence. Then he'd given the chronum to Rakanian to save Susie. Now he didn't even have the anti-venom.

The anti-venom! It wasn't lost! It must still be right where he found it in the past.

"Are you all right?" Jürgen ran up and helped him stand. "Joromwor threw you pretty hard."

"I'm okay." Kyle limped back to the overturned table. He couldn't use his left arm. It felt broken. He spotted the orange vial and grabbed it. "This can save Susie!"

The boys rushed to their Native American friend, who was writhing with agony. Veeksha held her as if her life depended on it.

Kyle opened the vial and pressed it to Susie's mouth. "Drink this." Within seconds of the elixir passing her lips, her convulsions eased and she managed a weak smile.

"Oh, that's much better," she whispered.

"*Wunderbar!*" Jürgen said, smiling like a lottery winner. "It worked!"

"Oh, thank you, Kyle!" Veeksha cried. "You saved her!"

"Yes, I saved her," Kyle said, throwing away the empty

vial. "But I doomed the world to suffering under Rakanian. Or destruction by Savakala."

"What do you mean?" Veeksha asked.

As the Zurans fought, Kyle quickly explained what Rakanian had told him about Savakala's plans to destroy Earth. He told them that Rakanian wanted to rule the world by traveling through time.

"You went back in time?" Jürgen was amazed. "I want to go back in time. And forward! That would be so fun."

"Is that all you can think about? Having fun? Quit being so selfish!" Veeksha fumed. "We have to save the world!"

"From both Rakanian and Savakala," Susie added, her strength returning with the departure of the venom.

"Without our quintessence," Jürgen sighed, "we can't do anything!"

Kyle noticed Bozabrozy hiding behind some rubble. "I don't know about that," he said.

CHAPTER 76

Kyle limped across the chamber. Jürgen and Veeksha followed, helping Susie. The quadrimental still towered above them as it stormed within the mosaic, watching the Zurans fight for the chronum.

"Hi," said Bozabrozy.

"Hi," said Kyle.

"Hi!" said Jürgen. Veeksha hit him in the arm and shushed him.

"What are you doing, Bozabrozy?" Kyle asked.

"Waiting to see who wins."

"Shouldn't you help them?" Susie suggested.

"In case you didn't notice," the rascan said, "I'm not much of a warrior. I'm a sneak."

"That doesn't mean you can't do something to defeat Rakanian," Susie insisted.

"With the chronum, Rakanian is too powerful. Only Joromwor's Indomitable Armor has saved him from the venom so far. It won't for long."

"But you have all sorts of magical items," Kyle said, pointing to Bozabrozy's pouches and bandoliers. "You must have something that can help."

"True. But Flakes of Freezing and Drops of Melting are for close quarters only. And I wouldn't last long enough to use them. Rakanian would bite me before I could throw them."

"We're not threats to him," Susie said. "We don't have our quintessence any more. He doesn't think we can do anything."

"She's right," Kyle said. "We can try to hit him with the Flakes of Freezing! Then we could take the chronum."

"What are we going to do with the chronum?" Veeksha asked.

"I could be a time traveler!" Jürgen exclaimed.

Susie said, "We can't give it to Savakala. We can't give it to anyone. We can't trust anyone."

Bozabrozy turned from watching the battle. "Why can't you give it to Savakala?"

"Rakanian told me that Savakala wants it so she can destroy the Earth," Kyle said.

"Oh," Bozabrozy said, his eyes downcast. "Rakanian told you that, did he?"

"Is it true?" Veeksha said.

"No, absolutely not." Bozabrozy looked at his paws and sighed sorrowfully. "Okay, well, yes."

"What?" Kyle yelled. "You knew that all along? And you never told us?"

"Why does she want to destroy Earth?" Susie asked.

"To save Zura. Without Earth's quintessence, Zura is doomed."

"And you were going help her do it?" Kyle was shocked.

"What choice do I have?" Bozabrozy pleaded. "What choice do any of us have? It's either Earth or Zura."

"But you know us," Susie said. "You know Earth! You've seen the cities and people. Millions of people. Billions! And you're still going to let it happen?"

Bozabrozy frowned, his whiskers drooping. "Zura is my home…"

"Well, we're not going to let it happen," Kyle said angrily. He grabbed one of Bozabrozy's pouches and yanked it away. "Which of these bottles have Freezing Flakes?"

"The cold ones." Bozabrozy slumped behind a collapsed pillar.

Kyle rummaged in the pouch and found four fragile-looking bottles. Snowflakes danced inside each, like a Christmas snow globe. He passed them out to his friends.

"What's the plan?" Susie asked.

"Throw them on Rakanian and freeze him," Kyle ordered. "Then take the chronum and don't let anyone else have it."

"Shouldn't we freeze everyone else, too?" Veeksha suggested.

"Yeah," Jürgen nodded. "That's a good idea, also."

"But not before we freeze Rakanian, otherwise he'll be on his guard."

"Whatever you do," Kyle said, "don't let Savakala get the chronum. She'll use it to make the quadrimental destroy the world."

"Let's go!" Susie stepped out from behind the rubble, followed by Jürgen, Veeksha, and Kyle.

CHAPTER 77

Rakanian continued to increase his control of the chronum. He was moving so quickly now that, by comparison, Joromwor and his Sundering Bardiche looked like they were stuck in molasses. Despite his supernatural speed, however, the sleesh could not successfully bite the urgra. His venomous fangs repeatedly bounced off the Indomitable Armor.

Machadaro coordinated with the urgra. The sky captain was quick and agile, accelerated by the magic of the pyrophyra in the Burning Blade. An experienced and vigorous warrior full of shrewd lunges and immediate parries, the rasha remained a mortal threat.

Not only did Rakanian need to contend with the impenetrable urgra and the flaming rasha, but that cursed uburu's lightning bolts forced him to keep an eye on her, too. The sleesh realized that, ironically enough, his command of the chronum was not progressing quickly enough to save him from the trio of Zurans. If he didn't do something soon, Machadaro's blade would find its mark or Savakala's lightning would electrocute him. Rakanian needed more than his fangs. He needed a weapon.

And then he saw it, emerging from the rubble. The human children walked toward the battle. The children! Devoid of their quintessence, they were as harmless as lambs. As Bannecker, he'd used them to get the four quintessences to Cairo. He could use them again.

Rakanian knew that Joromwor cared less for the

children than he did a leg of mutton. The urgra would happily slice any of them in half to kill Rakanian. Savakala was cold and calculating and solely intent on her quest. Even though the children had rescued her, they meant nothing to her. She planned to destroy an entire world and would not hesitate to sacrifice them to achieve that goal.

Rakanian grinned as he barely avoided yet another deft swing of the Burning Blade. He felt the fires lick his scales as the sky captain lunged and then ducked a counterattack. Veeksha obviously had a deep affection for Machadaro, but was that warmth returned? Rakanian had no choice but to gamble on it. But first he had to make his way to the children while avoiding death.

Oddly, however, the children were moving straight toward him. He laughed inwardly at their ignorant compliance with his scheme. Soon he would stand victorious in the elemental temple. After Machadaro fell, he could wrest the Staff of the Sky from Savakala. Then it would be an easy task to electrocute Joromwor into submission.

Rakanian coiled himself. With a speed thrice that of an attacking cobra, he struck out as Veeksha neared. Her face contorted in shock and fear as he caught her in his arms. He turned to gloat, but saw that Machadaro was far too cunning a warrior. He had obviously predicted Rakanian's ploy and was positioned to strike where he would not hit the girl.

A fraction of a moment too late, Rakanian realized that his attempt to use Veeksha as distraction had been too much of a distraction for himself. The Burning Blade slashed him, deep enough to sear bone. Pain surged within him. He dropped the girl and clasped the chronum in both hands.

Machadaro saw an opening and lunged to attack again, but the opening was a ploy. Rakanian had feigned greater injury. With the chronum firmly in hand, he dodged Machadaro's second attack and struck out. He tasted the rasha's flesh as his fangs delivered their lethal venom into the captain's flame-shrouded arm.

372

CHAPTER 78

"No!" Veeksha screamed. She threw the bottle of Freezing Flakes at the sleesh's tail. It broke open and immediately a little whirlwind of snowflakes blew around him. Frost quickly spread across Rakanian's scales.

"What have you done?" Rakanian looked over his shoulder to see himself freezing, the cold seeping swiftly toward his chest and arms. "Stop! No! The chronum must stop it!"

"I'll take that!" Machadaro jerked the chronum from Rakanian's stiffening hand, then leaped away to avoid the chilly storm.

"Stupid child." Rakanian glared at Veeksha. "You have doomed... your... world... to..." He was frozen solid before he could finish the sentence.

Machadaro sheathed the Burning Blade and his nimbus of flame dwindled away. He held the chronum like a well-earned trophy.

Jürgen walked up to the immobilized Rakanian and rapped his knuckles against it. "He's an icicle."

Savakala bent down and helped Veeksha to her feet. "Good work, little one," she said.

"Now!" Kyle yelled, throwing his potion bottle at Joromwor. "Jürgen!"

Jürgen suddenly remembered their plan, and threw his bottle at Savakala, as Susie threw hers at Machadaro.

The rasha captain saw the bottle and ducked beneath it. Savakala, too, was prepared, and she waved the Staff of the

Sky. A gust of wind caught the bottle and it flew wide, breaking against a distant pillar. Kyle's bottle shattered against Joromwor's magical armor. The snowflake storm swirled to life and the Indomitable Armor glistened white. But a moment later Joromwor walked out of the blizzard with only a soft dusting of frost on his fur.

"This armor protects me from such simple magic," he laughed.

Savakala yanked Veeksha close, her talons digging into the girl's flesh. "So, you've learned of our plans, have you?"

"We're not going to let you destroy our world," Kyle said, drawing closer.

"How are you going to stop us?" Savakala said. "With more help from that idiot rascan?" She squinted at Bozabrozy, peeking from behind the crates. "Stealing the emperor's artifacts again, you cowardly pest?"

Joromwor grabbed Kyle's broken arm. He yelled in pain as the urgra yanked away Bozabrozy's pouch and threw it aside. "No more tricks from you!"

"Machadaro, give me the chronum," Savakala said. She looked up at the tumultuous quadrimental, still imprisoned in the mosaic. "I must repair the damage the boy did to history."

"No!" Veeksha cried. "You can't do it, Machadaro. You have to stop her! You have to help us!"

Machadaro glared from his one eye at Savakala and Veeksha, his face twisting as the sleesh's venom seeped up his arm. "My world cannot exist lest yours end, little one," he said sadly.

"No. Please don't do it!"

Savakala chuckled. "Your pleas fall not on deaf ears, child. Machadaro does wish to help you. He wishes to stop me. But he cannot. I have seen him give me the chronum. His choice has already been made, and will be made. He's already done what needed to be done, and he will do what needs to be done now. He has no decision to make. He has but one option, to continue to do what he has always done."

Jürgen shook his head in confusion. "What does that mean?"

"Fate," Veeksha wept. "She's talking about fate. She means that Machadaro is destined to help destroy our world."

Savakala laughed. "Silly child. Fate? Destiny? Those are but pale shadows to what is really happening here."

"What is happening here?" Kyle asked.

"Your feeble minds could not comprehend the enormity of the truth. Machadaro, give me the chronum."

Machadaro hesitated. The venom spread an ache across his chest. He watched the tears flow down Veeksha's face. He walked toward Savakala, holding out the chronum.

"Please..." Veeksha sobbed.

CHAPTER 79

Savakala released her hold on Veeksha and took the chronum from Machadaro. "You have done the right thing, Captain." She stared fixedly at the chronum orb, completely captivated by its majesty.

"No, I have not," Machadaro whispered. He raked Savakala with his claws. Feathers and blood sprayed and the chronum fell from her grasp. Machadaro grabbed the uburu and bent to clamp his vicious fangs on the slender feathered throat. An enormous peal of thunder shook the chamber and Machadaro was thrown into the air by a bolt from the Staff of the Sky.

"Kill that traitor!" Savakala gasped, pointing at the rasha. Joromwor swung the Sundering Bardiche at the stunned captain.

But the captain was not as stunned as he seemed, though smoke wafted from the charred flesh where Savakala's bolt had struck him. He dodged the urgra's attack, and the Sundering Bardiche sliced deep into the floor. Joromwor yanked the weapon from the stone as Machadaro drew the Burning Blade.

"At long last," Joromwor growled.

Machadaro merely nodded, and the flames from his sword once again wrapped him in a blazing shroud.

The warriors clashed with a titanic fury.

Machadaro danced around the legate, swift and agile, evading and striking, forward and back like a coiled spring. His tail waved and twitched as the Burning Blade swung in fiery arcs. But, the armor that slowed the legate also prevented Machadaro from inflicting any damage. Each strike produced a dazzle of multicolored sparks, but the Burning Blade could not penetrate the magical defense.

Joromwor, slower yet powerful, encased in a shell of geopsium armor, channeled his fury into exacting lunges, parries, and counterstrikes. His onslaught was flawless but not fast enough to connect with the pyrophyra-accelerated nimbleness of the rasha.

Savakala rose unsteadily to her feet. Blood seeped from dire wounds, but victory was in her grasp. Only the rasha stood between her and the successful completion of her quest. She pointed the Staff of the Sky at the captain and unleashed another bolt of lightning. It struck him in the back, throwing him toward the mosaic. He collapsed in a convulsing heap.

"Hey!" Jürgen yelled at the uburu. "No fair ganging up!"

Joromwor ran at Machadaro and swung his weapon. The captain, still staggering, raised his sword to protect himself. The Sundering Bardiche descended on the Burning Blade like a guillotine, cutting it in two, and slicing deeply across Machadaro's chest. The rasha dropped the broken blade as his shroud of flames sputtered out.

The legate gloated over the sky captain, relishing his impending victory. He raised the Sundering Bardiche for the killing blow. Machadaro jumped up and grabbed his foe. Turning on his heel, he used Joromwor's own momentum to throw him off balance and pull him into the mosaic. The quadrimental engulfed them, dragging them into its chaotic maelstrom. The two Zurans tumbled like leaves in a tornado. Fire and stone and storm and ice scorched and gnashed and pummeled and bit.

After what seemed an eternity, the quadrimental spat them both out in geysers of water and flame. Joromwor crashed onto a pile of crates, sending Bozabrozy scuttling out of the way. Machadaro slammed high against the wall and slid to the floor, where he lay motionless.

Veeksha screamed.

"Finally!" Savakala cackled at the fallen sky captain. "Joromwor! How do you fare?"

Pushing away the splintered crates, the legate slowly rose to his feet. His Indomitable Armor was scratched and singed and dented and bent, but intact. The Sundering Bardiche was nowhere to be seen.

"I live."

"And now nothing stands against us. Let us collect the chronum." Savakala turned to see the orb at Veeksha's feet. "Give it to me!"

Veeksha grabbed the chronum, but realized as the uburu neared that she couldn't escape with it. She threw the orb, and it bounced and rolled across the rubble-strewn floor until Kyle picked it up. But Joromwor picked up Kyle and plucked the chronum from his grasp.

"I have it!" the legate said triumphantly.

"Not really," said Bozabrozy, who jumped up to snatch the chronum and scampered off before Joromwor could catch him.

"Yay for Bozabrozy!" Jürgen yelled.

Joromwor tossed Kyle aside and gave chase to the rascan.

Bozabrozy fled from the lumbering legate. "Yes!" he shouted. "I did it! I have it! What do I do with it?"

"Die!" Savakala said. The Staff of the Sky spoke, and Bozabrozy dodged just in time to avoid the full brunt of the blast. But he dropped the chronum and it rolled free again, bumping and hopping and spinning.

Joromwor chased after it, but sure-footed Susie ran faster than the battered urgra. She caught the chronum and sprinted away.

"I'll eat you if you don't give that to me," Joromwor threatened.

She dodged behind frozen Rakanian, but Savakala blocked her path.

"Over here! Over here!" Jürgen yelled, waving his hands. "I'm open!"

Susie threw the orb and Jürgen caught it with delight. He marveled at the metallic swirls on the strange surface. His fingertips, he noticed, sank into it slightly. He could barely see a reflection of his face. When he looked up, Joromwor and Savakala stood only a few steps in front of him.

He yelped. "How did you get over here so fast?"

Savakala smirked. "Chronum alters time, you fool. Now give it to me before Joromwor mauls you."

Joromwor looked at Savakala. "Are you sure about this? Something is wrong. Machadaro was not supposed to betray us."

"Kyle's interference in the past is already having repercussions. Events are changing. I must quickly repair history lest the damage ripple even further into the future and past."

Jürgen stumbled backward fearfully. "Kyle! What do I do?"

"Don't give it to them!"

"I know that part," Jürgen yelled. The two Zurans advanced on him. "What's the next part?"

"Use it to speed yourself up!"

Jürgen shook the chronum, tilted it, and stared at it. "It's not working!"

"Throw it to me!"

Savakala and Joromwor towered over him. "If you do," Savakala said, "Joromwor will mangle you."

Jürgen quivered. He realized he was standing on the edge of the mosaic and he suddenly knew what to do. He bent and threw the chronum backwards between his legs.

Savakala shrieked.

The chronum entered the quadrimental and erupted

with a temporal fury, breaking into shards that shot through the mixture of elements. For the longest instant, the quadrimental froze in place. Stone, fire, water, wind, steam, dust, smoke, mist, mud, and magma all stopped.

Then, with the finality of creation, it exploded back into proper time with a concussion that seemed to shake the entire planet. Pillars toppled, tiles fell from the ceiling, and one of the walls collapsed, pouring tons of sand and stone over the doorway. Winds blew fire and dust and water everywhere. Boulders and infernos and geysers swirled throughout the room.

Joromwor stared at the tumult. "This can't be good."

"Stupid human!" Savakala screeched in dismay. "You have doomed us all!"

"No." Jürgen grinned. "Now I get to command it! Short, controlled bursts of chaos. First, I'll command it to not destroy the Earth. Then I'll tell it to give me all the quintessence I want!"

"You don't have the knowledge to do that," Savakala yelled, hurrying away from the quadrimental. "It will rupture time and space. All you have wrought is havoc and destruction!"

Joromwor scrambled after Savakala.

Jürgen stood resolutely and yelled at the quadrimental. "I order you to calm down! Stop shaking everything!"

The shaking continued.

Jürgen took a step backward, looking up at it fearfully. "I order you to give me back my geopsium."

The elemental clamor continued, unperturbed by the boy's feeble demands.

"I order you to obey me?" Jürgen said uncertainly.

The quadrimental said but a single word. "NO."

A blast of heat and cold washed over Jürgen. Suddenly, he wanted to be very far away.

"Jürgen," Susie screamed. "What have you done?"

"Get away from there," Kyle warned, but Jürgen was so

380

scared he couldn't get his body to obey any more than the quadrimental.

Kyle ran up to Jürgen and pulled him away just before a pillar smashed down where he had been standing. "Let's go!"

Jürgen stumbled along behind. "Go where?"

Kyle did not have an answer. He found Susie and the three hid behind a chunk of pillar as the storm raged around them.

"Where's Veeksha?" Kyle yelled over the tumult.

Susie pointed to the far wall, where the Indian girl knelt beside the prone sky captain.

"What's she doing over there?" Jürgen asked.

"Saying goodbye," Susie replied.

They scampered over to their friend, miraculously avoiding incineration and other even less pleasant forms of elemental death. Surprisingly, they found a relative calm around Veeksha and Machadaro. And the sky captain was still alive!

"Please don't die, Machadaro," said Veeksha, weeping uncontrollably and holding his huge hand in hers. "You can't die. You tried to save us. You have to live." He was burnt and battered, and blood flowed from numerous injuries. He had lost his eye patch, and one of his fangs was broken.

He coughed, and wiped a tear from her cheek. "Worry not, little one. We shall meet in another world. There, we shall sail together...far across the wild blue yonder. And if I frighten you, please forgive me."

"You never frightened me!" Veeksha objected.

His arm fell to his side, and his breathing slowed. "But I will... Far across the wild...blue...yonder..."

CHAPTER 80

As life left Machadaro, Veeksha fell across his chest, hugging him and sobbing hysterically. Susie bent down to embrace her friend, and tears flowed down her face as well.

Jürgen wiped his nose. "He's right. We'll meet him real soon. This whole place is going to cave in and kill us all."

Bozabrozy peeked over Kyle's shoulder and squeezed it affectionately. Kyle jumped in surprise at the rascan's sudden appearance. "He's died, then?"

"Yeah," said Kyle, wiping his eyes. "Just like we're going to."

"Don't be too sure." Bozabrozy took off one of his bandoliers and handed it to Kyle. "Here, you might need this."

"For what? How can anything help us in this chaos?"

"Oh, chaos can't last forever. That's the thing about chaos. It must include calm and order, otherwise it wouldn't really be chaos, now would it?"

"What's that?" Susie asked, sitting up.

"What?"

"It's not so noisy."

Susie was right. The noise level was dropping. The quadrimental's wild seizures slowed, and the chaos in the room subsided.

"It looks like it's getting stuck in time again," Kyle said, and he was right. The maelstrom stopped moving entirely. Flames froze in mid-flicker, stones suspended in the air. Serenity descended on the elemental temple.

"What does this mean?" Jürgen wondered.

Joromwor hobbled from behind a fallen pillar to help Savakala out from under the rubble.

"Did we fail?" the urgra asked.

Battered, bloody, burned, and frozen, with nary a feather left on her scrawny frame, Savakala struggled to stand as the urgra supported her. She gazed at the unmoving quadrimental. Wisps, grains, drops, and sparks of chronum floated languidly around the temple.

"Loose chronum shards," she gasped. "If one should strike us, we'll be killed. Or worse!" She stumbled away through the rubble. A long string of chronum drifted toward her.

"Look out!" called Joromwor, who rushed forward and threw himself between the shard and the aeromagus. The chronum wrapped around him like a lasso. He tried to tear it off, but it sank through his armor. As it touched his body, a bright flash erupted from his fur and leaked out between the armored plates. An instant later, the Indomitable Armor collapsed to the floor, empty of all but the skeleton of Imperial Legate Joromwor.

Savakala stared in panic. "It will kill us all! I must escape. I may still... have... time..."

But she did not.

The quadrimental popped like a bubble and vanished, only to reappear an instant later and detonate with a horrific boom. Fire and stone and water and sky inundated the elemental temple. Even worse than that, shards of pure chronum exploded outward in all directions, and where they struck, chaos reigned.

A shard wrapped around Rakanian's frozen form, and he vanished. A wave of chronum sprayed over the bodies of the soldiers. Some disappeared, while others rotted in an instant. Savakala hopped away, her long featherless arms flapping uselessly as she ducked behind a pillar. A bright chronum shard floated through the pillar and enveloped her. The aeromagus walked backward and away, as if someone hit a rewind button. She stopped near Joromwor's empty armor and disappeared.

A string of chronum spun toward Kyle, but Bozabrozy pulled him to the floor and it flew overhead.

"Thanks!" Kyle said.

The rascan opened his mouth to respond, but jerked his head around as he felt the chronum string catch on his ringed tail.

"Uh oh." Bozabrozy jumped to his feet. "Now listen, Kyle, when this endsyouneedto–"

The children couldn't understand the rascan, who was talking fast like an auctioneer, then faster than that. Then he vanished.

The quadrimental blinked out of existence, the raging elemental storm died, and the shattered temple plunged into silence and darkness.

CHAPTER 81

A single bright beam of light appeared from the center of the mosaic.

"Are we going to live?" said Jürgen, breaking the silence.

"I don't see any more chronum," Veeksha said. "Or the quadrimental."

"Did we save the world?" Susie asked.

"We're still here," Kyle said hopefully. "We must have."

"We saved the world!" Jürgen shouted, pumping his fists in the air. "Woo hoo! We saved the world!"

"All we know is that this part of the world isn't destroyed," Veeksha said. She still clenched Machadaro's fur in her hands.

"Don't be such a sourpuss," Jürgen argued. "The quadrimental is dead. Savakala, Joromwor, and Rakanian are dead. Everyone else is dead. We're the only ones left. We won!"

"And we're alive," Kyle said. He broke another glow stick. "Let's go check out that light."

"Maybe it's a way out," Susie agreed. "Come on, Veeksha. We can come back for him."

Veeksha looked down at the fallen sky captain, her tears still wet on her face. Susie took her hand and slowly pulled her away.

They picked their way carefully through the rubble. Blocks of masonry impeded them. They maneuvered around broken tables, crumpled wheelchairs, shattered computers, and other debris. Finally, they reached the edge of the mosaic. The beam of light was very bright. It glared upward from the exact center of the temple.

"Look," Jürgen said. "The mosaic wasn't damaged at all."

Susie pointed. "One tile is gone. Where the light is coming from."

"Must be a tunnel," said Jürgen. He hurried to the center of the mosaic and looked into the opening revealed by the missing tile. "Ow! That's bright."

Kyle joined him, and held up his good arm to shield his eyes. Before he could get a good look, the tile beneath his feet gave way. He stumbled backward.

"Watch out!" he warned. "It's unstable."

More tiles sank beneath the floor. More light shone up.

"Help!" Jürgen yelled as the tiles around him collapsed. He slid toward the widening hole. Kyle grabbed his outstretched hand and Susie and Veeksha quickly came to their aid, pulling them back from the hole. Light from beneath now filled the temple. As they scrambled away from the gap, they saw many of the diamond tiles floating in the air, while the rest fell into hole.

"There's nothing down there," Veeksha exclaimed, watching tiles and sand and rubble toppling downward into an azure blue emptiness.

"Wow!" Jürgen gawked. "We're way up in the sky. That's the ocean down there. We're too far up to see the waves. It's like being on a plane."

Kyle had only been on a plane high over the ocean once, and this did look like that. Then he noticed something else.

"Is that a mountain?" Indeed, a huge mountaintop had swung into view below them.

"It's an island."

"Floating in the sky!"

"There's another one," Veeksha said. A second island

soared into view below them.

Kyle realized that this is what he had seen in his chronum-induced vision. It hadn't been mountaintops below him, but floating islands. These floating islands! And it wasn't ocean way down there. It was more sky. An endless sky!

"*Unglaublich!*" Jürgen whispered. "This is impossible. There aren't any floating islands on Earth."

"The quadrimental destroyed the Earth," Veeksha gasped.

"No, it didn't," said Kyle. "We're not on Earth."

"Where are we?" Susie asked.

Kyle breathed one word:

"Zura!"

The adventure will continue in

TALES OF ZURA

BOOK TWO

WHERE MAGIC REIGNS

Acknowledgements

This book would not have been possible without the encouragement, understanding, and love of my wife, Shari. She never once complained about all the hours I spent in the back room typing away on the manuscript. Nor did she complain about me hijacking our vacation and taking us to South Dakota for research on the first chapters of the book. (By the way, South Dakota is a great place for vacations if you like monuments, hiking, wildlife, and scenic vistas. ;)

I'd also like to thank all the following people who helped me:

My parents, Ron and Linda, for all their support and encouragement and for supplying me with as many books as I wanted to read as a kid.

Jordyn Kruse, the first young adult reader of this novel. She gave me a huge amount of great feedback, and she'd make a great editor when she grows up.

Nathan Levin, the second young reader, and a pretty smart kid.

Dustin Turnage, a great person to have as a fan and pre-reader.

Igor Kieryluk for the great cover. He's easy to work with and puts up with my change requests without a complaint.

My editor, Joel Palmer, for his speedy and great editing. He catches all my mistakes and extra commas.

Volunteer Park Ranger Deborah Ehr for all the help and information she provided to me at Mt. Rushmore National Memorial.

Wikipedia and Bing Maps for all the vast information they provide. Once upon a time, it would have been a long and laborious process to research all the exotic and far away places in this book. But, with Wikipedia I can learn all about South Dakota, Peru, Easter Island, Rome, and Cairo from my office desk. And, Bing Maps gives me bird's eye views of the Roman Forum and Easter Island! Is that amazing or what?

Finally, I'd like to thank all my readers who continue to enjoy my stories and give me encouragement. I love imagining and writing these stories. But, it sure is nice to know that there are others out there who enjoy reading them and get a few hours of entertainment and escape.

Pronunciation Guide

Bold indicates the stressed syllable.
The zh sounds like the s in measure.
The ahy sounds like the i in hide.

Aethrial = **Eeth**-ree-uhl
Aquosia = Uh-**kwoh**-zhuh
Azuria = **Azh**-oor-ee-uh
Barathrina = Bair-uh-**threen**-uh
Bozabrozy = **Boh**-zuh-broh-zee
Canar = **Kay**-nahr
Geopsium = Jee-**ops**-ee-uhm
Grunk = **Gruhnk**
Joromwor = **Johr**-uhm-wohr
Jürgen = **Yer**-gen
Machadaro = Motch-uh-**dair**-oh
Mumba = **Muhm**-bah
Pyrophyra = Pahy-roh-**fahy**-ruh
Rakanian = Rah-**kayn**-ee-uhn
Rascan = **Ras**-kin
Rasha = **Rah**-shah
Reid = **Reed**
Savakala = Suh-**vok**-ah-lah
Sleesh = **Sleesh**
Uburu = Oo-**boo**-roo
Urgra = **Ur**-gra
Veeksha Das = Veek-**shuh** Doss
Zura = **Zoo**-ruh

About the author

Derek J. Canyon graduated from the University of Washington in 1990. He's been working as a professional technical writer in the software industry since 1997, and released his first fiction ebook in September of 2010. Derek and his wonderful wife live near Seattle with their jealous long-haired Chihuahua.

Connect online
Website: www.derekjcanyon.com
Email: derek@derekjcanyon.com
Blog: derekjcanyon.blogspot.com
Twitter: twitter.com/DerekJCanyon
Facebook: Derek J. Canyon

Books by Derek J. Canyon
Available in print or electronic format

TALES OF ZURA SERIES (young adult adventure)
The Elemental Odyssey

DEAD DWARVES SERIES (gritty adult science fiction)
Dead Dwarves, Dirty Deeds
Dead Dwarves Don't Dance

OTHER SCIENCE FICTION
Twelve Worlds (contributor)

NON-FICTION
Format Your Ebook for Kindle in One Hour

Made in the USA
Lexington, KY
24 July 2011